Enchanted

Kay
Hooper

BERKLEY BOOKS, NEW YORK

B

A Berkley Book
Published by The Berkley Publishing Group
A division of Penguin Putnam Inc.
375 Hudson Street
New York, New York 10014

Copyright © 2003 by Kay Hooper
Kissed by Magic copyright © 1983 by Kay Robbins.
Originally published under the pseudonym Kay Robbins.
Belonging to Taylor copyright © 1986 by Kay Robbins.
Originally published under the pseudonym Kay Robbins.
Eye of the Beholder copyright © 1985 by Kay Robbins.
Originally published under the pseudonym Kay Robbins.
Text design by Kristin del Rosario
Cover design by Rita Frangie
Cover photo by Marty Heitner

PRINTING HISTORY
Berkley trade paperback one-volume edition / January 2003
Kissed by Magic published 1983 by Second Chance at Love
Belonging to Taylor published 1986 by Second Chance at Love
Eye of the Beholder published 1985 by Second Chance at Love

Library of Congress Cataloging-in-Publication Data
Hooper, Kay.
Enchanted / Kay Hooper.
p. cm.
Contents: Kissed by magic—Belonging to Taylor—Eye of the beholder.
ISBN 0-425-18825-6
1. Love stories, American. I. Title.
PS3558.O587 A6 2003
813'.54—dc21   2002027929

PRINTED IN THE UNITED STATES OF AMERICA

10 9 8 7 6 5 4 3

Contents

Kissed by Magic
1

Belonging to Taylor
175

Eye of the Beholder
327

Kissed by
Magic

For
Alvin Robbins, my favorite uncle,
and
Brenda Robbins, my favorite fan.

"I daresay you haven't had much practice," said the Queen . . .
"Why, sometimes I've believed as many as six impossible things before breakfast."

—*Lewis Carroll*

Chapter One

Rebel read the final page of Knight's report and then lifted her head to glare across the desk at her executive assistant. "What is Lennox, anyway," she demanded irritably, "a dinosaur? I've seen more liberated views in my great-great-grandfather's diary!"

"He doesn't like dealing with women," Knight murmured. "Particularly female company presidents. He feels that a man should always have control. And he won't deal with a female executive. No exceptions."

The president of Sinclair Hotels flicked the neat papers in front of her with one short, unpolished nail. "Then I'm glad you'd heard those rumors about him," she said. "He certainly would have refused to sell that land to us if I'd approached him myself." She leaned back in her comfortable chair and sighed. "Well, I shouldn't be surprised, I guess. I was bound to run into Lennox's type sooner or later. I've just been lucky so far. I've been president of this company for six months, and I hadn't faced his kind of Neanderthal attitude yet. Dad warned me to expect it, though."

"There aren't many of his type left," Knight pointed out.

"No." Rebel studied her assistant, her customary abstraction lifting to reveal an unwontedly personal curiosity. "You're not his type, are you, Donovan?"

"I wouldn't work for you if I were." Donovan Knight folded powerful arms across his massive chest and returned her gaze with the faintest hint of a smile.

"You were hired to work for my father when he was president," she reminded him.

"But I stayed on when he retired. I could have left. However, I happen to enjoy being your secretary."

"Executive assistant," she muttered, dismayed as always by the title he invariably gave himself.

"You're splitting hairs," he informed her calmly. "Basically, I'm your secretary. I answer your mail, type your letters, keep your appointments straight, et cetera."

He could have added, Rebel thought dryly, that he did all those things—and more—with utter perfection. In six months she had never seen the man make a single mistake. Oddly irritated by the thought, she pushed it aside.

Determinedly, she got the conversation back onto its proper track. "About Lennox: How much do you think he knows about Sinclair Hotels? Is he aware that I'm president?"

Donovan shook his head slowly. "I don't think so." A gleam of amusement lit his eyes briefly. "A good secretary knows almost everything the boss knows, and I spent some time talking to Lennox's secretary. She was under the impression that Marc Sinclair still runs the company, since he's chairman of the board. And Lennox had been out of the country for months."

Rebel drummed her fingers lightly on the report on her desk, the shrewd business brain inherited from her father working keenly. "We must get that land," she murmured almost to herself. "We don't have a hotel in the Bahamas, and we need one there."

"And the project's your baby," Donovan offered.

Amused, she looked up to meet the shuttered violet eyes. In one neat sentence he'd eliminated the possibility of her running to her father for help. Not that she had any intention of doing so. She wondered why she didn't resent Donovan's pointing out the obvious.

"My baby," she agreed. "You and I have done the preliminary work, and everything's set—except the land. And, aside from the fact that I *want* that particular piece of land, the architect used it as a base for his plans. If we have to find land somewhere else, he'll probably have to revise considerably, if not start all over again."

"True. You were taking quite a gamble when you gave the architect the go-ahead."

"You're a lot of help," Rebel accused mildly. She lifted an eyebrow. "Let's hear some suggestions."

Donovan leaned back in his chair and crossed one leg over the other, drawing Rebel's gaze in spite of herself. She felt vaguely confused as she suddenly found herself watching the way his tailored business suit easily accommodated itself to his powerful muscles and graceful movements. What on earth was wrong with her? She'd never been distracted by his appearance before.

"You can't deal with Lennox directly," he said, cutting into her bewildered thoughts. "He'd refuse to see you, and he wouldn't do it politely. You can't make the deal through lawyers or subordinates, because he wouldn't stand for that, either. It'll have to be a face-to-face meeting—a leisurely one, from what I hear—with the head of the company. He won't accept less."

"Wonderful." Rebel drummed her fingers again, mentally

pushing aside the crazy idea that had just occurred to her. "You've told me what I can't do; now tell me what I *can* do."

Her one-of-a-kind executive assistant shrugged with a faint smile. Donovan at a standstill? Impossible! Rebel wondered why that unnerved her.

The bizarre idea popped up again, and this time she considered it a little more carefully. Could they pull it off? A lot would depend on Donovan, she realized. She didn't doubt his trustworthiness one bit. His willingness, though . . . and another point would be her ability to relinquish the reins of the company technically and temporarily.

"Where's Lennox now?" she asked.

"At his vacation lodge in the Bighorn Mountains of Wyoming," Donovan responded promptly. "According to his secretary, he'll be there for at least two weeks—and I'd hate to tell you what I had to do to get that information out of her."

Rebel wanted to ask—badly—but she swallowed the sharp question. "Is he known for being a hospitable host?" she asked instead.

"Oddly enough, yes. Normally he fills the lodge to the rafters with guests when he's there, but not this time. He's due to leave for Europe in two weeks; this stay at the lodge is shorter than average, I gather. Aside from a domestic staff, Lennox has only his son for company. The son's about my age, I believe."

"Is business taboo at the lodge?"

"The opposite, if anything."

Rebel turned the nagging idea over in her mind one more time, looking for potential pitfalls and embarrassing possibilities. Her fingers drummed again; it was her only nervous mannerism. Absently, she watched Donovan's eyes drop to consider the movement for a moment and then lift, shuttered as always, back to her face. She felt a flicker of curiosity about what he was thinking, and then dismissed it as unimportant.

"How do you feel," she asked slowly, "about a little under-handed, unscrupulous scheming?"

Something unreadable gleamed for an instant in the depths of his eyes. "I've got an open mind," he drawled.

Rebel silently examined the idea one last time, looking for unpleasant gremlins lurking about in dark corners. Well, dammit, what choice did she have? She had to have that land.

"If I gave you temporary power of attorney for myself and the company, would you be willing to make a deal with Lennox as acting head of Sinclair Hotels?" Her voice was even, her eyes probing his expressionless face.

As usual, he appeared to grasp instantly what she had in mind. Rebel reflected that it was gratifying to have an assistant who never asked, "What do you mean by that?"

Donovan nodded slowly. "Of course—provided we can pull it off. As long as Lennox is out of touch and doesn't find any reason to check up on the company, it should work. But remember, this hotel is your baby. Even though I've been in on the planning, there are some questions only you could answer at this stage. And I hear Lennox is a big one for questions; he'll want to know exactly what's being planned for the land before he agrees to any terms for selling it."

Rebel thought for a moment, silently acknowledging the truth of his words, then nodded to herself. She had made a decision. "All right then. I'll go along as your secretary; if anything crops up, I'll be on the spot."

If Donovan was surprised at her suggestion, he didn't betray it by so much as the flicker of an eyelash. "It should work," he said simply. Then he added in a warning tone, "But if it doesn't—if Lennox finds out about our role-reversal—he'll be mad as hell."

"If he finds out, let him be mad." Rebel's lips twisted wryly. "Any twentieth-century man with his archaic notions deserves a jolt now and then; he'll learn that a woman can be as ruthless as a man."

Donovan merely nodded and rose to his feet. "I'll send off a wire to the lodge; we should hear something by this afternoon."

"Fine. If we get an invitation, call Buddy and have him warm up the jet. I don't want to waste any more time than necessary in getting that land." As an afterthought she added, "I assume there's somewhere we can land the jet in Wyoming?" She spoke with the natural distaste of someone who had lived her entire life in urban areas; she couldn't help considering Wyoming the back of beyond.

His lips twitching slightly, Donovan murmured, "There's an international airport in Casper. The lodge is northwest of the city; we'll have to rent a car."

"We'll probably have to rent a snowplow," she retorted. "Wyoming in December—and in the mountains, no less!" She rubbed the tension-knotted muscles at the base of her neck, pushing aside the heavy coil of silver-blond hair lying in a smooth chignon.

Disregarding her sarcasm, Donovan asked a logical question. "How do I introduce you to Lennox?"

A point—and a good one. It would hardly do to be introduced as Rebel Sinclair! She'd reverted to her maiden name after the divorce. Why not use her married name in this little charade? At least something useful could be retrieved from her fiasco of a marriage. "I'll use my married name: Anderson."

Donovan exhibited no curiosity, although presumably he wouldn't know that she'd been married. "Good enough. Single or married?"

"Single." Her voice was definite. She'd borrow the name, but she'd be damned if she'd reclaim the title.

"Right." He started for the door. "I'll send off that wire." With one hand on the brass door handle, he turned to look back at her as though struck with a sudden thought. "By the way—don't bother to change your appearance; you look as prim and efficient as any good secretary."

Rebel looked at him sharply, suspiciously, sensing criticism, but he seemed perfectly grave. "Right," she responded evenly.

Donovan left her office, closing the door softly.

Rebel drummed her fingers on the report still in front of her and stared at the closed door, trying vainly to shake off a sudden uneasy feeling. Without conscious direction, her mind flew back to her first meeting with Donovan Knight, more than a year before.

Loaded down with a pile of reports and statistics, she had literally run into the mountain of a man in the hall outside what was then her father's office. Other than astonishment at his size and a fleeting impression of startling violet eyes, Rebel had paid little attention to him. She'd been preoccupied with business.

Had they spoken? Probably. Yes, she remembered now. Stilted, faintly embarrassed conventionalities.

"Oh! Excuse me! So sorry. . . ."

"Don't mention it. No, don't bend over—you'll only drop something else. I'll get it. There. Can you manage?"

"Yes, of course. Uh . . . thank you."

"My pleasure." A graceful, oddly old-world bow.

Rebel frowned. For someone who'd been preoccupied with business, she certainly remembered that brief conversation clearly!

She stirred restlessly in her chair and tried to determine why she was so uneasy. Because of this business trip with Donovan? No; although the circumstances were somewhat different, this certainly wouldn't be their first trip together. And how many business lunches and practically all-night work sessions at her apartment had they shared during the past six months?

They had worked together like a well-practiced team from the very beginning. Donovan had become her right hand, and Rebel had never questioned that or looked any deeper. In all truth, she admitted to herself, she had never really seen him as a man. She'd been under a great deal of pressure since she'd taken over her father's chair as president. He'd been traveling and had left her alone to find her footing. And after three years with the company full-time, and summers during college, she was qualified. She had since proven that she could run the company.

So she was beginning to relax now. And in relaxing, she had discovered that her "secretary" was a very attractive man. No—she was splitting hairs again. The truth was, she silently acknowledged, that the man was devastatingly handsome. He was every woman's fantasy walking around on two legs.

Rebel frowned irritably and tried to shake off the thought. She wasn't interested in men at the moment; she had a company to run. And Donovan had never shown any interest in her as a woman. He treated her with respect, supplied her with information and shrewd, sound advice, and never stepped over the line between employer and employee.

And if she had gotten the impression from time to time that there was a teasing glint in his eyes, she had instantly banished it as a misconception.

Long hours of working closely together had put them on a first-name basis rather quickly, but neither had probed the other's personal life. Rebel knew that he wasn't married, was thirty-six years old, and lived here in Dallas—all items from his vague personnel file. She knew that her father had been enormously impressed with Donovan—so much so that he had hired the younger man as his assistant after only a fifteen-minute interview.

And that was everything she knew—factually—about Donovan Knight.

Intuitively and from observation, she could make a few guesses. If there was a woman in his life, he kept her well hidden, and the lady was either a paragon of understanding about his long hours or she was slavishly devoted. Occasionally, Rebel had detected a faint Southern drawl, and she mentally made a stab at Virginia or North Carolina for his birthplace.

He drank brandy and occasionally beer, ate his steaks rare, disliked Chinese food. He drove a car well—and fast—was never rattled by anything or anyone, and had somehow amassed a great deal of knowledge about the hotel business somewhere along the way.

Rebel pushed away the thoughts. She had a lot to do if she was going to fly off to Wyoming for an unspecified length of time. There was the board meeting tonight; her father would be coming home for that. She would have to clear up all minor business matters on deck at the moment and instruct her staff whom to contact if there was trouble while she and Donovan were gone. It would certainly ruin everything if someone called or wired Rebel Sinclair at the lodge!

There was no time for personal curiosity or inexplicable uneasiness—only business.

The wire from Lennox came late that afternoon, a jovial invitation for Mr. Knight and his "assistant," Miss Anderson, to visit the lodge for a week or so to discuss the property in question.

After Donovan had returned to his own office to continue gathering the material they would need, Rebel frowned down at the wire for a moment and then reached to pick up her phone. She'd have to call Bessie and have her pack a suitcase.

Her hand stopped just short of the receiver, her mind flying back to Donovan's words of this morning: *You look as prim and efficient as any good secretary.*

Still frowning, Rebel rose from behind the modern and masculine oak desk and crossed the large room to the full-length mirror beside the compact bar in the corner.

Prim and efficient? Halting before the mirror, Rebel took a careful, considering look at her appearance. She looked like a businesswoman, she thought defensively. To be sure, the tailored skirt and blazer were a bit severe, and the neutral color was not terribly flattering, but the outfit was both functional and comfortable. And while the white blouse might be plain, it *was* silk.

She lifted a hand to tuck back a strand of silver-blond hair, simultaneously noting both her blunt, unpolished nails and the almost total lack of color in her face. She seldom bothered with makeup.

Rebel felt suddenly shaken. When had this begun happening? She couldn't remember a time in her adult life when she hadn't played up her femininity, her attractiveness. When had she become this—this caricature of a businesswoman? Was this what her father had meant when he had given her an odd look six months before and warned her not to let the business take her over?

Rebel bit her lip for a moment, then nodded decisively and went back to her desk. She sat down and picked up the phone, placing a call to her apartment. Her housekeeper answered and gave Rebel no opportunity to say more than hello.

"Mister Donovan called about the trip," Bessie said cheerfully, a slight Spanish accent tinging her voice even after forty years in Texas. "He told me you'd be leaving in the morning and what to pack."

Hesitating slightly, Rebel dismissed the question of just what Donovan had said to pack. "Bessie . . . pack a few pretty things this time, please. I'm getting a little tired of suits."

"About time, too." Bessie sniffed. "You'll never catch another husband wearing those drab suits, Miss Rebel."

"I don't want another husband, Bessie," Rebel responded dryly. "I'm quite happy with the company."

"Well and good, Miss Rebel, but a company can't keep you warm at night," Bessie said flatly.

Rebel sighed and abandoned the familiar debate. "Never mind. Just pack the case. Oh, and keep out that dark blue dress I bought a while back; I'll wear that for the trip."

"It's lovely," Bessie said, sounding pleased. "I'll leave it out. Will you and Mister Donovan be working here tonight, Miss Rebel?"

"No. There's a board meeting. I'll probably be late, so don't wait up for me."

"Be sure you eat something," Bessie ordered tartly. "You're far too thin these days."

Thinking of the reflection she had just studied, Rebel silently agreed with her. "I'll eat. Did Donovan tell you to expect Dad? He's flying in tonight for the meeting and then going back to Paris and Mother tomorrow."

"Mister Donovan told me. Fine thing, your father flying all over the place at his age! You get him home at a decent hour, Miss Rebel, so he can get his rest."

"Dad and Mom enjoy travel, Bessie; you know that's why he retired early," Rebel said patiently. "But I'll try to get him home quickly. See you later."

"Take care," Bessie said automatically before hanging up.

Rebel sat back and stared at the phone, feeling an inexplicable sense of alarm. *Mister* Donovan. How long had Bessie called him that? The affectionate, semiformal address was her mark of approval—had been for years. She used it only with the family she'd been a part of for as long as Rebel could remember, the family and a very few select friends. And she didn't use it lightly; with Bessie, one had to earn respect and affection.

It was . . . funny. Even after nearly three years of marriage and numerous attempts on his part to charm her, Jud had never been called anything but Mr. Anderson. Rebel's husband had never won Bessie over.

Why did that make her suddenly uneasy?

She was tired, that was all. She was just tired, and that was why she was receiving all these crazy impressions and being attacked by ridiculous uncertainties. With a sigh and an effort, Rebel drew forward the agenda for that night's meeting and began to study it.

The Sinclair lawyers drew up the necessary documents giving Donovan power of attorney in the short time allowed. But what with one thing and another, the Sinclair company jet didn't leave the Dallas/Fort Worth airport until well after lunchtime the next day. She had had lunch with her father and Donovan, and she had been puzzled more than once by the former's unconcealed amusement.

Her father had seemed to think something was terribly humorous, but feeling a bit cramped by Donovan's presence, Rebel hadn't asked him what it was. She had a feeling, though, that it was the job-switch between her and her executive assistant, which she had told him about. He had, to Rebel's surprise, approved of the deception, but the laughter in his blue eyes had unnerved her for some reason.

Now, away from Dallas, the company, and her father, Rebel tried to relax in the comfortable lounge of the jet, but she found it impossible. She had unfastened her seat belt as soon as they had reached cruising altitude, and she shifted about restlessly. The luxurious cabin was silent except for the soft whisper of pages turning, and she sent a guarded glance across to Donovan.

He was apparently absorbed in the papers he had taken from his briefcase, his dark head bent and a slight frown between his slanted brows.

There had been half a dozen such trips in as many months, usually overnight whistle-stops at one or another of the Sinclair hotels, for reasons ranging from on-the-spot inspections to managerial meetings. On all such occasions, the journeys to and fro had been made in relative silence unless business matters had to be discussed.

For the first time, the silence bothered Rebel.

Body language, she thought vaguely, studying Donovan covertly. He looked indolent, slumping as though to disguise his great size. He gave the impression of a large, languid man of latent physical power and no more than average mental abilities.

The giveaway was his eyes. Although Rebel couldn't see them at the moment, she conjured in her mind's eye a vivid image with astonishing ease. She saw dark-fringed violet eyes, striking and startling and alive with intelligence. There was nothing lazy in those eyes, and certainly nothing stupid. Violet eyes with a dozen mysterious shades.

As if he sensed her steady regard, Donovan's eyes lifted suddenly to meet hers, and Rebel felt a sharp, physical jolt. Shock sent tingles all the way to her toes, and she wondered dimly what in heaven's name was wrong with her. There was nothing in his eyes to cause such a sensation, nothing unusual. Just a faint question.

"Is something wrong?" he asked quietly.

"No." But Rebel couldn't seem to look away, and butterflies abruptly emerged from chrysalises inside her stomach and began fluttering madly. Odd . . . she had the absurd feeling that she'd never really looked at him before, never really seen him.

He stacked the papers neatly in his case and then got to his feet, returning her stare rather searchingly. "You look a little pale. Drink?"

She nodded slowly and watched while he made his way to the bar near the door leading to the cockpit. Automatically he began mixing her favorite drink, a screwdriver. Rebel wasn't really paying attention to his actions, though. She was busy having an attack of sheer panic.

Always mistrusting extremes in anything, Rebel had never been overly susceptible to masculine beauty. Her ex-husband had been an average man in looks, temperament, and intelligence. Other men she had been attracted to in her twenty-eight years had also been average, she reflected.

But Donovan Knight was not average. For one thing, the man was *big*. Close to six and a half feet, Rebel judged, and built on noble lines. He had shoulders that an all-pro tackle would have happily sacrificed his Super Bowl ring for, a massive chest, and long, powerful arms and legs. Not a spare ounce of fat anywhere. He moved with the unthinking, sensuous grace of a stalking jungle creature. His voice was deep and resonant and almost incongruously soft for such a large man. His black hair was thick, and a little shaggy, and strikingly silvered at the temples.

And his face . . . his face was the closest thing to pure male beauty that Rebel had ever seen or imagined. Lean and strong, with high, well-molded cheekbones, straight dark brows, a finely chiseled aquiline nose, and a strong jawline suggesting a great deal of character. His curved, faintly amused-looking mouth possessed the odd trait of seeming to be both hard and soft at the same time.

Studying him in profile as he mixed the drinks, Rebel thought about that mouth in a crazily detached way. Hard, but not really, she decided finally. Softened by humor. Not a cynical humor, but a fun-loving humor—a humor that enjoyed life and people.

Rebel's panic returned. What was wrong with her? Why was she suddenly looking at Donovan in this entirely new and unwelcome way? Oh, this whole situation was going to become impossibly complicated.

Picking up the drinks from the bar, Donovan suddenly seemed to freeze, his head snapping around and startled violet eyes meeting hers. Rebel tried vainly to read the play of emotions across his face, but she captured only a few fleeting impressions. Astonishment, bemusement, uncertainty, faint shock. And then a curious sort of satisfaction.

What in the world—?

Donovan almost immediately thawed—or whatever—and came toward her with the drinks. He seemed undisturbed now by whatever had struck him. But there was a new expression in his veiled eyes.

Rebel was granted only a few seconds to try to read that expression, and it wasn't enough time. But she got the impression that he was suddenly pleased with something.

She controlled a start of surprise as he sat down beside her before handing her the screwdriver. She reached to accept the glass, uncomfortably aware that she was trying to avoid touching his fingers. But she did touch them—did he move them at the last minute?—and nearly dropped her glass. Hastily, she sipped the drink.

"This trip should be interesting," Donovan said, his voice just a shade more friendly—a shade more intimate?—than usual.

"Oh? Why is that?" she asked, knowing the answer.

"I get to boss around the boss-lady."

It wasn't so much what he said as how he said it that caused Rebel to turn her head and stare at him. "Looking forward to that, are you?"

"Sure. It's what every underling fantasizes about."

Rebel frowned at the term *underling* and then ignored it. "Why do you work for me?" she asked suddenly, honestly curious.

"Because I want to," he replied, unperturbed. An odd little smile curved his lips as she watched. "I have to work for someone."

"No." Rebel shook her head slowly. "I don't think you have to work *for* someone. Don't try to tell me you couldn't be your own boss if you wanted to. I assume you have to work, though; most of us do."

"You don't," he said coolly.

Rebel felt a surprisingly sharp stab of bitterness. She turned her attention back to her drink, her lips twisting slightly. "You mean the country-club route? Rich man's daughter, and all that? I've tried that, thanks. Never again."

"No, I can't see you spending your days playing tennis or golf and your nights attending boring parties," he agreed softly, something strangely intimate in his voice. "I'll bet it bored you silly."

"Something like that."

"So you divorced the man and married the company."

Rebel felt another jolt of surprise. How had he managed to associate her country-club days with her marriage to Jud? Her father hadn't told him; that wasn't Marc Sinclair's style. Still, gossip ran rampant in the company; perhaps he'd heard about it that way. She brushed the thought aside. "The company's less trouble," she said lightly.

He chuckled unexpectedly. "Easier to control, anyway."

For some reason his remark stung. "If you're implying that I have to dominate," she said defensively, glaring at her drink, "then you couldn't be more wrong."

"I didn't say that, boss."

Yet another jolt. He'd never called her that before. And why was it, she wondered desperately, that he said "boss" the way another man might have said "honey"?

"Then just what did you say?" she demanded.

"That a company's easier to control," he said patiently.

She darted a look at him, finding his face grave but his eyes twinkling slightly. Deciding that discretion was the better part of valor, she changed the subject. "I hope Lennox doesn't give us the runaround; we've wasted too much time in getting the land as it is."

Donovan followed the change of subject and then promptly gave it a new direction. "He should be reasonable about it. By the way, I should warn you about something. According to what I've heard, Lennox will automatically assume that you and I are having an affair."

Rebel choked on her drink and turned watering, disbelieving eyes to Donovan. After a moment she said with dangerous restraint, "That man should be stuffed and mounted as a relic of a bygone age! How in heaven's name did he reach his position in life believing such stupid, utterly ridiculous—"

Soothingly, Donovan murmured, "He inherited the money, the power, and the arrogance. I hear he always has affairs with his secretaries, including the present one."

Rebel wouldn't let herself be soothed. "I don't care about his sexual habits! I'll soon disabuse his mind of the idea that you and I are—"

"I wouldn't, if I were you," Donovan interrupted dryly. He went on in the same tone of voice when she gave him a glare. "He'll just assume that I'm stupid and that you're—excuse the expression; it isn't mine—fair game."

A militant spirit entered Rebel's heart. "I'll handle him," she said evenly, almost relishing the prospect. It occurred to her that tacking a "Mrs." onto her name might have discouraged groping hands, but she refused to consider it. Not even for the best of reasons could she pretend to be happily married while wearing Jud's name.

"I'm sure you know how." Apparently engrossed in a study of his brandy, Donovan missed the suspicious glance she threw him. "Better be prepared for a pass right off the bat, though. That dress you're wearing would arouse the hunting instinct in a cigar-store Indian."

In the act of raising her glass for another sip, Rebel froze and felt heat sweep up her throat. So he *had* noticed her change of appearance! The offhand compliment, though, gave her a sudden impulse to tug up the low V-neckline of her blue silk dress.

Not that she did, of course.

Still gazing at his brandy as though into a crystal ball, Donovan went on conversationally, "That hairstyle, too, is very sexy. Just a few strands to soften your face and the rest in a knot on top of your head. It gives a man an almost overpowering urge to take all the pins out and watch it cascade down your back in a shower of silver fire. Very sexy."

Rebel, the glass still frozen halfway to her lips, found herself staring at him and experiencing a profound sense of alarm. Was he still talking about Lennox? Somehow she didn't think he was.

She found herself listening silently to his drawling, resonant, musical voice, feeling hypnotized. Like a rabbit watching the hawk circling lazily above it.

"It's a curious thing about women. They often change their appearance abruptly for no apparent reason. But there's always a reason. Always. Maybe they get bored and just want a change. Or maybe it's some . . . outside influence, something someone else says or does. Or maybe it's the seasons. Hard to tell for sure."

Why had he changed the subject? Or had he?

"Anyway, you'd better watch Lennox." Donovan's voice remained in the low, pleasant drawl. "He thrives on pursuit. Would you like me to play knight-errant and chase him away? Warn him off? You know: 'She's not mine yet, but I'm working on it'?"

Rebel lowered her glass slowly, realizing that somewhere along the way she'd lost her desire to "handle" Lennox. "Let's do whatever you think best. If Lennox believes I'm off-limits, maybe he'll concentrate on business."

"Whatever you say, boss."

Was there a quickly hidden gleam of satisfaction in his eyes? she wondered uneasily.

Donovan leaned forward to place his glass on a low table in front of them and then rose to his feet, casually patting her silk-covered knee along the way.

"I'll go talk to Buddy and find out when we'll arrive. Can I get you anything first?"

Highly conscious of her tingling knee, Rebel could only shake her head silently. She watched him lift a hand in a half-mocking salute and then move forward. Moments later she was alone in the quiet, luxurious cabin.

Rebel lifted her own hand and methodically drained her glass of every last drop. There was a little gremlin in the back of her head whispering the unsettling conviction that she should have remained in Dallas and allowed Donovan to perform this task solo.

Chapter Two

Rebel snuggled her chin down into the fur collar of her coat, jammed her cold hands a bit deeper into its pockets, and sent a glowering look up at the equally glowering sky. It looked like snow, she decided unhappily. It looked like a *blizzard*. Any minute now.

For a brief moment, she flirted with the idea of buying land from somebody other than Lennox. Anybody. Anybody, she amended silently, without prejudices against female company presidents.

With another murderous glare at the leaden sky, Rebel sighed and resolutely delved into the heart of the matter. She was uneasy about this role-reversal business. Period.

It was fine to tell herself that it was just for the sake of convenience and very temporary. It was also fine to tell herself that the ploy was necessary in order to acquire that land. What was *not* fine was the inescapable knowledge that a ruthless man could easily take advantage of the situation.

And the sixty-four-thousand dollar question was: Was Donovan ruthless?

Until today, Rebel would have sworn that he was not. She would have said that Donovan Knight would put the interests of Sinclair Hotels above his own. She would have said that he was not interested in lining his own pockets. She would have said that he was not interested in taking advantage of the situation, or in stepping over the line that fate had drawn between them.

She would have said all of that. Until today.

Rebel looked around in an effort to rid herself of her unnerving thoughts. The airport runways stretched before her. It was as interesting as any other airport, which meant not very. And the view coming in on the jet had been daunting, to say the least. A native of Texas, she was used to flat land, but as much of Wyoming as she'd seen had looked like a flat, unfriendly desert.

Rebel stepped sideways to get the jet out of her line of sight and stared into the distance, where mountains reared to an imposing height. Snowcapped, some of them. Buddy had assured them that there had been "very little" snow this year and that the roads should be clear. Wonderful. They'd get there, but would they ever be able to leave?

Thinking about getting there spawned another thought, and Rebel cast an impatient glance toward the terminal. How long did it take to rent a car, for heaven's sake? Donovan was probably talking to a pretty clerk, and here his boss was, freezing her . . . The thought vanished into nothingness as a sleek new Mercedes pulled up on the tarmac beside the jet and Rebel.

"That doesn't look as though it can climb a mountain." She directed her annoyed comment to Donovan as he got out of the car.

"Don't let looks deceive you." He was busy stowing their cases in the trunk.

Stubbornly, Rebel refused to let the subject drop. "Well, I hope you insured it; I'd hate to have to pay for that thing if a rock fell on it or something."

Donovan shut the trunk lid firmly and then cocked a knowing eyebrow in her direction. "Cold getting to you, boss? I told you to wait in the jet."

Rebel toyed with the idea of pulling rank, then discarded it. "It was stuffy in there," she muttered instead, and she was immediately alarmed to hear the defensive note in her voice. What was wrong with her? *She* was the boss, not he!

Donovan bounced the car keys a couple of times in the palm of one hand. "You or me?"

"You." Rebel sighed and headed for the passenger side. "I'm too depressed to drive." To her surprise, he came around to open the door for her.

"Why depressed?" Before she could either answer or get into the car, he added. "Better take off your coat; the heater's going full blast, and it's a good one."

Rebel would have preferred to leave the coat on, knowing that the wide fur lapels hid her low-cut dress, but she silently removed the garment and watched him toss it onto the backseat before getting into the car himself. And she didn't answer his question until he had slid behind the wheel. He had discarded his own coat, tossing it in the back with hers.

When Donovan started the car and drove toward an exit, she finally answered him. "Why should I be depressed? After all, I'm only leaving my home two weeks before Christmas to spend a lovely week or so in the back-of-beyond mountains of Wyoming with a man who has the mentality of a feudal lord and the hands of an octopus." Taking a breath, she repeated sardonically, "Why should I be depressed?"

"I'm not that bad," Donovan murmured innocently.

"Funny man. I'm talking about Lennox, and you know it."

"Well, I'll be there, too, you know. Any interesting insights into *my* character?"

"You're a dark horse," Rebel answered promptly. She shot a glance at his face. "And getting darker all the time."

"And you should never bet on a dark horse, right?" Donovan seemed to be paying attention to the traffic leaving the airport.

Momentarily, forgetting that they were talking about personalities, Rebel answered automatically. "Oh, I don't know. Dad always says that you should never count a dark horse out of the running until it crosses the finish line."

The Mercedes changed lanes smoothly, and Donovan smiled oddly without looking at Rebel. "Thanks, boss. You've given me hope."

Rebel feverishly cast about in her mind for a change of topic. She didn't understand Donovan's remark—at least, she hoped she didn't—but she didn't like it. Before she could come up with anything, however, Donovan changed the subject himself.

"Why 'Rebel'? I've always wondered."

She accepted the topic gracefully. At least it was better than the other one! "Well, Dad's Irish and Mother's German. Dad said that any child of that union was bound to be a rebel."

Donovan chuckled. "That sounds like Marc."

"Uh-huh." She sighed. "He says he's just glad that I didn't get his red hair."

"My mother says the same thing about me—that she's glad I didn't get her red hair, I mean."

Rebel looked at him curiously. She was strongly aware that the conversation was on a more personal level than was customary between them. She knew that she should change the subject and avoid personalities, but curiosity won.

"Are both your parents living?" she asked.

He nodded, still paying attention to his driving. "In Virginia."

While Rebel mentally gave herself high marks for perception and observation, he went on, "Like you, I'm an 'only.' Mother's been pestering me for years to marry and settle down."

Rebel hastily spoke. "Virginia's a long way from Texas. How did you wind up there?"

Donovan shrugged. "After college, I decided to see a bit of the world. I kept traveling, working as I went, until I ended up in Mexico, and then Texas. When I heard about the opening at Sinclair, I decided to settle down and try that for a while."

"Indefinitely?" Rebel asked dryly, registering that a lot of his knowledge of hotels probably came from the years of traveling.

"That wasn't my idea when I entered the building," he admitted cheerfully. "It was when I came out."

"I suppose Dad persuaded you?"

"Not exactly. You might say that I wished on a star. And, having wished, I had to stay until the wish came true."

Rebel had the confused desire to remind him that the interview with her father had been conducted in broad daylight, but she knew he had been speaking metaphorically. "What did you wish for?" she asked finally.

He sent her a reproachful glance. "You know better than that. If I told you, then the wish wouldn't come true."

"I never knew you were fanciful."

"There's a lot about me you don't know, boss."

Rebel sighed inwardly. He was right. And it made her nervous.

They left Casper far behind them, the silence in the car as companionable as could be expected. The mountains ahead of them loomed ever larger and ever closer and a few snowflakes drifted down lazily, unthreateningly.

When the Mercedes came to a stop some time later, Rebel tried to blink away the sleepiness born of inertia. "Why are we stopping? We haven't even started to climb yet."

Donovan was sitting with one arm over the steering wheel, smiling and obviously amused. "This is as far as the car can take us, I'm afraid. The last leg of our journey demands alternate transportation."

Short on sleep, unnerved and unhappy, Rebel wasn't disposed to humor. "First by jet, then by car—what's next? Don't tell me! We get into the nearest covered wagon, or climb onto a mule. Did you remember to pack the beads to soothe the natives with?"

He chuckled. "The natives are friendly. And the transportation isn't that primitive. Take a look."

Rebel's eyes followed his pointing finger. She craned her neck and looked, and then she looked again. When she spoke, her voice was deadly calm. "I'm not getting into one of those."

"It's the only way," Donovan said patiently.

Rebel ignored him. "We'll take the road."

"There *is* no road."

"There *has* to be a road. They couldn't have built a lodge up there without a road."

"Your needle's stuck," Donovan murmured, a slight tremor in his voice.

Rebel rounded on him with a glare. "You knew! You knew all about this, didn't you? Why didn't you tell me?"

"You wouldn't have come," he replied simply.

She felt her heart give an ungentle lurch, and then she reminded herself that he needed information only she possessed about the proposed hotel. That was why he wanted her to come; that was why she was here. The thought fueled her anger.

"I will not get into a helicopter," she told him with careful restraint.

"You fly in the jet about once a month," Donovan said reasonably. "What's the difference?"

Rebel hated his rationality. "Those things fly nose-down, and it makes me dizzy. I won't get into one. There must be a more civilized way to get to the lodge."

"The one I rented won't fly nose-down, and—"

"What do you mean the one you rented? Are you saying that that octopus-handed feudal lord builds a lodge on top of a mountain and then makes his guests *rent* helicopters to get to him? Of all the— Do you remember the top price we're willing to pay for that land?"

"Of course I remember."

"Well, knock it down a thousand, dammit."

Donovan was openly grinning. "Right. If I can get a word in here, I wanted to tell you that there's no road. There *was* one when the lodge was built, but a rockslide destroyed it. Lennox decided to leave it as it was. And since it's a private road . . . well, call it a rich man's whim."

"Wonderful. And if a guest doesn't have the taxi fare?"

"Beats me, but he didn't offer to pay ours."

Rebel gritted her teeth. "*You* go. I'll go back to Casper."

"I'll need you here, and you know it."

"If he asks a question you can't answer, excuse yourself and find a phone. I'll be in that cute little motel next to the airport."

Donovan gave her a measuring look. "That's a very childish attitude, you know," he said conversationally.

Not at all offended or provoked, Rebel responded cordially, "I know—isn't it terrible? We all have our little fears, and that's mine."

"Why?"

"Why what?"

"Why are you afraid to fly in helicopters?"

"I can't be rational about it, for heaven's sake! I'm just afraid. I won't go, and that's final."

"You're just being stubborn."

"You bet I am."

"Rebel, it's a short flight. Ten, fifteen minutes. You can close your eyes."

"And what'll I do about my stomach?"

Donovan changed tactics. "Do you want that land?"

"Yes."

"Then you have to come with me."

"No. You can wing it—no pun intended."

"Rebel—"

"*No.* Donovan, I'm *not* going!"

"Rebel . . ."

It took nearly half an hour of patient arguing for Donovan before Rebel finally gave in. By that time she'd been backed into so many corners that she felt rather like a hunted animal. She was still arguing when Donovan calmly picked her up and set her on the backseat of the blue-and-white helicopter he'd managed to drag her to. He fastened her seat belt just as she was telling him in an aggrieved voice to be sure to call her father should she die of heart failure.

Donovan simply grinned and shut her door, climbing into the front beside the pilot.

Rebel realized two things in that moment: one, that he'd picked her up; two, that she was going up in this thing whether she liked it or not. Neither thought did anything to settle her nervous stomach or calm her disordered senses.

She promptly covered her eyes, silently berating herself for the phobia but not at all ashamed of it. As she'd told Donovan, everyone has some sort of fear.

She had been up in a helicopter one time in her life, and that had been one time too many. Surprisingly, though, she didn't feel all that frightened this time. Hesitantly, she parted the fingers covering her eyes and peeked between them. Not too bad, she decided a little sheepishly, as long as she watched the sky and ignored the ground rushing past below.

Donovan had half turned on his seat, watching her with a faint smile. When she finally dropped her hands into her lap, he told her, "See? It's not bad at all." He had to practically shout to be heard over the roar of the aircraft.

Irritated by his composure and her lack of it, Rebel yelled back rashly, "I'll get you for this!" She saw his lips move in a reply, and she blinked as he turned around again. Not that she was adept at reading lips, but hadn't he replied, "Oh, I hope so"? No . . . ridiculous.

They left the small heliport, with its rescue and private craft, far behind, and within moments were surrounded by imposing mountain ranges. Rebel didn't bother to look for signs of civilization, convinced that there weren't any. She didn't even look for Lennox's infamous retreat. She just stared at the back of Donovan's dark head and wished vaguely that she had a star to wish on.

Rebel was so wrapped up in her own muddled thoughts that when Donovan turned and gestured, it took her a moment to realize what he meant. She leaned forward and looked out the side. And her eyes remained glued to the sight before her until the helicopter settled gently on one of three concrete pads beside the lodge.

What had she expected? A lodge. Logs maybe, and native rock. Rustic, cozy, practical. But this lodge was, indeed, a rich man's whim. If Cinderella had been an American story, this would have been the prince's castle.

It perched—literally—on the side of a mountain, hosting the most spectacular view Rebel had ever seen. Above it, its base mountain was snowcapped and majestic. Below it was a sheer drop, a couple of smaller mountains, and then the flat, desertlike plains of eastern Wyoming. Aspen and pine covered the slopes.

The lodge itself was magnificent. No wonder guests didn't complain about the taxi fare.

The wood was not rough-hewn logs but beautifully weathered timber, and the native rock was plentiful. But the rest was glass. There were huge windows on every side, taking full advantage of the views. The central structure was a tremendous A-frame, at least fifty feet from base to apex, its multipaned glass front facing southeast. Twin wings swept out to either side and ended in smaller versions of the central A-frame. Behind the first level was a second one, rising to follow the lay of the land. It, too, held an A-frame, slightly off-center to the left. A third level rose behind it, its A-frame off-center and to the right.

How many rooms did it hold? Thirty? Fifty? Rebel's opinion of Lennox—provided that he had guided the architect—rose. This lodge wasn't just grandiose, it was a perfect jewel in a perfect setting. And it was breathtaking.

She accepted Donovan's help getting out of the helicopter, her eyes still fixed on the lodge. Moving to the foot of the stone steps that led from the helipad to the central A-frame, she finally turned away, shaking her head, and watched Donovan get their cases out of the aircraft. He talked briefly to the pilot and then joined Rebel at the steps, and both watched as the helicopter rose gracefully and soared away.

"Sure this is it?" Rebel asked dryly, gesturing with one thumb over her shoulder.

Facing the lodge, Donovan looked over her head to gaze up at it. He nodded. "This is it. Some altitude, too. Notice how thin the air is?"

"I noticed. If the helicopter ride didn't kill me, the lack of oxygen certainly will."

Donovan looked down at her and grinned. "You don't usually complain, boss. Something bothering you about this trip?" His eyes were wickedly innocent.

Rebel said the first thing that came into her head. "Look, an octopus is still an octopus, even if I do admire his house. I'm not exactly looking forward to this."

"I offered to assume the role of knight-errant," he reminded her. "Come to think of it, I'd probably enjoy the part; it's one I've never played. Shall I post a no-trespassing sign, boss?"

Rebel found herself staring at his mouth, and she hastily looked away. "It's freezing out here; let's go in."

He glanced over her head and up at the lodge again. "Someone's coming. I'm afraid I'll have to take the decision out of your hands. If I have to watch Lennox pawing you—or trying to—I'll probably knock him off his own mountain. Not good for business, boss."

"What—?" Rebel barely had time for the one strangled word before she found herself held securely against a massive chest. She could feel the powerful arms wrapped around her even through the thickness of her winter coat, and she wasn't sure if her breathlessness was due to the thin air, his sudden action, or her pounding heart.

"Donovan!"

"Command decision, boss," he murmured just before his head bent and his lips covered hers.

For a split second Rebel made no move either to push him away or to respond. She had a weird, distorted image of something crashing down within her, and she wondered idly if she was seeing her own defenses bite the dust. She found her fingers clutching the lapels of his coat, and she felt one of his hands coming up to cradle the back of her head.

After that, there was only sensation. He tasted of brandy and exuded a piny scent matching the mountain they stood on. Cold air blew all around them, bringing a needle-sharp awareness to Rebel's skin. She felt his mouth moving gently on hers, and she was aware of her lips blooming and warming in response.

Rebel heard him mutter something against her mouth, and she tried to make sense of the words. But then he was kissing her in a new way, a probing, demanding, devastatingly possessive way, and she forgot his attempt at speech.

She wasn't on the side of a mountain; she was at its top, and a giddy sense of vertigo swept through her. Clouds rushed past, billowing like sails in the wind. Her heart was pounding like a jungle drum gone mad. She thought that she was falling, but the fall was insidiously comforting, and she made no effort to save herself.

A sound intruded. Someone clearing his throat? But that was impossible; they were all alone on top of the mountain. It was absurd to think that anyone could get up here without wings.

She found herself staring blankly up at Donovan's face as he held her shoulders to put her gently away from him. His eyes, she noted dimly, were clouded, more deeply purple than she had ever seen them. He was breathing as roughly as she, and he shook his head slightly as if to clear it. Rebel was aware that her hands were still clutching his lapels, but she was unable to make them let go.

Rebel watched Donovan turn his head at last, apparently to greet the throat-clearer, and she heard a painfully British voice speak. "Good afternoon, Mr. Knight. Miss Anderson. I am Carson, Mr. Lennox's butler. If you'll follow me, please? I'll send someone down for your bags."

Emerging from her trance, Rebel looked at the butler with a flicker of interest. Where had Lennox found him? she wondered. The man had more dignity than Sinclair's entire board of directors. And his voice had been almost inhumanly devoid of expression, as was his face. He was as correctly attired as any butler would be expected to be . . . in a ducal mansion.

Donovan gently removed Rebel's clinging hands from his lapels and tucked one into the crook of his arm. "Carson." He nodded cheerfully. "Lead the way."

Halfway up the steps, Rebel realized abruptly that she was being awfully meek about all this, and belatedly she attempted to pull her hand from beneath Donovan's. His hand tightened to prevent the move, and she cast about in her mind for some suitably cutting remark. For Donovan's ears only, she hissed, "That was a wasted effort—for the butler!"

"Not at all," Donovan murmured in response. "Good practice."

Desperately certain that she'd made a total fool of herself by responding to his kiss, Rebel had a sudden impulse to push him down the steps. With any luck, he'd roll right off the mountain and she could avoid facing him.

"If you keep glowering," Donovan murmured, still not looking at her, "Lennox will think we've had a lovers' spat and he'll try to catch you on the rebound."

Rebel wondered where she had lost control of this situation. When this loony idea had first popped into her head? When she had *seen* Donovan for the first time on the jet? When he'd managed to get her into a helicopter entirely against her will? When he'd kissed her with a hunger she didn't understand?

Oh, Lord . . . would this day never end?

The inside of the lodge was as magnificent as the outside. It had been, Carson told them, dubbed Eagle's Nest by the workmen who had built it, and the name had stuck. Not very original, Rebel noted, but certainly appropriate.

It looked as if a decorator had been allowed free rein inside, given his head and an unlimited budget. The front doors opened into a great room, and it was entirely open from the plushly carpeted floor to the rafters—solid oak beams, from the looks of them—fifty feet above. The carpeting was off-white and ankle deep, the scattered chairs and couches a rust color and nearly as plush as the carpet. A tremendous fireplace graced the back end of the A-frame, occupying nearly the entire wall. Made of stone and beautifully crafted, it was large enough to roast a whole steer.

Carson gave them the grand tour—apparently the customary practice—and Rebel was exhausted when it was over. She had lost count of the rooms, and was bewildered by the number of dens, lounges, and living rooms. She also felt a bit dizzy at the decorating schemes, which changed from wing to wing. One modern, one Early American, one Louis XIV, and so on. And she had deduced early on that every stick of furniture and every bit of porcelain was a genuine whatever-it-was-supposed-to-be.

It wasn't until Carson was leading them toward their suite that Rebel noted two significant things. One was the conspicuous absence of their host, and the other was the dangerous word *suite*.

Wanting to put off the moment of confrontation with Donovan as long as possible, Rebel hurried into speech as Carson was opening the door to their suite. "When do we meet our host, Carson?"

If Carson thought the question odd coming from the secretary rather than the boss, he didn't show it. "Mr. Lennox's apologies, Miss Anderson, but he was forced to fly to Denver on urgent business. He should return tomorrow afternoon, and he asked that you and Mr. Knight enjoy yourselves until he returns."

The butler related the information with a perfectly expressionless face, but Rebel read all sorts of hidden meanings into Lennox's message. She could easily imagine the leer that had probably accompanied it. And the hand still captured by Donovan's arm tightened in sheer temper.

She tried to remember how badly she wanted the land, but she knew she'd be hard put to keep from greeting Lennox with a haymaker he wouldn't soon forget!

Carson led them into the apartment, explaining that each suite had been designed with guests in mind and was made up of a sitting room, two bedrooms, and two baths—which relieved one of Rebel's cares. Their suite was at the front of the house and in the modern wing. The furniture was ultra-modern but looked comfortable: a modular couch and a love seat of sorts, a couple of chairs, a desk in one corner. The floor was polished hardwood with rugs scattered here and there, including a white fluffy one in front of a huge fireplace. That rug, Rebel thought, positively invited one to sink bare toes into it.

The bedrooms, too, looked comfortable, although Rebel looked into hers only long enough to see that her luggage had been placed at the foot of the wide bed.

Carson told them when and where dinner would be served, pointed out the bell in the sitting room, which they could ring if they wanted anything, politely invited them to explore the house further if they wished, and then bowed himself out.

Rebel barely waited until the door clicked shut behind him before jerking away from Donovan. She took off her coat and tossed it at a chair, feeling her polite expression dissolve and the glower return. She wanted very badly to vent her confused emotions on somebody and Donovan made a large and inviting target. But he took the wind out of her sails.

"I know you're upset about what happened on the steps," he began directly, his coat joining Rebel's on the chair, "but surely you see that it's the best way. Lennox will concentrate on business, and you won't have to worry about being pulled into dark corners."

Momentarily deprived of ammunition, Rebel quickly made up

for the lack. "It was the *butler!* Would you like to tell me why the butler had to think we're having an affair?"

"It was good practice," he returned, unperturbed.

"You don't need any practice," she snapped. She immediately regretted the remark.

"Thank you," he murmured, a smile tugging at his lips.

Rebel crossed her arms defensively over her breasts and the low-cut dress. "I didn't mean it like that," she said in confusion, determined to get control of herself. She drew herself up to her full and usually imposing height of five eight and glared at him. "I don't like playing that kind of game," she announced coldly.

"Afraid?" he asked softly.

It was a direct challenge, and Rebel felt some of the steel melt from her spine. "Afraid of what?" she asked uneasily.

"Afraid of letting go of that strictly-business facade and allowing the real you to emerge?"

Rebel suspected that that was the point when she should call for a helicopter and leave without another word. But she knew for sure that Donovan was challenging her and that Marc Sinclair's daughter had never refused a challenge.

She lifted her chin and deepened the glare. "There's no 'facade' to let go of."

"Oh, no?" Donovan strolled over to one of the wide windows and gazed out at the spectacular view. Then he turned back to her and spoke calmly. "Rebel, you've wrapped Sinclair Corporation around you so tightly that it's like a chrysalis. If that's just a stage of development, then it's fine; butterflies emerge from chrysalises. But if you don't break out, then there's no development. No growth, no change. Just stagnation."

Rebel kept her voice level with an effort. "And you want to help me break out of the chrysalis, is that it?"

Donovan hesitated for a moment, his veiled eyes searching

hers as though looking for something. Whatever it was, he apparently didn't find it, for his sigh held resignation. "You're going to take this the wrong way, but yes, I'd like to help you do that."

"Gee, thanks." Rebel didn't know what other way she could have taken it. "To what do I owe the honor?"

He sighed again and leaned a hip against the desk by the window. "Don't lose your temper, please. I'm not talking about our so-called affair. I'm talking about the fact that you've forgotten how to relate to someone on a one-to-one level. You look at people, boss, as though you're sizing them up across a bargaining table. With you, it's always black or white—no shades of gray."

"Anything else?" she asked tightly.

"Yes," he answered levelly. "There is one other thing. Your appearance. Over the past year, I've watched you strip yourself of layer after layer of femininity. Your hairstyles became more severe; you cut your nails and stopped polishing them; your suits became more formal, more masculine. No jewelry, no ruffles or frills. Even your walk changed, became brisk and businesslike. You've become a caricature of a businesswoman."

Rebel felt a chill as he echoed her thoughts of the day before. Before she could speak, he was going on.

"Until today. Today you look very feminine, very sexy, and very much a woman. Today you look like a business*woman*, rather than a *business*woman. You're breaking out of that chrysalis—or trying to."

Mercifully, Rebel thought, he didn't speculate on the reasons for her change. "I want to be taken seriously," she defended herself, troubled to realize that she had taken that idea to its farthest extreme.

Donovan shook his head. "You're respected for what's inside, Rebel, not what's outside. Your first duty is to gain the attention of whomever you're dealing with. So why not use the ammunition God gave you?"

Rebel wanted to consider that a sexist remark, but somehow she didn't think it was. She met his eyes, noticed the searching expression in them, and strove to keep her own blank.

After a long, silent moment, Donovan sighed. "Look, forget the business angle for the moment. According to Marc, you haven't had a vacation since you left school, and that's been three years. Until Lennox gets here, why don't we both relax and consider this a brief vacation? It won't hurt, and it'll probably do us both good."

Rebel nodded slowly, thoughts of her "chrysalis" flitting through her mind. Had it really gotten that bad?

"Good." Donovan's voice was unusually gentle, as though he saw or sensed her weary confusion. "Now, why don't you lie down and try to rest before dinner? It's been a long day."

Silently, Rebel turned and went into her bedroom, closing the door behind her. She told herself that she was only agreeing to his suggestion because she was tired.

But the real reason was that she had felt tears sting her eyes suddenly. Inexplicable tears. And she didn't want Donovan asking questions that she couldn't answer.

Chapter Three

*D*inner was a strange affair. It was as if, Rebel thought, she and Donovan were strangers. Careful, tentative questions elicited guarded answers. The company wasn't mentioned, nor the reason that had brought them to Wyoming. They tacitly avoided potentially dangerous topics, falling back on the trite and commonplace.

Carson—white gloves and all—served them in a dining room that could have seated twenty people without crowding. The pheasant was delicious, as was the remainder of the meal. But Rebel, desperately aware of the deteriorating conversation, hardly noticed. She finally excused herself before Donovan could resort to polite conjecture about the Superbowl this season.

She found her way into the central greatroom and sat down in a chair near the fireplace, watching flames lick at what looked like half an oak tree. Moments later she nearly jumped out of her skin when large hands came to rest on her shoulders.

"You're as tense as a drawn bow," Donovan said quietly from behind her chair. His fingers began to move in a gentle, soothing massage. "Relax."

Rebel wanted to tell him that it was impossible to relax with him touching her, however innocently, but she managed to bite back the words. She couldn't, however, halt the sensations rushing through her body. The warmth of his hands easily penetrated the thin silk of her dress, setting her nerve endings on fire. Her heart was pounding, and she felt again the dizzying sense of vertigo. What was the man—a warlock? Why did he make her feel this way? She had never felt this way before, not even with Jud. And she'd *loved* Jud. Once, she had loved him. Before she found out . . .

Donovan spoke again, quietly, calmly, cutting into her thoughts. "You know, of course, that I want you."

Rebel stiffened and stared blindly into the fire. "Do you?" She was amazed that her voice was so calm.

"Very much."

"You never mentioned it before," she observed, for all the world as though they were talking about something unimportant.

"You never looked at me before. Not the way you've been looking at me today."

"You're imagining things," she scoffed.

"No. Until today you had never really seen me as a man, had you, Rebel?"

Rebel shifted uneasily and found that his hands, gentle though they were, would not let her escape. She wondered suddenly why he was standing behind her. The thought had barely crossed her mind when he came around the chair, drawing forward a hassock and sitting down to face her. Deliberately or not, he had chosen a position that made it impossible for her to get away.

"You've been so wrapped up in that damned company that you never noticed anything else—until today."

"How you do harp on this supposed transformation of mine," she managed lightly.

His jaw tightened—the first sign of temper she had ever seen in him. "Rebel, don't try to avoid the issue."

"And just what is the issue?" she asked evenly.

"Us. And what we could have together."

Rebel didn't like the question that was plodding with deadly slowness, deadly clarity, through her mind. But it was there, and it hurt her in a way she hadn't been hurt in years.

What was Donovan really after—her, or Sinclair Hotels?

If she asked him, he'd only deny any interest in the company, she thought cynically. But Rebel strongly mistrusted his sudden interest in her as a woman. So . . . what? A confrontation now was the last thing she needed or wanted.

"Oh, damn," she murmured at last. "I forgot the key."

Donovan blinked. "Key? What key?"

"The key to my chastity belt."

Looking for the effect of her soft words, Rebel watched as Donovan leaned back slightly and stared at her. Somewhat to her surprise, he didn't become angry with her flippancy, but instead seemed thoughtful. After a moment, he nodded slightly as though coming to a silent decision. And when he spoke, his voice was as light as hers had been.

"We could always call a good locksmith."

"Wouldn't work; the belt's an old model."

"At least a few years old," he murmured innocently.

Rebel started to snap at him, and then remembered that she was supposed to be taking this whole conversation lightly. "At least," she agreed limpidly.

It was Donovan's move, and she waited to see if he would at least try for a stalemate. But Donovan neatly retired from the board, and Rebel didn't know whether to be relieved or disappointed.

"Ah, well, forgive the trespass, milady. I'm abashed."

"A bashed what?"

"Cute. Is that what they call rapier wit?"

"It's what they call tired wit. If you'll kindly get out of my way, I'll go to bed."

Donovan got to his feet and politely moved aside so that she could rise. He made no move to follow her, and he didn't speak again until she was at the archway leading to their wing.

"Fair warning," he said cheerfully. "I'm very adept at picking locks."

Rebel turned to look at him. "I'll just bet you are," she deadpanned. "So—fair warning to you: This lock's booby-trapped."

Donovan inclined his head slightly at the warning. "Good night, boss," he said, his cheerfulness not diminished by one iota.

"Good night."

Rebel managed to find her way to their suite—no mean feat considering that she wasn't really paying attention to where she was going. Going through the sitting room, she noted that someone had built a fire in the fireplace, and she wondered if Carson believed the night would be filled with romancing. Shoving that curiously painful thought aside, she went into her bedroom.

The busy "someone" had turned down the quilted spread on her bed and laid out a peach satin nightgown. Rebel methodically got ready for bed, her blank mind a result of weariness rather than effort. As she slid between cool sheets and reached to turn out the lamp on her nightstand, she wondered how on earth she was supposed to sleep. . . .

Rebel didn't remember closing her eyes, but when she opened them light was flooding the room. She lay there for a moment and blinked at the ceiling before sitting up.

The events of yesterday rushed through her mind in a kaleido-scope of impressions, ending at last at the semiconfrontation of the night before. She'd been wrong, Rebel realized now, in believing that Donovan had retired from the board, conceding defeat. He had merely retreated to a tactical holding position.

So whose move was it now?

Shaking off the question, Rebel slid from the bed. A glance at her watch on the nightstand told her that it was nine A.M., which meant that she'd slept nearly eleven hours. No wonder she felt rested! During the past few years she'd averaged no more than six or seven hours of sleep a night.

Now she felt wide awake, clear headed, and ravenous. Probably the mountain air was responsible for the last, she thought.

Since her cases had been unpacked the day before, Rebel searched through drawers until she had the clothing she wanted. She told herself fiercely that Donovan's comments had nothing to do with her decision to put the businesswoman away in her briefcase for a while. She told herself that . . . but she didn't believe herself.

In the bathroom, she resisted the invitation of the sunken tub large enough to host an elephant, opting instead for a quick shower. Some time later she stood in front of the full-length mirror in the bathroom and stared at her reflection critically.

Apparently Donovan had told Bessie to pack some casual clothes, because the jeans were certainly not something Bessie would have automatically included. Faded and growing shiny in the seat, they hugged her slender hips and thighs. She had chosen a blue cowl-necked sweater to go with the jeans. It was bulky, but not so much so that it hid the curves beneath. After a brief struggle with herself, she put up her hair in a casual, girlish ponytail, trying to ignore an urge to leave it down and see if Donovan said anything. She had applied her makeup carefully and deliberately, and now she studied the overall effect.

She looked years younger and not in the least like her mental image of a businesswoman.

Smiling with satisfaction, Rebel returned to her bedroom and searched for shoes. She found scuffed riding boots and lifted her eyebrows briefly in silent surprise, then shrugged and pulled on the boots. At that moment she would have bet half her company that there were horses somewhere about.

Leaving her bedroom and going through the sitting room, she glanced into Donovan's room and saw the bed neatly made and very empty. That didn't surprise her; she would have bet the other half of her company that he was an early riser.

Rebel took her time finding the dining room, partly because she got lost and partly because she wanted to explore some more anyway. She wandered from wing to wing, gazing at furnishings and decorations and becoming increasingly puzzled. One room in particular—in the Early American wing—disturbed her. There was a rectangular spot on one wall that indicated that a large painting was missing, and that bothered her, although she couldn't have said exactly why.

She was gazing at the bare patch on the papered wall when she became aware that she was no longer alone. Turning slowly, she felt her eyes widen in surprise.

At first guess, it was at least half timber wolf. A closer look told Rebel that she was staring at one of the largest specimens of Siberian husky she had ever seen. And the ice-blue eyes were narrowed and suspicious.

Rebel didn't waste any time. With a dog of that size, the smart thing would be to become friends as quickly as possible. She dropped down to her knees and held out one hand, palm down. "Hello, fella. Where did you come from?"

The husky advanced, a bit stiff-legged, and examined the hand held out to it. A sniff, and then the curled tail wagged tentatively.

Within moments, the big dog was practically sitting in Rebel's lap and busily washing her face with a tongue the size of a hand towel.

Rebel held on to the thick silver-gray ruff of the dog's neck and giggled as she tried to save her makeup. "Stop that! I won't have a face left when you get through."

"I see you've met Tosh."

She jumped to her feet as the dog abandoned her to dash to the large form leaning against the doorjamb. Watching the dog frisking around Donovan's feet, Rebel mentally discarded the formality she'd planned on assuming today. It didn't fit her new image, and besides, she didn't need formality as a shield. Did she?

"He's beautiful. Why didn't we see him yesterday?"

Donovan bent slightly to scratch a blissful Tosh behind one ear. "Carson said he was at the stables."

Rebel silently gave herself a gold star for intuition and studied Donovan while he was paying attention to Tosh. He was dressed more casually than she'd ever seen him, in jeans and a ski sweater. Like her, he was wearing boots. He looked relaxed and cheerful, and for the first time, she noticed the laugh lines at the corners of his eyes.

When he looked up and met her gaze, Rebel said the first thing that came into her head. "I wonder why that painting's missing," she murmured, jerking a thumb over her shoulder.

Donovan looked at the naked wall and then shrugged. "Ask Lennox, if he ever gets here."

Rebel felt a sense of foreboding. "What do you mean if he ever gets here?"

"You didn't look out your window this morning, did you?"

"No." Rebel frowned. "Why?"

"We had a little snow during the night. Denver had more than a little."

"Lennox isn't coming?"

"Not today. I just talked to him on the phone. Apparently Denver is snowed in. Doesn't happen often, but it does happen."

Rebel sighed. "Uh-huh. It figures."

"Cheer up," he directed lightly. "We get another day of vacation. Now, how about breakfast? Then we can saddle up and explore some of the trails around here."

"In the snow?"

"Why not? The horses are used to it."

"How do you know I can ride?" she challenged.

"That picture Marc used to keep on his desk," Donovan supplied instantly. "I think you were about sixteen and had just won some kind of rodeo final."

Rebel felt a twinge of pain as she remembered those carefree days. How long had it been since she'd ridden? Not since the divorce. Seven years. Where had the time gone?

"Hey." Donovan had crossed the room to stand in front of her. "Sorry if I struck a nerve; I didn't mean to."

"You didn't." She stared fixedly at some point near the middle of his chest.

"No?" His hand lifted to firmly tip her chin up. "Then why do you look so sad?"

Gazing into his quiet, curiously shuttered violet eyes, Rebel felt suddenly that she could tell him this, that he would understand. She couldn't remember the last time she'd confided her feelings to anyone, and she wondered dimly if she'd really lost touch with other people so completely.

"Tell me," he urged softly.

She uttered a shaky laugh. "For a minute there—when you mentioned that picture on Dad's desk—I felt old. And I wondered what had happened . . . and why it happened so fast."

The hand beneath her chin shifted to gently cup the side of her neck. "And you felt lost and alone," he finished quietly.

Rebel nodded mutely.

Donovan drew her into his arms and held her firmly, resting his chin on the top of her head. "It happens sometimes," he said pensively. "Odd moments when everything screeches to a stop and you wonder where the time has gone. You wonder if you've made a wrong turn somewhere, and what would have happened if you'd turned left instead of right."

He *did* understand, and Rebel let herself relax in his comforting embrace. "It's a scary feeling," she whispered.

"Very," he agreed. "But don't let it throw you, boss. I won't let you get lost for long, and you're never alone."

Rebel carefully stepped back, vaguely disappointed when he made no effort to stop her, and stared at him. "Why am I never alone?"

"Because you've got me." The words were uttered lightly, and he immediately took her arm and began leading her from the room. "I'm your man, boss. Always have been. Ready for breakfast?"

Breakfast was a lighthearted meal, thanks largely to Tosh, who begged shamelessly for bacon. Thanks also to Donovan, who kept up a steady flow of utterly meaningless, totally absurd conversation.

"Did you know that there's a legend about an old prospector who climbed this mountain and never came down?"

"Is there?"

"Yes."

"And so?"

"And so what?"

"Is there a point to the story?"

"Not really."

"Then why did you bring it up?"

"Seemed the thing to do."

"I'm going to dock your pay."

"Ssshh—Carson will hear you."

"I don't care."

"You should. There's another story—"

"I don't want to hear it, Donovan."

"—about a mermaid who lives in a cave near here."

"Mermaids live in the ocean."

"This one lives in a cave."

"Yeah? How do you know?"

"Carson unbent enough to tell me about it."

Rebel casually slipped a piece of bacon under the table for Tosh. "Unbent? He'd have to un*ravel* to tell you something like that."

"Stop feeding the dog; he's half grizzly bear already."

"Who's feeding the dog?"

"You are. That's the third piece of bacon you've snuck to him."

"You're seeing things."

"And you're going to split hell wide open if you keep lying like that."

"You're playing Russian roulette with your future, buddy."

Donovan shook his head, blatantly feeding Tosh a piece of bacon. "I know. My boss is a holy terror. No sense of humor."

"Your boss is currently having her ankle chewed on by half a grizzly bear. What did you do, drop that bacon on my foot?"

"Tosh, stop that!"

"Forget it. I'll just have to buy a new pair of boots."

"Speaking of boots, are we going riding or aren't we?"

"You just want to see me suffer, don't you?"

"It's been a while, huh? Since you've ridden, I mean."

"A while," she agreed wryly. "Seven years. An hour in the saddle, and I'll be sore tomorrow."

"I'll ask Carson for some liniment and give you a good massage. How's that sound?"

It took Rebel a moment or so to remember that she wasn't going to take him seriously. Just the thought of his hands on her bare body was enough to send a flame through her veins. "Thanks, but I think I can handle it," she managed at last.

"Spoilsport."

"That's me. Shall we head for the stables?"

Donovan didn't appear at all downcast by her offhand rejection. "After you, boss."

"As it should be."

"Why?"

"Because if you go first, nobody sees me."

"There's nobody here to see either of us."

"It's the principle of the thing."

"Oh."

With a laugh, Rebel serenely preceded him to the door, halting only long enough to don a thick flannel jacket that Donovan pulled from a closet.

"How did you know that was there?"

"Carson."

That figured. "Whose is it?"

"Beats me." Donovan pulled another jacket from the closet and put it on. "This one's mine," he said before she could ask. "I left it here earlier this morning."

Rebel accepted the information. He could hardly have pulled a jacket from the closet that just happened to fit him; his size wasn't exactly average.

He led her unerringly from the lodge to the stables along an almost invisible path. Their boots crunched in the two or three inches of snow, and a slight cold breeze blew all around them. The morning was pleasantly brisk; in fact, it made Rebel feel very alive.

The stables were tucked away beneath trees and on the gentle slope of the mountain, built on levels like the lodge. There were roughly twenty separate stalls opening into various wide halls, a feed room, and a tack room. And two horses were tied near the tack room, saddled up and ready to go.

"You called ahead?"

"Came down this morning. The palomino's yours; her name is Sugarfoot."

Rebel reached to stroke the mare's golden neck and then tugged at the snowy white mane. "Lennox sure does himself proud," she murmured almost to herself. "This has to be more than just a lodge. I've counted four stable hands; the house staff is made up of Carson, a housekeeper, four maids, and a cook; and there are twenty horses here. Not to mention Tosh. He keeps all this on tap just for vacations? Doesn't make sense."

"It does if you're rich apparently. Want a leg up?"

"No, thanks." Rebel untied Sugarfoot, glancing over at the big muscled bay gelding Donovan was preparing to mount. "Does he have a name?" she asked, swinging into the saddle lightly.

Donovan grinned at her as the horses moved out of the wide hall. "Sure. His name's Diablo."

Rebel couldn't bring herself to comment, but it struck her as vaguely unnerving that Donovan was riding a horse named Devil.

Their ride lasted for nearly two hours and covered several different trails, including one that passed by a hollowed-out place in the side of the mountain that could have been taken for a cave.

"Told you there was a cave."

"Where's the mermaid?"

"She must be hibernating."

"Cute."

Beginning to feel chilled and definitely stiff, Rebel gratefully accepted Donovan's suggestion that she dismount at the lodge and let him take the horses back to the stables. She felt long-unused muscles protest as she swung down, and she winced slightly as she stepped over to hand Donovan the reins.

"I think you've killed me, and all for nothing. I didn't leave you a thing in my will," she told him darkly.

He chuckled. "You'll recover. I'd advise a hot bath."

"I'm way ahead of you. Don't fall off the mountain on your trip down to the stables."

"Concerned, boss?"

"Dreadfully. You have to be alive to keep me from killing Lennox when he finally arrives."

"Is that all I'm good for?" he asked, wounded.

"Don't ask loaded questions. 'Bye." Rebel turned away and headed for the door. She passed two of the maids and Carson on her way through the house, and she wondered again about Lennox's lodge.

Something about this whole place bothered her, but she just couldn't pin it down. She probably could have pinned it down, she realized wryly, if only her mind would assume its normal habit of working properly. But she'd been off balance and rattled since this trip had begun. And she had a sneaking suspicion that this state of affairs was entirely due to the sudden change in her relationship with Donovan.

In her bathroom, Rebel located bubble bath provided by her thoughtful and still-absent host, poured it into the huge sunken tub, and then rapidly stripped while the tub was filling.

At all costs, she thought, she had to avoid a confrontation with Donovan over what he was really after. A confrontation would ultimately end in one of two ways: Either she would fire Donovan, or he would quit—neither of which would do. She told herself that her concern was because of the land; she needed Donovan to bargain with Lennox.

For the first time, Sinclair Hotels felt like an albatross around her neck. No, not for the first time. But for the first time in years. And this time it hurt terribly to understand that she could well be only the means to an end—the end of controlling a vast and profitable corporation.

Shoving the thoughts into the small and rapidly overflowing room in her mind reserved for "tomorrow," Rebel wound her ponytail into a knot on top of her head, stuck a few pins in it, and climbed into the tub.

She turned off the taps and leaned back in the hot water, letting the bubbles and the heat pamper her. The tub was deep, and the bubbles reached nearly to her chin.

The thoughts in their little room continued to tease her, and Rebel finally gave up the attempt to ignore them. They wouldn't wait for tomorrow. She admitted to herself, silently and painfully, that Donovan's "I want you" had stirred something inside her. If she had felt nothing, the possibility that he was after the company would not have bothered her, would not have hurt.

But it did bother her; it did hurt. For the first time since the divorce, she was interested—no, fascinated—by a man. Setting aside their roles as employer and employee, could she have any sort of relationship with a man whose eyes were fixed on the president's chair? The nontraditional roles didn't really bother her, and she didn't think they bothered Donovan either—although that was easy to say here, far away from the office.

No, the real question was what Donovan wanted. If it was the company, no relationship was even conceivable. But if he wanted just her, well . . . Rebel closed her eyes and let herself think about what that might mean.

A sharp knock sounded on the bathroom door, followed by a cheerful, "Are you decent?" and just barely preceded by Donovan's entrance into the room.

Rebel instinctively grabbed a woefully small washcloth and held it to her breasts, covering what the dissolving bubbles were beginning to expose. Caught totally off guard, she stared at him in speechless indignation.

Dressed only in jeans, which left bare an unexpectedly furry chest, Donovan casually perched on the raised edge of the tub and gazed down at her. His eyes flitted briefly over white flesh visible between disappearing bubbles and then swiftly returned to her flushing face. And Rebel had the odd feeling that he was holding on to some private resolution with both hands.

"Cocoa." He held out a large mug. "To warm up the inside."

"I don't like cocoa!" she snapped. "Leave!"

"You could at least be polite," he observed reprovingly.

"To a man who charges unannounced into my bathroom? Not bloody likely! Take your cocoa and leave!"

Donovan set the mug down on the tiled floor. "I thought I'd wash your back for you."

Rebel felt her heart bump against one hand. She tried desperately to assume the boardroom dignity she'd acquired over the years, but she found that dissolving bubbles and a half-naked man did nothing to promote any kind of dignity at all. The assurance of twenty-eight years and a corporate presidency notwithstanding, she had never felt more vulnerable in her life.

"Leave," she whispered finally. "Donovan, please leave."

His violet eyes were slowly darkening to purple. "You don't really want me to go." He leaned forward to press his lips briefly to one soapy shoulder. "Do you?"

"I don't want things to change," she managed, not even sure what she meant by that.

"Things have already changed." One of his hands had cupped the back of her neck, and he was drawing her slowly toward him. "You can't turn back the clock. It might not have happened except for this trip, but it did happen. Nothing will ever be the same between us, Rebel. Not now. And you know that as well as I do."

Rebel watched his face coming closer, lost herself somehow in the depths of his purple eyes, and a last protest died in her throat.

When his lips touched hers, she felt something flare inside her, something primitive and hungry. One of her hands abandoned the cloth she was still holding against her breasts to touch his lean cheek with a need beyond thought, beyond reason. Her lips parted willingly, eagerly, beneath his.

Donovan explored her mouth slowly, as though all the time in the world was theirs. He defied any resistance, seduced and defeated it. She could feel tension in him, and a burning heat, and she realized dimly that he was holding himself rigidly in check.

Rebel couldn't believe that she could be so deeply affected by a simple kiss. Every nerve ending in her body came vividly alive, throbbing with feelings and sensations she had never known before. The warm water flowed all around her; his fingers brushed lightly, gently, against the side of her neck; his lips held hers like an insidious trap made of satin. Colors whirled behind her closed eyelids—reds and purples and sparks of silver fire. Tension grew in her like a living thing.

And when his lips finally, abruptly, left her, Rebel wanted to scream aloud in frustration and disappointment. But she didn't make a sound; she simply blinked up at the man who had risen and was now towering above her.

Donovan murmured something beneath his breath and shook his head slightly, a gesture she remembered from the day before and that electrifying kiss at the bottom of the steps. When he spoke, his voice was only a shade more hoarse than usual.

"Lunch will be ready in half an hour. I'll meet you in the dining room. Okay?" He barely waited for her silent nod before leaving the room.

Rebel tried to think clearly, tried to make her mind work in its usual shrewd and logical manner, but to no avail. Only one thing kept revolving in her head. What he had said beneath his breath a moment ago, what he had muttered against her mouth yesterday at the bottom of the steps.

"A year," he had muttered hoarsely. "My God . . . a year. . . ."

Chapter Four

Once again, *Rebel decided to treat her relationship with* Donovan lightly. It would not be easy, she knew, because Donovan had made the next move. He had made it clear to her that role-reversals and a pretense of knight-errantry notwithstanding, he wanted her.

And Rebel had realized when Donovan had left her alone with her bubbles that she wanted him as well. Had that been his intention? The soul-destroying kiss ending abruptly and leaving her unsatisfied? Perhaps. If so, then she could expect other interludes calculated to wear down her resistance.

Her resistance . . . oh, that was funny. If Donovan only knew, her resistance to him was absolutely nil. And that was why she had to keep things light between them. Because if she didn't—if she turned left instead of right and jumped blindly into a serious relationship—then she would never be able to be sure that it was her and not the company that Donovan wanted. And that would blast her self-respect, leaving it as tattered as her marriage had.

So Rebel slowly and carefully got a grip on her bewildered senses as she climbed from the tub, dried off, and dressed. She used every mental trick she had ever learned, pouncing on traitorous desires and wrestling them into sheltered corners of herself. She did not examine her own feelings, flinching away as one would to protect a raw wound. She simply repressed them.

She dressed in slacks and a light sweater, thoroughly brushed her hair, and refastened it into the casual ponytail. Then she composed her face into calmness and headed for the dining room.

One of the many phones throughout the lodge was in the dining room, and Donovan was talking on it when Rebel entered. She was too preoccupied to listen closely to what he was saying for a moment or so, merely noting silently that he had donned a Western-style flannel shirt over the jeans and reclaimed his boots. She also noticed that his black hair was damp from a recent shower, and she felt a flicker of interested speculation as to whether it had been hot or cold.

Then she pushed aside the thought and stared at his broad back, his end of the conversation breaking through her abstraction.

". . . and one day more or less *will* matter. Because the timing has to be perfect, that's why. No. No, blindly unsuspecting. What do you mean sudden? It's not sudden at all. Never mind that now; I'll explain later. Just do it." His level voice roughened suddenly. "I don't care if it upsets airline schedules all over the world; this is important to me!"

He was silent for a few moments, apparently listening to the person on the other end of the line. "All right, then. No, he's still in Denver. Well, it's obvious, isn't it? Wouldn't you smell a rat? Right. I'll make the arrangements. See you then."

As Donovan replaced the receiver, he stiffened suddenly and then turned slowly to meet Rebel's watchful gaze. He looked startled and ill at ease for a split second, and her suspicions climbed a good three or four notches.

"Who was that?" she asked mildly.

Donovan slid his hands into the back pockets of his jeans, matching her own stance, and seemed to brace his shoulders. "Josh—from the office."

"I know who Josh is, Donovan."

"Sorry."

"Well?"

Donovan sighed. "I talked to Lennox again a few minutes ago, and I think he's decided to play hard to get. He claims that an emergency business meeting has postponed his return to the lodge indefinitely."

Rebel's vague suspicions dissipated, and she felt herself beginning to do a slow burn. "Dammit! Then we'll go back to Dallas and look for another piece of property—"

"I have a better idea."

She studied him curiously. He appeared a bit different, and she wondered if that was why he'd looked uncomfortable when he'd turned and seen her listening to the conversation. Was he worried about taking the initiative?

"What have you been up to, Donovan?"

He grinned slightly, a wicked twinkle in his violet eyes. "I'll have to ask you to trust me on that point. Let's just say that I think I can get Lennox here by the first of the week—and he'll be more than willing to talk business. Nothing illegal," he added hastily. "Just a bit underhanded. And since we're already being slightly underhanded, I didn't think you'd mind if I . . . upped the ante?"

Rebel had a burning curiosity to know exactly what Donovan

had planned, but something stopped her from asking the question, and she didn't know why. "All right. But I'll expect to hear the whole story before this is over with, Donovan."

"Oh, you will, boss. You certainly will."

During the light lunch of soup and salad, which followed hard on the heels of their conversation, Rebel reflected that this new turn of events meant at least four more days alone with Donovan. Of course, she could have flown back to Casper and then on to Dallas until Lennox was due to arrive here. But that would have entailed a sinful waste of the Lear's expensive fuel. No, she would remain here.

But her often-repeated resolution to treat her changing relationship with Donovan lightly would be sorely tested. Was, in fact, being tested right now. His new and disturbing way of looking at her—born on the jet coming out here—had increased in intensity. The warmth in his eyes was decidedly unsettling.

Her one serious romantic relationship had not prepared her for this man who looked at her as though she were an oasis come upon suddenly in a bleak and barren desert. A part of her wanted to give up and give in, to explore the possibilities and the promises she could see in his eyes. Another part of her resisted the urge, unable to bear the thought of laying what she was at his feet and watching him walk over her as Jud had. She wouldn't go through that again.

Rebel managed to make it through the afternoon, primarily because Donovan seemed bent on keeping her relaxed and amused. He unearthed a Monopoly game shortly after lunch and engaged her in a life-and-death battle on the floor of the central greatroom. Tosh lay before the roaring fire, wagging his tail from time to time.

"You cheated!"

"That's slander."

"So sue me, but move that piece back."

"Command order, boss?"

"You'd better believe it. Ha! I own that property—pay up."

"All right, but I'll have my revenge. See? That puts you in jail. Now who's one-up?"

"Don't gloat; it isn't becoming."

"You gloated when *I* landed in jail."

"That was different."

"Uh-huh. Want to buy your way out, jailbird?"

"Stop waving that card under my nose! All right, let's bargain. What do you want for it?"

"The key."

"What key?"

"How soon we forget. The key to the chastity belt."

"Too steep. Try again."

"No way. The key or nothing."

"Look, it's snowing."

"Stop avoiding the subject. The key."

"I'll give you all my property on that side of the board. Total control for you. How about it?"

"Nope. The key."

"Forget it, chum. The lady of the castle takes a dim view of someone else's holding her key."

"What about the lord of the castle?"

"There isn't one. He was pinching the maids, and I kicked him out. I can run the castle very nicely on my own, thank you."

"The jousting tournaments must be hell."

"Funny."

"The dragon-fighting, too."

"*Will* you be businesslike?"

"Knight-errants are romantic, not businesslike."

"Well, knight-errants don't own keys to chastity belts. It's a rule. They just borrow them."

"Oh. Can I do that?"

"No. Look what happened to Launcelot."

"Unlucky devil, wasn't he?"

"What do you expect? He tampered with the king's lady."

"Tampered. That's a new description."

"Don't be crass. How much for the card?"

"No key, huh?"

"Nope."

"Then let's try the barter system. Knights are good at that. I'll trade you this little card for another piece of paper."

"How many dollar signs are on that paper?"

"Just a couple."

"You want two bucks for the card?"

"No. I want a small piece of paper that *costs* two bucks—or thereabouts."

"You've lost me. What's this paper?"

"It's called a marriage license."

"Sorry. Not an even trade."

"You want out of jail, don't you?"

"Not that badly."

"Ouch. That hurt."

"Good. A hundred bucks for the card?"

"Plus the property?"

"Yes, dammit."

"Deal. If I can't have what I want, I'll take what I can. You're a shrewd businesswoman, boss."

"Right. I just lost control of one whole side of the board. My father would have a heart attack if he knew."

"You kept the key, though."

"Of course."

"And left a poor knight to eat his heart out."

Rebel began to soulfully hum the theme from *Gone with the Wind*, and Donovan threw a little red house at her.

"Frankly, my dear—"

"Don't say it!" she begged, laughing.

"—I think we should finish the game."

Sadly Rebel observed, "It wouldn't work without the moustache, anyway."

"Roll the dice, Scarlett."

The game was temporarily interrupted by dinner, the passage of time surprising both of them, but was picked up almost immediately after the roast chicken was demolished. Treading softly, Carson came into the greatroom once to build up the fire and was nearly out of the room before Rebel saw him.

"Carson, arrest Mr. Knight—he's cheating!"

"Sorry, Miss—this isn't my jurisdiction."

Rebel looked blankly at Donovan when the butler had gone. "Did Carson make a joke?"

"I think so."

"I wonder if he meant to?"

"Beats me. Are you going to put a hotel on Park Place?"

"It takes nerve to ask me a question like that."

"I beg your pardon, I'm sure."

Rebel finally called a halt to the game some time later, saying virtuously that she would no longer do business with an out-and-out shyster. Donovan looked so wounded that she nearly giggled, but she managed to keep a straight face as she wandered over to browse through a magazine rack. Donovan put away the board and the game pieces, then stretched out on a couch with a sigh of contentment.

"This is the life," he murmured.

"Don't get used to it," she warned wryly, locating a fashion magazine presumably left by one of Lennox's lady friends. Deciding to get back in touch with current styles, Rebel took the magazine to a chair and curled up to study it. Both she and Donovan had shed their heavy boots right after dinner, and it was easy to get comfortable.

Physically. Mentally was another matter. Rebel quickly discovered that without the light banter that had been the rule for the afternoon, she had entirely too much time to think—and not about fashion.

She blanked her mind and flipped listlessly through the magazine, then set it aside on an end table. She found both her glances and thoughts straying to Donovan's apparently sleeping form, and she grew steadily more restless. The silence was unnerving.

Rebel got to her feet with the idea of turning on the extensive stereo system in one corner of the room. She needed background noise. Badly.

"In the cabinet by the left speaker," Donovan murmured.

Rebel froze and turned slowly to gaze at him, puzzled. He was lying with his eyes closed. "What?"

"The tapes. They're in the cabinet beside the left speaker."

"How did you—?" Rebel stared at him blankly.

Donovan's eyes opened abruptly and lifted to her, a startled, bemused expression flickering in their violet depths. "Oh . . . well, you looked as if you wanted to hear some music."

"I did?"

"Sure."

Rebel wondered briefly what her I-want-to-hear-some-music expression looked like, and then she realized something. "You weren't looking at me," she pointed out.

"Of course I was. How else would I know what your face looked like?"

That made sense. Rebel shrugged and went over to the stereo. It only took a few moments for her to figure the thing out. She chose a tape at random and pulled it from its slot, not even bothering to see what it was before she placed it in the player and flipped a switch. Immediately, loud music filled the room.

She hastily turned down the volume, inwardly cursing and horribly embarrassed. And not because of the volume.

Brilliant move! she silently and caustically applauded herself. Lennox probably kept this particular tape for the purpose of seducing his secretaries. It was Ravel's "Bolero." In Rebel's opinion, it was the most erotic piece of music ever written.

The heavy, sensuous rhythm filled the room even at low volume. She didn't dare snatch the tape from the player, knowing that her reason for the move would be easily understood. Instead, she wandered with apparent aimlessness toward the fireplace, hoping that Donovan would attribute the pink in her cheeks to the heat of the fire. She felt uncomfortable and unnerved, and her heart was beginning to match the beat of the music.

She wished that Tosh hadn't left with Carson; she could have made a fuss over him and maybe drowned out the damned music. Unfortunately, she and Donovan were alone.

"Lovely music," he murmured from the couch.

Rebel stared determinedly into the fire. "Lovely."

His next words came from right beside her. "Dance with me."

"You can't dance to this music," she objected quickly.

"Want to bet?" He took her hands and placed them at the nape of his neck, placing his own hands at her waist and drawing her close. Then he began moving. Slowly, sensuously, following the music.

Rebel kept her gaze fixed on his chin and attempted to keep a respectable distance between them. But his hands slid down to her hips, pulling her closer until their lower bodies nearly merged. Fiercely, she tried to ignore the sensations that caused.

"Do you know," he murmured conversationally, "that you're a beautiful, brilliant, incredibly exciting woman?"

It took all the willpower at Rebel's command to return a light, bantering response. "Be still, my heart."

He grinned. "Flattery doesn't move you, does it?"

"Not an inch."

"How about truth?"

"Truth is nice. I have a fondness for truth."

"Okay. You're a beautiful, brilliant, incredibly exciting woman."

"That's still flattery. Spanish coin."

"No. Truth."

"Gilded truth. You have a silver tongue."

"Really?"

"Oh, yes."

He was looking down at her with a sleepy sort of smile, eyelids heavy and lips just faintly curved. Lazy. And deceptive. Because she could *feel* the wide-awake awareness behind the sleepy look. And she wondered suddenly how she had ever managed to under-rate this man to the point of not even seeing him.

"Who did this to you, Rebel?" he asked very quietly.

She blinked at him, startled. "Did what?"

"Battered your self-respect. Wounded the woman in you until she curled up and hid herself away. Damn near destroyed you. Who was it, Rebel? Your ex-husband?"

Rebel stiffened and tried to pull away, but he held her firmly, moving slowly to the heavy beat of the music. He continued to speak in a drawling, thoughtful voice.

"Oh, you're good at keeping things light. You didn't even turn a hair when I mentioned marriage. You're quick and you're witty, and you pass off everything as a joke." One hand slid up her back and began toying with her ponytail. "But there's no joke in your eyes. So tell me, Rebel. How badly did he hurt you? Was he a rotten husband?"

Rebel felt her lips twist into a bitter smile, heard her voice answer his question, and wondered why she was telling him this. "Oh, he was the perfect husband. Charming, attentive, romantic. Flowers for no special occasion. Little gifts on my pillow. We played tennis and golf and rode horses. We went to parties and out to dinner, and had marvelous vacations." She felt her smile harden. "And he satisfied me in bed. Anything else you want to know?"

Donovan's jaw tightened. His eyes had totally lost the sleepy look now and were reflecting what he saw in her eyes: something diamond-hard and painful. And the expression beneath the reflection of hers was searching, sober. "Were there other women?"

"Not that I know of," she responded brightly.

His hands gripped her shoulders. They had stopped dancing; neither of them was paying attention now to the music that throbbed seductively. "Why did your marriage break up, Rebel? Why did you divorce your husband?"

"Because it wasn't real!" she cried. She flung off his hands and turned aside trying to control herself and keep the bitter words inside. "I . . . don't want to talk about it, Donovan. Just let it drop."

"I won't do that, Rebel. I can't do that." He caught her hand, preventing her from escaping him. "You've kept this inside you for too long. Even your father doesn't know the whole story, and he—"

"My father?" She stared at Donovan, incredulous, furious. "You discussed me with my father?"

Donovan released a short, impatient sigh. "No, I didn't discuss you with him. I asked Marc a few questions, Rebel. Because I wondered what kind of bastard could destroy a woman the way that ex-husband of yours obviously destroyed you. But Marc didn't know what had happened. The only thing he was sure of was that you'd left your husband after less than three years and filed for divorce. You wouldn't talk to him, your mother, or Bessie about it."

"You had no business discussing me," she shot back tautly, tenaciously holding on to a subject less painful than her marriage. But she sent a silent thanks to her father. He'd known why her marriage dissolved; he had known long before she why Jud married her.

Donovan ignored the red herring. "Rebel, you have to talk about it. It's been eating away at you for years! Until you get it out of your system once and for all, you'll never be able to shed that chrysalis. You'll be just the shell that he left you with and nothing more! *Tell me.*"

"No!" Vainly, she fought to free her hand, finding it trapped in a gentle vise. "It's none of your business—"

"It *is* my business! Dammit, Rebel, what do you think I've been trying to get through to you since we got here? I want to become a part of your life, and that means knowing where the shadows are. How can I fight something I can't even see? How can I prove to you that you're a beautiful, desirable woman when I don't know what your ex-husband did to destroy your confidence in yourself?"

Rebel was still struggling vainly, forgetting dignity. She was trying desperately to avoid talking about what had happened, because it hurt now as it hadn't hurt in years. The confrontation she had wanted to avoid at all costs was here, and it hurt because she didn't know what Donovan wanted—her or the company.

"Rebel, tell me!"

"No!" She was utterly dumbfounded when she burst into tears. Dimly aware of his arms holding her, of her face pressed against his flannel shirt, she realized that it was the first time she'd cried since childhood. She hadn't shed a tear after leaving Jud. Dry-eyed and hollow, she'd simply picked up the threads of her life and gone on.

But she was crying now.

Donovan picked her up, holding her as easily as he would a child. He carried her to the couch and sat down with her in his lap. She could feel the tenderness in him, and somehow it made her cry harder. And the crooning, wordless sound of his voice pulled tears from wells she hadn't known existed.

It was a long time before she finally stopped, drained and weary. Donovan produced a handkerchief and dried her cheeks, then held the cloth and gently ordered her to blow her nose. Meekly, Rebel did as he commanded. Even in her emotional state she was conscious of the absurdity of the situation.

"Some boss I am," she sniffed woefully.

"You're a terrific boss." He held her firmly when she would have removed herself from his lap. "No man could have a better one. Now tell me why it wasn't real."

Rebel didn't have to ask what he meant. The music had ended, the player automatically shutting itself off, and when she spoke her voice was the only sound in the room other than the pop and crackle of the fire.

"It wasn't real because it wasn't. None of it was real. The charm, the attentiveness, the romance. The love he was so good at voicing— and making. It was fake, phony . . . a sham. All of it."

"Start at the beginning," Donovan urged quietly.

Rebel sighed and sniffed one last time. She felt small and vulnerable, and there was a dull ache inside her. Perhaps the tears had blunted the pain; she didn't know.

"I was eighteen and had just started college. I met Jud at a party. He . . . He made me feel special right away. He was charming and attentive, and he made me laugh. We spent almost all of our time together during the next two weeks. And then we eloped."

She laughed harshly. "Eighteen! What do you know about love at eighteen? But you're so sure. I don't think you can ever be as sure of love as you are at eighteen. Nothing else matters, nothing else is important. Just starry-eyed dreams."

Donovan tightened his arms around her slightly. "Go on."

"I dropped out of school, and we set up housekeeping. Dad gave us a house as a wedding present. I didn't think anything of it then. Jud had taken a business degree in college, but he earned his living as . . . as a tennis instructor." She flung back her head almost defiantly, expecting to see scorn or contempt in Donovan's violet eyes. But only gentle understanding met her searching gaze as he waited for her to go on with her story.

With an effort, Rebel swallowed the lump in her throat. "I knew Dad didn't approve, but he never said a word against Jud. He only wanted me to be happy, and if Jud could do that . . . well, he was willing to wait and see.

"It was a country-club lifestyle. We played tennis or golf during the day and went to parties at night. We had a maid—courtesy of Daddy—and two cars and a poodle." Rebel became aware that she had reverted to childhood's use of "Daddy."

"Jud didn't make very much money at this job, but I had an allowance and charge cards. We spent money like it was water, buying things we didn't really want or need on the spur of the moment."

"When did things start to go wrong?" Donovan asked softly.

Rebel shook her head. "That's the whole point: Things *didn't* start to go wrong. I mean, it wasn't a gradual thing. I was so completely and utterly blind that I didn't suspect anything.

"I thought that I had the most perfect husband in the world. I knew that he loved me as much as I loved him. There were no fights—not even small disagreements. I should have suspected something when I realized that; two different people can't live together every day without some disagreements, some . . . adjustments. But Jud made sure that the water was always smooth.

"It wasn't a marriage at all. It was just a play staged for my benefit. Oh, Jud said all the right words and made all the right moves . . . and it was all cold-bloodedly planned."

"How did you find that out?" Donovan asked.

"Brutally," Rebel answered shakily. "I was supposed to meet Jud for lunch, and I stopped by the office to see Daddy, since we hadn't talked in a couple of weeks. The outer office was empty; the secretary had already gone to lunch. I started to open the door to Daddy's office, and I heard Jud's voice."

Rebel closed her eyes and tried to forget the words she had heard that day. But her memory was cruelly accurate, every word and nuance of voice etched in her mind like neon.

"You'll never run this company, Anderson—I'll see to that!"

"Why else do you think I married your daughter, old man? Rebel does what I tell her to, and when you're gone, the company's mine."

"Rebel?"

She opened her eyes to see Donovan's anxious expression, his violet eyes worried as he tipped her chin up firmly and stared at her. "What did you hear?"

"Jud and Daddy were arguing," she replied flatly. "Jud was saying that Daddy should retire and leave the company to him. He said he'd get it anyway, once Daddy was gone. That he'd only married me for the company."

"Bastard!" Donovan muttered roughly.

Rebel barely heard him. In a toneless, faraway voice, she went on. "I've never heard Daddy so furious. Jud was jeering and confident, and Daddy was shouting that if I was hurt Jud would have him to answer to. Jud just laughed. He asked Daddy if he really thought I'd believe anything against him. He said that he—that he'd done his work well, that I'd never guessed the truth."

Donovan swore softly, roughly, one large hand cradling the side of her face. "The man was a fool, Rebel," he told her insistently, his voice still rough. "He didn't know—didn't have the sense to know—that companies are as common as flies, but a woman like you is one in a million!"

Rebel managed a watery smile. "Gee," she murmured.

He smiled tightly. "I mean it, dammit! He was an idiot, and I'd feel sorry for him except that I'd dearly love to break him into a few thousand pieces."

Her smile died a weary, painful death. Donovan went very still, something savage flaring in his eyes. The thought of what Jud had done chilled her, and she wanted desperately to be held tightly, comfortingly. To her vague surprise, Donovan immediately pulled her closer, wrapping his big arms around her in a warm bear hug. Her cheek was resting against the flannel covering his broad shoulder, and she could feel his chin moving gently against her forehead.

"What did you do, Rebel?"

She sighed raggedly. "I walked for hours after I left the office. I was numb. Stupidly, I finally thought that maybe I had misunderstood somehow. So I went home. He was waiting for me, supposedly worried because I'd missed our lunch date. I confronted him with what I'd heard."

She was silent for a long moment, then shook her head slightly. "I should have remembered that Jud was a sore loser. He was always very even-tempered, except when he lost. At a game, or something small and petty. He'd blow up. I should have remembered that."

"Did he hurt you?" Donovan asked gratingly.

Rebel felt the words rushing from her, and knew that Donovan had been right; she'd held it inside for far too long.

"Not in any physical way. At first, he tried to deny it. But I could see the deceit in his eyes, and I knew he was lying. When he realized that I meant to leave him, he became cold and cruel. He . . . said things. Things that sickened me," she finished starkly. She was shivering now, in spite of the arms holding her close.

Donovan's arms tightened convulsively. "Forget what I said about feeling sorry for that bastard. If I ever come face to face with him, I'll kill him." His voice was flat and deadly.

Rebel lifted her head to look at him uncertainly. She saw pain in the violet eyes. Pain for her, she realized. Rage for her. It moved her oddly, and she had to swallow hard before she could tie up the loose ends.

"He stormed out afterward. I packed a few things and went to a motel. I stayed there for a few days until I could face things. I never told anyone what had happened. I just said the marriage was over and filed for divorce. Jud didn't fight me. I think he was afraid of Daddy. Anyway, it—it ended."

"Did it?" Donovan asked quietly.

Rebel looked at him and knew what he meant. It hadn't ended. Not really. She was still carrying the emotional scars from what had happened that day. And her response to Donovan proved that Jud's form of brutality had not destroyed her ability to feel desire. She was not afraid of men because of him.

But she was afraid of being a woman. Afraid to trust her instincts. Her self-confidence had never recovered from the blow Jud had dealt it.

Chapter Five

After a long moment, Donovan sighed softly. *"You think I might be after the company. That's it, isn't it?"*

Rebel dropped her eyes to stare at the hands gripped tightly together in her lap. "I don't know what I think," she said dully.

"But you aren't . . . afraid of me, are you?" There was a thread of anxiety in his voice.

Rebel felt a flush rise in her cheeks. "No," she whispered. "No, I'm not afraid of you." She felt a sigh of relief from him.

"You're just afraid that I have my eye on the president's chair," he said finally.

She stirred uneasily but remained silent.

"Rebel, there's no way I can convince you. I could tell you that I don't give a damn about the company except about how it affects you, but I can't prove that. I could promise to stay totally away from the office, find a job somewhere else, but I happen to enjoy working with you."

He laughed shortly, a bitter humor in the sound. "I sure picked some shadow to box, didn't I? Even now that I know what it is, I can't really fight it."

Rebel stole a glance at his face, bewildered by the urgency in his deep voice. What did he want from her? What part did he want to play in her life? And why did she want suddenly, desperately, to believe that he had no overwhelming interest in the company?

"It's up to you, Rebel," he said soberly. "You have to decide for yourself what kind of man I am. You're not eighteen anymore; you have more experience in judging people."

Rebel had nearly forgotten that she was still sitting in his lap. He was still holding her, comfortingly and undemandingly, and that was soothing her and making her feel oddly cherished. She hung on to the feeling, trying to work through the dilemma in her mind.

"It happened so fast," she murmured at last. "One moment you were the perfect assistant, and the next . . . the next, I didn't know what you were."

"I was slightly insane," he said dryly. "And after a year, I think I had a perfect right to be."

She looked at him hesitantly, remembering that he'd muttered something about a year twice after kissing her. "A year?"

"Uh-huh." His tone was wryly self-mocking. "You were the star I wished on, Rebel—a year ago. Remember that first day, when we ran into one another in the hall outside your father's office?"

"I remember."

"Well, that's why I hired on with Sinclair. After seeing you, I was damn well going to stick around for a while. It didn't take me two seconds to realize that you were wrapped up in the business, but I figured you'd have to come out of it sooner or later. And I wanted to be around when that happened."

Rebel had a small feeling that her mouth was open, and she hastily closed it. "You mean you—you took the job just because you wanted *me*?"

"I've always been impulsive," he drawled consideringly.

His eyes were veiled, oddly watchful, and that suddenly made Rebel very nervous. She didn't know him. How many times had she looked at him unexpectedly and seen that expression in his eyes? Waiting, searching, watchful. She had noticed it only in passing, abstractedly, indifferently. His eyes were always quickly shuttered again, and she had dismissed the look. But now she wondered what lay behind it.

"Rebel, stop it!" His hands cupped her face, and his eyes were no longer veiled but dark and troubled. "Don't look at me as though you're afraid of me, honey. It hurts."

"What do you want from me?" she asked in a whisper, trying to ignore the bump her heart had given at the endearment.

He hesitated, a flicker of indecision showing on his face. Then he sighed roughly. "The hell of it is," he muttered, "that I've waited a long time to answer that question, and now I know damn well you won't believe me."

Rebel was trying to understand what he meant by that when he pulled her forward abruptly and kissed her. His lips were warm, demanding, and achingly hungry. He kissed her as though it were the last thing he would ever be able to do in this life—a final, desperate action before oblivion.

And she couldn't help but respond to that. Her mouth opened willingly beneath his, her hands lifted to tangle in the dark, thick hair at his collar. She could feel and sense the passion in him, the thread of restraint stretched nearly to the breaking point, and a part of her wished that it would snap. She didn't want to have to think . . . only to feel. And what Donovan made her feel was astonishing and strangely addictive.

His hands moved caressingly over her back, pulling her nearer and nearer until her breasts were crushed against the hard wall of his chest. She felt them swell and harden even through the clothing separating her flesh from his, and she heard a groan rumble from the depths of Donovan's throat.

When he finally tore his mouth from hers, it was with an obvious effort. A heavy shudder shook his strong body, and his breath came raspingly.

Rebel was left staring at him, her lips hot and throbbing, her heart pounding crazily. When she'd finally gotten her own breath back, she said shakily, "I guess that answers my question."

He shook his head slightly, the violet eyes slowly clearing. "Not entirely." His voice was hoarse. "Oh, I'm not about to deny that I want you. I'd have to be blind, stupid, or made of stone not to, and I'm certainly none of those. What we have together is magic, Rebel, but I want more than that."

"What—" she had to clear her throat before the words would emerge properly—"what do you want?" Her arms were still around his neck, her fingers still tangled in his hair.

"I want your trust, Rebel. Your trust, and your faith, and your heart. I want your love."

When the steady words finally sunk into Rebel's brain, she could only shake her head miserably. "You want too much," she whispered raggedly, feeling tired and confused and terribly afraid to probe her reaction to his words. "Even if I wanted to, I—I can't give you what I don't have to give."

"You're coming out of the chrysalis," he responded softly. "And that's a big move. Today—in spite of your trying to keep things light—you were more relaxed than I've ever seen you. And you laughed. Do you know that I'd never heard you really laugh until we came on this trip? And now you've told me something you've never told anyone else. Don't you realize that you had to trust me a great deal just to do that? I'm willing to build on it, Rebel. If you'll let me."

"Are you saying that you . . . that you—"

"That I love you?" His voice deepened, taking on colors and shades filled with meaning. "I think I've loved you ever since we bumped into each other in that hallway."

Rebel wanted to believe him. Something inside her urged her to believe him. But the suspicious little gremlin born of Jud's deception jeered at her. She shook her head silently, numbed and bewildered by the conflicting emotions of the past hours.

After a moment, Donovan rose to his feet as easily as if he weren't holding a grown woman in his arms. He made his way toward the archway leading to their wing. "I think you need to sleep on it," he told her gently. "And I," he added with a sigh, "need to take a long walk in the snow."

She was too tired to make sense of the remark. "In the snow? But it's freezing out there." Fascinated, she watched a muscle tighten in his lean cheek.

In a very dry voice, he responded, "Honey, you're looking at a man who's holding on to his willpower with both hands and his teeth. Believe me, I need to walk in the snow for a while."

"Oh." Rebel hastily tucked her chin in and tried to control the flush rising in her cheeks. It occurred to her that she should be making some protest over the fact that he was carrying her, but for the moment it was comforting to be carried like a child.

Donovan whisked her into their dimly lit sitting room and then through to her bedroom. He set her gently on the foot of the bed, grimacing slightly at the sight of her peach satin gown shimmering in the lamplight beside her. Quickly, he bent to give her an almost brutally short kiss.

"Good night, honey. Sleep well."

Rebel waited until he was at the door. "Donovan?"

He half turned to look back at her, and she could have sworn that he stiffened. "What is it, honey?"

She swallowed, the gremlin keeping back the words she wanted to say. "Be careful when you go out."

"Bet on it," he said lightly. He left the room, closing the door quietly.

Rebel stared at the door for a long moment, hearing the sitting room door shut, and then silence. She got up and automatically undressed, donning the peach gown before sliding between the sheets and turning off her lamp.

She had looked at the luminous dial of her watch twice, and an hour passed before she heard the quiet sounds of Donovan returning. Only then did she let herself slip into sleep.

When Rebel was awakened the next morning by a steady thumping sound, her first thought was that she'd certainly had peculiar dreams. Castles and jousting knights and golden keys dangling enticingly from turrets. Enticingly? Odd. Definitely odd.

The thumping sound connected itself to knocking in her mind just as Donovan poked his head through the door.

"Hey, sleepyhead, want to go look for Christmas trees?"

He was disgustingly bright-eyed and bushy-tailed, and Rebel glared at him for a moment before making an attempt to rub the sleep from her eyes. She had the irritating feeling that there was something she should remember, but it remained just out of reach.

"Christmas trees?" she responded grumpily, raising herself on her elbows, the better to see Donovan. "Can't Lennox find his own trees? There's a mountain full of them."

"Carson suggested it. I think his British soul is offended by the lack of ornamentation about the place. Want to help me repair the lack?"

Rebel smothered a yawn with one hand. "Can we have breakfast first?" she asked plaintively.

"Certainly. It's ready when you are, love."

The "love" triggered Rebel's memory, and her eyes widened as the events of the day before rushed through her mind. Given half a chance, she would have pulled the covers over her head and attempted to hibernate until spring.

"Don't panic on me now," Donovan ordered lightly, apparently rooted in the doorway. "Today's just for fun—I promise. No serious discussions about anything. Are you game?"

Rebel found herself nodding in what she knew to be a very weak way. "I'm game," she murmured wryly.

"Then get a move on, milady—the forest awaits," he informed her cheerfully before leaving her alone with her muddled thoughts.

The forest awaits. Uh-huh. With her luck it would turn out to be an enchanted forest.

Sighing, Rebel pulled herself from the bed. It was better, she decided, not to think. She'd just take the days one at a time and try to get to know this impossibly large man who said he was in love with her. And maybe somewhere along the way she'd figure out what her own confused emotions were.

Donovan was as good as his word. A day for fun.

After breakfast, they bundled up in coats, scarves, and gloves burgled from various closets and they tramped over a winding trail to what Donovan said was the tree farm.

The tree farm turned out to be on a gentle slope some distance from the stables. A number of unhappy-looking stumps were mute testimony to this field's having been victim to Christmas-tree hunting for some years, but a larger number of seedlings also gave evidence of great care to replace what was taken. Spruce and cedar were the rule, with sizes ranging from the seedlings to one sixty-foot giant. Snow made a four-inch thick pristine blanket beneath the trees and provided a lovely contrast to the various shades of green.

Rebel had tucked her hair beneath a wool cap, and now she turned up her collar to ward off a blast of cold air. "You dragged me out of bed for this?" she grumbled once they stood in the center of the tree farm.

"Let's hear some Christmas spirit," Donovan chided.

"Bah humbug," she muttered.

"The ghost of Christmas past'll get you for that. Pick a tree, boss—for the central greatroom."

"What are you going to cut it down with—your teeth?"

"That's all taken care of. Pick a tree."

"Decorations?"

"Carson's digging them out now. Are you going to pick a tree?"

"Don't snap at me. I was just asking."

"I didn't snap at you, but I'm going to turn you over my knee if you don't get busy."

"You and what army?" she challenged huffily.

Donovan's violet eyes gleamed impossibly brilliantly in the bright reflection of sunlight off snow as he grinned. "Don't push me, boss," he warned gruffly.

Rebel hastily went tree hunting. Trying to ignore the fact that Donovan was dogging her footsteps, hands in his pockets and whistling cheerfully, she finally picked a tree. It was a beautifully shaped ten-foot specimen. "This one."

Donovan studied it. "Nope. Too small."

She went looking again, and this time found a lovely fifteen-foot tree. "This?"

"Too small."

The next one was twenty feet. "Well?"

"Too small."

"Donovan, if you want a redwood, we'll have to go to California."

Ignoring her sarcasm, he turned in a slow circle, surveying the trees. Then he pointed. "That one."

Rebel stared at the majestic, thirty-foot cedar expressionlessly. "Shall I yell for Paul Bunyan?" she asked finally.

"Why?"

"Because we'll need his ax to cut that thing down, and his ox to drag it back to the lodge."

"Funny." He pulled a roll of bright red tape from a pocket. "Be a good girl and mark the tree. At the base there, high enough to see."

"Who's the boss here?" she wanted to know.

"I think we're still jockeying for position," Donovan said wryly.

Prudently not rising to the bait, Rebel silently marked the tree. When she had done so, she returned to Donovan and handed him the tape. "Why did I mark that tree?" she asked politely.

"So the men can find it. The stable hands are going to cut the trees for us."

"*Trees?* More than one?"

"Several." Donovan began ticking off rooms on his fingers. "This one's for the central greatroom. Then there are the two front dens, three lounges, the butler's pantry—"

Rebel was shaking her head. "Never mind. Just let me know when we're through. Are you sure there are enough decorations for all those trees?"

"Carson says so."

"Won't Lennox feel offended if we do this?"

"Do you care?" Donovan asked cheerfully.

Rebel thought it over. "Not really. However, I draw the line at decorating all these trees. It would take a week."

"Okay. Then we'll just decorate the one in the central great-room and leave the rest to the staff. How's that?"

"Fine. But I feel sorry for poor Santa."

"Why?"

"All the chimneys at the lodge."

"We'll leave out a glass of brandy so he can refresh himself."

"I sincerely hope we won't even *be* here. And what kind of man would try and get Santa drunk?"

"Not drunk. Just pleasantly warm."

"Uh-huh. You pick the next tree."

The morning flew past as they argued the merits of each tree selected. Most of the trees were on the large side, but the one Rebel fell in love with was just barely six feet tall. A misguided bird had built a small nest among the needles and then abandoned it, and that lonely little nest touched something in Rebel. She didn't say anything about it to Donovan, but she thought more than once of suggesting that they select a tree for their sitting room. *That* tree.

She didn't, though.

After lunch, they repaired to the greatroom, where the stablehands had managed to set up the thirty-foot cedar far enough from the fireplace to be safe. Boxes of decorations, strings of lights, and tinsel were grouped about at its base.

Rebel tucked a strand of silver-blond hair behind one ear and sighed as she surveyed the Herculean task before them. "How did I let you talk me into this?" she asked mournfully.

"My fatal charm," Donovan answered, busily engaged in untangling a string of lights that had probably been packed away neatly but had mysteriously tangled during the preceding year.

"Right." She hastily grabbed a handful of silver fur. "Tosh! Stay out of the tinsel, dummy. No, I don't want to play catch, and that isn't a ball! Lie down over there like a good boy."

"*Your* fatal charm," Donovan observed as the big husky obediently stretched out in front of the fireplace.

"Tosh knows the voice of authority when he hears it," Rebel said disdainfully. "Which is more than I can say for certain other members of this household."

"Has Carson been disobeying your orders, boss?" Donovan asked innocently.

"You know very well whom I meant. And how you've got the gall to call me 'boss' is beyond me!" she told him sternly.

"Well, because I'm yours to command," he replied, wounded.

"Then go find a ladder. Unless you plan to sprout wings and fly to the top of this tree."

"Yes, ma'am. Right away, ma'am." Donovan pulled an imaginary forelock and bowed with mock awkwardness several times until Rebel threw a plastic angel at him.

Tosh happily retrieved the angel, thinking that they were going to play catch after all. By the time Rebel managed to wrestle it away from him, Donovan was back with the ladder.

Rebel made one attempt to climb the ladder and got dizzy halfway up, so it was left to Donovan—loudly gloating—to string the lights.

He gloated so much, in fact, that Rebel enormously enjoyed the fact that he missed the bottom step of the ladder on his first descent and sat down rather hard in an empty ornament box.

"Try again, hero," she invited with a giggle.

"Unkind," he groaned. "Help me out of this damn—"

"I'm busy." She was sitting cross-legged on the carpet, sorting ornaments into small, neat piles. "Tosh, help him."

It was several minutes before Donovan managed to get Tosh

off his lap and himself out of the box. "Was that nice?" he demanded after putting Tosh bodily on the couch and out of his way.

"Was it nice to make fun of me when I got dizzy?"

Donovan sighed. "Touché. Hand me that next string of lights, will you?"

Rebel did as he asked, then frowningly regarded the ornaments piled all around her as he went back up the ladder. "How many kids does Lennox have?" she called up to Donovan.

"Since we're living in his house," Donovan called back, "maybe we'd better call him by his first name."

"I don't remember his first name."

"It's Astaire."

In a bemused voice, Rebel murmured. "Astaire. How could I forget a name like that?" Then, in a stronger voice, she said, "All right then—how many kids does Astaire have?"

"Several." Donovan was making his way back down the ladder, this time negotiating the hazard carefully. "But only the one son. Why?"

Rebel fretfully rubbed her forehead. "Well, it's these decorations. There are at least a dozen with 'Baby's First Year' on them, some of them recent. And a bunch that were obviously made by kids. Everything from plastic to crystal. It looks like a family—and a big family, at that—collected these things over the years."

"So what's wrong with that?" Donovan asked, making his way back up the ladder. "I imagine that Astaire, like many men of his age, has grandchildren."

"I guess." Rebel frowned again. "But it seems out of character. The man you've told me about just wouldn't have these things lying around for years on end. And why here? Does the family meet here every year for Christmas? Because if so, we'd better make tracks."

"It's more than a week until Christmas; we have plenty of time to close the deal and be out of here before then."

Rebel silently conceded the point but stubbornly went back to her original observation. "I still say it's out of character for him to keep these decorations."

"Why?" Donovan asked reasonably. "Even a rake can have a soft spot for his own flesh and blood, can't he?"

Defeated but still disturbed for some reason, Rebel gestured helplessly. "Okay, okay. I'm outgunned; I can see that. I hate thoroughly rational people."

"Would you love me if I were irrational?" Donovan asked anxiously from halfway up the ladder.

With an effort, Rebel ignored the question. "Are you going to be finished with that any time soon? I've found the angel for the top, and I want to see how it looks."

"The angel comes last," he informed her, apparently undisturbed that she hadn't answered his question.

"Well, hurry up, then. I hope you realize this is going to take all day."

"You have someplace else to go?"

"No, but it's the principle of the thing."

"Always in a hurry. You're going to have to learn to slow down, boss, or you'll have an ulcer before you're thirty."

"I started developing an ulcer the day we met."

"Ouch." Donovan set aside the ladder and began stringing the last group of lights. "Well, at least I've had *some* effect on you."

"Stop fishing."

"My father used to say that one should either fish or cut bait."

"So?"

"So I think I'll keep fishing. Never know what I might catch."

"You might catch something you can't handle," she warned lightly.

"I'll take my chances. Shall I hang the decorations on the top, or will you brave the ladder?"

Rebel blinked at the abrupt change of subject. "You get the top."

"Okay. Stand back."

Rebel found herself relegated to one of the archways while he moved boxes and repositioned the ladder. That done to his satisfaction, he calmly walked over to her, took her in his arms, and kissed her with deliberate thoroughness.

Emerging from the embrace to find her fingers clutching his sweater and her heart pounding, Rebel stared up at him dazedly. "Um . . . what . . . ?" was all she managed.

Donovan gestured upward with one thumb. "It was too good an opportunity to pass up," he said gravely.

Rebel tipped her head back to stare at the sprig of mistletoe hung neatly in the archway above them. "When did that get there?" she asked blankly.

He managed to leer with his eyebrows. "When you weren't looking, boss." He patted her on the bottom and headed back for the tree.

Rebel wanted to get mad. Donovan was taking shameless advantage of this entire situation, and she had a perfect right to be furious. The problem was, she didn't feel mad. In fact, she felt like laughing.

Choking back the urge and sighing inwardly at her own inexplicable emotions, Rebel went to help with the tree.

Donovan was frowning down at the decorations on the carpet. "You didn't happen to find a key among this stuff, did you?" he asked hopefully as Rebel joined him.

"What kind of key?" she asked innocently.

"A key suitable for unlocking stubborn chastity belts, as if you didn't know."

"Sorry. Nary a one."

"Damn. I'd hoped I might get lucky."

"I told you—knights don't get custody of keys."

"Then how can I become the lord of the castle?"

"With great difficulty. Here"—she dumped a handful of ornaments into his outstretched palms—"hang these."

"Will that get me a castle?"

"It'll get you gold star. Castles come later."

"Oh, really? How much later?"

Rebel gave him push toward the tree. "If you don't get busy, we'll have this tree decorated just in time for *next* Christmas."

With a gusty sigh, Donovan began climbing the ladder again. "Since you won't answer that question, how about another one?"

"You can ask, but I don't promise to answer." Rebel got busy hanging ornaments on the lower third of the tree.

"Well, I'm curious. When the lord of the castle gets the key, exactly what rights does that give him?"

"Oh, the works." Rebel filled a small box with ornaments and handed it up to him the moment his hands were empty again.

"Define that, please," he requested politely.

"The works? Well, actually, it's more of a partnership deal. The lord and his lady share joint ownership of the castle and everything therein. Tasks are divided according to who does what best. And of course the lady is responsible for the castle whenever his lordship is out jousting or defending the realm from invading hordes, or things like that."

Donovan was shaking with silent laughter. "I'd love to hear you give a talk on medieval history," he murmured.

"Who's talking medieval?" Rebel muttered, but only to herself. Aloud, she said, "Will you please start working your way down? We've got a bare spot in the middle, and I can't reach that high."

"You're rushing again."

"Sorry."

"Forget it. Can I buy a key, by the way?"

"Absolutely not. It has to be given freely."

"Oh. Coercion is out then?"

"Definitely."

"How about blackmail?"

"Unchivalrous."

"What's a knight to do?"

"All things come to he who waits."

"Is that a promise?"

"It's a proverb."

Donovan dropped a cardboard reindeer on her head—deliberately. And then gave her an innocent "Who, me?" look when she glared up at him.

"That wasn't smart, hero. One push from me and we'll be scraping you off the hearth for a week."

"Sorry. It slipped."

"I'll bet."

"Okay, so it didn't slip. But you shouldn't have dashed my hopes like that."

"It hasn't bothered you so far."

"Good thing I thrive on rejection," Donovan responded philosophically.

For once Rebel didn't have a snappy comeback.

The tree was given its finishing touches after dinner that night, and a toast was gravely drunk to usher in the holidays in style. The remainder of the evening was quiet and companionable as they listened to music and watched the lights blinking cheerfully on their gaily decorated tree.

Rebel excused herself fairly early and headed for her room, feeling Donovan's eyes following her and torn between relief and disappointment when he made no move to stop her.

She took a long shower and then climbed into bed with a book she didn't really want to read. When she discovered herself reading the first page for the sixth time, she turned out her lamp and tried to go to sleep.

But sleep eluded her. She tossed and turned, checking the watch on her nightstand at fifteen-minute intervals. The earlier conversations with Donovan, bantering but with an undertone of seriousness, kept playing like a recording in her mind. The kiss beneath the archway flitted through her thoughts.

A muffled thump from the sitting room temporarily interrupted her thoughts. She frowned, listening in the darkness for a few moments, then dismissed the sound. She pounded her pillow energetically and tried to sleep once more.

Finally, Rebel threw back the covers and slipped from the bed. In darkness, she crossed the room to the sitting room door, easing it open. Maybe a change of location would help.

But she didn't leave her bedroom.

Very still, she gazed into the sitting room for a long moment and then soundlessly closed her door again. She leaned against the door, thinking about what she had seen.

Donovan. He'd been standing with his back to her, humming softly to himself and hanging decorations on a lovely, six-foot tree in the corner by the window.

The tree had not been cut like the others, but dug up and potted. And a small, abandoned bird's nest nestled among the needles. While she had watched, Donovan had carefully placed a crystal dove in the nest.

She went back to bed and crawled between the sheets, wondering how he had come to pick that tree. She was certain he hadn't seen her looking at it. Then she dismissed the question. It didn't seem to matter somehow. She knew that she was smiling in the darkness, and she knew somehow that she wouldn't have any more trouble sleeping.

And she didn't.

This time, her dreams were different. This time, no golden key dangled enticingly from a turret. But the drawbridge was lowered to welcome the knight riding triumphantly home. . . .

Chapter Six

Rebel woke much earlier than usual the next morning, her sense of expectancy puzzling her for a moment. But then she remembered.

Quickly, she rose and began dressing, anxious to go into the sitting room and see the completed tree. She donned an attractive slacks-and-sweater set in an ice-blue color, then pulled on a pair of thick, warm socks. She debated the matter of shoes briefly, but chose not to wear any. She and Donovan seemed to spend most of their time running around in their stocking feet anyway.

Rebel glanced over at the boots placed neatly in one corner and grinned faintly. No matter where she left her shoes, they always reappeared in her room. Their host certainly possessed a well-trained staff!

She brushed her hair thoughtfully, gazing at her reflection in the mirror above the dresser. She looked . . . different. Her eyes were bright and sparkling, the weary look she had noticed at the office gone now. There was a glow to her face, the pallor a thing of the past.

A little wryly but not regretfully she realized that the caricature businesswoman had slipped quietly away. And along with her had gone a few other things as well. The strictly ordered business mind had opened up to allow for feminine thoughts; the company no longer seemed the most important thing in her life; the tension, the guardedness, of years had relaxed.

She felt like a woman again.

Rebel placed the brush on the dresser, seeing in her reflection the smile she had felt last night and feeling strangely light-hearted.

Donovan, she realized, had said little about her "letting her hair down"—literally as well as figuratively—since she'd worn it loose yesterday. And she had a sneaking suspicion that that was because he knew her better than she had ever realized. If he had pounced on the change in her, Rebel would probably have reverted to habit out of sheer perversity. And she was suddenly filled with the amused certainty that he had known that.

There was something, she decided, both unsettling and strangely satisfying about being known that well.

Deliberately leaving her hair hanging straight and shining down her back, Rebel left her room and went into the sitting room. Donovan's bedroom door was closed, and she softly crossed the polished floor to the tree.

It was decorated with shining simplicity, the ornaments all glass and crystal. Rebel wondered how he had managed to find all of them. There were stars, tiny glass reindeers, and turtledoves. Elves winked at her out of crystal eyes, and snowflakes glistened pure white among green needles. And at the top of the tree was not the traditional star or angel, but a miniature castle made of glass, perfect in detail down to the lowered drawbridge.

"Like it?"

The soft question made Rebel turn slowly, and she stared at Donovan as he leaned casually in the doorway to his bedroom. He was dressed, like her, in slacks and a sweater—his a deep blue—and was gazing at her with warm eyes.

"I love it . . . it's beautiful," she answered huskily. "How did you know I wanted this tree?"

"I just knew."

Rebel shook her head slightly with another glance at the tree. "The ornaments?"

"Questions, questions," he chided gently, walking toward her with his sure-footed grace. "I wanted to do it, and you like it, so that's all that matters."

"Why did you want to do it?" she whispered.

His big hands came to rest on her shoulders, and he smiled down at her with those warm, caressing eyes. "Because I love you."

In that moment, Rebel could have believed him. But it was too perfect, too easy, and the little gremlin in her head wouldn't let her believe. Donovan must have seen the doubt in her eyes, because he immediately drew her into his arms.

"I can't blame you for not trusting," he said with a sigh, resting his chin on top of her head. "Not after what you've been through. Give it time, Rebel. I've been patient this long; I'm not about to pressure you now."

But Rebel could sense the hurt in him, and it disturbed her deeply. She didn't want to hurt him. Even less, though, did she want to expose herself to the kind of hurt another ambitious man could bring.

With his uncanny understanding of her, Donovan seemed to sense that she just wasn't ready to talk seriously. Keeping one arm around her, he began leading her toward the door. "Ready for breakfast, boss?" he asked lightly. "I believe that waffles are on the menu for this morning."

Friday and Saturday followed the easy, playful course they had set for themselves, but tension inevitably grew. Rebel could feel the awareness between them as powerful as a current beneath a thin layer of ice, and it became harder and harder to ignore.

And for that, Donovan was largely responsible. Although the bantering continued, he was clearly determined to show her how much he wanted her. And he found ingenious ways to do that— ways she could find no defense against.

Except, perhaps, for laughter.

It all started with the mistletoe. Donovan had apparently found an enormous cache of the stuff somewhere and had spread it all through the lodge. Every time Rebel turned around, she found herself beneath a sprig of it.

"Donovan!"

"Well, I couldn't ignore the mistletoe."

"Look, Carson saw, and you've offended his dignity."

"Not at all. He's just making himself scarce like the tactful soul he is."

"That mistletoe wasn't there a minute ago!"

"It is now."

"What'd you do—hire a squad of elves?"

"Damn, you guessed it!"

Rebel was attacked beneath mistletoe even where it was nearly impossible for mistletoe to be.

"How much did you pay the stable hand to hang out that window, Donovan?"

"He volunteered. Out of the goodness of his heart."

"You're making a spectacle of me."

"Not at all. All the world loves a lover."

"You're impossible."

"Nothing is impossible. Only improbable."

"All right then—you're improbable."

"Thank you. I'd hate to be dull."

Apparently possessing a singular talent for garnering good-will—or maybe it was because of the holiday season—Donovan somehow managed to draft the housekeeper, the maids, and Carson as allies. More than once Rebel found mistletoe dangled over her head by a helpful hand—and it wasn't Donovan's.

"How much did you pay her?"

"Nothing. She likes standing on chairs."

"You can get down now, Mrs. Evans. Donovan, you're absolutely, certifiably insane!"

"Sneaky, too."

"Unfair as well. How am I supposed to think when you keep grabbing me?"

"Who's grabbing? I'm just indulging in a holiday tradition."

While the mistletoe was serving its purpose, the entire staff got into the act. Donovan was bent on wooing, and everyone at the lodge was apparently just as bent on helping him.

Candlelight and soft, romantic music graced meals—even breakfast. Books of love poetry began appearing wherever Rebel chose to sit down. Red paper hearts began adorning the various Christmas trees. Even Tosh sported a red ribbon around his neck, from which dangled a paper heart.

"Where did he get that?"

"The elves must have given it to him."

"A six-and-a-half-foot elf, maybe?"

"Christmas makes anything possible."

Wavering beneath the bombardment, torn between laughter

and tears half the time, Rebel nonetheless found the strength of mind to bawl out Donovan.

"All right! Breakfast in bed was the last straw! Do you know how embarrassing it was to have Carson and two maids setting a gargantuan feast in my lap?"

"I helped you eat it."

"That's not the point! It was embarrassing!"

"You looked lovely."

"I looked half asleep, dammit. Why don't you just take the easy way out and get me drunk?"

"Would it work?"

"Forget that I said that. You're driving me crazy!"

"Have a glass of wine, boss."

"Donovan, I am going to kill you. Do you hear me? If possible, with my bare hands!"

"That sounds like fun. The bare hands part, I mean."

"What will Astaire think?"

"I'll handle him."

"Why doesn't that comfort me?"

"I don't know."

"And another thing," Rebel began wrathfully, loath to admit herself outgunned yet another time, "I want to know—"

"I can't tell you my little plan to get Astaire here yet."

"*Stop* answering my questions before I ask them!" she wailed, feeling definitely put-upon. "You've been doing it all day! Do you know how unnerving that is?"

"We're attuned," he murmured, a tremor of laughter in his voice.

"I don't care if we're a song!" she snapped, in no mood to search for a better pun. She dropped her head into her hands, muttering to herself. "Why did I come here? Everything's been crazy since I came here. The whole world's gone nuts. . . ." Her head lifted, and she glared at Donovan. "Would you at *least*," she snapped, "have the decency to stop grinning? It's very difficult to yell at a man who won't yell back!"

Standing before the fireplace with his arms folded across his massive chest, Donovan made no attempt to squelch his lopsided grin. "Two flints make a fire; you'll strike no spark off me, boss," he told her cheerfully.

Rebel lowered her head again, uttering a sound midway between a groan of despair and an ill-suppressed giggle. "You're fired. Go away."

"Who's going to bargain for that land?" he asked practically.

Sitting back on the couch, Rebel carefully crossed one jean-clad leg over the other and stared at him. Truth to tell, she had completely forgotten about the land, and she hoped to heaven that her face didn't give that away. "You're rehired. Temporarily. When's our host returning?"

"Monday afternoon," Donovan answered promptly.

"How did you manage that?"

"Chicanery."

Rebel blinked and fought to hide a smile. "And I'm not to ask exactly what you mean by that?"

"I'd appreciate it."

"What assurance do I have that you're not doing something I wouldn't approve of?"

"None at all. You wouldn't approve."

"Donovan, am I going to have to fire you by the time this is over with?"

"You already have."

"I rehired you. Will I have to fire you again?"

He appeared to give the question serious consideration. "You'll probably want to kill me," he answered at last, his voice oddly whimsical. "Slowly. With your bare hands."

Rebel sat up with a jerk, staring at him in dawning horror. "Donovan . . . what have you done?"

"Would you believe . . . had Astaire Lennox kidnapped?"

It took Rebel only a moment to realize that her leg was being pulled—by an expert. She sat back with a sigh, the stiffness draining away. "Don't do that to me, dammit. I thought you were serious. What did you really do?"

"Nothing illegal."

Rebel gave up. He wasn't going to tell her. It didn't really bother her, because in business matters she trusted him completely. It was this sudden interest in *her* that she mistrusted.

Donovan came over to sit down beside her on the couch, lifting one of her hands and rubbing it against his cheek. "I wish you wouldn't let it worry you," he said soberly.

Her senses spinning at the loverlike gesture, Rebel said the first thing she could think of. "What—how you're getting Astaire here?"

"No." He sighed roughly, the cheerful teasing gone. "Me. And whether it's you or the company I want."

Rebel made a useless attempt to pull her hand away, still not ready to talk seriously. Still not ready to take *him* seriously. But this time, Donovan wouldn't be denied.

"Rebel, I look at business the way your father does." His voice was quiet, but it held an undertone of urgency. "It's great to build something with your mind and your wits, to watch it grow until it's established. But it's the challenge of the thing that counts, not the end result. I'd be just as happy training horses, or laying bricks, or watching my kids grow up.

"I'm not interested in power. Hell, you said it yourself—I could be my own boss. And I wouldn't need to step on you to do it. I could have started my own company ten years ago; I had the chance. But I passed it up, Rebel. I didn't want or need the headaches, the ulcers, or the backstabbing and the power plays."

Rebel looked at him steadily, trying to understand, trying to believe. "Then why do you work for me?" she asked finally. "You still end up with twelve-hour days, hurried lunches, board meetings lasting until midnight. No time for a personal life. No time to relax. Just stress and tension and potential ulcers."

"I work for *you*," he agreed, stressing the last word softly. "I took the job a year ago because I knew I'd be working for you; Marc made no secret of the fact that he was ready to retire and that you would take over for him. I wanted to lighten the load for you, Rebel. The company could have gone to hell in a bucket for all I cared—and for all Marc cared, although you don't realize that. But you were totally wrapped up in the business, buried in it, and because of that, I wanted to help you."

"Nobility," she managed with feigned lightness, wondering if what he'd said about her father was true.

"No—enchantment. You were trying to give everything you had to the company—everything your bastard of a husband left you with. It was draining you. I tried to lighten the load for you, but there was only so much you'd let me do."

A faint thread of humor brightened his voice suddenly. "You don't realize the conspiracies your . . . dedication . . . caused. The entire staff did everything possible to help you. A great many minor problems never reached your desk or mine. Business was discussed over lunch or dinner whenever possible, because we'd want to make sure you ate something that day. Bessie deliberately turned off your alarm clock many mornings, just so you'd sleep an extra hour or so. Marc was after me constantly to try to get you to slow down, to convince you that the company wasn't the be-all and end-all of everything. Not that I could. You didn't even see me."

Rebel winced at that last oddly bleak comment. She knew, somehow, that what he said about his efforts, the staff's, Bessie's, was true. With the veils of abstraction stripped away now, she could look back and see much more clearly. And what she saw was, as Donovan had said, a conspiracy—with her in the center of it.

Scolding Bessie because she hadn't awakened her. Donovan's smooth "Don't worry, I handled everything" when she'd rushed to the office an hour later. Her executive staff seemingly running itself. Problems solved by the time they filtered through to her. Meetings finished in record time. Bessie mothering her, pestering her to rest, to eat. Donovan making lunch or dinner reservations as a matter of course, arranging discussions across a food-laden table whenever possible.

Donovan . . . always the needed bit of information, the shrewd suggestion, the sound advice. Always there when she needed him. Lifting as much of the burden as she allowed—scheming to lift even more. Final decisions always hers, but with his thoughts on them flowing through her mind.

She looked at him blankly, stunned by the fact that she had never seen, never realized. "But, why?" she whispered. "Why did you—all of you—go to all that trouble?"

He pressed a gentle kiss into the palm of her hand. "*We* never doubted you, love," he told her quietly. "From Marc down to the typing pool, none of us doubted that you could run the company—and run it well. But you doubted yourself. You gave the company more than it needed, and it was draining the life out of you. We could all see that. A blind man could have seen it. And none of us wanted to see the company break you."

"This trip . . . ?" Rebel stared at him.

Donovan shrugged slightly, and a glint of mischief showed itself briefly in his eyes. "I could have handled this on my own," he admitted. "But you were strained to the breaking point, and I couldn't stand it any longer. I had to get you away from the office, if only for a few days."

He looked down at the hand he still held firmly, and then he met her eyes again, his own somber. "Honey, I don't want your company. I wish to hell you didn't want it, either, but I know you do. And I respect that. You're a natural businesswoman; you're shrewd and you're strong and you're capable. Anything less than the full use of your abilities would be sheer waste.

"But there are other things beside business, Rebel. Challenges to stretch your mind the way business does. I think you're beginning to see that now. Or at least considering the possibilities. I hope so. If you ever decide that the business has served its purpose—that you don't want to be chained to a company—I hope you'll let me be there beside you, exploring the possibilities of another kind of life.

"And if not—if the business wins in the end—then I'll still be there. I'll share that with you. Shoulder as much of the load as you'll let me. Bully you, if I have to. I won't let the company have all of you, Rebel."

She tried to shake off the spell of his quiet, almost hypnotic voice. "You—you make the company sound like a rival," she said with an uncertain little laugh.

His smile was twisted, a curious bitterness flashing briefly in his eyes. "Ironic, isn't it?" he said roughly. "You suspect me of wanting the company and intending to use you to get it. And a hundred—a thousand!—times during the past year, I've silently consigned Sinclair Hotels to the fiery depths of hell. If I could bargain with the devil to free you from that company, I'd do it. No matter what the price—except for your unhappiness. I won't bargain with that."

Rebel tried to let his words—and the incredible commitment

he had made a year before—sink in and be recognized for the truth she sensed it was. But the little gremlin sneered at her.

Another man had said wonderful, moving things to her. Another man had made lies sound like truth. Another man had acted a part for three years, had possessed her body and her mind and her heart, leaving her shattered and betrayed when the deceit was revealed.

It was too much to think about, too much to unravel. She didn't know whom to trust, what to believe. She knew only that she wouldn't—couldn't—be hurt that way again.

Rebel rose to her feet, gently pulling her hand from Donovan's grasp. "It's late. I think I'll go to bed. Maybe read for a while." She wondered at her own calm, detached voice, the meaningless words. What was wrong with her? Why couldn't she respond to the pain in his eyes, the look of defeat on his face?

"Good night, Rebel." His voice was toneless.

She turned away from him and walked steadily through the archway and into their wing. Something was pulling at her, ordering her, screaming at her to go back to him. Something was telling her that she was walking away from something infinitely precious.

Steadily, she walked on.

In her own room, she showered, changed into a fresh, flower-sprigged satin nightgown, and brushed her hair. Then she paced. Back and forth, from window to door, steadily, constantly.

Images flashed through her mind. Bantering conversations. A mythical key. A Christmas tree decorated with laughter. One decorated in secret, as a gift. Kisses beneath mistletoe. The dammed-up tears of too many years, shed at last. Strong arms holding her, a gentle order to blow her nose. Questions answered before they were asked. Burdens lifted, burdens shared. Light comments taken seriously. Serious comments taken lightly. A smile in the darkness, and dreams of castles and knights.

Rebel heard Donovan go into his bedroom; still she paced. There was something teasing her, something battering for admittance into her mind. But pain-filled violet eyes kept haunting her. She had never intentionally hurt another human being before. But tonight she had hurt Donovan.

Defeated. Donovan defeated. She couldn't bear to see that, couldn't bear to see the chinks in his armor. It hurt her. In hurting him, she had hurt herself. That meant something. That had to mean something. But what?

Gradually the fragments and questions faded into blankness. Her pacing slowed, finally stopped. She felt, oddly, that she had been walking in her sleep. Quietly, she opened her bedroom door and went out into the sitting room. A fire had been freshly built in the hearth, as it was every night.

Unable to resist the thick fur rug in front of the fireplace, Rebel sank down into its white softness. The room was lit only by firelight, the silence disturbed by pops and crackles and an occasional soft moan as the wind picked up outside.

Rebel rolled over onto her stomach, propped up on her elbows as she stared into the fire. The gremlin was silent. There were no more arguments to voice. Donovan's strength she could fight with her own, but his defeat left her defenseless. She couldn't think anymore; she could only feel. And what she felt was the desire, the need that had been building for days.

This room demanded a lover, she realized dreamily, and she made no attempt to banish the thought. A lover, coming out of the surrounding darkness and into firelight, silent and strong and as raw as nature had made him. A man filled with tenderness and sensitivity and aching need.

Eyes slitted against the fire's shifting orange glow, she allowed her mind to sketch the lover. Big. A big man with broad shoulders and a massive chest, long, powerful arms and legs. Moving like a jungle cat. Black hair a little shaggy, going silver at the temples. A face that might have been hard but wasn't. An elusive dimple in one lean cheek. Striking, startling, incredibly vivid violet eyes.

Donovan. She needed him. She needed his warmth and his closeness. Needed to try to heal the hurt she had inflicted. Needed him to begin to heal the hurt inside herself. She needed to make a commitment she could not yet make in words.

The thoughts had barely peaked in her consciousness when a small sound drew her eyes. And there the lover stood. Her lover.

Firelight glinted off his body, naked but for the towel knotted around his lean waist. Even as she watched, the towel fell. Huge, silent, he was overwhelmingly male and devastatingly handsome. And the aching need she had dreamed of was evident in every taut, hard line of his body.

And in his eyes was the look of a man reprieved from hell.

Rebel turned off her conscious mind at that point. He had come to her, and nothing else mattered. For this night, at least, he would belong to her. Her man.

Donovan moved toward her slowly, as if he were approaching a deer he was wary of frightening. Muscles rippled smoothly beneath his shimmering flesh, drawing her fascinated eyes. She remained on her stomach as he knelt beside her on the fur rug. Even as she looked away from him she could feel his presence through her every pore and nerve ending. And her body tensed like a drawn bow when she felt his big hand come out to rest lightly on the small of her back.

Still, she didn't turn her head, waiting breathlessly for the next touch. It came. His free hand brushed aside her long hair, and she felt his warm lips moving over the sensitive nape of her neck. Rebel bowed her head slightly, one kind of tension melting away and a new kind taking its place. The hand on her back was moving gently, a finger languidly tracing her spine through the sheer satin of her gown. His other hand had brushed away the lacy straps, fingers exploring the delicate bones of her shoulders with the seeking touch of a blind man.

Neither of them uttered a word or made a sound.

She could feel his powerful thigh against her side, the darting touch of his tongue on her flesh, and a shiver began somewhere deep inside her, radiating outward in ripples of sensation. His hand slid down over her hip, her thigh, using the silky material of her gown to create a sensual friction.

Unhurriedly, gently, as though they had all the time in the world, Donovan guided her with soft pressure until she was lying flat on her stomach, arms at her sides and face turned toward him. Her eyes were nearly closed, her breath coming shallowly from between barely parted lips. She was completely quiescent, allowing him to do what he would.

The gown was slowly pulled down, a strong hand beneath her stomach lifting slightly until the material was past her hips and gone. She felt cool air on her skin, heard a soft, rough intake of breath from him, and still didn't look directly at him, didn't move. Now she felt the length of him beside her, felt the thick mat of hair on his chest brushing her back as his lips returned to her neck.

Large hands moved over her body—her back, her hips, her thighs. Touching, stroking, shaping. His mouth followed, tongue darting out again and again to find shiveringly sensitive areas, teeth nipping lightly. Only when he had explored every inch of her flesh between neck and ankles did he gently turn her over onto her back.

Rebel's lashes drifted up as she looked fully at him for the first time since he'd begun touching her. His oddly fixed stare was gliding down her body slowly, leaving a trail of fire. And then his eyes met hers, and the breath caught in her throat. She had never seen such hunger in a man's eyes, such aching need, and for a moment it frightened her. But only for a moment.

His dark head bent toward hers slowly until their lips were only a breath apart. Teasingly, he kissed her once, twice, kisses no heavier than dew. It was Rebel who finally broke the silence between them, moaning softly as her arm moved at last to encircle his neck. As though the involuntary sound were the signal he'd been waiting for, Donovan abandoned his tormenting, taking her mouth in a surge of ravenous hunger.

And it *was* hunger, the same almost desperate hunger she'd seen in his eyes. Like a man lost and wandering in a bleak desert for a very long time, he came at last to an oasis, drinking from a clear pool and devouring tender fruit. He couldn't seem to get enough, couldn't slake his thirst or satisfy his hunger.

His strange, inexplicable desperation moved Rebel in some way she couldn't name. She could feel his heart pounding out of control in the massive chest pressed against her, could feel the rigid desire throbbing against her thigh. His intense, fervent need transmitted itself to her, and her own need spiraled crazily.

Her fingers locked together with almost bruising strength; tongues met, clashed, possessed, dueled as though to the death—or to life.

The need for oxygen finally proved stronger than anything else—but barely. Donovan drew a single harsh breath when his lips reluctantly left hers. She was granted only a glimpse of his taut expression, a flash of violet eyes darkened to purple, and then his face was buried between her breasts.

Rebel pulled air into her starved lungs in shaken gasps, her fingers still tangled in his hair. Large hands slid up her body to shape full breasts; lips moved from one hardened tip to the other. He lavished her breasts with adoring kisses, his tongue curling voraciously around the hard bud his mouth held. Sensually abrasive hands spanned her waist, traced the curve of her hips, feathered along the inside of her thighs.

Jerking involuntarily, Rebel moaned when his searching fingers found the warm, wet center of her desire. Her body arched of its own accord, her fingers sliding from his hair to dig into the muscles of his back. His probing touch was sending her senses on a crazy, cartwheeling spin, and she couldn't find the breath to tell him what he was doing to her.

Oh, God, he was so gentle! In spite of the desperate need she could feel burning in him, in spite of the almost inhuman control that made his muscles bunched and rigid beneath her fingers, he was so very gentle. And she couldn't even tell him what that meant to her.

He raised his head at last, and Rebel tugged mutely at his shoulder, unable to even whisper a plea. But he knew; he understood. Her legs shifted restlessly as he slid between them, and she suddenly knew a fierce need to feel his heavy body bearing down on her, crushing her into the pile of the rug beneath them.

But he hesitated, staring down at her, breathing like a marathon runner at the end of a very long race. She saw something flicker in his desire-darkened eyes, something uncertain, oddly defensive, and understanding came clearly to her mind. He was afraid he'd hurt her!

Her arms encircled his neck, pulling his head down until she could reach his mouth, telling him in the best way she knew that he wouldn't hurt her.

Donovan's groan rumbled from deep in his chest, accepting her silent assurance as his wonderful weight bore her down into the rug. Rebel's breath somehow got lost, leaving her body as he entered it. She felt like a virgin again, knowing a man for the first time, being known in a way one could never describe but only feel. And it had never felt this way before.

He was with her, filling the hollowness that had ached for him, filling her until she was conscious only of him. He was still for a moment, as though possessing her satisfied something in him that was beyond words, beyond description. And then he was moving gracefully, powerfully, but with great tenderness, his eyes blazing darkly out of his taut face.

Rebel held him, moved with him, feeling the primitive, driving tension building within her until she felt that she would shatter into a million pieces. And for one eternal second, she thought that she had done just that. She was flying apart, jagged pieces of herself soaring with exquisite agony. She was unable to cry out; only a strangled, kittenlike sound escaped her. She was aware dimly of a shuddering groan torn from Donovan's throat.

Donovan's heavy weight continued to crush her body into the rug, but Rebel felt only contentment. As though they were the epicenter of some massive earthquake, she could feel aftershocks, shudders in his body and her own. His face was buried in the curve of her neck; his harsh breathing gradually steadied in her ear.

He rolled slowly onto his side, taking her with him, his lips seeking hers almost blindly. Powerful arms held her securely to him, bodies touching, merging. He kissed her hungrily, as if only the sharp edge of his need had been blunted.

He had left a tiny glowing ember deep inside of her, and expertly he fanned it to flame again.

Rebel was aware of very little clear, conscious thought during the hours that followed. But her occasional, stray thoughts were delighted ones. She had never known, never believed, that lovemaking could be this way. He silently taught her things about herself, her body, that she had never known before, and Rebel learned each lesson blissfully.

With the openness of old lovers, the silent, instinctive under-standing of soul mates, they explored each other long into the night. The need continued to drive them both, each touch and kiss sensitizing their flesh until the brush of fingers and lips—even the meeting of eyes—was like a torch branding raw nerves. It was almost unbearable, and yet it was borne; almost agony, and yet it was sweet . . . so sweet.

Again and again they made the journey of lovers, leaving earthly ties far behind them and passing an occasional shooting star along the way, then drifting slowly down, only to begin the dizzying climb again.

Dawn's light was beginning to creep into the room, the fire in the hearth long since ashes, when Rebel finally yielded to ex-haustion. His hands were caressing again with a touch she recog-nized, the hunger in him apparently insatiable, but she was just too tired to respond. With an apologetic murmur, she buried her face in the damp curve of his neck, utterly limp and delightfully weary.

Immediately his touch changed, becoming gentle and soothing. He stroked her back, her hair. She felt his heart beating steadily against her, the warmth of his body offsetting the chill of the room. The imprint of his large body, the touch of his hands, the throb of his heart, all followed her into dream.

Chapter Seven

When Rebel awoke, she didn't open her eyes for a long moment. Somehow, she was aware of being watched, and she knew instantly who was watching her. Donovan. She could feel his warmth beside her in bed, hear his steady breathing. When had he carried her to bed? She didn't remember. But she remembered everything else.

Physically, she'd never felt better. Emotionally, she was teetering on the edge of a precipice, clinging to finger- and toeholds. One sudden or wrong move, and over she'd go.

Rebel didn't bother to belatedly acknowledge—even to herself—that she was in love with Donovan. She'd known that for quite some time now. What she did silently acknowledge was the fact that she was still confused. She needed time.

"Are you going to feign sleep all day?"

The deep, amused voice brought Rebel's eyes open with a snap.

She was lying on her back, close beside Donovan. He was raised up on one elbow, watching her with mock gravity.

"Good morning," she murmured. "Or is it?"

"Actually, it's after noon," he told her.

"Oh." For the life of her, Rebel couldn't think of a thing to say. She was highly conscious of the hard length of his body beside hers, and she wondered what on earth she should talk about with the man who had ravished her delightfully for the better part of a night.

"You're blushing!" he said in a delighted voice, beginning to chuckle softly.

"I am not." She forced every ounce of dignity possible into the three small words. "You're seeing things."

"No, you're definitely blushing."

"Stop harping."

"Yes, ma'am." He leaned over to kiss her, his lips warm and lazy. Last night's desperation was gone, but his hunger had not diminished a bit.

Rebel found her arms creeping up around his neck, her mouth responding to his, and decided that conversation wasn't all that important anyway. She felt his arms drawing her close. In the back of her mind the gremlin remained silent.

Donovan raised his head slightly, gazing down at her with smoky purple eyes. "Tell me something, lady of the castle," he murmured. "Is the key mine, or am I just . . . borrowing it?"

Rebel didn't lower her arms, her fingers still tangled in his shaggy black hair. His steady eyes demanded honesty, and she gave it, quietly, her voice a little husky. "I need time, Donovan. Time to . . . get my priorities in order."

He was silent for a moment, and then he nodded. In a voice of utter calm, he told her, "Take all the time you need, honey. But I'd better warn you about something. The only way you'll keep me out of your bed from now on is with a loaded gun."

Rebel blinked at him. "Masterful, aren't you?" she murmured, chuckling.

"I'd be glad to demonstrate," he muttered, beginning to nuzzle her throat, "exactly how masterful I can be."

She decided that there was something wicked about making love in the middle of the day. Wonderfully wicked.

Whatever constraint had existed between them vanished rapidly. If Donovan was disturbed by her continued reluctance to make a verbal commitment, he gave no sign of it. He was cheerful again, teasing, bantering. The only difference in his manner toward her was an indefinably male look in his eyes whenever they rested on her.

They shared a bath in the huge tub in Rebel's bathroom and then dressed casually and ate a well-prepared brunch in the dining room. Rebel wasn't even surprised to find the meal ready and waiting for them; she'd already come to the private conclusion that Carson was a wizard.

After brunch they went for a walk outside, their boots crunching through the additional two inches of snow that had fallen during the night. Rebel had hoped that the cold air would clear away the remaining cobwebs in her mind, allowing her to think clearly but she was granted no such luck.

Donovan held her hand firmly, swinging it between them cheerfully like a teenager, warm eyes on her almost constantly. And she couldn't resist that. She felt cared for, cherished, and not even the occasional whisperings of the gremlin could fight that.

Wandering along one of the many trails that spread out from the lodge, she finally worked up the courage to ask about something that had been puzzling her. She wasn't sure she wanted to know the answer, but the questions wouldn't leave her alone.

"Donovan . . . this past year . . ."

"What about it, love?"

How easily the endearments rose to his lips, she thought. That had never been easy for her. Never. She shunted aside the thought.

"I never noticed—I mean, there was never any sign of . . ." Floundering helplesssly, she sent an oblique glance up at him, silently begging him to help her out.

"Women?" he supplied, his faintly amused eyes meeting hers before she quickly looked away again. "That's because there weren't any—except for a certain company president."

"None at all? I mean, not even casual . . ." Floundering again, she silently cursed her stumbling tongue.

"Not even casual," he murmured. "I wanted you, Rebel."

A year, she thought faintly. She tried to understand what he must have gone through. And worst of all—worst of all was that she had never known, never *seen*.

This new revelation made his gentleness of the night before even more astonishing. It spoke volumes for his self-control, his restraint. She had felt the desperate need within him, had seen it in his eyes, but never once had he rushed her, never once had he hurt her.

"It wasn't easy," Donovan murmured musingly as both of them came to a stop.

The curving trail provided a natural vantage point here, the ground falling away in a sheer drop beside the path. The entrance to a snow-blanketed valley lay before them, the pristine beauty of the snow untouched by man or machine. Lonely and beautiful.

"There were times," Donovan continued, "when I wanted to just grab you and shake you until you looked at me. Saw me. Hell, I wasn't even sure you'd like what you saw. But I was willing to take that chance. I had to. I never had a choice. So I stuck around and tried to become important to you in any way I could."

"My right hand," she murmured, staring out over the valley but not really seeing it.

"Yeah." He sighed roughly. "It wasn't what I wanted, but it helped you and kept me near you. I spent a lot of nights pacing the floor and wondering if I were . . . tilting at windmills. Then I'd look at you in the office the next morning and know that I was stuck there. For however long it took."

Rebel gently disengaged her hand from his and moved to the edge of the path. "I'm sorry," she murmured, again staring without seeing the view.

He came up behind her and put his arms around her, drawing her back against him. "Don't be. You couldn't help not seeing me any more than I could help staying."

She stirred slightly but made no attempt to leave the warmth of his embrace. "I still don't know very much about you. You said you were an only child?"

"No, I said that I was an 'only,' " he corrected. "An only son. I have sisters."

"Really? How many?"

"Six—all older than I." He chuckled softly. "Dad said that he wasn't going down without a fight. If I'd been another girl, he was going to throw away his vitamins and try something else."

Rebel found herself smiling. "And your mother?"

"She said that six girls were enough; they already had more than they needed for a basketball team."

Awe in her voice, Rebel asked, "Are they all as tall as you?"

"No, but none of them is small."

"I've always wondered what it would be like to have a large family—no pun intended."

He laughed again. "Marry me and find out," he invited easily. "My family's generally pretty far-flung, but we manage to get together a few times a year. Want to meet them?"

Rebel ignored the suggestion in favor of the question. "Maybe someday," she answered evasively, then immediately changed the subject. "Whom do you resemble—your mother or father?"

"Both," he responded, allowing the subject change. "I have Dad's coloring and Mom's features. And, before you ask, the girls all got Mom's red hair."

"All of them?"

"Various shades, but all red."

"Must be a temperamental family."

Donovan reflected for a moment. "Not really. Helen—she's the next step up in age after me—has a temper like a drunk marine. But she cheerfully lets her kids bully her, and although my brother-in-law says they go through at least one set of china a month, he doesn't seem to mind."

Rebel laughed, then urged, "Keep climbing the steps. This is getting interesting."

"Are you sure you're warm enough?" he asked. "We could continue this inside, if you'd rather."

"I'm warm enough." Rebel tipped back her head to rest against his shoulder. "Keep climbing."

"Whatever the lady wants. Next is Geneva."

"Unusual name," Rebel commented.

"You don't have to tell me that. Gen's complained bitterly about it for as long as I can remember. It means 'juniper tree,' and she's never forgiven Dad for that; it was his inspiration."

Victim herself of an unusual name, Rebel could well imagine how Donovan's sister felt. "I'm surprised she's still speaking to him. What's she like?"

"She . . . *arranges* things," Donovan said carefully. "Ruthlessly and with every good intention in the world. She imagines boredom in every silence, and inactivity drives her crazy. So she keeps people busy—whether they want to be or not. Her kids claim that any general could use her expertise to straighten out his troop movements. And her husband, Adam, told me that when they spent a few weeks in Hawaii last year, Gen arranged two marriages in a bewildered island family and then topped off her vacation by preventing a volcanic erruption. Singlehandedly."

This time, Rebel hooted with delight. "She sounds daunting."

"Not at all. Adam adores her, and the kids listen respectfully to her advice and then do exactly as they please."

"Brave kids. Next step, please."

"Charley—Charlotte. She's vague, absentminded, and creative. Talks a mile a minute and never makes sense—although she never misses a thing. Her husband, Rick, calls her half-pint because she's the smallest of us all."

"Back up a minute," Rebel requested. "Who's Helen's husband?"

"Burke."

"Okay. I'm trying to keep the names straight. Next step."

"Ami. Her kids are all out of the nest, her husband is Steve, and she's the original 'iron hand in the velvet glove.' She could smile sweetly at opposing sides in war and have them laying down arms before they'd know what hit them. Steve says he was on his honeymoon before he came out of the daze, and by then he didn't have the energy to protest."

Rebel bit her lip. "Next step," she ordered unsteadily.

"Judith," Donovan said obediently. "And Judith is sunshine. She's happy and cheerful and never sees the bad in people. Her husband, Larry, and her kids say that she could daunt the devil. Everyone she meets is a friend, and nobody ever has to ask her for help with a problem."

"Is my counting off," Rebel murmured, "or are we at the last step now?"

"Last. Or first, depending on which way you're going. Oldest of us all is Kelly. She's . . . queenly. Reminds me of a battleship under full steam." After a moment and a giggle from Rebel, he added fairly, "That could be pure prejudice on my part; eleven years' age difference rendered my childhood hideous with bullying."

"Forgive me if I don't believe that," Rebel murmured wryly.

"Shrewd of you. Actually, she's got a heart like oatmeal, although you'd never guess it. Kelly is loud and astringent and will hotly debate anything at the drop of a hat. Her husband, Robert, trails along in her wake, bemused and soft-spoken. Contrary to appearances, Robert can shut Kelly up with a word or a look; she absolutely adores him."

"Interesting family," Rebel said at last.

"We have an opening. Want to enlist?"

Rebel ignored that. "Are you a great-uncle yet?"

"Well, of course I'm a great uncle."

"You know what I mean."

Donovan chuckled. "Right. Well, Ami, Judith, and Kelly all have kids who married fairly young, so there are several babies and toddlers in the family. I'm definitely a great-uncle."

"Must be a madhouse when you all get together," Rebel said, hearing the note of envy in her own voice.

"Utter bedlam. Mom and Dad are both in their seventies, and Dad swears after every gathering that he'll never make it through another one. But he's usually the first to suggest we all get together for Arbor Day or something. One year he called us all together to celebrate the first rose in his garden."

Rebel smiled. "He sounds terrific."

"He is." There was a wealth of pride and affection in Donovan's voice. "I wish I had half his energy and a quarter of his wisdom. He's the undisputed patriarch of the family, and Mom rules *him* with a iron hand." After a pause, he added, "They remind me a lot of your parents. Totally devoted to one another, but still individuals after years of marriage."

Bemused, Rebel murmured, "I didn't know you'd met my mother. When she and Dad make flying visits to Dallas, she never comes to the office."

"She did in July. You and Marc had flown to Tahoe to check on that hotel and left me to mind the store. I took Vanessa out to lunch and then we went to the zoo."

"You did?" Rebel said blankly.

"Sure we did. Actually, I would have met her sooner, except that while I was working for Marc she was already in Paris decorating the house they'd bought. A charming lady, Vanessa."

Rebel wondered vaguely why she wasn't shocked at Donovan's familiarity with her parents. His next words, however, drove the speculation from her mind.

"We spent the afternoon talking," he added musingly. "She was quite pleased when I told her I was going to marry her daughter."

"You did *what*?" Rebel broke free of his hug and whirled to stare up at him. "You told her—"

"That I was going to marry her daughter." His violet eyes laughed down at her. "One day or another. Fair means or foul. Even if I had to use caveman tactics."

"Donovan, you—you—" Rebel was torn between incredulity and wrath.

"You can hit me if you want," he told her soothingly. "I promise to take it like a man."

Rebel lifted her hand, but it was only to jab a finger into his chest. Each jab emphasized a word. "How dare you tell my mother something like that! What makes you so damn sure—"

Donovan caught her hand and lifted it to his lips. "Honey, one way or another, I'm going to get you to the altar. I don't expect it to be easy, and truth to tell, I wouldn't miss the fight for anything. But I'll win." Disarming her immediately, he added softly, "I have to. Nothing else bears thinking of."

"Don't *say* things like that!" she very nearly wailed, glaring up at him. "You're boxing me in, dammit!"

He grinned and, still holding her hand, began leading her back along the path to the lodge. "I'll give you all the time you need," he offered cheerfully.

"Oh, sure," she muttered. "I can just *feel* all the time you're giving me. Shall we dance the 'Minute Waltz' while we're waiting?"

"Not in the snow," he responded gravely.

She ignored that. She was getting very good at ignoring most of his cute comments. "Donovan, you're taking entirely too much for granted. This is the twenty-first century, remember? Standards have changed. *People* have changed."

"All of which has nothing to do with us."

Rebel tried again. It was difficult to think of sensible things to say and watch her footing in the snow at the same time, but she managed. "What I'm trying to say is that nothing in—our relationship automatically implies marriage. It's not written in stone anymore. No one would be shocked if we decided to live together—"

"I would."

"You'd be shocked?"

"Certainly I would. What kind of man do you think I am?"

Rebel bit back a giggle at his offended tone, and then fiercely tried to hang on to her objections. "Donovan . . ."

"Honey, don't waste your breath," he advised calmly. "I don't like unofficial vows with plenty of escape clauses thrown in, and that's what living together would mean. I want everything official. I want the kind of marriage your parents, my parents, and my sisters have—an enduring marriage filled with love."

Rebel swallowed hard. "You're an idealist," she murmured.

"I am that," he agreed, tucking her hand into the crook of his arm as they neared the lodge. "But I'm also blessed with a streak of practicality a yard wide—from my Scottish ancestors, no doubt. And I'm old enough to know what I want, Rebel. You and I will have many a disagreement, I'm sure. You're Irish-German and I'm Scottish-English—with an Indian or two a few generations back—and if anything, that's a combustible mixture. But we'll make it work for us. I have a lot of faith in what we have together."

In the face of that kind of determination, there wasn't much Rebel could say. Although it was true that a part of her was warmed by that determination, she knew what the biggest problem was between them, and she reluctantly brought that up.

"Donovan, even if—even if I'm sure you don't want the company, it's still *there*. And to you, it's a rival."

He stopped on the path and turned to face her, his hand still covering her hand as it rested on his arm. His lean face was serious, his violet eyes grave. "That's true. But understand something. Rebel—I won't ask you to give up the company. If you decide to keep on running it, that's fine. I'll help in every way I can. I won't like it, but I promise not to try to stop you.

"On the other hand, I think we'd both be happier out of the rat race. There are all kinds of possibilities to explore. Sinclair Hotels is an established corporation. The growth potential is still there, but where's the challenge? What's the point of working the same job day after day? Slight ups and downs due to temperamental coworkers or other people you have to deal with; high-pressure meetings; whirlwind flights around the country. It all gets routine after a while."

Rebel was staring up at him, halted in a seven-year journey by a fork in the road. Which way to go? Slowly, she asked him, "What would you like to do, Donovan? I mean, if it were completely up to you to decide?"

"Besides spend the rest of my life with you?" Donovan gazed off into the distance, thoughtful, considering. "Have a ranch somewhere I think. Raise horses. That's a business, too, of course, but it has enormous benefits. No stuffy offices, for one thing. No high-pressure meetings. No traffic jams to contend with. Just lots of fresh air and sunshine and working with your hands."

His eyes dropped back to hers, and he smiled slowly. "Like I said, I'm not interested in power. I'd much rather . . . plant a fig tree, nurture it, and watch it grow."

"You're an . . . unusual man," she murmured.

"Not really. I think most men would give up the corporate game in a minute if they had a choice. Aside from a relatively rare power-hungry one."

"But you're so good at the corporate game."

He shrugged slightly, his eyes distant again although still fixed on her face. "I suppose, but I'm not really comfortable with it, Rebel. Maybe it's the idealist in me. What's the point of having a success label stuck on me, or money I'll never need? I'd rather enjoy life."

Donovan paused for a moment, and then smiled suddenly. "Remember a while back during that last solar eclipse? There was some guy selling cans of 'solar dark' at a buck a throw. Now that man enjoyed life—and its absurdities."

Rebel felt a smile tugging at her lips. "How many cans did you buy?" she asked, beginning, at last to understand this man.

He grinned. "Just one."

"I bought two," she told him solemnly.

Donovan laughed and began leading her toward the lodge again. "See? We're more alike than you thought."

"I'm beginning to think so. Did you have a pet rock?"

"A niece sent me one for my birthday. How about you?"

"A present from Dad."

"Sounds like Marc. Who gave you the teddy bear?"

Rebel stopped walking abruptly, drawing him to a stop. "How did you know about that?" she asked blankly, thinking to herself that this was the most disjointed walk—and talk—they'd ever had.

Donovan had the grace to look slightly sheepish. "I snooped. One of those work sessions in your apartment. You went to answer the phone or something, and I spent the time looking around. That battered, moth-eaten teddy bear stuck out like a sore thumb in your beautiful Oriental bedroom. It gave me hope."

"It did?"

"Sure. It didn't fit in with your solid businesswoman front. I decided that somewhere underneath all that gray flannel there had to be a woman who could still hang on to a part of childhood."

Rebel thought about that as they started walking again. "You shouldn't have snooped," she said at last, weakly.

"I'm ashamed of myself," he said in a voice that held no sign of shame.

"Sure you are."

"Really."

"Uh-huh."

"And if you believe that," he murmured thoughtfully, "I have a bridge I'll sell to you. Across the San Francisco Bay. Or there's a big clock in a tower. Or there's the Great Sahara Forest—"

"I get the point. And I'm surprised you weren't selling cans of 'solar dark' yourself."

"Don't be ridiculous. I have the stardust concession."

"Shame on you. Taking advantage of gullible people."

"Nonsense. Want to buy a pinch of stardust? Guaranteed to cure all aches and ills."

"I'm not gullible."

"You bought the dark," he pointed out gravely.

"Don't rub it in. Besides, you bought some, too."

"Ah! But I never claimed not to be gullible."

"There's probably a word for what you *are*, but if there is, I don't know it."

"Charming?"

"I don't think so."

"Lovable?"

"Not quite what I had in mind."

"Irresistible?"

"Hardly."

"Now you've cut me to the quick."

"I'll bet." Rebel sighed. "Never mind. I'll come up with it eventually. I have a feeling it's more along the lines of impossible."

By this time they had crossed between two of the helipads and reached the bottom of the stone steps leading up to the lodge's main entrance. Rebel glanced up at the central A-frame as Donovan laughed, and then she froze, adding yet another temporary halt to their walk.

There was a man standing at the top of the steps. He was tall, lean, hard. He didn't look to be in his late sixties, although Rebel knew he was. He had a full head of copper hair, touched by gray only at the temples. He stood with arms folded, looking down on them from Olympian heights.

"Master of all he surveys," Rebel murmured involuntarily.

"Damn. He's a day early." Donovan did not sound pleased.

Rebel gave him a curious look as they started up the steps, belatedly remembering to remove her hand from his arm. "I thought you had it all arranged for him to come tomorrow."

"I thought the same thing." Donovan glanced down and met her puzzled look. He grimaced slightly. "I was hoping we'd have more time to be alone."

"Before the charades, you mean?"

"Something like that."

An elusive note in Donovan's voice bothered Rebel, and she tried to pin it down. Constraint? Uneasiness? Was he worried about carrying off his role as boss? As soon as the question posed itself, she gave it a mental dismissal. That wasn't it. Then what?

"Mr. Lennox," Donovan called out coolly as they reached the top of the steps and their host, "I'm Donovan Knight. This is my assistant, Rebel Anderson."

As Astaire Lennox held out a hand to Donovan, smiling with some inner amusement, Rebel was experiencing a weird and muddled sense of *déjà vu*.

She had seen this man before somewhere. Not a photo—in the flesh. But she couldn't recall where or when. In the moment or so granted to her for a quick memory check, she studied his face carefully. Lined with age but alive, vital, deeply tanned. His eyes were deep-set, shrewd, and as clear blue as her own. He looked like a tough man, but by no means a stupid one. And although it certainly didn't jibe with Donovan's description of the man, met across a business desk she would have instinctively trusted him. But she couldn't for the life of her recall where she had seen him before, or why he would otherwise seem so familiar.

"Miss Anderson," he said, holding out a hand to her.

"Rebel," she murmured. His grip was firm and friendly without being the slightest bit supercilious. The blue eyes met hers in an amicable, slightly measuring look.

Obeying his almost courtly gesture, she silently preceded the men into the lodge, hearing behind her Lennox cheerfully apologizing to Donovan for the delay in his arrival. Rebel and Donovan removed their coats along with their host, Carson appearing magically out of nowhere to whisk them away. They made their way into the greatroom and sat down.

Rebel listened quietly as the two men talked casually. Her silence was due not to the reticence expected of a secretary but rather to her mental activity.

There was, she decided, something very rotten in the state of Denmark.

She tuned out the conversation. Bits of conversation were briefly reviewed in her mind—light comments, warning comments. Feudal lords with octopus hands. Knight-errantry and an unexpected kiss on the steps.

A method to the madness? Oh, yes. Definitely yes.

"Don't you agree, Rebel?"

She looked up, blinking at the jovial question from Lennox. "I'm sorry?"

"I said that your boss certainly goes after something once he's made up his mind. Wouldn't you agree?"

Rebel turned a limpid gaze to her "boss." In a voice that could have put honeybees out of business, she murmured, "Oh, I certainly agree. He doesn't let anything stand in his way."

Donovan very nearly winced.

"Pass the soap, please."

"Get it yourself."

"Rebel, I've explained why I—uh—exaggerated certain of Astaire's characteristics. I was trying to get through those walls of yours, and I thought that a bit of knight-errantry—"

"You've explained."

Donovan sighed and tried a change of subject. "Did you have to use lilac-scented bubble bath? Astaire will think I'm crazy."

"Just be glad I didn't follow my impulses and pour acid in the tub. You deserved that."

"Rebel . . ."

"You're an impossible man. Pardon me—improbable. Tell me, is it at least true that Astaire doesn't deal with female executives?"

"You read my report."

"Big deal."

"It's true. Just ask him."

"If I didn't want that land—"

"I know, I know. Forgive me?"

"Stop that. You want me to drown?"

"I have marvelous balance."

"You'd have to. And nerves of steel. A sane man wouldn't try that maneuver in a bathtub full of bubbles."

"Look at the fun he'd be missing."

"Donovan, we have to get ready for dinner. Donovan? What're you—? I think that's illegal."

"I must break the law more often."

"Donovan . . . ?"

"Astaire won't mind if we're a little late. . . ."

Chapter Eight

During the next two days, Rebel found that her role as secretary made her an observer, a listener, and she was surprised to find that very little different from her actions as a boss. It was eerie in a way, she decided—the extremely thin line separating one link of the executive chain from another.

As a boss, she had listened to opinions and recommendations, bits of information needed to make a decision. It had usually been Donovan who had given her the pertinent facts, along with his opinions and advice. She had listened, thought about it, and then decided.

They had worked as a team, each half as important as the other, she realized. Slowly the line in her mind separating employer from employee thinned even more.

Several small things were coming together, pieces assembling a jigsaw puzzle. The first pieces had come together when she had realized on meeting Astaire that Donovan had created a rake where none existed.

Astaire Lennox treated her rather like a daughter. He was friendly, amusing, and unusually down-to-earth for a man of his wealth and power. He made not a single sneering reference to women in corporate positions, women as sexual toys, or anything else that could have been considered sexist.

Those several pieces gradually formed a corner of the puzzle in Rebel's mind. Donovan had been determined to get her up here to this lodge, and he had been perfectly willing to resort to subterfuge to do it.

She could have accepted his reason for that: She was tired and strained, and he'd wanted to get her away from the office. Added to that was his impatience after a year of waiting for her to come out of her chrysalis. Hence the knight-errantry and his immediate moves to take advantage of the situation he had created.

But the puzzle still wasn't complete.

Silently, Rebel watched and listened to the fencing between Donovan and Astaire. It was highly skilled, adroit, and never seemed to accomplish a thing. Rapidly losing interest in the land she needed and increasingly absorbed by the human drama unfolding around her, Rebel made no attempt to berate Donovan for his lack of progress in acquiring the property.

It was slowly dawning on her that Donovan—and perhaps Astaire as well—was deliberately dragging out the negotiations. She didn't know why, but for some reason neither was in any hurry to close the deal. It gave her food for thought.

Rebel wouldn't have been so tolerant of the situation had she not gotten her own priorities into order. She wasn't certain exactly what had finally decided her. The nights with Donovan might have had something to do with it. Making love with him, she had discovered, was a very special kind of sharing. Donovan gave totally of himself, sometimes tenderly, sometimes lustily passionate.

He never pressed her for a verbal commitment, although she had a feeling that he took it for granted in a sense. He seemed to understand her better than she did herself. Rebel had ceased being surprised at questions answered before they were asked, accepting that as on a par with this puzzling situation.

By Tuesday night, Rebel had come to several private decisions and conclusions. And the result of those was that she would have to make a trip into Casper. Alone.

"Donovan?"

"Hmmm?"

"Look at me when I'm talking to you."

"I was contemplating your navel."

"I noticed. Did you find the secrets of the universe?"

"No. I just got dizzy."

Rebel resolutely pulled up the covers. "Get out from under there and pay attention to me."

Donovan emerged from the covers. "I *was* paying attention to you. Strict attention. Undivided attention." He began to languidly explore the flesh of her throat.

"Donovan . . ." Rebel locked her fingers in his thick hair and had to clear her throat before intelligible words would emerge. "I called the heliport today."

The dark head lifted abruptly, startled violet eyes staring into hers. "You did? Why?" his voice was careful.

"I'm going into Casper tomorrow."

"Why?" he repeated.

Gently, she said, "Donovan, I didn't plan on staying this long. I have some shopping to do."

"I'll go with you," he said rather hastily.

Still more gently, she said, "You have to stay here and work on Astaire. Remember? The land? The reason we're here?"

He just stared at her.

"Afraid I'll slip my leash?" she asked sardonically.

"I'm afraid you'll catch the first mule train back to Dallas," he said frankly.

"Oh, no. I'm going to see this thing through. Observe the final curtain, so to speak."

Donovan looked with some suspicion at her bland expression. "I can still go with you," he said at last. "Astaire mentioned some calls he needed to make in the morning, so . . ."

Rebel shook her head slowly.

"Pulling rank, boss?"

"Oh, can I still do that?" she asked with mock surprise.

"Rebel, you know . . ."

Yes, she knew. She knew that Donovan had chosen to follow her, even though he was innately a leader himself. Knowing him better than she had before, Rebel no longer questioned his willingness to work for her, to take her orders. He followed because he wanted to, and that implied a strength she found intriguing.

Unwilling to enter into a discussion about that right now, and still seeking the pieces of her puzzle, she cut him off with a sudden change of subject.

"Tell me something. Why did you tell Carson that I was allergic to shellfish?"

"Because you are."

"Yes, but how did you know that? I only found out myself a few months ago." She watched the startled, bemused flicker in his violet eyes and tried once again to figure out what it meant.

"You must have mentioned it," he said finally.

She shook her head firmly. "No. The subject never came up."

"Then Marc must have mentioned it."

"He doesn't know."

Impatiently, Donovan said, "Then it was Bessie. Or you mentioned it and just don't remember. Or something."

"Right. Or something." That part of Rebel's puzzle was still empty. The pieces were flitting elusively through her mind, and she hadn't been able to grasp them yet. But she would.

"Are we going to talk all night?" he demanded.

Rebel wound her arms around his neck with a smile. "Perish the thought," she murmured.

The helicopter Rebel had rented picked her up at the lodge the next morning and flew her directly to Casper. She kept her eyes resolutely up for most of the trip, not daring to look down until she had to get out of the craft.

Donovan had made one last attempt to convince her to allow him to come along with her. She had resisted firmly, although she still felt a bit weak-kneed when she thought about his blandishments.

She got a taxi at the airport and was driven to a large shopping center that looked promising. For a while she simply wandered, picking up a few odds and ends she needed.

Then she located a phone booth and placed a collect call to her apartment in Dallas. She was supposed to be joining her parents in Paris for Christmas, and something told her that she'd better be prepared to forgo that trip. It was beginning to look as if she'd be in the Bighorn Mountains for the holiday. She had to at least alert Bessie.

Puzzlement reigned, though, as she listened to the operator identify the caller, get permission to reverse the charges, and then get off the line.

"Dad? What are you doing in Dallas?"

"Oh, your mother had a hankering to spend the holidays in the States," the elder Sinclair told his daughter in an offhand voice. "When're you coming home?"

"That's why I called." Rebel felt a little uncomfortable, but she wasn't quite sure why. "It looks like I may be stuck here for a while."

"Lennox being troublesome?" Marc asked sympathetically.

"Not really, but he just won't be pinned down. It may take another week to close the deal."

"It's a shame for you to miss Christmas," her father said with a curious lack of regret in his voice. "Your mother and I will be disappointed if you don't make it home. But—I know—business comes first."

Rebel held the receiver several inches from her ear and stared at it for a moment. Then she got back on the line. "Is Mom there? Can I talk to her?"

"Sorry, honey, she's out shopping. You know your mother; she always waits until the last minute."

"I suppose Bessie's with her?"

"Sure is. They were out at dawn and left me to sleep in."

"Oh." Rebel frowned at the stream of holiday shoppers flowing past her. "Well, give them both my love and tell them I'll be home as soon as possible."

"I will, honey. You take care, and we'll see you soon."

"All right. 'Bye, Dad."

" 'Bye."

Rebel hung up the phone slowly, continuing to stare at the people rushing past. Her father, she realized, had seemed awfully anxious not to prolong the conversation. That hurt a little. But what really hurt was that he hadn't seemed at all upset by the possibility of her missing their traditional family Christmas.

Frowning, Rebel bent to pick up her shopping bag and joined the throng. Pushing the brief conversation from her mind, she went to find a restaurant and have lunch.

After lunch, she wandered again, something definite in mind now. It was, in fact, the entire point of this trip into town. She was looking for something special, and she had to visit three jewelry stores before she finally found it.

Luck or fate was with her; it was exactly what she wanted. The small package was carefully and gaily wrapped in the store, and she hid it in the bottom of her shopping bag before leaving.

She wandered for a bit longer. After passing three phones in the mall and looking thoughtfully at each of them, Rebel finally gave in to the urge and placed another call—again, to Dallas. Ordinarily she wouldn't have even thought of checking up on Donovan . . . but she had to know.

Josh was surprised by her question. Except for one routine call to make certain that everything was all right at the office, he hadn't heard from Donovan. Orders? No, no orders in regard to Lennox, except to ask for Donavon rather than Rebel if he needed to call the lodge for anything. And, by the way, everything was fine at the office.

Rebel hung up the phone slowly. "You forgot to cover that base, Donovan," she murmured to herself.

The conversation she had overheard days before now assumed new importance. Whom had Donovan talked to on the phone that day? He'd said, "He's still in Denver," and to her mind that meant that he hadn't been speaking to Astaire. Who, then? And what about? He'd talked of something upsetting airline schedules all over the world. He'd said, "Well, wouldn't you smell a rat?" He'd said that timing was important. That someone was "blindly unsuspecting." That it was important to him.

It? What was *it*?

Rebel found an unoccupied wooden bench in the mall and sat down to think. Donovan and Astaire were in cahoots—that much she was sure of. And she had the peculiar feeling that this was another one of those conspiracies entered into for her own good.

For a moment she was sorely tempted to dig the buried package out of her bag and dump it into the fountain a few yards away. But she didn't. *That* decision had been made, and nothing short of sheer betrayal would alter it. And the possibility of Donovan's being after her company had long since been banished.

But what was the point? Why keep up the tenuous fiction of bargaining for that property? And why keep her in the dark about whatever was going on?

The pieces of her puzzle were falling into place, but the overall picture *still* didn't make sense.

It was, Rebel decided irritably, like waiting for the jaws of a trap to slam shut.

Sighing, she got up to go hunt a taxi. She'd go back to the lodge and confront Donovan. He'd talked about boxing the shadows of her past; she had no intention of boxing the shadows of his present. One way or another, she was going to find out what lengths his devious mind had gone to. And if she found out—as she strongly suspected—that he'd simply wanted to get her alone and away from the office . . .

Well, she could accept that. What woman wouldn't? It was flattering, and it made her smile the same way she'd smiled when she had watched him decorating a Christmas tree in secret.

The trip back to the lodge was uneventful. She was so wrapped up in her thoughts, in fact, that the helicopter ride didn't bother her at all. She even managed a cheery wave to the pilot as the small craft lifted off one of the pads at the lodge.

Carson met her at the door with the information that Mr. Knight and Mr. Lennox were in the library, in the Early American wing. Rebel merely nodded and allowed the butler to take her coat, purse, and shopping bag, asking him politely to put the bag in the closet in her bedroom. Being Carson, he immediately went to do so.

Rebel wandered in search of the library, passing the kitchen en route and puzzled by the loud activity going on in there. It sounded, she thought, as though they were getting ready to feed an army. She wondered if Astaire's family was coming for the holidays after all.

That thought didn't remain long in her mind, because she reached the door of the library. It was slightly open, and she paused instinctively when she heard two male voices. It came to her that she could make a career out of overhearing conversations not meant for her ears. But she didn't announce her presence.

"That's slander, my boy. Character assasination. No wonder the poor girl gave me such a look when I finally showed up."

"It served its purpose." Donovan's voice was amused.

Astaire snorted. "Well, it'll serve you right if she takes the first carrier pigeon back to Texas when she finds out what you've done. Most women would."

"Rebel isn't most women."

"For your sake, I hope not. Couldn't you have found a simpler way of convincing her that you loved her? You get her up here on the flimsiest of pretences, keep her here for days while we pretend to argue about land she could have for the asking, go to great lengths to 'arrange' things when she isn't looking. . . . How long do you expect to keep this up?"

"As long as necessary."

"Sure. And from what I've seen and heard of her, when you paint her into a corner and announce your engagement, she'll probably hit you in the face with the paintbrush."

"Probably." Donovan chuckled. "Look, I want her to decide for herself that I'm not after that damned company. Once she's made up her mind about that, I'll tell her everything."

"Better hope that's soon. Damon's chewing nails; he says he's going to shoot you for keeping him in Denver all this time."

"If he comes up here before I've explained him, I'll shoot *him*. If Rebel gets a look at him, I'm finished."

"What about when she gets a look at the rest? You've got everyone heading this way; they'll start rolling in tomorrow. It won't take Damon to point out the family resemblance, you know; your mother and I look like twins."

"I know, I know."

"You'd better work fast, my boy."

"Tell me about it." Donovan sighed. "I didn't even know until we got up here that I'd have a chance with Rebel. And I sure wasn't certain I could keep her here until Christmas. Still, it seemed the best way."

"Because you want to be loved for yourself."

"Don't point out that I'm being idealistic; I know that."

Astaire laughed suddenly. "You know, for two people who want exactly the same thing—to be loved for themselves—you've managed to hellishly complicate the situation."

"That has occurred to me."

While both men laughed, Rebel crept away silently, having heard all she wanted to hear. She made her way back to the great-room. Crossing to the bar, she poured herself a snifter of brandy—a large snifter—and began to pace. The first gulp of liquor burned all the way down. The second gulp followed the well-blazed trail and scalded only slightly. The third gulp pleasantly warmed.

The puzzle was assembling itself in her mind—be it ever so increasingly fuzzy a mind—and the picture justifiably roused her temper.

The whole thing had been a plot! Donovan's plot. No wonder Carson and the rest of the staff had backed him up in his ridiculous wooing—he'd probably spent half his childhood at this lodge!

Unscrupulous, conniving, deceitful—aahhh! She'd kill him. With great pleasure and malice aforethought. She'd boil him in oil and dangle him from a turret. Turret? No . . . from the point of one of the A-frames.

No wonder she'd felt that Astaire looked familiar—there was a definite, although elusive, resemblance to Donovan. And the painting missing from that wall was probably a family portrait—with Donovan squarely in the middle.

Damn the man! Making her agonize over whether it was she or the company he wanted, when all the time his family could have bought and sold Sinclair Hotels a dozen times over. It just wasn't fair!

She didn't let herself consider the fact that Donovan had apparently wanted only what she did herself—to be trusted and loved until nothing else was important. That was not the point. Not at the moment. She was mad, and it felt good to be mad, and good to have something definite to be mad *about*.

Damn the man. Getting her into helicopters and hanging mistletoe and decorating Christmas trees and making love to her until she couldn't think and reading her mind when she *could*, and—

Reading her mind?

The fanciful thought skittered through her mind and screeched to a halt. She sat down rather abruptly and tried to focus her eyes on the opposite wall.

Psychic? Oh, no—ridiculous! That was a weird thought. A definitely weird and unnerving thought. Still . . .

She remembered the past six months. Her seemingly uncanny

affinity with Donovan—or his with her. All the things she'd not had to tell him. His ability to anticipate her wishes, to see what she had in mind before she was certain herself.

And then there was this fateful trip. The moment on the jet when she had *seen* him for the first time—and he had realized it. The small things: questions answered before they were asked; his telling her where the tapes were when he'd been lying there with his eyes shut and couldn't have known that was what she had in mind; the very tree she'd fallen in love with selected and decorated in secret; his knowing she was allergic to shellfish.

Then came the clincher—and Rebel was appalled that she hadn't realized it sooner.

The night he had tried to convince her that he had no interest in the company, she had left him believing that he hadn't been successful. She had seen the defeat on his face. But then she had paced and wrestled with herself and gone out into the sitting room and dreamed of a lover. And he had come to her.

Rebel rather hastily got to her feet and poured more brandy. It had a reasonable explanation—all of it. She did *not* believe in ESP and mental telepathy and precognition . . . it hadn't been proven yet, after all. But wouldn't it be just like the man to have something like that up his sleeve!

This time Rebel took the bottle back with her to the chair. She'd get completely blotto, and then she'd mop up the floor with Donovan. And tomorrow she'd tie her head on with a piece of string or something, call the heliport and rent another damned copter, and go back to Dallas.

By the time Donovan and Astaire came into the greatroom about an hour later, Rebel could have picked a fight with a saint.

"I want to talk to you!" she announced clearly, rising to her feet with wonderful balance and pointing one of the fingers not wrapped around the snifter at him.

The two men, she noticed with mental clarity, looked as though they were about to be confronted by a volcanic eruption. It was a vastly pleasing thought, since either of them would make two of her.

"Sure." Donovan came toward her rather carefully.

Astaire made haste to vacate the battleground. "You two want to be alone, I'm sure—"

Rebel leaned sideways, coming perilously close to tipping over. "Don't rush off, *Uncle* Astaire," she said gently, peering past the bulk that was Donovan. "That is who you are, isn't it?"

"Uh-oh," Donovan murmured with resignation.

"I'm too old for this," Astaire said plaintively. "If you'll excuse me, I'll—uh—go check on dinner."

"Don't bother." Rebel walked cautiously around the coffee table, reasoning that battles took space and she didn't want to be trapped beside the couch. Very sweetly she told them, "I've already spoken to the cook. He will shortly serve up two man-sized portions of *hemlock*!"

While Astaire made himself scarce, Donovan murmured, "You've been drinking."

Rebel toasted him with her nearly empty snifter. "I would have been disappointed if you hadn't noticed."

"We'll talk about this tomorrow—"

"We'll talk about it *now*! Would you like to try to explain this web of lies you've got me tangled in?"

"Rebel—"

She pursued her prey relentlessly. "You lied about Astaire's being a rake; you lied about his prejudice against women executives. You lied by—by implication when you didn't tell me he was your uncle—"

"How did you find out?" he interrupted.

Rebel drew herself up and glared at him. "I eavesdropped," she announced defiantly. "When you were in the library."

Donovan sighed. "We didn't hear the helicopter."

"Well, lucky for me! Otherwise, you might never have let me in on the secret."

"Rebel, that was only because—"

"And another thing!" she interrupted, wanting to air all her grievances before he could somehow manage to outgun her yet again. "You've been reading my mind! That's an invasion of privacy, and I'm going to *sue*!"

"They'd throw it out of court," he murmured, a tremor of mirth in his deep voice.

"If you think I'm going to marry a man who knows what I'm thinking before *I* know what I'm thinking, you're crazy!"

"You have to marry me," he said calmly. "We're going to make the announcement at the party. I've disrupted airline schedules all over the world to get everyone here."

Rebel blinked at him. "What party?" she asked, pieces of the puzzle still busily falling into place and confusing her.

"The Christmas party," Donovan told her gently. "Both our families will be here."

"Here?" Some part of Rebel's mind felt relief as she realized that *that* was why her father hadn't sounded disappointed at the unlikelihood of her attending the traditional family Christmas. but the full import of his statement didn't sink in for a moment. "Who's Damon?" she demanded abruptly, her wayward mind latching onto the vaguely puzzling name.

"My cousin. He's coming to the party, too."

"Astaire's son?" she hazarded.

"Bingo," he murmured. "You're not as tipsy as I thought."

"I am not tipsy," she announced with tipsy dignity. She made a horizon-sweeping gesture with her free hand. "I'm blotto."

"It's nice to know you can lose control occasionally," Donovan observed musingly. "I mean, out of bed and with your clothes on."

Rebel had to try twice before the words would emerge. "Ohhh—that was a low blow!"

"Sorry," he murmured.

Rebel glared at him owlishly for a moment, and then the needle dropped into its proper track. "Party. What's this about a party?"

"A Christmas party," he repeated patiently. "And an engagement party. Both our families will be here."

"All your daunting sisters?" she asked easily.

"All my daunting sisters. And my parents. Assorted in-laws, nieces, nephews, cousins—the Lennox side of the family, you know. And your parents, and Bessie."

Rebel could feel the horror overtaking her face, and Donovan choked on a laugh.

"Am I fired, boss?"

"Fired? *Killing's* too good for you! Donovan," she wailed, "how could you do this to me?"

"I admit it's a little underhanded, but—"

"It's the most infamous, deceitful—" Shock went a long way toward dispersing the mists of brandy. She set the snifter down carefully on the coffee table and then straightened. Glaring at the fiend, she said with vast politeness, "Would you mind very much telling me exactly who your family is?"

He obviously knew what she wanted to know—and just as obviously wished he didn't have to tell her.

"Ever hear of the Knoxx Group?" he asked casually.

"Well, of course I have. It's a worldwide conglomerate." She was pleased that the difficult word emerged correctly.

"That's the family," he murmured. "Dad and Astaire merged their companies forty years ago. Over the years, the family grew and scattered to take care of the expanding businesses. So now we have diversified companies all over the world."

Rebel wanted to sit down, but she forced her knees to lock and continue to support her. "And you work for me," she said dazedly. "A worldwide conglomerate as your birthright, and you work for me."

"I told you I wasn't interested in power," he pointed out.

Rebel stared at him as the last piece of the puzzle dropped into place. Now the picture made sense.

Donovan sighed. "I never wanted to have much to do with the business, and Dad—thankfully—understood. But I did want to help out without actually getting into the rat race myself. So for about ten years I acted as a sort of troubleshooter for Knoxx. I traveled all over the world—I told you that. I just didn't tell you why.

"By the time I met you, I was ready to settle down. The last thing I wanted was an executive position, but I didn't have much choice. So I joined Sinclair."

"Dad knew," she murmured.

"Of course. I was very honest with Marc."

It was a poor choice of words. Rebel didn't need the fumes of brandy this time. She got mad all by herself.

"You swine!" she yelled in a fine imitation of Vesuvius. "Do you know what you put me through? Do you know how I agonized over the possibility that you could be after the company? That nearly drove me crazy!"

"Rebel—"

"And do you know the worst part? I stopped caring whether you were after the company or not! I would have handed the damned thing to you on a plate! And do you know what that did to my self-respect? Can you possibly guess?"

He stepped toward her quickly, a sudden glow in his eyes. "Rebel, are you saying—?"

"I'm saying that I love you, dammit, and you tricked me!" she snarled wrathfully.

Immediately, she was a caught in a bone-crushing bear hug. Hard lips found hers in a bruising, possessive kiss. "Thank God," he muttered against her mouth. He literally picked her up and swung her in a happy circle, which did absolutely nothing to restore her brandy-and-kiss-disordered senses.

And then he laughed, resting his forehead against hers and gazing down at her with tender eyes. "Oh, honey, I'll treasure that declaration all the days of our lives!"

"I'm still mad at you," she managed weakly.

"That's all right," he said comfortingly. "You're magnificent when you're angry. And I deserve it."

"You certainly do," she said promptly, swaying lightly as he set her back on her feet.

Donovan put an arm around her and began leading her from the room. "Let's get some food into you to balance the brandy," he said wryly. "You will definitely have a head tomorrow."

"Somebody else's," she agreed, wondering where the anger had gone.

He stopped in the archway. "Tell me again."

Rebel looked up into shining violet eyes and felt her whole face soften with the glow of a love acknowledged at long last. "I love you," she whispered.

"And I love you," he murmured, bending to kiss her tenderly.

He was taking advantage of the mistletoe above them. Again.

Rebel knew that, even now, Donovan couldn't be sure that she had made her decision before finding out who he really was. Being Donovan, he had accepted what she'd said. But he couldn't be *sure*.

The proof was in a shopping bag in her closet. And at an appropriate moment, she'd give it to him. But not just yet. She intended to let *him* be uncertain for a while.

Food cleared more of the cobwebs from her mind, and she managed to resurrect her glare during dinner. He didn't have to have everything his own way, after all. And she *was* mad.

She kept glaring until the lights went out in their bedroom.

Then he wooed her.

Chapter Nine

Rebel awoke the next morning with someone else's head, and she hated every living thing. Donovan didn't waste time or effort in trying to convince her that she would actually get better; he simply inserted her efficiently into a steaming hot bath and met her occasional fading moans with spurious sympathy.

Rebel knew that she was dying, and she intended to make quite a lot of noise about it. She had never been one to suffer in silence. No one in the long and eventful history of mankind, she thought with some vague satisfaction, had suffered as much as she was suffering now.

Added to her agony was the unmercifully vivid memory of how she had acted the day before. She was by no means ashamed of her temper, nor did she regret the brandy-induced scene with Donovan. It had cleared up several puzzling matters after all. But she hated losing control of herself, and announcing her love to Donovan with a wrathful snarl had not been the way she had planned it.

Turning her head carefully and literally hearing the creak of rusty hinges, she glowered over at the vanity, where Donovan was busy shaving. "Tell me it didn't happen," she requested faintly. "Tell me that I didn't hear you announce that an entire battalion of your relatives is arriving today."

"Sorry, love." He sent a look brimful of laughter her way. "It did happen. And they are coming."

"Donovan, I am going to kill you. Slowly, and taking great care to prolong your agony, I am going to kill you." She rested her head carefully on the lip of the tub and closed her eyes. "And after that, I'm going to climb this mountain and, like that prospector, I'm never coming down again."

"The aspirin should start working any minute now," he told her consolingly.

"You think it's just the hangover, but it isn't. You have grossly deceived me all along, and I'm going to get you for that. I will turn into six kinds of a shrew and make your life hideous. Are you listening to this?"

"No, sweetheart, I'm shaving."

"Donovan, would you for once—just once—get mad and yell back at me?"

"In your condition? It'd kill you."

"Well, when I'm better, you'd better yell at me."

"What is this masochistic desire to feel my anger?"

"It isn't masochistic at all. It's just that if you don't get mad, I'll live in terror of hearing the other shoe drop."

"There's a crazy kind of logic in that," he observed thoughtfully.

Rebel opened her eyes long enough to send him a pained stare. "Tell me again who's coming. Then I can drown myself."

"Everyone's coming."

"Can you at least give me a *number*?"

"Well, to be honest, I've kinda lost count. I can give you a reasonable estimate of the Knight clan, but the Lennox clan seems to sprout like weeds. Damon isn't married, but Astaire had eight daughters, and they have innumerable kids—"

Awed, she murmured, "Girls must run in your family."

"They do," he told her cheerfully. "And it's odd when you think about it. Since sex is determined by the male, you'd think my sisters could have logically expected to have a roughly even number of boys. But between the six of them, there are only two boys: Kelly and Geneva each have one. And the boys are always dark; the girls tend to get the red hair."

Rebel decided that the aspirin was beginning to take effect; she was fascinated by this. "Tell me more."

Donovan came over to sit on the edge of the tub, a towel knotted around his lean waist. "I'm afraid it'll make you take to your heels," he said wryly.

"If I haven't run by now, I won't. I seem to have lost my sanity somewhere along the way." Her voice was bemused.

"That's the second-nicest thing you've ever said to me, love." He leaned over to kiss her briefly, then straightened. "What do you want to know?"

"I think I have a fair grasp on the Knight clan; how about the Lennox side? Do you have uncles other than Astaire?"

"No, but I have six aunts. They all have children and some grandchildren—mostly girls. At last count, I think there were three boys other than Damon, all dark."

Rebel made a stab at mental multiplication but gave up very quickly. "My God," she murmured faintly. Backing up a bit, and not sure she wanted to hear the answer, she said, "Your father. He can't be an only child."

"One of six. The rest—"

"Don't tell me. Girls."

"Bingo."

Rebel thought it was no wonder Donovan didn't have a chauvinistic bone in his body. If he'd had any notions of sexual inequality, the girls in his family would have blasted them out of existence at an early age. "I wonder why the boys are all dark," she murmured absently. "Those Indians in the family history you mentioned?"

"That's our theory. By the way, the girls tend to marry young, but not the boys."

She stared at him. "All these people are coming up here?"

He nodded cheerfully. "Yep."

"Donovan, I am going to kill you. . . ."

She was still repeating those same words as she peered around Donovan and out one of the front windows, trying to get a look at the suddenly busy helipads. "Donovan, I am going to kill you. Is that a troop carrier, for God's sake?"

"It pretty much has to be, don't you think?"

"Oh, Lord—that has to be your father. *Damn*, I'm going to kill you. Why didn't you warn me? And why didn't you let me out of that bathtub in time to at least fix my hair—"

"You look beautiful. And I happen to love your hair down. Will you stop worrying? They'll love you."

Rebel nervously smoothed her denim-clad thighs. "I should have worn a dress. Why didn't you let me wear a dress?" She would have felt more sure of herself confronting the army of a hostile nation.

"Because you look cute as a button in jeans."

"I've never seen so many redheaded people in my life!"

She didn't have a chance to say much of anything else before the deluge began—and went on all afternoon. At some point she began to feel that she was looking at a film rushing past, with an occasional still-frame stopping the motion temporarily. It was those moments she remembered.

"Mom, Dad, this is Rebel."

"So this is the lady you've been moving heaven and earth for, eh, son?" Randall Knight was as tall and upright as his son, although age had turned his black hair silver and sapped the muscles from his thin frame. But the years had done nothing to dim the mischief in his violet eyes. "Well, she looks like she's worth it."

"Don't tease the poor girl, Randall—can't you see she's bewildered by all of us? You should be ashamed, Donovan! Welcome to the family, my dear." Leslie Knight was as upright and very nearly as tall as her husband, silver-haired and blue-eyed. And both she and her husband gave Rebel a warm and welcoming hug.

"And this is Geneva."

"Well, thank God, not another redhead! Maybe we can have a few nicely neutral kids in the family instead of carrot-tops or Indians!" Geneva topped the six-foot mark and moved with the brisk determination of someone who couldn't bear to be still.

Shaking hands with Donovan's brother-in-law Adam, Rebel felt duty-bound to mention the unlikelihood of that. "My father's a redhead," she pointed out meekly. "And I think there are a few more on the family tree. . . ."

"Oh, God! Will this redheaded curse never be broken?"

"You're blocking traffic, Gen. Move aside and let the rest of the army in."

"Donovan, you're a snake. If you weren't my only brother, and I hadn't been *insatiably* curious to find out what kind of woman had finally managed to catch you—"

"Who caught who?" Rebel mumbled involuntarily.

"Whom," Geneva corrected automatically, and then immediately completed her sentence. "—I never would have dropped everything in Japan and come rushing out here on that excuse for a plane—"

"Adam, can you do something with her? Preferably take her into the greatroom and gag her?"

"Come along, darling."

"That pilot should be ashamed of himself. . . ."

"Charley, Rick, this is Rebel."

Rebel looked at the slender, auburn-haired woman who was perhaps five-ten in her stocking feet, and said weakly, "They call you half-pint?"

"Well, Rick does—isn't it terrible of him? My, how pretty you are! And so tiny! I met your father; he's so sweet. And your mother's just lovely. Donovan, you look so happy! I'm so glad for both of you. Three children at least, and *maybe* a boy. . . ."

Still reeling under the shock of being called tiny, Rebel shook hands with Rick and watched as he followed the wife who had drifted away on a wave of half-sentences and fragments.

"Marc, Vanessa—glad you could make it. Vanessa, you look as lovely as usual."

"Flatterer. Merry Christmas, darling! How are you holding up?"

"Mom, how could you let him do this to me?"

"Well, darling. I didn't have much to say about it, you know. Bessie, *will* you stop hovering over that box? It doesn't contain the crown jewels!"

"It's got my cake in it, and that's more valuable." Black eyes snapped with a peculiar sort of Latin satisfaction as Bessie took in the picture of Rebel leaning somewhat weakly against Donovan. "Took you long enough!" she announced, and she sailed off to the kitchen with her carefully baked cake.

Rebel met her father's laughing blue eyes resignedly. "Hi, Dad."

"Merry Christmas, honey," he chuckled in response.

The onslaught continued. Rebel rapidly lost count of the adults and didn't even try to keep track of the younger generations. It was like being hit in the face with a tidal wave of good wishes and loud voices, and once Rebel recovered from the initial shock and began to relax, she found herself enjoying it.

The huge lodge, so empty until now, was packed to overflowing with people ranging in age from six months to their mid-seventies. Everyone was warm and welcoming to Rebel. They were a close and affectionate family, cheerfully insulting one another but never with malice. The whole lodge fairly throbbed with them.

And enough redheads to start their own country. No redheaded boys, though. Not a single one among the younger generations.

"Rebel, this is Damon."

She looked up into twinkling, clear blue eyes and murmured involuntarily, "Well, no wonder you didn't want him here."

Damon Lennox was very nearly a carbon copy of Donovan. The same size, the same black hair silvered at the temples, uncannily similar features. Except for the blue eyes. One look at him, and she would have instantly known the two men were related.

With a laugh, Damon said, "I was ready to shoot him for keeping me in Denver, but I see now that it was worth it."

Even the voice was nearly identical.

"Hands off, cousin," Donovan warned lightly. "She's taken."

"Pity," Damon murmured, eyes twinkling as he went to join the throng.

The still-frame image that Rebel would cherish for years she literally stumbled on the next day. Passing by one of the lounges in search of her missing fiancé, she glanced through the doorway and stopped in her tracks, a hand over her mouth to halt the giggle.

Carson, not a hair out of place or a shred of dignity lost, was on his hands and knees on the floor. On his back were two tiny copper-haired girls who periodically shrieked, "Horsey!" in unison.

Standing in front of the butler, nose-to-nose and peering solemnly, was a black-haired boy of perhaps four. "Cookie," he said firmly. "Want a cookie."

"May I have a cookie," Carson corrected austerely.

The child thought it over. "May I have a cookie," he finally repeated carefully. "Now."

Rebel retreated hastily, giggling. When she ran Donovan down in the greatroom, she related the story with a laugh. Donovan shared her amusement but wasn't at all surprised. He told her gravely that he had learned manners from the butler at about the same age.

Having been indecently rushed for nearly two weeks and practically railroaded into her engagement, Rebel planned Christmas Eve carefully. Knowing full well that the next day would be a day of noise and confusion after Santa's visit, she wanted this night to be a special one for her and Donovan alone.

So when Donovan came before midnight, having been kept occupied by both her father and his at her request, she was ready.

The champagne was icing in its silver bucket, near at hand. A fire blazed cheerfully in the hearth. Pillows were piled on the white fur rug in front of the fire. And Rebel reclined against the pillows, her blue satin-and-lace nightgown shimmering in the fire's shifting glow.

She looked up as he entered the room, watching him as he halted for a moment and then reached back to lock the door.

"You're reading my mind again," she murmured.

"Don't be ridiculous." He came toward her, handsome and devilish in his stark black shirt and slacks, violet eyes glowing. "That would be impossible."

"Sure it would."

"Really."

"Uh-huh. Once more with feeling."

"Are we going to talk about impossible things all night?" he demanded, kicking off his shoes and sinking down beside her.

"And cabbages and kings," she murmured. "I thought you said that nothing was impossible?"

"Don't fling my own words back at me."

Rebel calmly pushed the champagne bucket his way when he would have reached for her. "Why don't we drink a toast to Christmas," she suggested limpidly, producing two hollow-stemmed glasses and smiling sweetly at him.

Donovan sighed and began working on the bottle. "If that's what you want. But I don't need champagne . . . I've got you."

Rebel smiled but said nothing, waiting until the cork had popped and bubbly liquid filled both glasses. Then she lifted her glass and said softly, "To Christmas."

His glass touched hers lightly. "To fifty more Christmas toasts made together," he responded firmly.

The toast was duly drunk, and then Donovan reached into his pocket and drew out a small black velvet box. Setting aside his glass, he opened the box to reveal a beautiful sapphire engagement ring. "To make it official. I've been carrying this around with me for months." He slid the ring carefully onto the proper finger. "Merry Christmas, darling."

Rebel stared at the glittering ring and swallowed hard. "It's lovely." Her smiled turned teasing. "I haven't actually heard a proposal, you know. Lots of statements and commands, but not a single very simple question."

Donovan smiled and lifted her hand to his lips, kissing it gently. "I've loved you for a very long time," he said quietly, gazing into her eyes, his own flaring with a savagely simple feeling. "I used to watch you in the office when you weren't looking. So close . . . and so far away. We'd be working at your apartment and you'd sit down beside me on the couch—and I had to fight every instinct screaming to grab you.

"After one of those twelve-hour days topped off by an interminable board meeting, you always looked so tired. I wanted to take you in my arms, to share some of the burden you were so determined to bear alone. But you wouldn't let me."

He sighed heavily. "So I plotted and I schemed—and I lied to you. I created a problem where none existed, building it around that land—land that I could have gotten for you with a phone call. I had to get you away from the office; I had to somehow break through that chrysalis you'd wrapped yourself in.

"I knew that I was taking a chance. God, I knew. And when you told me about your husband and what he'd done to you, I understood how hard it would be to convince you that it was you I wanted and not the company. The truth would have convinced you—the truth about my family, I mean. But I wanted you to trust me and believe in me. So I kept trying to convince you."

He paused again, and Rebel sensed that he wanted to say something more, that he wanted to be certain she had made up her mind about his motives before finding out the truth about his family. But he didn't question her.

"Rebel, I love you with everything inside of me. I want to spend the rest of my life with you. Will you marry me?"

Rebel couldn't answer him with words. Silently, she reached behind the pillows and pulled out a small, gaily wrapped box, handing it to him and feeling suddenly shy.

Donovan looked at the package and then at her, puzzled but smiling. "Is this your answer?"

She nodded. "I got it that day I went to Casper."

Beginning to unwrap the box, Donovan looked up at her suddenly, and she could see the realization in his eyes. After a moment, he somewhat hastily tore the colorful paper away and opened the box. She saw a tremor in the long fingers as he slowly lifted her gift from its box, and that evidence of deep emotion moved her almost unbearably.

"Every lord of the castle should have one," she said shakily.

Silently, Donovan slipped the fine golden chain over his head, looking down for a moment at the exquisitely crafted gold key resting in the palm of his hand. "Given freely," he murmured huskily.

"Given freely . . . and with all my love. I love you, Donovan. I've known that since the night I opened my bedroom door and saw you decorating a Christmas tree in secret."

He reached out to frame her face in his hands, looking at her as though at the secrets of the universe. "You realized that I wasn't interested in the company—that I loved you."

"More than that." She fumbled for the explanation that was only now beginning to crystalize in her mind. "Donovan, when I found out that Jud had only wanted the company, something happened. The company was never important to me until then. But after that, I felt—in a crazy way—that I had to prove my ability to master what had very nearly destroyed me. If I could control it, it wouldn't be a threat to me any longer. I didn't blame Jud for what had happened—I blamed the company. So I set out to master it.

"And then we came up here. I was away from the company; I could see it—and myself—clearly for the first time in years. And listening to you talk about it put the company in perspective for me. It's just a business, just a small cog in a huge wheel. It didn't ruin my marriage—Jud did.

"The company doesn't matter anymore. It stopped being the most important thing in my life the first time I looked at you . . . and *saw* you. It isn't your rival any more than it's mine."

Donovan pulled her fiercely into his arms, holding her tightly for a long moment. "Thank God," he muttered. "I was afraid that company would always stand between us."

"Oh, no," she murmured, sliding her arms up around his neck and smiling tenderly into his shining eyes. "Who needs a company? I've got you."

"You certainly have. . . ." Impatiently, he pushed aside the silver bucket, their glasses, and the empty jeweler's boxes and pulled her down into the furry softness of the white rug. "And I'll never let you get away from me now."

Happily absorbing the weight of him, Rebel blindly sought the buttons of his shirt as his mouth found hers. The ember flared to new and blazing life within her, and need coursed through her body like molten lava as tongues met in a hungry duel.

His shirt was cast aside, falling unnoticed to provide a black dustcover for the champagne bucket. Her gown and the remainder of his clothing swiftly followed.

"You're so beautiful," he whispered, lips searching out the hollows of her throat, hands shaping willing flesh. "So exciting. I'll never get enough of you!"

"I have a lot to make up for," she murmured throatily, her fingers tangled in his thick black hair as she thought of the year he had waited patiently.

"No." He pressed warm kisses over her face. "That wasn't your fault; you couldn't help it. And the wait was worth it, love."

But Rebel understood now the strain of his patient wait. And she wanted to make it up to him somehow. Fiercely, she pushed against his shoulders until he rolled onto his back. Half lying against his side, she eagerly explored his neck and shoulders with her lips.

"On the other hand," he rasped, "if you feel obligated . . ."

Rebel nearly giggled, but passion swiftly pushed the laughter aside. She used her teeth and tongue to torment and then soothe, experimentally tasting his flesh and finding the sensation addictive. Her mouth continued to search, finding the flat male nipples and teasing them with a flicking tongue. His groan of pleasure spurred her on, and she only dimly noticed that his hands were far from still, threading through her hair, stroking her back.

She followed the narrowing trail of black hair down over his flat belly until she reached the throbbing desire he felt for her. She felt him jerk involuntarily as she touched him, held him, and a primitive and loving hunger enveloped her.

Donovan groaned harshly, a shudder shaking his strong body. "Rebel! Honey, you're driving me out of my mind!"

Some distant part of Rebel's mind silently acknowledged that she wanted to do just that. She wanted controls splintered, restraint lost. The need in her was beyond thought, beyond reason. She wanted layers of civilization stripped away, leaving only the primitive bonding of man and woman.

And that hunger drove her relentlessly. She tormented, teased, incited, using the knowledge these past days with him had given her. She found feminine instincts within her she had not known existed. She became woman incarnate.

And Donovan wasn't about to resist. He lifted her back up into his arms frantically. The strength of him was almost bruising now, and Rebel gloried in every moment of it. She met strength with strength, bending without breaking to the savage need she had kindled to life within him.

Lips clashed in a firestorm of desire, hands caressed with blind urgency. Time tunneled, focused on an eternal second, and then ground to a halt.

Their joining was explosive, devastating in its intensity. They loved and fought like the primitive beings this moment had made them. Both taking, both giving, merging in a driven effort to share one body, one soul.

And for one shattering moment they did just that, two souls clinging in an instinctive recognition of affinity.

"Donovan!"

"Rebel . . ."

Rebel decided she was never going to move again if she could possibly avoid it. She'd just lie here on this fur rug in front of a crackling fire and in Donovan's arms. The world could go on without her.

"Good Lord," Donovan murmured, his voice drained and more than a bit awed. "Did I dream that?"

Rebel stirred slightly, eyes closed and an extremely feminine smile on her face. "You've been branded, milord," she told him softly. "Now you're all mine."

"It wasn't just your sense of obligation, then?"

"Not really. Just a desire to mark what's mine."

"Does it show?"

"What?"

"Your mark."

"Does it matter?"

"Well, the guys at the club will never let me live it down."

"What club? Do you have a club?"

"Just a figure of speech."

"So is the mark—a figure of speech, I mean."

"No, it's definitely there. I can feel it."

"Good. Then you won't stray."

"Who wants to stray? I know a good thing when I find it, love."

"Which reminds me—" She opened her eyes and rose on her elbow with an effort, frowning down at him.

"Reminds you of what? Have I been caught in another lie?" He opened his eyes and grinned at her.

"I think so." Rebel held on to the frown. "If you didn't want an executive position at Sinclair—before we ran into each other, I mean—then what were you doing in the building in the first place?"

"Oh . . . that." Donovan toyed absently with a strand of her silver-blond hair.

"Yes, that. Well?"

"Look, it's snowing. Isn't that nice?"

"Donovan."

"We can drag the sleigh out of the stables tomorrow, and—"

"Donovan."

He sighed. "You wouldn't want to just let it drop, I suppose?"

"Not really, no."

"You'll think I'm crazy."

"I doubt that. What were you doing at Sinclair?"

Donovan sighed again. "I followed you there."

Rebel knew that her mouth was open. "What?" she asked faintly.

"I saw you in a restaurant having lunch, and I followed you back to the office."

"Donovan, that's crazy."

"Yeah, well. . . . Anyway, I happened to overhear a couple of the staff talking about how you were slated to take over the company. And about an opening for an executive assistant. So I called Marc and made an appointment to talk to him. It was for the next day, and that was when we ran into each other. Not quite by accident, I'll confess."

"You mean you deliberately ran into me?"

"Not exactly. I just put myself into a position where *you* ran into *me*."

"My God," Rebel murmured wonderingly. "You were plotting and planning even then. But, Donovan, you didn't know me!"

Donovan looked thoughtful for a moment, and she could see that he was considering that in his own mind. "No, I did know you," he said finally, musingly. "I can't explain how, but I did know you. It was as if I'd been waiting for something—some-one—and when I saw you, a bell went off."

Rebel had silently thanked fate for sending him to her, and now she realized in some amusement that she should have thanked Donovan. Solemnly, she said, "Do you know that I love you?"

"Yes, I do know that," he said conversationally, his eyes show-ing something not at all casual. "Finally. It was a long time in coming, but I have to admit that the delay added a certain spice. And I trust you know that the love is returned?"

"There were a few hints of that."

"Just a few?"

"Let's say I'm convinced."

"Well, if you need a few more hints—"

"Donovan, stop that!" She pushed his wandering hand away and pulled on a serious face. "We have one more thing to settle."

"Really?" He didn't sound very interested.

"One at least. This used-to-be rival of ours."

That sobered him. "The company. Honey, if you want to go on running Sinclair—"

"I told you, it's not important to me anymore," she interrupted softly. "I don't have to prove anything now."

He went very still. "Rebel?"

She rested her chin on the hands folded atop his chest and smiled whimsically. "I was thinking that we could look around— maybe in Texas. Find a ranch. Plant a fig tree or two and watch them grow."

"Rebel . . ."

"Merry Christmas, darling. . . ."

Chapter Ten

Rebel totaled the last column of figures and turned off the calculator. She rubbed the small of her back as she studied the paper in front of her, then flexed her shoulders to ease the slight ache.

"Come to bed, love."

"I'm not sure that's safe." She sent an amused glance across to the man sprawled out on their king-sized bed. "I think you're still mad at me."

"Don't remind me."

Rebel smiled to herself and began putting the ranch records away in her desk. "At least now I know what you're like when you get mad. Very loud." She paused in her tidying up to stare pensively into space. "And you swear a lot, too. Carl said he hadn't heard words like that since he left the navy."

"Carl should be shot for letting you into the corral with Ruffian. He's lucky I didn't fire him. And you're lucky I didn't turn you over my knee."

"Donovan, I only—"

"I know what you 'only'—you've told me. You *only* wanted to see the new stallion. You *only* wanted to see if he hated women the way he hates men. You *only*—"

"All right, all right. But he didn't hurt me. And you scared the poor horse to death charging up like that. He turned tail and ran, and Carl wasn't far behind him. That was the only good thing to come out of the situation: Carl and Ruffian became brothers in terror. They're buddies now."

"You're a funny lady."

"Well, really, Donovan! You stood there swearing for ten solid minutes and never once repeated yourself. When the other shoe dropped, I never expected it to make such a loud thump."

"I was completely justified. In your condition—"

"We've been through this. And stop saying my 'condition,' as if I were in the grip of some dreaded disease. I'm a perfectly healthy woman, darling, and as strong as the proverbial horse. The doctor's more worried about you than me; he said he'd read about it in the medical books but didn't believe it until he met you. I think he's writing a paper on you."

Donovan sighed. "I'm never going to hear the end of this."

Rebel slipped off her robe and crawled into bed beside her husband, allowing a giggle to escape at last. "Well, you kept telling me it was some bug you'd picked up. I had to hear about it from the doctor. And he looked so bemused that I wasn't sure what he was trying to tell me."

"It was something I ate, that's all." Donovan drew her close to him with a long arm and sigh. "The doctor's nuts."

"Is my mother nuts? She noticed the other day when she brought that pizza by and you couldn't stay in the room for more than five minutes. She said that it was touching to see a husband who—um—shared in his wife's pregnancy so thoroughly."

"What do you mean, share? You've breezed through the past six months. And stop changing the subject. The point is, you should never have been in that corral. That horse could have killed you. Scared me out of a good ten years."

"Sorry, darling. I won't do it again, I promise."

"The heat out there didn't do you any good, either."

"Donovan."

"Just wanted to make my point."

"You did. And then some."

"Good. While I have stubborn Sinclairs on my mind—"

"Donovan . . ."

"—Bessie said that Marc called today. I thought he and Vanessa had gone back to Paris."

"No, they're still in Dallas. Dad just called to repeat that Josh is doing a fine job running the company—except he's complaining that he can't find a decent secretary. Want a job?"

"I have several, thank you. Running a ranch. Looking after a wife who's as stubborn as she is beautiful. Helping to decorate a nursery. Trying to keep from stepping on those kittens you've adopted. And when Astaire sends us that puppy—"

"You can housebreak him."

"Wonderful. I don't know why Astaire decided that Tosh needed a family at this late stage in his life. And I don't know who named the she-wolf Tiffany—"

"Don't insult Tiffany. Tosh will get you; he's insufferably proud of her."

"I know the feeling. I'm insufferably proud of my she-wolf."

"You know, it's a funny thing," Rebel mused aloud, "but your compliments just don't sound like compliments."

"Shall I rephrase?"

"Unless you want to sleep alone."

"I'm insufferably proud of my beautiful, charming, multitalented wife. How was that?"

"Better."

"I wish she'd take better care of herself and not take chances with dangerous horses. I'm terrified of losing her, you know."

"Well, I could say the same." Rebel snuggled a bit closer to her husband, frowning slightly. "About losing you, I mean. Who decided to help break the three-year-olds to saddle in spite of paying trainers to do it for him?"

"You weren't supposed to hear about that."

"I heard."

"I'm going to fire Carl yet."

"It wasn't Carl; it was Bessie. When she went down there to drag you back here for lunch, she saw what I wasn't supposed to know about. I'm sure that she swore at you all the way back to the house."

"She did. In Spanish."

"I'm not surprised. She says I look terrible in black."

"I was *not* thrown."

"Just trying to fly without a plane, huh?"

"The way you stroke my ego is just wonderful."

Rebel bit back a laugh. It had become a habit, these late-night conversations before the lights went out. Sometimes whimsical, sometimes serious, they were a warm and intimate part of her marriage that she cherished.

"Well," she murmured, "wives are like that."

"Mine is, anyway."

"If you were a Bedouin, you could trade me in on a new model."

"I'd have to throw in a couple of goats and a camel, though."

"Not at all. Arabs are fascinated by blondes. You'd probably even get a tasseled saddle or two."

"Ruffian would love that."

"Only if you wore it instead of making him."

"Never mind. I'll keep you for at least another year."

"Gee, thanks. That's big of you."

"My pleasure." Donovan shifted suddenly and muttered. "What the hell—?" He reached under the covers and withdrew a yellow tabby kitten, who blinked at him sleepily. "Rebel . . ."

"Well, she was asleep; I didn't have the heart to wake her."

Donovan set the kitten on the floor beside the bed, a gesture she immediately and loudly protested. "She can join her brothers and sisters in the kitchen," he said firmly over the heartbreaking mewing.

"Darling, it's a big house; she'll get lost."

"Rebel . . ."

"Darling . . ."

"Dammit."

When Donovan returned from his trip down to the kitchen and climbed back into bed, he said resignedly, "I had to feed them again. Honey, if you adopt one more homeless creature, I swear I'll—"

"Oh, dear . . ."

"*Now* what?"

"Rabbits, I went into town this morning, and there was this little boy. His mother told him he had to give them away, and—"

"Where are they?"

"Carl put them in an empty stall for me. They're white, and the little boy named them Jack and Jill."

"Male and female. And Carl put them in a stall together?"

"Of course he— Oh. I never thought . . ."

"Great. I'll definitely fire Carl in the morning."

"I suppose we'll be raising rabbits now?"

"I don't think we'll have much choice."

"Sorry, darling."

Donovan sighed. "That's all right. Some wives collect hats; mine collects animals."

"I suppose it's my maternal instincts," Rebel murmured wryly. "They seem to be flourishing."

"Speaking of which . . ." Donovan rose up on an elbow to gaze down at her. "Have we reached the definite possibility of a firm maybe with the names?"

"Lots of suggestions. Geneva called yesterday."

"Don't tell me. Romeo or Juliet?"

"You're not far wrong. Algernon or Clementine. She said they had definite possibilities."

"Oh, God!"

"That wasn't why she called, though. She called about natural childbirth. I told her we were taking classes."

Donovan groaned. "Don't remind me!"

"Hey, fella, I didn't get into this condition on my own, you know." Rebel pointed to her rounded belly.

"I should hope not," he murmured. "Anyway, I said I'd be brave, didn't I?"

"I'm not sure. Getting that yes from you was like pulling teeth."

"Don't make fun of my cowardice. It isn't wifely."

"Maybe not, but it may be a moot point away. If you keep on 'sharing' my pregnancy, they'll have you up on the table instead of me." She fought to keep from laughing at his expression, adding hastily, "Never mind, darling. We'll get through it together."

"Let's get back to the names," he responded wryly. "It's a safer topic."

"Right," she murmured.

"Dad suggested Daniel or Crystal."

"Mom said Clinton or Nicole."

"We'll pass on Geneva's suggestions."

"Agreed. Astaire voted for Taffy or Tamara."

"What do you expect from a man who names a she-wolf Tiffany?"

Rebel ignored the remark. "Your mother said Jeremy or Selena."

"And your father suggested Logan or Danica."

"Donovan?"

"What?"

"I don't hear a single suggestion from us."

"I've noticed."

"Don't you have a preference?"

"Just a few prejudices. *Not* Algernon or Clementine. And not Puff or Spot. Other than that, I've an open mind."

Rebel sighed. "Well, then, why don't we ask the baby what name to pick."

Donovan looked at her as though he thought the sun might really have gotten to her that day. "Want to run that by me again?"

"You heard me. We can ask the baby." Rebel smiled at him innocently. "Or rather, you can. First, find out the sex. Then ask what name the baby prefers. It'll solve all our problems."

"Rebel . . ."

"Come on, Donovan the Great; pull on your wizard suit and ask the baby for a name."

He lifted an eyebrow to her. "I get this feeling that I'm being taunted. You don't think I can do it."

"Like Alice's queen, I've believed as many as six impossible things before breakfast," she said gently.

He lifted the other eyebrow. "If you're going to quote, you

should remember Shakespeare. You know, the part about there being more things in heaven and earth . . ."

"I'll keep that in mind."

Donovan shifted position until he could rest one ear against Rebel's rounded stomach. He remained there for a moment, frowning in obvious concentration. A little while later, he was back beside Rebel and drawing her into his arms.

"Well?" She gazed at him laughingly, her arms creeping up around his neck. "Boy or girl?"

"Boy," Donovan informed his wife firmly. "Boys, really. We are going to have twins, love."

"That," Rebel said immediately, "isn't possible. There are no twins in my family, and I've never seen a sign of them in your family. You're wrong this time."

"Twins. Boys."

Looking at her husband's calm face and suspiciously twinkling eyes, Rebel asked mildly, "Did they happen to mention a date? The doctor said October—"

Donovan shook his head. "November third." He paused, tilting his head to one side as though listening to a far-off voice . . . or voices. Then he added casually, "Between ten and eleven A.M."

Rebel blinked. Vaguely, she remembered a great-uncle who had been able to predict a baby's birth to within a few hours after a single look at a pregnant woman's stomach. Did Donovan possess that curious talent? Or had he—? No, ridiculous.

"Bet you're wrong," she told him. "The doctor, my father, two old ladies I met on the street, *and* Geneva all said that I'd have a girl in October."

Donovan smiled. "Twin boys. Born November third between ten and eleven A.M." When Rebel stared at him, he added, "We'd better start doubling up on supplies. And we'd better be careful with colors. They're redheads."

Rebel felt victory in her grasp. "Now I *know* you're wrong! There is absolutely no way on earth we'll have redheaded *boys*. It won't happen."

"They want to be called Eric and Patrick," Donovan said as if she hadn't spoken.

"No way."

"You don't like the names?"

"They won't have red hair, Donovan. It isn't possible."

"You want me to call my sons liars?"

"They can't have red hair. It'll upset the Indian theory."

"One theory shot to hell."

"We'll have your entire family flying out here to observe the miracle."

"We'll wait until Christmas and then spring it on them."

"You're wrong this time. I *know* you're wrong."

"They're redheads," Donovan repeated stubbornly.

"Care to make a small wager?" Rebel invited spiritedly.

"Certainly. You'll be my slave for a week."

"Or you'll be mine!"

"Agreed, wife."

"Donovan?"

He was busy kissing her neck. "Ummm?"

"Oh . . . never mind. I don't think I want to know."

Patrick Daniel and Eric Shannon Knight were born on November third between ten and eleven A.M. And the doctor, who had been apprised of both the lack of twins in both families and the Indian theory, spent a lot of time muttering to himself.

Tired but happy, Rebel looked at the tiny bundle her husband bent down to place in her arms. She gently stroked the copper-colored fuzz covering the small head and gazed into violet-blue eyes that stared seriously back at her. Then she looked up at Donovan, still wearing his hospital gown, mask dangling, and holding an identical bundle in his own arms.

"What if you'd been wrong?" she asked.

He smiled. "But I wasn't."

"But what if you *had* been?"

"I wasn't."

Under her breath, Rebel said something about six impossible things. Then she murmured, "Donovan, did you really . . . ?"

His violet eyes held tender laughter. "Did I really what, love?"

Rebel thought it over for a moment, then shook her head. "Never mind. I don't think I want to know."

"I had a feeling you'd say that, love. . . ."

Belonging to
Taylor

For Eileen:
"This rough magic"

O! she's warm.
If this be magic, let it be an art
Lawful as eating.

—William Shakespeare,
The Winter's Tale

Chapter One

Trevor King had never thought of himself as a busybody, but when a man came across a young lady crying her eyes out noisily in the middle of a very lovely and peaceful garden, he decided, there was surely some justification for trying to find out what was going on. Accordingly, he sat down on the stone bench beside the distressed damsel and asked a pointed question.

"Excuse me, but what in hell is wrong?"

Stunningly electric blue eyes, no less potent for being tear-drenched, gazed at his face for a moment and then were hidden once more behind slender fingers as the dam burst in earnest.

Conscious of innate male helplessness when confronted by irrational female tears, Trevor ran bewildered fingers through his thick black hair and stared at her warily. Those incredible eyes, he reflected in astonishment, had held a rueful gleam of amusement. Hysteria? he wondered, studying her long, lustrous chestnut hair—which was all he could really see.

No, not hysteria. He didn't know why he was so sure of that, but he was. Sighing, and wryly condemning his own curiosity, he dug in his pocket for a handkerchief and held it out to her. "Here," he offered brusquely.

She couldn't have seen it through her tears and fingers, but she reached out anyway to grasp the snowy cloth and press it to her eyes.

Trevor gazed off across the garden, waiting patiently for time or exhaustion to stem the tide. It took another five minutes before the sobs lessened to sniffles and finally faded into silence. He heard her blow her nose fiercely and turned his head to intercept another curiously amused look from those wet, vivid blue eyes.

"I—uh—I have this problem," she murmured.

"I guessed as much," he responded politely.

She squared her shoulders and met his bemused gaze defiantly. "I cry," she announced as though to a blind man with bad hearing. "I cry over sad movies, sad books, the national anthem, and commercials with cute kids and puppies. I cry over spring showers, rainbows, bad days, *good* days, and dead butterflies. I cry," she summed up, leaning forward to emphasize the point, "when my *laundry* comes back!"

Trevor blinked. He found himself gazing into a striking face, in which the electric blue eyes dominated all other features. He was vaguely conscious of a small nose, high cheekbones, straight winging brows, cupid-bow lips, and a stubborn chin. Viewed separately, the features didn't seem to fit together, and yet they made a more than pleasing whole. In fact, it was an endlessly fascinating face.

And there were absolutely no signs of the tears that had so recently halted. No red-rimmed eyes. No pink nose. No flushed splotches.

Resolutely, Trevor pulled himself together. "What were you crying about this time?" he asked.

"Oh, don't! You'll start me off again!" She caught her under-lip firmly between white teeth to stop a slight quiver, then apparently controlled a last urge to sob again. "It wasn't important anyway. It never is," she added in the wry tone of someone resigned to a troublesome but irrepressible trait.

Trevor grappled with that for a moment in silence. "I see. Then you're all right?"

"Oh, yes. It was kind of you to be concerned, though."

Given an opportunity to accept her thanks and walk away, he found himself unable to do any such thing. "My name's Trevor King," he said as if it was an afterthought.

She gravely held out the hand not clutching the handkerchief. "I'm Taylor Shannon."

As his fingers closed around her slender ones, Trevor felt a very curious sensation. Startled, he stared down at their hands, aware of what felt like a genuine electric shock and then a spreading warmth. A soothing blanket crept up his arm, over his shoulder, and down his body, lending a feeling of security that was as strong as it was surprising.

"Well!" She, too, was staring at their clasped hands. Then her vivid eyes lifted to his face, and there was something in them he almost flinched from because it was so nakedly honest. "I'll be damned," she added blankly.

He rather hastily reclaimed his hand, feeling it tingle as it left hers. And the "security blanket" left him as if it had been a visible quilt ripped away.

"I didn't expect to meet you so soon," she said thoughtfully.

"What?" he managed, but she was going on, unhearing.

"It's really not the best time. In another five years, I would have—Oh, well. It's no use fighting these things. But I don't know anything about you," she accused irritably, staring at him. "You might be an ax murderer or something!"

"I'm not," he offered somewhat weakly, unable to get even the slightest handle on what was going on.

She was abruptly cheerful. "Oh, I know that! You like kids and animals; your favorite color is blue; you love Italian food and old movies; you live alone—at the moment," she added sapiently. "You have a younger brother who adores you, and you're a criminal lawyer."

Trevor was unable to hide his astonishment. "How'd you know all that?" he demanded.

She cocked an eyebrow at him. "On target?"

"All the way across the board!"

"That clinches it," she said cryptically. "I've never gotten so much from one touch."

He flexed the fingers that had held her hand, looking down at them for a moment. Then he stared at her warily. "Who are you?"

"Don't you mean what am I?" she corrected, seemingly amused.

"All right, then—*what* are you?"

"I'm the woman you're going to marry," she told him solemnly.

"I beg your pardon?"

Taylor began laughing. "Don't look so horrified! It'll probably work out very well, you know. You have more than a spark yourself, and that'll make things even better."

"A spark of what?" he asked, choosing the lesser of two evils.

"Raw talent."

Trevor ran fingers through his hair and stared at her. He couldn't help wondering if this undeniably fascinating woman was spending the odd day away from the funny farm, but he couldn't seem to make himself get up and walk away from her. "I don't know what we're talking about," he confessed finally.

She laughed again. "I'm sorry—I seem to have overpowered you! It's a fault of mine, I'm afraid, because I've lived with psychics so long I sometimes forget others aren't so familiar with it. We're talking about 'esper'—that's shorthand for psychic or parapsychological—abilities; that's what you have a spark of raw talent in."

He shook his head instantly. "I don't believe in that stuff."

Taylor sighed. "Oh, dear. I can just see the rocks looming in my path. If you don't believe, I've got my work cut out for me."

Ignoring this, he said firmly, "Jason put you up to this; that's how you knew so much about me."

"I've never met your brother."

"Then how d'you know Jason's my brother?" he pounced.

"The same way I know so much about you." She sighed again, murmuring to herself, "Parlor tricks. I knew it'd come to parlor tricks. And I hate them. Why did fate do this to me?"

"If you can read my mind—" he began, challenging.

"I'm way ahead of you," she interrupted dryly. "You want proof. You want me to do something that will instantly convince you I'm psychic. All right then, dammit—if it's parlor tricks you want, parlor tricks you shall have! Think of something very obscure—something only you know. Something I couldn't *possibly* have learned from anyone else."

She held out her hand commandingly, and Trevor, with only an instant's hesitation, closed his fingers around hers. He felt the warm blanket creeping up his shoulder, closed his mind to that, and began to concentrate.

Taylor's face was serene, her vivid eyes fixed on his face. And when she spoke, it was not in some blurred, trancelike voice, but in a calm and matter-of-fact tone.

"You're very young. There's a man you know. A friend of your parents. No, more than that. He's your godfather. He did something—no. They *said* he did something. They said he killed a man. You know he couldn't have done it. You think his lawyer believes him guilty. You think that's why he's been convicted. And why he's—"

She broke off abruptly as Trevor jerked his hand away. Apparently undisturbed by his sudden retreat, she gazed into his shocked eyes and said quietly, "I see. That's why you decided to become a lawyer. And you never told anyone that, did you." It wasn't a question.

Trevor drew a deep, shaken breath. "My God," he said unsteadily.

After looking at him for a moment, she began to talk lightly. "I'm like a sponge—soaking up information. It doesn't tire me, which is a bit uncommon among psychics. It *does* tire me if I have to reach out farther than touch; for instance, if I'm trying to find someone and have only a bit of clothing or jewelry to go on. My mother's a touch-telepath, too. Daddy's the precognitive one; I inherited a bit of his talent, but I'm not too strong in that, thank God."

Stirring slightly, Trevor made an attempt to untangle the threads of disbelief, panic, and finally belief. He only partially succeeded, but he was grateful for her obvious intention to give him time to get hold of himself. "Why . . . thank God?" he murmured.

"About not being strongly precognitive?" She shook her head slightly. "Looking into the future isn't usually comfortable. You tend to see disasters rather than triumphs. Thankfully, Daddy can't see his own future or that of anyone he really cares about. And I just see bits and pieces."

Recalling the troubling statement she'd made, Trevor challenged, "Then how d'you know we'll be married?"

"Oh, that's different," she told him cheerfully. "I knew that instantly, the moment I touched you. I always expected to know, but I really didn't think it'd be this soon."

"How old are you?" he demanded suddenly.

"Twenty-six. And you're thirty-two, right?"

"Right." He sighed, wondering if "esper" abilities became more believable simply by being casually discussed. He found his own disbelief fading—speeded along by her earlier demonstration— and a growing discomfort taking its place.

She was smiling just a little. "That's always the second reaction," she mused softly. "First comes disbelief—then comes discomfort. Then fear."

He looked at her for a moment, seeing no self-pity in her remarkable eyes, but aware, suddenly, that it couldn't be a good feeling to inspire fear in others. Instinctively trying to close down his own mind—and uneasily aware that fear drove him—he changed the subject. "Surely you weren't serious about marriage?"

Taylor seemed disturbed for the first time. She looked at him, the naked honesty in her eyes, her face hurt. "Is the idea so distasteful to you?" she asked diffidently.

Gazing at that fascinating, hurt face, Trevor was disarmed totally against his will. "It isn't that," he said with more firmness than he'd intended. "But we're strangers! I mean—well, *I* can't pick facts about you out of thin air. Besides, I don't like having my future planned for me. And, if you want brutal honesty, I don't much like the idea of having a wife who reads minds!"

Oddly, she seemed less disturbed now. "Well, if that's all it is," she said dismissively. "I was afraid the thought of seeing my face across the breakfast table was giving you the horrors."

He laughed in spite of himself. "Hardly that. You . . . have a fascinating face, Taylor Shannon. I suspect there's a lot about you I'd find fascinating. However," he added hastily, "the timing isn't right for me either. I'm at the midway point of a vacation, after which I have a heavy load of court cases." He got to his feet.

What was intended to be a polite and final leave-taking turned out to be no such thing. Taylor rose to her feet also, looking up at him hopefully. "I don't want to impose," she said guilelessly, "but could you possibly give me a ride home? It's getting dark, and—"

"Of course." Uneasily suspicious, Trevor was nonetheless too polite to question her motives. He glanced down as she walked beside him along the path, noting absently that the top of her head barely reached his heart.

It was difficult to see clearly now in the gathering twilight, but he'd already noticed that her blue jogging suit and shoes closely matched his own red outfit. It was casual, comfortable wear, seen often on the streets these days and not always meant as exercise suits. He'd not been jogging himself, but rather had driven out here for what he'd meant to be a half hour or so of air and scenery.

And found a crying psychic! he chided himself mentally.

Taylor seemed content to walk in silence, saying nothing until they reached his car. Then she looked at the hulking Jeep and laughed delightedly. "I knew it! Rugged, strong, and practical— just like you!"

Not entirely sure he liked the comparison, Trevor merely opened the passenger door and gestured silently. When he went around to his own side and climbed in, he found Taylor staring intently at the stuffed unicorn hanging form the rearview mirror. She sent him a glance as he started the engine, and he wasn't quite certain he had caught her words.

He hoped he hadn't, hoped that with the intensity of a man caught in some act believed to be unmanly. Had she really said something about the soul of a dreamer?

The Jeep, in accordance with Taylor's directions, drew into the driveway of a large three-story house possessing that indefinable air of having been lived in over many years. Trevor felt curiously drawn to the house; it was a sensation he'd never felt before and now profoundly distrusted.

Deciding that this leave-taking *would* be final, he opened his mouth to utter some polite and evasive words.

But he never got the chance.

The side door of the house, located by the drive, burst open just then, revealing a girl who looked nothing at all like Taylor. She was raven-haired, tomboyish, definitely tousled, and all of ten years old. Literally swarming up Taylor's side of the Jeep, she peered through the open window and shrieked, "Taylor! Agamemnon stole Mother's best blouse and Dad says the preacher's coming and Solomon's had her kittens *somewhere* and Jamie lost my *favorite* sheets and Dory's locked herself in the closet *again* and won't come out and somebody let Jack and Jill loose and I think they're under the washing machine and Solomon will *eat* them unless I get them out and we've got *chicken* for supper and *please* can't you *do* something or I'm going to join a *nunnery*!"

And, putting a period to her extraordinary sentence, the moppet slid back down the side of the Jeep and vanished into the house.

Murmuring, "Oh, dear," Taylor opened the door. Glancing back over her shoulder at her stunned companion, she added cheerfully, "Come on in."

And Trevor, betrayed once more by his curiosity, followed her meekly into the house.

Chapter Two

Trevor had little opportunity to note the furnishings of the house, for the inmates instantly overpowered everything else. He found himself standing in a den and had the general impression of tasteful decorating overlaid by the clutter of a lively and populous family. There were various clashes, bangs, and thumps coming from distant parts of the house; in this room, the moppet's strident voice reigned.

Taylor was ignoring the importunities of her sister in order to ask a brief question of a strikingly lovely raven-haired woman.

"Which, Mother?"

Standing in the center of the room, Mrs. Shannon, who was dressed in jeans and a peasant blouse but wore vagueness like a cloud, blinked gray eyes at her daughter. "The blouse, I think, darling," she said in a soft lilting voice. "Because of the Reverend. Then Dory out of the closet; she wanted you and you weren't here, so she hid. Your father's looking for the kittens."

"My sheets!" the moppet wailed, tugging at Taylor's sleeve.

Taylor removed the fierce clasp on her sleeve, saying briskly, "Help me find the blouse, Jessie; then we'll find your sheets." She led the protesting child from the room.

Trevor found himself the focus of the vague gray eyes. "Hello," she said encouragingly. "Any good with hamsters?"

He blinked, not really sure what was expected of him. "Animals in general," he offered.

A slight frown disturbed her beautiful face, then vanished. "It'll have to do," she said in the tone of one who didn't expect a miracle. "Jamie—the hamsters."

From an adjoining room came a slender wraith of a girl. About sixteen or so, she was blond and bore the same mismatched, fascinating features of her sisters eclipsed by the dreamy gray eyes of her mother.

"All right, Mother," she said softly. She took Tevor's hand and led him, unresisting, down a short hallway and into a laundry room. Then she sat on a tall stool and gestured toward the washing machine. "They're under there, we think," she said helpfully.

Presented with a definite task—however bizarre—Trevor felt some relief. He pushed up his sleeves, stretched out on the floor, and worked one arm around behind the machine.

"It'd be easier," he panted, feeling around gingerly, "to pull the washer away from the wall. But there's no room."

"And it's bolted to the floor," Jamie explained serenely. "It walked around and made noise, so Daddy fixed it. Do you belong to Taylor?" she added politely.

Disconcerted, Trevor peered up at her even as he found and grasped a warm, furry body in his searching hand. Suppressing a wild impulse to answer, "I think so," he pulled the hamster from under the machine and said instead, "Want to hold this while I get the other one?"

Jamie bent forward to accept the hamster, cuddling it against her sweater. "Nobody but Daddy has an arm long enough," she said suddenly. "And he's looking for the kittens."

Again disconcerted, Trevor realized that she'd answered his mental question: why no one had retrieved the hamsters before now. Remembering something Taylor had said earlier, he thought, *Oh, Lord—all of them?*

He found the second hamster and held it in one hand as he got to his feet. "Where do they belong?" he asked, perforce adopting the verbal shorthand of the family.

"They live in Dory's room. I'll take them up." She got the second hamster and stepped toward the door, pausing only to smile at him over her shoulder. "I hope you belong to Taylor. I like you," she said naively.

Trevor stood there for a moment, absently pulling his sleeves down, then sighed and made his way back to the den. He wondered in sudden amusement when it would occur to this absurd family that there was a total stranger in their midst; he had a feeling it might never happen.

Reaching the den, he found Taylor's mother exactly as he'd left her. She stared into the middle distance but turned her head when he came into the room. "Name?" she asked abruptly.

"Trevor," he answered a bit helplessly.

She appeared to consider. "Good. That's good. Two syllables and same first and last letters. Last name?"

"King," he supplied.

After a brief frown, she nodded, satisfied. "Not bad. At least, unless there's a German shepherd in the room."

"I beg your pardon?" he managed, faint but pursuing.

"They always name them Prince or King," she explained vaguely. "Confusing if you're in the same room."

Trevor leaned against a wall for support, staring in utter fasci-

nation at the woman. He couldn't, for the life of him, get a handle on Taylor's mother. The niggling suspicions that she was
hardly as vague as she seemed wasn't confirmed by any outward
sign, but his courtroom-sharpened senses told him there was
much more to the lady.

Before anything else could be said, Taylor returned to the den.
Under one arm she carried a clearly disgusted toy poodle, and in
her free hand was the missing blouse. Jessie skipped impatiently
at her side, still nattering about her mislaid sheets, and a newcomer clung fiercely to the jacket of Taylor's warm-up suit.

The newcomer, Trevor decided, must be Dory. If Jessie was a
talkative moppet and Jamie a serene wraith, then Dory was a pixie.
She was all of six years old, her red hair cut short around a face
uncannily like her sisters'. But in her small face glowed the huge,
vivid blue eyes only Taylor shared.

That there was an affinity between the two was obvious; Dory
stared up at her sister adoringly, and Taylor, after handing the
blouse to her mother, reached to absently smooth shaggy red hair.

Trevor was trying to convince himself silently that he really
should leave when he realized he was under scrutiny. Dory had
released her grip on her sister and crossed to stand before him,
looking up at him solemnly.

Instinctively going down on one knee to be closer to eye level
with the child, he returned her stare as gravely as she offered it.
"Hello," he said gently.

"Hello." Not a piping, childish voice, but one far too gruff and
serious for the young face. And, astonishing the man, she asked
the same question her sister had asked. "D'you belong to Taylor?"

He found himself uncomfortable beneath that solemn stare as
he'd not been with Jamie; this one, he knew, wouldn't accept eva-
sion. "I just met her," he explained seriously.

She frowned a little as if the answer was unsatisfying, then reached out and laid a tiny hand on his shoulder. A shy, elusive smile flitted briefly across her mismatched features and was gone. But she nodded to herself as she withdrew her hand. "You belong to Taylor," she told him firmly, her tone that of a wise teacher to a dim pupil.

Trevor blinked. She wandered away before he could say anything, and he rose to his feet slowly. He saw that Mrs. Shannon had vanished—apparently to don the found blouse—and watched as Dory stood on tiptoe to whisper into Taylor's attentive ear before wandering from the room.

"My sheets!" Jessie cried impatiently. "Taylor!"

"All right, Jess!" Taylor glanced around briefly, then said dryly, "They're in the piano bench, where you left them! Next time, don't blame your absent-mindedness on Jamie."

Taylor turned to Trevor as her sister shot from the room, exclaiming immediately, "Hasn't anyone asked you to sit down? Do, for heaven's sake!"

He removed a Teddy bear from a chair and sat down, telling himself that he merely needed to recruit his strength before fleeing the madhouse. "D'you have a mirror?" he asked carefully.

She sank down in a chair across from his, still holding the poodle and gazing at him quizzically. "Not on me. Why?"

"Because I think there's a brand of possession on my forehead, and I'd like to see it."

Taylor laughed. "Have they been pestering you? I'm sorry!"

He sighed. "Not pestering. Just asking in the most natural, innocent way if I belong to you."

"And what did you answer?"

"I evaded Jamie's question. I told Dory—I assume the littler one's Dory—that I'd just met you. That didn't satisfy her; she touched my shoulder and then told me reprovingly that I belonged to you." He reflected for a moment, adding thoughtfully, "And your mother liked the sound of my name but hopes there won't be a German shepherd in the room, since they're always named Prince or King."

Taylor was giggling. "My family's a little . . . original," she gasped. "I should have warned you."

"Are *all* of you psychic?" he demanded.

She nodded. "To varying degrees. Of my sisters, Jessie has the least natural ability and Dory the most. And Jamie's sporadic; we never know whether she'll predict tomorrow's news or ask someone to help her find a lost shoe."

Before Trevor could respond, a tall, disheveled blond man appeared in the doorway leading to the main hall, announcing in a deep, satisfied tone, "I've found the kittens."

He earned Taylor's instant attention. "Oh, good! Where?"

"In that old sewing basket some idiot got your mother years ago," her father explained. "There's never been any sewing in it, so it's perfect."

Trevor, on his feet and watching silently, noted that Taylor and Dory had gotten their electric blue eyes from their father. He also noticed that both parents looked ridiculously young. At a guess, they were both in their fifties, but neither looked a day over thirty-five. *Does being psychic make you age slower?* he wondered abstractedly, then realized that a vivid but benign stare had fixed on him.

Then Taylor's father looked back at her. "Polite," he noted approvingly.

"Very," she agreed.

Her father bent a sudden frown on her. "No organ music, or I won't come! Your sister can play the piano, but I can't stand organs." He reflected for a moment, adding in the tone of a man who wishes to be clear, "Five kittens." Then he disappeared into the hall.

Trevor sank back into his chair.

After a single glance at his face, Taylor burst out laughing. "We're not crazy, I promise you! It's just that we forget how to talk to people outside the family, and when you get into the habit of not finishing sentences or even thoughts, it's very hard to remember."

"Try," he begged ruefully. "And would you mind explaining exactly what your father said? I think I missed most of it."

She smiled a bit. "He said he found five kittens in an old sewing basket he got Mother years ago."

Trevor remembered the mildly uttered "some idiot" and wondered if Taylor's father often called himself that. "Yes, I got most of that, but what else did he say? Did he mean I was polite? And what was that about organs?"

"He meant you were polite—because you stood up when he came in. And that about organs was . . . um . . . in reference to weddings."

"One wedding in particular?" Trevor managed evenly.

"Uh-huh."

He stared at her. "Is there a shotgun pointed at me where I can't see it?" he asked finally.

"Of course not." Her smile was trying hard to hide.

"Then why does everyone in this house assume—without even knowing my *name* for godsake—that I belong to you and that we're going to be married?"

Remaining silent, Taylor meditatively pulled at the poodle's ears and watched Trevor, clearly waiting for him to realize. He'd already realized, but he wasn't a man to go down without a fight.

"Because they're psychic?" he muttered.

She nodded.

Trevor made a valiant effort and produced a lightly mocking tone. "It's completely ridiculous. You realize that, don't you?"

"Completely," she agreed blandly.

"I mean, there is such a thing as free will."

"Certainly."

"I'm the captain of my fate," he insisted firmly. "The master of my soul. In charge of my own destiny."

Taylor nodded with grave agreement.

Glaring at her, Trevor said, "You don't believe a word I've said!"

"Of course I believe."

"But you also believe we'll get married?"

"I know we will."

Trevor dropped his head into his hands, massaging aching temples. "A prudent man," he said helplessly, "would run screaming into the night."

"Are you a prudent man?" she asked interestedly.

Lifting his head and gazing into those electric blue eyes, Trevor found to his disgust that he couldn't lay claim to prudence, logic, rationality, an instinct for self-preservation, or any other sane trait. "I think I've been bewitched," he groaned in answer.

She laughed, then asked briskly, "Can you cook?"

The very normality of the question was a welcome relief. "Yes."

"Good." She set the poodle on the floor and rose to her feet. "Mother's got the chicken baking, but I know she hasn't done anything else. Come help me."

Some moments later, Trevor found himself meekly donning a large chef's apron with HIS emblazoned across it in huge letters, while Taylor absently put on a matching one marked HERS. The kitchen was large and done in redbrick and butcher-block counters, with copper pots hanging abundantly around a central work island. Everything was neat and clean, well-organized and arranged. And Trevor's instant feeling that this was Taylor's domain rather than her mother's was borne out by her cheerful words.

"I had the chicken ready to bake before I left this afternoon, and the oven all set. Mother's a disaster in the kitchen unless she has step-by-step instructions, and even then she's apt to wander off and forget she's left something on a burner."

Her tolerant amusement sparked Trevor's curiosity. He stepped around the poodle sniffing suspiciously at his trouser leg to obey her gesture and begin to prepare the ingredients she'd assembled for a salad. "Your mother can't be as vague as she looks," he objected, having finally realized that what may have seemed rude anywhere else was commonplace with this family.

Taylor laughed. "Well, she isn't, really. I mean, she's hopeless at most practical things. Cooking, cleaning, balancing a checkbook. If she goes to the store for a gallon of milk, she's likely to bring back shoes for Dory or a new collar for Agamemnon. Once she came home with a new car—and she got it for a really good price, too. We never did figure out how, because she doesn't seem to know how to bargain."

"But she isn't really vague?" Trevor prompted, amused.

"Not when it matters. She's got a disconcerting ability to go straight to the heart of things, and in a real emergency she's so efficient that it's scary." Pausing after whisking a cloth off homemade bread dough left to rise, Taylor looked reflective. "Daddy says he's terrified of her. He says she's the most utterly ruthless woman he's ever met in his life."

Trevor blinked, chopped cucumber for a moment, then said, "I have to hear about your father."

"Daddy?" She placed the loaf pan in the second of the two ovens, then straightened, thoughtful again. "Well, unlike Mother, who only says what she thinks is necessary, Daddy talks quite a lot. And you have to sift the chaff from the grain, if you know what I mean. He's apt to bury a vitally important sentence underneath a ton of absurdity. Animals adore him; I've seen totally wild creatures come up to him as gentle as you please and follow him around like puppies."

Scrabbling through a drawer, she located a ribbon, which she used to tie her long chestnut hair at the nape of her neck. Then she continued describing her father. "He cooks like a dream, can fix anything with an engine, and can do things with wood that'd have master cabinetmakers green with envy. He has a black belt in karate and was on the Olympic boxing team. Oh—he's a doctor," she finished in an obvious afterthought.

"A medical doctor?" Trevor asked, surprised.

"Uh-huh."

"*Chicken,* Taylor!" wailed a voice suddenly from the doorway.

Taylor turned and stared, exasperated, at her sister. "Jessie, nobody's going to make you eat the chicken; there'll be bread and salad."

The moppet sighed and, slouching against the doorjamb, subjected Trevor to a long, thoughtful stare, as if she'd just noticed him. She, too, had gray eyes, he realized. And he could have predicted her sudden question.

"D'you belong to Taylor?"

Sighing, he threw Taylor a *See?* look and refused to answer.

"He's Trevor King," the oldest sister explained calmly. "Now, be helpful, Jessie, and go set the table."

Ignoring, for a moment, the request, Jessie straightened and said gloomily, "The preacher came, but just to drop off a flier about something. Mother's upstairs threatening to kill Daddy."

"Go set the table," Taylor repeated, and Jessie, with a last depressed sigh, vanished.

"Not seriously?" Trevor wondered aloud, not surprised when he didn't have to elaborate.

"Of course not. If I know Mother, she just said 'Dammit' and went off to change again. Jessie exaggerates. Constantly."

Trevor finally mentioned something that had been hovering like a troublesome insect. "The blouse. A special blouse?"

"For the Reverend. And don't ask me why. Mother always wears that blouse when the Reverend comes." She giggled suddenly. "If he were a noticing kind of man, he'd probably wonder about that."

"But he isn't, darling."

The soft voice, wafting toward them from the doorway, startled Trevor. Taylor, of course, was undisturbed. "I suppose not, Mother."

Mrs. Shannon glided into the room with a feline grace that disconcerted Trevor; he realized only then that it was the first time he'd really seen her move. She was back in her jeans and peasant blouse, her raven hair caught at the nape of her neck like Taylor's. And she smiled vaguely on them both.

"Milk for Solomon, darling. Your father says."

Taylor nodded and went toward the refrigerator, snaring a bowl from a cabinet along the way.

Her mother continued to smile at Trevor. "I'm Sara. And Taylor's father is Luke. We forgot to tell you."

Rudderless yet again in her confusing wake, Trevor said uncertainly, "Nice to meet you . . . Sara."

She laughed softly, the gray eyes for a moment—an instant—not the slightest bit vague. There was something of the electric intensity of Taylor's eyes in them. Nothing at all threatening or ruthless, but an enormous strength and intelligence—and kindness. Then she was accepting the bowl from Taylor, and her eyes were vague again.

"Thank you, darling. Did I do it right?" she asked absently.

"Exactly right, Mother. Dinner in half an hour."

Sara Shannon drifted from the room, bearing the bowl of milk in both hands.

Trevor took a deep breath. "I agree with your father. She's frightening."

Giggling, Taylor said, "She must have turned the Power on you. Daddy says her eyes could topple mountains or stop armies in their tracks, but only when she *really* looks at something or someone. Strong men have been known to blench."

"Then," Trevor said definitely, "that's the way she just looked at me. I felt as if my dentist had just said all my teeth had to go."

Taylor laughed even harder. "I'll tell Mother that; she'll love it!"

He found himself staring intently at the clean, delicate line of her throat, his eyes skimming down over the small, slender body and back up to her fascinating face. And he thought, *Hell, I am bewitched!* But that realization didn't lessen his sudden desire to kiss her.

"Trevor? Is something the matter?"

Abruptly, he demanded, "Can you always read thoughts when you touch someone? Always?"

"Oh, no," she denied instantly. "Some people instinctively mind-block. And the mood is an influence, too. It's funny, but strong emotions either broadcast powerfully or else throw up their own barriers."

In the grip of several strong emotions, Trevor decided to test the premise. At least, that's how he defended his actions to a sneering inner voice. He carefully laid aside the knife he was holding, wiped his hands thoroughly on a towel, and turned to Taylor. Without giving her a chance to do or say anything, he drew her firmly into his arms and bent his head to hers.

He didn't really know what he was expecting, but he very quickly abandoned any pretense of "experimenting." And some dim and distant part of his mind wondered vaguely if "belonging to Taylor" meant having some indisputable right to these incredible feelings.

He'd felt desire before. And strong passion. What he'd never felt before was this odd, soul-deep warmth. He wanted to luxuriate in it, to bask in a golden glow of brilliant light and . . . magic. Never before had he felt so completely, acutely aware of his own body as it literally *became* two bodies. He didn't believe what he felt, tried to disbelieve, but the essential *rightness* was too powerful to deny.

He knew the instant she took fire in his arms, felt the shiver of her body as if it were his own. He felt her little hands tangle in his hair, felt her rise on tiptoe to fit herself against him. Urgency gripped him; compulsion drove relentlessly toward an imperative, critically necessary joining.

But it was he who drew away suddenly, shaken by a violence of emotion that tore at something vital. *Just a kiss*, he thought dazedly, staring into vivid blue eyes that looked as shocked as he felt.

Taylor took a deep, unsteady breath and stepped back, automatically reaching to turn off the oven timer as it prosaically announced normality in a loud buzz. She turned off the oven itself with the same absentminded awareness, her eyes still fixed on Trevor. And when she spoke, she sounded as shaken as she looked.

"I've never felt anything like that before," she said, nakedly honest.

"Neither have I," he muttered hoarsely.

Taylor was quiet for a moment, gazing at him. Then she said with a sudden dry humor, "You really do think you're bewitched."

"Can you blame me?" he shot back. "All afternoon I've been told I'm going to marry you, asked if I belong to you, *told* I belong to you . . . and now this—this—"

"Feeling," she supplied quietly.

It stopped him cold. Shaking his head slightly, he said, "This is out of my league. I'd better go." He began fumbling with the ties of the apron, but she stopped him.

"No. You helped fix dinner; you'll stay for the meal at least. Besides, if you go now, Dory'll hide in the closet again."

He knew he was being betrayed again by curiosity, but he couldn't seem to help himself. "Why would she do that?" he asked blankly.

Taylor, completely herself again, was busily removing the chicken from one oven and the bread from another. Over her shoulder, she explained, "I told you that Dory has strong natural ability; she's very sensitive. And she hasn't learned to deal with herself yet, so practically anything sends her to hide in the closet. She likes you; if you leave so suddenly, it'll scare her."

A little diffidently, Trevor suggested, "Maybe she should be taken to see a . . . doctor."

"You mean a psychiatrist?" Taylor wasn't the least bit offended; she appeared to consider the suggestion seriously. "No, I don't think so. We all went through the same thing at her age: Jamie clung to Daddy, Jessie hid under her bed, and I was always creeping out into the woods by myself. We're all here for her when she needs us; that means a lot. She'll be fine."

"Dinner, Taylor?" asked a plaintive voice from the doorway. "Solomon's hidden the kittens again and Dory's lost Jack and I'm hungry."

"Just coming, Daddy," Taylor replied absently, concentrating on transferring the chicken from baking pan to serving dish.

"Your mother didn't ruin it?" her father asked anxiously.

"No, it's fine. Round everybody up, will you, please?"

"Yes, they're all waiting. But Jack? I suppose Trevor can get him out later if Solomon stays with her kittens and doesn't eat him. D'you play poker?" Luke Shannon demanded suddenly of Trevor.

"Yes." Trevor, an afternoon's accumulation of shocks and absurdities belatedly catching up with him, was holding on to control by force.

"Well, there's nothing to laugh about in that," Taylor's father chided reprovingly, shattering the last remnants of Trevor's control. Gazing at his daughter's guest as he leaned against the refrigerator and laughed himself silly, Luke directed an interested question to his daughter. "Is he staying, Taylor?"

"For dinner, at least," she murmured, crossing to hand her father the serving dish. "Take this in, Daddy."

"All right. Milk for your mother because of the baby, but I want wine."

Taylor nodded and turned back to quickly and efficiently slice the bread, watching with amusement as Trevor's laughter was cut short and replaced by astonishment.

"Your mother's—"

"Pregnant? Yes."

"But . . ." He didn't quite know how to frame his question.

Taylor laughed, understanding. "Her age? Mother's only forty-four, Trevor. I was born when she was eighteen. There's a certain risk for her age group, but her history is a good one. Our people tend to have large families and to space them all through the childbearing years. Mother says she was born to have babies because it's the only thing she does really well. But she also says this one's change-of-life and the last."

Removing his apron as she removed hers and automatically helping her gather the rest of the meal for transference to the dining room, Trevor reflected silently for a long moment. Then he began to laugh—silently this time.

"I wasn't ready for this," he muttered despairingly as he followed Taylor from the kitchen. "Nothing in life *prepared* me for this!"

Chapter Three

Looking back on that meal later, Trevor realized that the hunted feeling he'd been conscious of had been more the result of his own acceptance of the situation than anything Taylor or her family said or did. It bothered him that he felt so comfortable so quickly, no longer startled or amazed, but simply quietly fascinated. The entire family had instantly and in their respectively vague, cheerful, solemn, offhand, or matter-of-fact ways accepted him as a part of them. And he began to enjoy it.

That was why he felt hunted. Absorption into this absurd family, however painless the process, boded ill for his bachelorhood. Not that he'd been clinging to *that* with rabid intensity, but a man liked to have at least *some* say in the selection of his wife, he thought uneasily.

But when Dory, who had taken a chair beside his, slipped her tiny hand confidingly into his, and when he looked across the table to meet Taylor's smiling, vivid blue eyes, he found himself oddly disinclined to fight for his freedom.

Definitely hunted.

Taylor was aware, more by his reactions than anything else, that Trevor was still a bit unnerved. She watched his lean, handsome face across the dinner table, seeing the fascination, seeing his features soften whenever he looked at Dory, who sat so quietly beside him.

She watched him gradually relax in the company of her family, bemusement reflected in his keen gray eyes. He responded easily to any question or comment addressed to him, catching on quickly to the family's unconscious shorthand and even replying in kind after a fashion. Several times he seemed to swallow a sudden laugh, amusement lightening his rather stern eyes and curving the firm lips.

Lips.

Taylor ruthlessly dragged her mind away from memory and back to inspection. She was gazing at the man she would marry, and she knew that with a certainty that wouldn't be denied. She even could have told him how many children they'd have.

Psychic abilities, she thought ruefully—not for the first time—certainly took away some of life's little mysteries. Still, she didn't doubt that her trip to the altar would be troubled; Trevor, though accepting the clear proof of her abilities, was uncomfortable with them.

And they'd only known each other a matter of hours, after all.

Trevor found his apartment door unlocked and remembered even as he opened it that Jason had said something about stopping by. He found his brother stretched out on the couch, a bowl of popcorn on his flat stomach and a mug of beer in his hand as he stared at the television.

"Make yourself at home," Trevor invited dryly, tossing his keys onto a table in the foyer before stepping down into the living room.

"Don't mind if I do," Jason responded cheerily. He sat up and placed the bowl on the coffee table, smiling. Then his smile faded, and he came abruptly to his feet, staring at his brother. "What is it?" he asked in an altered voice.

"What?" Trevor responded blankly.

"You look like you've been hit by a train—mentally, that is."

Trevor sank down in a chair and frowned at his brother, irritated to hear that his tangled emotions showed so clearly on his face. "Well, I haven't," he said, further irritated by the defiance in his own voice.

Jason's eyebrows lifted and a grin began working at his mouth as he slowly sat back down. "Dare I guess the train was female?" he ventured solemnly.

"I wouldn't if I were you," Trevor warned.

Grinning openly now, Jason instantly demanded, "Who is she?"

"She isn't what you think!" Sighing, Trevor knew that Jason wouldn't give up until he heard at least part of the story. So he set his mind to editing certain things, telling the rest as briefly as possible.

"A whole family of psychics?" his brother exclaimed when he'd finished. "No wonder you look stunned. But I want to hear more about Taylor."

Trevor started slightly. He'd deliberately glossed over any details regarding Taylor, and his brother's ability to home in on that surprised him. After an evening with psychics, he hardly needed his own brother reading his mind. He sent Jason a guarded look;

his brother was gazing back with innocently lifted brows. "Never mind Taylor."

"Why?"

"Because."

Jason chuckled. "So she's the one. I thought so, considering the way you carefully didn't mention her much."

Stirring restlessly, Trevor glared at the face that was a slightly younger edition of his own. "There's no 'one' and nothing to talk about," he said with great firmness.

Jason made a rude noise.

"Little brother, you've enjoyed my television set, my couch, my popcorn, my beer—don't push your luck!"

His "little" brother, who easily equalled his own six-two, pulled on a ludicrously injured expression, which he could still get away with after twenty-four years of perfecting it.

"Well, if you feel that way about it—"

"I do."

Jason sighed. "All right, all right. But I would like to know if you're planning on seeing Taylor again."

"No," Trevor said definitely. "I don't need the complication of a psychic in my life." And thereby, he realized ruefully, he'd tacitly admitted that Taylor had indeed been "the one."

His brother quickly mastered the grin and pulled on yet another in his repertoire of devious faces—this one solemn. "You're not going to see any of them again? You have no curiosity to find out what Solomon's kittens look like or if Jack and Jill escape again or what the significance of that blouse for the Reverend is? You don't want to find out if Jessie actually *does* play the piano and really *isn't* as psychic as the rest of them, or if Dory really *does* hide in closets? You don't want to know if Sara actually *could* topple armies with her eyes or if Luke's really a doctor?"

Trevor stared at him for a moment. Then, in a long-suffering tone, he said, "I always knew it was a curse to have a brother with total recall."

"It helped me a lot in college," Jason confided gravely. "I never had to take notes in class. Now, come on, Trevor, you can't tell me you aren't the least bit curious about that nutty family!"

"Not in the least," Trevor responded, spacing his words for emphasis.

Grinning openly now, Jason said oracularly, "I'll remind you of those words one day, dear brother. One day soon, I think."

It would have galled Trevor to admit it to his brother, but had Jason been present, he would have gleefully presented his "reminder" the following day.

Trevor didn't realize he was restless at first. He played tennis in the morning with a lawyer friend, had lunch with that same friend afterward, then returned to his apartment, planning on a relaxing afternoon by the pool with a good book. But somehow he never quite got into his suit and out to the pool. He did pick out a book he'd been planning to read for months, but he found himself wandering somewhat aimlessly around with no definite urge to do anything else.

It came to him only gradually, insidiously, that each time he passed his telephone, his hand reached absently for it. Halting by the seductive instrument, Trevor glared at it as if it were a thief caught in the act.

"I'm not interested. I'm just *fine*; no need of psychics in my life. I'm *great* . . . and I am talking to a phone!" He swore irritably. Dropping down into the chair beside the phone, he opened his book and began to read. Tried to read. But something nagged at him, a task needing doing, and he finally reached for the note pad by the phone, jotted down a few numbers with a feeling of relief, then went back to his book.

Half a paragraph later, he set aside his book with careful attention, picked up the pad again, and stared at the phone number he'd unconsciously written down. In one sense, it was not a familiar number; in another sense, it was very familiar. He realized then that at some point during their preparation of dinner the evening before, he had stared fixedly at the kitchen wall phone long enough to memorize Taylor's phone number.

So much for your indifference! he sneered inwardly.

"You've bewitched me!" he told the number severely, picturing a face with vivid blue eyes and fascinating mismatched features. Then he sighed and drew the phone toward him. He wasn't going to get involved, of course. No way. No chance. But he was bored halfway through his vacation, and they *were* an intriguing family. . . .

"Hello, Trevor! I knew you'd call and won't you *please* come over because Jack's under the washer again and Daddy's at the office and Solomon's going to show us her kittens I think and Taylor says not to pester you but won't you *please* come? Please?"

It was, of course, the moppet, and Trevor couldn't help but smile. "Hello, Jessie. How'd you know it was me?" He remembered Taylor saying that this sister had the least ability.

"I just knew! Isn't it great?" She sounded happily proud of herself. "I usually can't, you know, but I *did* this time and I think it's 'cause you belong to Taylor or maybe that's not it but anyway I *did*. Can you come, please?"

Trevor bit back a laugh. "Jessie, is Taylor there?"

"Well, she's at the office with Daddy, but I can switch you over."

"Switch me over?"

"To the other phone," Jessie said impatiently. "*This* phone is connected to the one in Daddy's office, which is next door—or something like that. Want me to switch you over?"

"Yes, please," Trevor said meekly.

"Okay—hang on."

There was a short silence filled with a faint buzz, then Taylor's cheerful, efficient voice.

"Doctor Shannon's office."

"Didn't *you* know it was me?" Trevor said severely.

Taylor replied instantly. "Of course, I just wanted to impress you with my businesslike manner."

"Damn."

She giggled. "Sorry, Trevor; it's difficult to surprise a psychic. Did you call the house first?"

"Yes. Jessie switched me over."

"After nattering at you, I'll bet."

"Jack's under the washer again, and Solomon's going to show her kittens," Trevor related automatically. Bemused, he realized that the family had quite definitely infected him with something, and it was spreading rapidly through his bloodstream; he was going to forget how to talk to normal people.

"Well, don't feel obligated. No matter what you think, Trevor, no one's pointing a shotgun at you or readying a matrimonial noose." Her voice was very dry, but amused as well.

Trevor could have argued the point, but wasn't in the mood, for some reason. And he didn't want to think about how utterly comfortable he felt talking to a woman he'd met less than twenty-four hours before. "We'll discuss *that* later," he said, sighing as he heard his own admission that there would be a future for them—of some kind. "You work for your father?" he added somewhat hastily.

"Uh-huh. I'm his receptionist this year."

"This year?" he managed blankly.

"Yes, I—Oh, hold on, will you?"

The receiver buzzed in his ear for a few moments; then Taylor was back.

"Sorry, the office is busy today. Why don't you come for dinner? You can go on over to the house; I'll be off in a couple of hours. If you'd like to, that is."

The last diffident sentence got him. "Oh, what the hell. Should I bring something for dinner?"

"Just willing hands," she told him softly, and hung up.

Trevor stared at the receiver in his hand for a moment, then thoughtfully cradled it. With rueful self-mockery, he wondered how on earth a logical, analytical lawyer could have gotten in so deeply over his head.

He continued to wonder about that while he was driving the Jeep out of the city and into the suburb where Taylor lived. But whenever he'd begin to wonder too deeply, a pair of vivid blue eyes would intrude. Trevor finally dispensed with the useless reflection, understanding wryly that neither logic nor analysis was going to produce an answer this time.

Jessie was beside the Jeep almost as soon as it stopped in the drive, and she had Trevor's hand in hers when his feet had barely touched the pavement.

"Oh, I *knew* you'd come! Hurry, Trevor, we have to get Jack before Solomon brings her kittens down and I've practiced a new song—would you like to hear it? You *do* like music, don't you?" She threw the last question anxiously over her shoulder, towing him along behind her like a tiny tugboat pulling a battleship.

Trevor laughed, but something about the moppet touched him in a way he'd never been touched before. It wasn't just her ridiculous sentences or apparently wild mood swings; he sensed that she needed something from him, something her clearly loving family couldn't provide. And he wondered if Jessie of the "least ability" felt that lack more than her family realized.

He kept his voice casual and friendly when he answered her anxious question, determined to do nothing to set up barriers between himself and the child. "I love music, Jessie; I took piano lessons when I was your age."

Her gray eyes were neither vague like her mother's nor brilliant like her father's, but were distinctively her own: deep smoky pools that brooded one moment and gleamed with a disconcerting wisdom the next. But they flared brilliantly when he claimed some knowledge of music.

"You know music? Really?"

A bit uneasily, Trevor sought to dampen her enthusiasm in the gentlest manner possible. As the side door banged just behind them, he said carefully, "It was a long time ago, Jessie. I haven't played in years."

"But at least you *know*," she said intensely. "No one else here knows. Oh, they all love music, but they can't play even a note. Not even Daddy, and he has clever hands."

Thoughtfully, Trevor noted that Jessie's sentences became much less tangled when she spoke of music. He filed that knowledge away in his mind as they entered the cheerfully cluttered den and were immediately addressed by Sara, who was sitting between Jamie and Dory on the couch.

"Jamie closed the laundry room door so Jack can't get out. Hurry and sit down; Solomon wants us to meet her babies."

Pulled firmly down beside Jessie on the love seat, Trevor wondered distantly why no one had thought to close that door yesterday, then silently chastised himself for trying to make sense of anything in this house. But he couldn't help wondering how they could be so sure the cat was about to present her kittens for inspection. Did cats even *do* that?

The Shannon cat did.

She came around the corner just then, ignoring the poodle,

which was sitting very still by the doorway. In a measured tread so careful that they could almost hear the music of a march, she entered the room—a tremendous Siamese cat with comically crossed blue eyes and a pure white kitten held securely in her mouth.

Like everyone else, Trevor found himself sitting very still and gazing at the mother and child with respectful eyes. He watched as Solomon gently deposited the kitten on the carpet squarely in the middle of the room, then sat down and gazed—or, at least, appeared to gaze—at Sara.

"How lovely, Solomon," Sara said instantly.

The cat released a peculiarly contented rumble, picked up the kitten, and marched regally from the room. She was back moments later with a kitten, and the little ceremony was repeated.

After she left with the fourth kitten, Trevor could no longer repress a burning question. "How do we know she isn't bringing the same kitten down every time? They're all identical."

Sara's vague eyes focused on him reprovingly. "Of course she isn't, Trevor. A mother knows her children."

Meekly, Trevor watched the fifth repetition of the ceremony. But when the cat had disappeared, he had another question. "Does she do this with every litter?"

"Oh, yes," Sara answered.

"Then why doesn't she wait for the whole family to be here?" Instantly, he felt abashed at the question, telling himself it was ludicrous to suppose the cat could count people or reason. But Sara's answer made his question quite logical and sane by comparison.

"To tease Luke, of course."

"I beg your pardon?" he managed.

"Luke won't let her hide the kittens. He always finds them. So Solomon shows them to the rest of us to get even with him."

"Oh." Trevor decided that there was absolutely nothing he could do with that explanation but accept it. Rather like the way, he reflected, he could only accept his absorption into this ridiculous family.

When Taylor came into the house some time later, she found him in a room off the den, seated in a comfortable chair with Dory nestled confidingly in his lap as they both listened to Jessie play the baby grand piano.

Trevor sent her a quick smile—instantly returned—but said nothing as she came to perch silently on the arm of his chair. And they listened intently as Jessie completed a rather difficult sonata with an expertise belying her young age. As soon as she'd finished, he asked, "D'you compete, Jess?" He'd adopted the diminutive of her name at her request.

She turned on the bench to regard him with bright eyes. "No, never have. I just love to play. D'you . . . think I'm good enough to compete?"

He replied with total honesty. "I went to a West Coast competition last year for kids under eighteen; if you'd competed, you would have won."

Her gray eyes glowed brilliantly. "Really?"

"I think you'd have won, Jess. I really do."

Jessie bounded up, excitement lighting her small face. "Taylor, d'you think Mother and Daddy'd let me?"

Taylor was smiling at her. "Why don't you ask them? Mother's digging up flowers out back; Daddy went out there when we came in."

Instantly, her sister raced from the room.

"Digging up flowers?" Trevor queried dryly.

Before she could answer, Dory wiggled from his lap, saying in her gruff little voice, "I want to watch Daddy comb his hair." She looked sternly at Trevor, her hand on his knee. "You won't go away?"

"Not for a while," he said gently, and watched her leave the room before he looked up at Taylor plaintively. "Digging up flowers? And what's that about your father combing his hair?"

She grinned faintly. "It's a little game Mother and Daddy play. At least I think it is, since it's been going on as long as I can remember. The flower bed's Daddy's, you see; he can get anything to grow. And Mother can't tell a flower from a weed until the former's bloomed, which they haven't as yet. So every day during the spring Mother wanders out to the flower bed just before Daddy's due home. And when Daddy comes in and is told by someone—Jamie today—that Mother's in back with a trowel, he lets out an anguished groan and bolts out there to save his flowers."

Fascinated, Trevor said, "What does he say to her?"

"Always the same thing. He takes the trowel away from her very gently and asks if she'd mind fixing him a cup of coffee. Then when she comes into the house, he rakes his hair with both hands—the 'combing' Dory was talking about—and hides the trowel in the garage."

"How's her coffee?" he asked, remembering Sara's ineptitude in the kitchen.

Taylor laughed. "Terrible! Daddy says it's strong enough to raise the dead; he pours it in the flower bed when she isn't looking. It seems to be a dandy fertilizer."

Chuckling, Trevor reached quite unconsciously to pull her down into his lap. "You have a remarkable family, lady."

"Never dull, anyway," she responded, smiling, utterly relaxed in his lap.

He realized then what he'd done. For a moment, he looked bemusedly at their positions, she on his lap and he with one arm around her shoulders and the other lying possessively across her thighs, then closed his eyes for a moment. "I knew it'd happen," he said mournfully.

"What?" she asked, polite, her hands resting on the arm across her thighs.

"I knew you'd entice me into this loony bin!"

"*I* didn't call *you*," she reminded.

"Didn't you?" his voice was rueful. "Now I know how Ulysses felt."

"If you're referring to a siren song, I'll point out that I've never warbled a note in your direction."

"You bewitched me!"

She giggled. "If it makes you feel better to think that."

"It makes me question my sanity slightly less than I would otherwise," he admitted wryly.

"Better bewitched than intelligently unresisting, huh?"

"Bewitched or not, I *am* resisting," he claimed stoutly. "For instance, I am manfully ignoring the ridiculously demure picture you present sitting on my lap wearing a skirt and frilly blouse."

She looked down at herself for a moment, then said thoughtfully, "Yes, you are, aren't you? I'll try for sexy rather than demure next time. Only this, you understand, was for Daddy's patients—not you."

"Oh, of course."

"They wouldn't feel very comfortable with a siren in the office."

"Perfectly understandable." He cleared his throat, deciding it would be better to change the subject. "Speaking of which, you said something on the phone about being your father's receptionist this year?"

Predictably, she didn't need the question to be clarified. "That's right. I've done something different every year since college. The first year, I went to France as—believe it or not—a governess to the young daughter of an American couple who were transferred over there for a year. The second year, I worked as an executive assistant to the manager of an American oil company based in Saudi Arabia. Since then, I've worked here in Chicago—first as a veterinary assistant, then as a private security guard."

Trevor lifted both brows as he gazed at the slender, dainty lady on his lap. "A private security guard?"

"Never judge a lady by her inches," Taylor advised serenely. "Daddy taught me karate as soon as I could walk, and boxing some years later. And since he's an expert marksman and has an excellent collection of guns upstairs in his study, I can handle weapons quite well."

"But a *security guard*?"

"Seemed the thing to do at the time. I like doing different things. As a matter of fact, I'm up for a job in Australia after the first of next year."

"Doing what?"

She grinned. "Assistant to a lawyer. I have some paralegal training."

He lifted only one brow this time. "If you go to Australia," he pointed out, "you can hardly marry me. I don't want to live down under."

"I said I was up for the job, not that I'd accepted it."

"But you'd be bored anyway, living with a dull lawyer like me."

"Oh, I don't know," she said easily. "I'm sure I'd be able to bear up under the strain."

"I work late most nights—"

"I love to read."

"—and take a vacation only every other year—"

"You obviously need a wife to make you take better care of yourself."

Trevor showed her a mock frown. "Right. Just a gentle little woman who could shoot me or throw me over her shoulder if she felt like it."

"My temper's not *very* bad," she explained anxiously.

"I can see it now. I'd be in a bad mood—we all have them, after all—and you'd read my mind and do something rash."

"No, because I'd *know* you were in a bad mood and understand."

"I'd snap at you, and you'd cry."

"There is that," she admitted ruefully. "It'd be just the thing to set me off, too."

Shaking his head, Trevor murmured, "Worser and worser."

"Not exactly traditional wife material, am I?" she mourned.

"Well, you can cook."

Taylor brightened. "I can, can't I? I can sew, too. And I'd never get mad if you brought home someone unexpectedly for dinner."

"You wouldn't?"

"Certainly not. A man's home is his castle."

A little wryly, Trevor said, "But I bet you'd expect me to clean the moat."

She giggled. "No, only mow the lawn and keep the drawbridge oiled. I can change lightbulbs, fix cars, and use a hammer and screwdriver, but I get a bit dizzy on ladders, and lawn mowers don't seem to like me."

"Lawn mowers don't like you? What do they do?"

"They run away with me. Daddy says it's because I forget where the brake is, but I always remember in cars, so I don't think that's it. And they always head for ditches, so I have to bail out."

Trevor blinked. "I see. Anything else I should know? In considering you as wife material, I mean?" He was enjoying the conversation, perhaps because it was filled with such relaxed solemnity.

Taylor considered the question for a moment. "Well, I'd be a dandy asset for a lawyer, because I could tell you in a minute who was guilty. And then there's the fact that you'd never have to explain why you were going to be late for dinner. And we'd never fight over—um—crossed signals, because I'd always know what you *meant*, no matter what you said."

He found himself torn somewhere between fascination and horror. "I'd never be able to call my soul my own!" he objected, half laughing and more than half serious.

"Wouldn't you?" Her arms lifted to encircle his neck, and she smiled at him very gently. "But you'd be able to call my soul yours."

Trevor was having trouble thinking clearly; the soft promises in those vivid blue eyes overpowered everything else. "I . . . could never be as sure about you as you could be about me," he murmured.

"Then I'll just have to teach you to read my mind."

He realized at that moment that he could read her mind, or at least read the intent in her nakedly honest eyes. "You wouldn't— you little witch," he managed, and he wasn't talking about her teaching him telepathy.

"I wouldn't?" She leaned toward him until their lips were just a whisper away. "Watch me."

Trevor was a strong-willed man and, at times, a stubborn one, but not even the stern inner voice clamoring for self-preservation had the power to keep his arms from encircling her and his lips from responding to hers. And this time he didn't draw away when he felt that incredible warm sense of well-being surrounding him. The insidious warmth lulled him, seduced him, until it blazed suddenly into essential need. His mouth slanted across hers hungrily, demanding what she gave willingly.

"Daddy kisses Mother like that," an interested voice observed.

The intruding voice drew them apart, but reluctantly, and both turned their heads to stare toward the doorway, where Jessie watched them with critical eyes.

"As a matter of fact," she added, "he just kissed her like that in the garden. I think it was because she caught him pouring the coffee on the flowers. But, guess what? They said I could compete if I wanted to! Isn't that *wonderful*? I have to practice!"

Chapter Four

Since Jessie began at once to practice with fierce concentration, Trevor and Taylor were more or less forced to vacate the room. Taylor went upstairs to change before beginning dinner, while Trevor was gruffly asked by Dory to retrieve the hamster shut up in the laundry room. Jack was safely back in his cage when Taylor returned to the den, and she entered just in time to hear Trevor addressed by her mother.

"Thank you for encouraging Jessie, Trevor," Sara told him in an absent tone. "She never believes us."

"She's very talented," Trevor responded. He listened for a moment to the sounds coming from those talented fingers. "I think you have a virtuoso blooming in there."

"Yes, and so nice for her," Sara said vaguely, then turned to Taylor. "Darling, I got some things for dinner and left them in the kitchen."

"All right, Mother." Taylor didn't wince visibly, but her vivid blue eyes threw a pained, laughing glance at Trevor, explained only when they were alone again in the kitchen.

"The last time Mother 'got some things' for dinner," she told him ruefully, "I found half a steer in the freezer—frozen, of course."

Trevor couldn't help but laugh. "Wonder what she got this time?"

Opening the refrigerator and peering inside, Taylor sighed. "Whatever it is, she didn't put it in here. Now where—"

"Here." Trevor, spotting an anomaly in the neat kitchen, had gone to stand by the back door, where a large metal tub reposed. Gazing bemusedly down at the contents of the tub, he added, "I only hope you know what to do with them."

Taylor joined him. "Oh no! Lobsters. *Live* lobsters."

"At least they're fresh," he murmured.

From the kitchen doorway, Luke announced, "I'll fix dinner, Taylor, if you'll keep your mother out of the flowers." He was holding a very much alive and indignant lobster in one hand. "One got away," he explained helpfully to them, "so I knew she'd bought lobsters." His benign gaze focused on Trevor. "Taylor hates to cook lobsters, but I'm very good with them. Not allergic to shellfish, are you?"

"No," Trevor managed to answer, ruthlessly swallowing the laugh in his throat.

"Good. Sara was craving them, I expect. She did with Dory. With Jessie it was watermelon, and with Jamie it was peaches. With Taylor—" He looked reproachfully at his eldest daughter. "With Taylor it was truffles. *Truffles!*"

"Sorry, Daddy," Taylor murmured, solemnly taking the blame for her mother's inexplicable long-ago cravings.

"That's all right," he said magnanimously, waving the lobster. "But go guard the flowers now; your mother's looking for the trowel again." Coming the rest of the way into the kitchen, he ab-

sently dropped the lobster—pincers waving in mute protest—
into the sink and reached for an apron, his vivid blue eyes abstracted. "Now, where did I put the— Oh, there it is."

Taylor caught a fascinated Trevor by the hand and gently
pulled him out the back door. "We have to guard the flowers," she
reminded him, grave.

Trevor found himself standing in a beautiful yard. It was large
for a suburban property, with a neatly trimmed flowering hedge
on two sides, several large and graceful oak trees providing plentiful shade, and innumerable rose bushes and flowering plants.
There was a hammock strung between two trees near a picnic
table, circular whitewashed wooden benches beneath two more
oaks, and a dandy playground area in the far corner, complete
with swings, slides, tunnels, and everything else a playful childish
heart could wish for.

The flower bed was a neat L-shaped affair that conformed to
the angles of the house, filled with a riotous growth that hadn't
yet bloomed but nonetheless showed vast promise.

There were only two occupants of the yard at the moment:
Jamie was stretched out in the hammock, reading a book, and
Dory was occupied with a tire swing in the play area.

Trevor pulled his eyes from the serene picture before him and
looked down at Taylor. Thinking of the cook busily working in the
kitchen, he asked carefully, "Does your father really have patients? People trust him with their bodies?"

Not in the least offended, Taylor giggled. "If you could see him
with his patients, you wouldn't have to ask. He's a wonderful doctor, very patient and gentle. And he's all business in the office, not
the least bit absurd. I suppose being ridiculous the rest of the time
is his way of unwinding."

Trevor shook his head, but made no protest as she pulled him
over to sit on one of the benches. "Did he plan this yard?"

"Every bit of it." She gazed off toward the play area, smiling reminiscently. "He built the playground when I was a toddler, and he and Mother would spend hours out there with me. My friends always envied me my parents. They were always ready to drop whatever they were doing to play games or plan a cookout, and they never worried about kids messing up the house or yard. Daddy may panic when Mother gets near his flowers, but he'd never think of scolding a child for trampling on the bed or carelessly uprooting a plant he'd nursed from a seedling."

Staring at her profile as she gazed back over time, Trevor softly encouraged the memories, no longer avoiding the knowledge that her life was important to him. "What about discipline?"

She laughed quietly. "I don't know if they planned their method—knowing them, probably not!—but it worked. None of us have ever been spanked or grounded or made to stay in our rooms. If we did something wrong, there were never any harsh words. All it took was a frown from Daddy or a hurt look from Mother, and we were honestly contrite. Maybe being psychic had something to do with it, I don't know. The house has always been noisy and cluttered, but there was never an instant's hesitation when a story was demanded or an umpire needed for a neighborhood ball game."

"Lots of love," he murmured.

Taylor nodded. "And plenty to spare. When I was in high school, the Homes for Foreign Students program was popular; at one point we had three foreign kids living with us. Then they started the Student Exchange program, and I spent a school year in London while an English girl lived here." She smiled. "All those kids still write and call Mother and Daddy; they were completely adopted in spirit."

Trevor chuckled. "I'm not surprised. I think I adopted your

mother when she approved my name, and your father won me over when he came into the kitchen carrying a lobster."

She smiled up at him. "I always thought my parents were the most fun of anyone I knew. Once some of my friends were sleeping over here—I was about Jamie's age, I think—and they all decided to test my claim that my parents were never upset by anything. So, in the middle of the night, they managed to get two goats into the house. We left the goats in the den and then crept back downstairs to the family room, where we were supposed to be sleeping, all of us giggling and expecting at least one of my parents to be awakened by the noisy goats."

"What happened?"

"Well, the goats were rummaging around above our heads, but we didn't hear anything else and finally went to sleep. The next morning we found Daddy in the kitchen cooking a huge breakfast for us, and he told us quite cheerfully that Mother was in back with the goats—for all the world as if they belonged here. Sure enough, Mother was sitting in the yard, feeding the goats bits of leftovers. When my friends went out there to see with their own eyes, Daddy said to me—in the gentlest way—that since the goats had made something of a mess in the den, perhaps we should clean the room after breakfast. And we did, too. Two of my friends begged me to exchange parents with them," she added, laughing.

"Your parents would be a hard act to follow."

"Idle observation?" she questioned with a smile. "Or are you contemplating parenthood?"

Trevor stared at her for a moment, then said firmly, "I make it a point never to answer loaded questions."

"Really? I'll keep that in mind."

He decided to change the subject. "I thought we were supposed to be guarding the flowers from your mother's fell hand. Where is she?"

"Probably in the garage looking for the trowel," Taylor responded readily, unperturbed. "Heaven only knows what she *will* find, though."

Amused, Trevor was just about to question this cryptic comment when the answer was presented to him by Sara.

"Look what I found," she said, appearing suddenly beside them with her gliding walk. She gazed in vague satisfaction at the object in her hands, which was a somewhat lopsided birdcage constructed of Popsicle sticks. "Is it yours, darling? I can't remember."

"No, Mother, it's Jamie's. She made it in third grade."

"How clever of her."

"What're you going to do with it?" Taylor asked in the tone of one who didn't expect a lucid answer.

And she didn't get one.

"A bird, I suppose," Sara murmured rather doubtfully. "Dory wants one. Or would it break, do you think? Little birds aren't very strong."

"Dory has hamsters," Taylor reminded firmly, "and Solomon doesn't like *them*. She'd definitely eat a bird."

"Would she?" Sara turned her dreamy gray eyes on Trevor. "Do you think she would?"

"Quite likely," he answered gravely.

"Oh. Well, then, I'll put this on the mantle." She smiled gently at him, then spoke to her daughter as she turned away. "I like him much better than that prince who followed you home from Arabia, darling."

"He was a sheik, Mother," Taylor murmured.

"Was he? How nice for him. But tents and things. I'm glad he went away." Serenely, she headed toward the back door.

Trevor stared at his giggling companion. "Sheik?"

Taylor got control of herself and returned his stare solemnly. "Well, yes. I met him while I was working over there."

"And?" Trevor prompted sternly.

She rubbed her nose in a rueful gesture. "And . . . he decided that what he needed was an American wife. He was a very stubborn man, too. When I came back home, he followed me and asked Daddy for my hand."

Choking back a laugh, Trevor said wistfully, "I wish I'd been here to see that. What'd your father say?"

"He told the sheik that since we hadn't any goats or camels for my dowry, he didn't think it would be fair and, besides, he really didn't want me to live so far away for the rest of my life. The sheik started talking about a mansion in Beverly Hills, and Daddy said *that* was too far away and, besides, he didn't trust California not to fall into the ocean."

"Did the sheik give up?"

"Not immediately. Daddy kept pointing out, very gravely, the differences in religion and lifestyle, and the sheik kept promising to change whatever was wrong. Every time Daddy seemed to be cornered, he found a new objection. Finally, he told the sheik that he really didn't want to lose his firstborn just yet."

"And?"

Taylor grinned up at him. "And then Jamie walked into the room. My fickle sheik instantly fell in love with her and offered Daddy the earth if he'd only consent to their marriage. He was horribly disappointed when he found out how old she was, but he stayed for dinner anyway, and when he left he promised he'd be back to court Jamie in a few years."

Passing by them just then, Jamie said softly, "I hope he does come to court me. He was a beautiful man, Taylor, and *such* nice manners. And I'd like to ride a camel. And at least he didn't yell like that Frenchman." With a gliding walk eerily like her mother's, Jamie moved on toward the house.

Trevor folded his arms across his chest and leaned against the tree at his back, staring down at Taylor. "Frenchman?" he queried with terribly polite patience.

She was gazing meditatively at nothing at all. "Hmm? Oh, him. He was just someone I met in Paris."

"He followed you back to the States?"

"Uh-huh."

"And asked for your hand?" Trevor's voice was growing more and more polite.

"Well, yes."

"And?"

Taylor sent him a sudden, glinting smile. "Judging by your tone, I think you would have loved Daddy's answer."

"Only," Trevor said grimly, "if he decked the man."

"He did."

"He did?"

She giggled. "Well, I'm afraid he took Daddy's amiability for weakness, and he became very demanding and—uh—abusive. And when he began shouting and frightening Dory, Daddy knocked him down. I must say it worked, too, because he begged pardon very meekly once he'd picked himself up off the floor, and he left without a murmur."

Trevor was clearly pleased by his mental image of that event, but he held on to his stern expression. "Do you make it a habit of bringing strange men home with you?" he asked severely.

"You should know," she told him blandly.

Without an instant's hesitation he said, "But you knew I was the man you were going to marry. What excuse did you have for the others?"

She choked on a giggle. "You make it sound like I've had men trampling a beaten path to my door!"

"I'm beginning to think that was exactly the case! I thought you waited for me!" he accused, aggrieved.

"A girl has to do *something* while she waits," Taylor explained gently.

"You shameless hussy, how many other men have you brought home?"

"Not many."

"Not many?"

She looked up at him soulfully. "And you're the only one who *mattered*, after all."

"Oh, sure!"

"I promise. It's just that I like making friends, you see."

Trevor made a rude noise. "Friends who propose?"

"Well, only three proposed—" She broke off abruptly with a comical look of guilty dismay.

"Three? And just who was the third?"

Taylor sighed. "Well, he was a man I met in—"

"Let me guess," Trevor interrupted in a voice of foreboding. "Just a man you met in London?"

She nodded, half laughing and half guilty. "But I was a schoolgirl, after all, so it didn't really count."

"You," he told her firmly, "should be barred from world travel! It's obvious you make a habit of ensnaring strange foreign men. I shudder to think of what you'd bring home from Australia."

Meditatively, she said, "I was planning on Italy after Australia."

Trevor fought with himself for a silent moment, then said calmly, "You'll probably catch a doge or a count over there. *Much* better than a stodgy American lawyer."

She started to laugh. "Damn! I hoped you'd take the bait!"

He lifted a superior brow at her. "And find myself engaged because I'd gone all primitive and possessive and ordered you not to go anywhere?"

"It was just a thought," she explained wistfully.

Manfully ignoring her pensive smile and mournful eyes, he said sternly, "Well, it won't work!"

"You'd let me go off to Australia with that other lawyer?"

"It's none of my business where you go," he said.

"You wouldn't lift a finger to stop me?"

"Not a finger."

"You wouldn't even *ask* me not to go?"

"It's none of my business," he repeated stoutly.

She stared at him for a moment, sad. Then, before his startled and horrified gaze, large tears pooled in the vivid blue eyes and rolled silently down her cheeks.

"Taylor!" Shaken, he took her hands in his and was just about to apologize fervently for making her cry. Then he remembered how easily she claimed to cry, and suspicion narrowed his eyes.

Slowly, she began to smile, amusement gleaming behind the tears. "You remembered. I wondered if you would."

"You—witch!" He released her hands and pulled out his handkerchief. "Here. Wipe those crocodile tears," he ordered.

She did so, still smiling as she handed the cloth back to him. "Well, it was worth a try," she confessed cheerfully.

"Can you always *make* yourself cry?"

"Oh, yes—except when I'm really upset. For instance, if you really did let me go off to Australia, I wouldn't cry at all. I wouldn't be able to," she said simply.

Trevor fought a desire to promise he wouldn't let her leave the country, ruefully aware of what would most likely happen if she *did* leave. "I'd probably chase after you anyway," he muttered.

"Would you?" She seemed entranced by the idea.

He stared at her for a moment, then reached out and hugged her. Hard. "Damn you," he said a bit thickly.

Taylor smiled up at him when his embrace loosened enough to allow her to do so. "I'm going to go on chasing you, you know," she said confidingly. "I know a good thing when I find one. And I have a slight advantage over most women."

"Which is?" he asked wryly.

"An unconventional upbringing. And a psychic certainty that we'll be married someday. So with me, it's no holds barred."

"I believe I've said it before," he murmured, "but a sane man would run like hell."

"I don't see you taking to your heels," she observed.

Abruptly, Luke stuck his head out the back door and waved a ladle at them. "If you want dinner," he called to them, harassed, "you'll come get your mother out of the kitchen, Taylor! She's got a birdcage. Why does she have a birdcage when we don't have any birds? And Jamie's sitting on the counter reading out loud, and I've lost a lobster—" The door banged shut on his last comment as Luke disappeared back inside.

Trevor rose to his feet, pulling her up with him. "Did I say a sane man would run? Well, it's obvious why I'm not running. Only an *insane* man would get involved with this ridiculous family," he said whimsically.

It was late before Trevor got home that night, mainly because Luke had instigated a poker game after the lobster had been consumed. They'd played for fantastic sums, and after losing every hand to one or another of the family, Trevor declared that he'd never again play cards with psychics.

But he thoroughly enjoyed the evening.

Sometime during the wee hours of the morning, alone and sleepless in his bed, it occurred to Trevor that if he wanted to preserve his unattached status, he'd better stay as far as possible from Taylor and her nutty but curiously attractive family. Instead of counting sheep, he kept repeating that to himself over and over, until sleep finally claimed him.

The end result was that Trevor kept himself fiercely occupied for the next three days. He played tennis and, if that didn't tire him physically, swam endless laps in the pool and even jogged every morning. He defeated his brother soundly at handball, all the while turning a deaf ear to Jason's innocent, persistent questions about Taylor. And at night, he buried himself in every literary potboiler he could lay his hands on until his tortured mind demanded sleep.

Jason said little about his brother's deliberately hectic vacation until the third night, when he came over to Trevor's apartment for pizza and a televised baseball game. The game was in the second inning when Trevor called to order the pizza, and when he hung up the phone, he saw that his brother was thumbing bemusedly through the latest potboiler.

Deadpan, Jason gazed at the lurid cover, then lifted shocked eyes to Trevor's face. "Your taste in literature's gone downhill these last few days," he remarked critically.

Ignoring this, Trevor said, "You start your vacation next week, don't you?" Jason worked as an electrical engineer with a large construction company.

"Yep. And, unlike you, I don't plan to fritter away my days off by exercising until I can't move or reading lousy books until I can't think. I'm flying to Wyoming, where I plan to spend a leisurely week hiking and fishing."

Jason's tone had been perfectly bland, but it caused Trevor to feel suddenly sheepish. "Is that what I've been doing?" he murmured.

"Yes," his brother told him cordially.

Trevor shifted a bit uncomfortably on the couch. "Look, it's *my* vacation," he said defensively.

"Of course it is. And who am I to say you're driving yourself into an early grave? I'm only your little brother. You're older, after all. Presumably wiser. Presumably, you know what you're doing. Now, if you *were* to ask my opinion, I'd just have to wonder why it is that you seem to be working so damned hard to get through your vacation. It's almost as if you want to be too tired to think. As if you're afraid to let yourself think—"

"All right! I get the point."

But Jason wasn't finished. Coolly, he said, "It isn't like you, brother. You've never been one to avoid facing whatever's bothering you. Or *who*ever." He hesitated, then added bluntly, "You faced up to the fact that you and Kara should never have gotten engaged."

Trevor said nothing, only frowned at the television.

Jason sent a searching glance at his brother's closed face. "But maybe that was different," he ventured quietly. "Maybe it didn't bother you then because you didn't care enough. Maybe it bothers you now because you care too much. She's gotten under your skin, hasn't she?"

"Where'd you get your degree in psychology?" Trevor countered with taut sarcasm.

Even more quietly, Jason said, "I got it from watching the brother who raised me while he was putting himself through college and law school."

Trevor's frown vanished. After a moment, he glanced at Jason and said gruffly, "Sorry, Jase."

Jason grinned a little in response. "Well, it isn't really any of my business. But I can't help thinking that since I loused up your last serious relationship—"

"What the hell are you talking about?"

It was Jason's turn to be uncomfortable, but he met Trevor's suddenly grim eyes squarely. "Kara didn't make any secret of it at the time. She didn't want a sixteen-year-old kid living with her. And who could blame her?"

Trevor turned on the couch until he was facing his brother, no longer making any pretense of watching the ball game. "Jase, we didn't break up because of you."

"I was a part of the reason, though," Jason said steadily.

Because they'd always been honest with each other, Trevor hesitated only a second. "In a way. Because I wasn't about to let my brother go live with some distant relative. But that isn't why we broke up, Jase. It just made me realize I could never be happy living with Kara."

Jason nodded but said, "I—used to worry about that. Blame myself."

Reaching out to grip his shoulder, Trevor said firmly, "Don't."

"Well, actually, I talked myself out of that pretty quickly," Jason admitted ruefully. "I never liked Kara."

Trevor laughed and shook his brother's shoulder briefly before releasing him. With the atmosphere eased, Jason instantly took advantage of it.

"And since we're discussing the women in your life, I'll go on being nosy. Are you going to come clean with me about Taylor?"

Trevor grimaced faintly. He stared at nothing in particular for a moment, then sighed. "What can I say about a woman who tells me—scant minutes after we meet—that she's the woman I'm going to marry?"

Jason blinked. "What? Straight-out like that?"

"Straight-out like that." Reflectively, he added, "Taylor doesn't pull her punches. She's quite possibly the most honest woman I've ever met in my life."

"Oh. Well, uh—what's wrong with that?"

Trevor stared at him. "She can read my mind any time she damn well feels like it."

Jason hid a grin behind the hand thoughtfully rubbing his face. "That . . . could be a drawback in a relationship," he admitted.

"And her family," Trevor continued, rueful, "may be sane, but if so, it's only by the skin of their collective teeth."

Jason choked. Controlling himself beneath his brother's pained eye, he finally managed to speak. "You went back and saw them that next day, didn't you?"

"Yes. I got the hamster out from under the washer again and encouraged Jessie to compete at the piano. Dory sat in my lap, and they all won imaginary money from me at poker. Sara got lobsters for dinner—live lobsters, which Luke prepared—but two got away and it took ten minutes to find the second one."

Fascinated, Jason asked, "And Taylor?"

"Taylor?" Trevor cleared his throat. "Well, Taylor told me some things about her life, including the information that she's worked in a different job every year since college. And sometimes a different country. A sheik followed her home from Saudi Arabia; a Frenchman followed her home from Paris; and an Englishman proposed to her in London."

"She told you that?"

"Only under duress, so to speak. Sara brought up the sheik; she likes me better than him, because of tents and things. Jamie compared the sheik favorably to the Frenchman, who yelled. And Taylor accidentally mentioned the Englishman."

"Did she offer an excuse for bringing home foreign men?" Jason asked solemnly.

"She likes making friends."

After a moment, Jason said carefully, "Don't bite my head off, but—uh—do you believe that *was* her reason?"

"Oh, yes. She's honest, you see. There isn't a doubt in my mind that Taylor hasn't had a serious relationship with a man in her life." Meditatively, he added, "She was waiting for me."

"Knowing you'd come along eventually?"

"Don't run away with the idea that she was waiting for Prince Charming," Trevor urged dryly. "It's just that she's psychic; she was always sure she'd know the right man when she met him."

"And you're the right man."

"So she says."

"Which is why you've spent the past few days carefully ignoring her existence?"

Trevor sighed, then said ruefully, "D'you know, I hadn't been in that house ten minutes before everyone assumed I belonged to Taylor? Luke said he wouldn't have organ music at the wedding. Jamie asked me innocently if I belonged to Taylor, and Dory *told* me I did after she touched my shoulder. As far as they're concerned, the wedding's only a formality." He stared at his brother. "D'you blame me for running?"

Before Jason could answer, the doorbell rang. Trevor went to answer it, remembering the pizza he'd ordered. But when he opened the door, he found a delivery man with an armful of something that definitely wasn't pizza.

"Trevor King?" the man queried, shifting his load to peer around it.

"Yes?"

A tremendous basket of long-stemmed red roses was thrust into Trevor's startled arms, and the delivery man said cheerfully, "These are for you; she must be crazy about you, pal!" Then he was gone.

Bemused, Trevor closed the door and carried the basket into the den, where he set it on the coffee table.

"There's a card," Jason offered gravely.

The card, opened, revealed a few lines Trevor recognized as a paraphrase from a work of George Bernard Shaw.

You believe it is your part to woo, to persuade, to prevail, to overcome, but you're the pursued.

The card wasn't signed. But then, it hardly needed to be.

Trevor knew he was smiling but couldn't seem to stop himself. "Damn that little witch," he murmured, and felt no surprise when the words bore a closer resemblance to a caress than to a curse.

Chapter Five

Two days later, with only a weekend left of his vacation, Trevor finally gave in and called Taylor. She answered the phone herself, and he wasted no time identifying himself; it was needless, he knew.

"Thank you for the flowers," he told her gravely.

"You're welcome," she said, equally solemn. "I hope you like roses."

"I like roses. I also liked the gardenias yesterday and the box of chocolates today. My entire apartment building is intrigued."

"Did I embarrass you?"

"Would it disturb you if I said yes?"

"Not particularly."

"I didn't think so."

Taylor laughed. "How does it feel to be pursued?"

"I haven't made up my mind yet." Trevor paused. "But my brother says he's in love with you."

"A man of obvious taste."

"No, just a radical sense of humor."

"Thanks a lot!"

Trevor laughed, but the sound held a sigh. "Taylor, you are not making this easy for me."

"That's supposed to be the lady's line," she said blandly.

"Tell me about it!"

"Well, if you want to fight about it, why not come to dinner and we'll fight over the pasta. You love Italian food," she added enticingly.

Trevor told himself quite firmly that he accepted this guileless invitation only because he was convinced the days away from Taylor and her family had put things rigidly into perspective. He told himself he was utterly and completely convinced of that.

Jason would have laughed uproariously.

So Trevor, after five days in which to put "things" into perspective, once again ventured a foray into Taylor's absurd family. He kept a close guard on himself, taking care to avoid being alone with Taylor for any length of time because he was determined to let nothing irrevocable happen between them.

He spent the better part of the weekend with the family, and even though he was ruefully aware that Taylor was amused by his guardedness, he couldn't help but enjoy himself.

He found himself giving Luke a hand with the gardening, listening to Jessie practicing the piano, reading to Dory, and helping Jamie groom the family poodle, Agamemnon. It became a ritual to help Taylor with the preparation of meals for the family. And Sara more than once requested his help in various bizarre chores he thought prudent not to question, such as looking all through the attic for an ancient pair of ballet slippers. And hunting through various closets for a hat with feathers. What she did with both his finds Trevor didn't dare ask, although he saw neither again.

Given the run of the house and the unshadowed trust of the family, Trevor grew far more comfortable than his self-preserving inner voice liked. Since no one displayed further evidence of ESP—even Taylor, if she read his thoughts, kept quiet about it— he was able to put from his mind the knowledge that this family was unusual in more than just behavior and personality. He was even beginning to understand them.

Luke, for all his softly hurried style of speech and all the "chaff mixed in with the grain," as Taylor ruefully described it, possessed a brilliant mind and a cool composure in emergencies. Trevor discovered the latter when Dory fell from a tree in the backyard on Sunday morning. Everyone was anxious, though all were calm, and Luke was gently expert in examining the sprained ankle of his youngest daughter while she sat in Trevor's lap. Trevor had to remind himself that this man was a doctor with quite a few years of practice behind him. The brilliant mind was discovered while they weeded and pruned in the backyard, when several of Luke's low and somewhat hurried remarks and questions forced Trevor to dredge into memories of college courses just to hold his own with the man.

He also, more than once, caught a gleam of laughter in Luke's vivid but benign eyes, and slowly realized that Taylor had been right: Her father very consciously used absurdity to unwind. His was a very demanding profession, and a serious one; obviously, laughter was Luke's way of dealing with that. And since every member of his family lovingly played their ridiculous parts, it was an easy and natural thing for him to do.

As for Sara, Trevor discovered to his own wry satisfaction that his court-sharpened senses had not been at fault: She was *definitely* not as vague as she appeared and acted. He came unexpectedly into the den on Saturday afternoon to find her engrossed in a book. That in itself seemed unusual enough, because Sara rarely sat, obviously preferring to wander about in the yard or house with a vague and fleeting interest in just about everything. But it was the title of the book that caught Trevor's astonished eyes, and long moments passed before it sunk into his brain that she was reading philosophy.

Clearly feeling a startled stare—or, for all he knew, feeling it telepathically—she lifted her eyes to meet his. In her vivid gray eyes was the intelligence he'd seen only once before, and in back of that was a rueful smile.

"You went to college," he said firmly, as if she were going to argue with him.

"Between babies," she answered sedately.

Suspicious, he demanded, "Phi Beta Kappa?"

Her smile was as sweet and vague as ever, but the vividness didn't leave her eyes. She nodded. Marking her place in her book with one slender finger, she rose to her feet. "Do you really think, Trevor," she said tranquilly, "that a stupid woman could have kept up with Luke all these years?"

"Not stupid," he protested.

"Just not all here?" She laughed softly at his bemusement.

"It's so dull being just like everyone else," she murmured. "And so boring for the children. We laugh at ourselves, you know, and most families can't." Her eyes were blue again. "That hat with the feathers. So pretty on the wall. I'll have to find a place for it somewhere."

"Sara—" he managed as she was turning away.

"Yes, Trevor?"

He sighed. "Nothing."

Her eyes gleamed at him briefly. "It so often is." She wandered away.

Trevor could hardly help but laugh. He shook his head and left the room, still laughing.

Of the other members of the family, he also discovered a great deal. Dory, the pixie, was a stoic physically but timid in her emotions; she clung to him often in a way that gripped at his heart, but she was gruff in speech and tended to hide herself away from curious eyes if she was upset. She was obviously secure in her family's love but insecure in herself. She clearly considered Trevor a part of the family and treated him like an adored older brother. And she talked to him with vast seriousness, even confiding, as he was reading to her, why she hid in closets.

"I like the dark. It's quiet."

Touched, he said gently, "Is it loud everywhere else, Dory?"

She reflected gravely, those brilliant, solemn eyes meeting his directly. "Sometimes. In my head. Taylor says I'll learn to close the door in my head and not need a closet. Sometimes I can. But sometimes I can't, so I go into the closet."

"I'm sure Taylor's right," he said, inwardly uncertain.

A shy, fleeting smile crossed Dory's face. "You keep your door closed a lot," she observed. "Did you learn when you were little like me?"

Trevor thought he understood. "I'm different from the rest of you, honey. I don't have to close a door because I don't need one. I can't—*hear* things the way you can."

Peering intently at him, Dory laughed suddenly, an odd, gruff little laugh. "You don't know."

Puzzled, he asked, "Know what?"

But Dory said no more on the vague subject, just smiled at him with curious wisdom and requested that he finish the story.

Baffled, Trevor had the elusive feeling that he should have understood her—and hadn't somehow.

It was just one more puzzle piece fitting nowhere.

Jamie, that serene wraith, saw everything—like her mother—and possessed the most even temperament Trevor had ever known; she was neither uncaring nor controlled, but simply calm and serene. She was sweet and confiding, never bored or restless. She was the seamstress of the family, willingly putting aside something else to mend a tear or sew on a button. In looks, she was the feminine image of her father except for dreamy gray eyes, and she had something of his soft, hurried style of speech. And, emotionally, of all the daughters she seemed the closest to her father.

Talking to Trevor casually, she told him that Luke hoped the fifth Shannon child would be another girl.

"Does he?" Trevor asked with a smile, thinking how tranquil her Madonna-like serenity was.

"Oh yes. He says he's had so much fun with girls, and girl babies are so sweet."

"Doesn't he know if it'll be a girl?" Trevor asked curiously, having already discovered that each of the daughters was utterly matter-of-fact about their psychic abilities.

Jamie giggled suddenly. "He always guesses the sex of his patients' babies, but he never can with Mother's. He says she hides it from him. The rest of us are sure it's a girl, but Mother won't say, and she's the only one who really *knows*."

Trevor recalled Taylor's remark about it being difficult to surprise a psychic. Another one of Sara's gently humorous games? he wondered.

With the Shannon family . . . who knew?

Jessie, the moppet, was temperamental, moody; she fought her way through highs and lows with equal energy and boasted incredible determination in her slender, tomboyish form. His own love and understanding of music had made him something of a demigod in Jessie's eyes, and she talked to him without any of the emotional emphasis she used with everyone else.

"D'you really think I'm good enough, Trevor?"

"You've got talent, Jess, real talent."

She smiled blindingly at him. "I'm glad you came here to belong to Taylor. I knew the mailman was coming this morning before he came around the corner, and I passed Jamie the salt before she asked for it. I didn't think I was psychic at all until you came."

"Not everybody's psychic, Jess," he reminded gently. "I'm not."

"You're not?"

"No."

Jessie frowned at him. "You're sure?"

"Very sure," he answered, amused.

She gave him a rather odd look, he thought, but seemed to accept his assurances.

He wondered, though.

And Taylor . . . Taylor. She grew more beautiful every time Trevor looked at her, her chestnut hair more vibrant, her candid blue eyes more vivid, her mismatched features more fascinating and alluring. She was intelligent, humorous, tolerant. She was, both ostensibly and actually, the briskly capable hub around which her peculiar family turned. Viewing her family with love and respect, she was nonetheless ruefully aware of their oddity and entirely tolerant of it. And she was the most honest woman he'd ever met.

He knew why men would be attracted to her; her beauty was certainly a part of it, but those eyes, those honest eyes . . . and since he knew well that the intelligence of American men was at least equal to that of foreign ones, he didn't doubt that men had been following Taylor around for years. He wondered about those others but didn't ask. He felt no conceit in the sure knowledge that only male friends preceded him, but he felt a strong responsibility in the knowledge that he had the power to hurt her, and hurt her badly.

He didn't consider his careful guardedness as nobility. He knew only that until he was as sure as she was, their relationship would remain platonic and feelings undeclared. And there was still a niggling unease in the back of his mind, a stout wall closing off a part of himself from her.

That vague, nebulous uncertainty assumed concrete form on Sunday evening. He and Taylor were, for once that day, alone. They were in the den, engrossed in a chess game. The board was before them on the coffee table, and both sat forward, elbows on knees, Taylor frowning over his last move.

"I think you've trapped me," she complained.

"Never say die," he advised her.

"Well, I won't concede anyway," she said, and reached out to make a brilliant move.

Trevor blinked. "Damn."

She giggled.

The phone rang out in the hall just then; both of them ignored it as they stared down at the board, Trevor taking his turn to frown.

Moments after the phone rang, Luke appeared in the doorway to say quietly, "It's Dave, Taylor. He says it's important."

She didn't get up and head for the phone, but instead gazed at her father for a long, unreadable moment. "All right, Daddy," she said finally in a low voice. "Tell him to come over."

Luke nodded and went back into the hall.

Trevor looked at her in puzzlement. She seemed suddenly a bit tense, a bit preoccupied. "I realize it's none of my business," he said, "but who's Dave?" He thought she wasn't going to answer, which was so oddly unlike her that it made him anxious—inexplicably, he told himself fiercely—about this unknown man. But then she did answer.

"Dave is a senior detective in the homicide division."

"A cop?"

"A very good one." Taylor sighed, and to the watching man, her eyes seemed abruptly older than they had any right to be. "A few years ago his sister, who's a friend of mine, told him he should ask me for help in a homicide case. He was broad-minded enough to appreciate the fact that police departments have used psychics in the past, and he was by no means too proud to ask for help."

"So you helped him."

She nodded. "On the understanding that my name wouldn't be mentioned anywhere. Not in his official reports and not to the press. He felt guilty about that when I was able to tell him where he could find the killer and then he got all the credit. But we had a long talk and straightened everything out. By now, he understands how I feel about it."

"And how do you feel?" Trevor asked, curiously.

Taylor looked at him with those too-old eyes and smiled faintly. "It isn't a pleasant thing to look into the mind of a killer; I couldn't handle that along with the attention the press would focus on me. I feel a responsibility to do what I can to help—but on my own terms. I won't be held up to the public as some kind of freak, and I won't have the police department ridiculed because they ask a psychic to help them."

Before Trevor could say anything—not that there was anything he *could* say—Luke came back into the room.

"He was calling from his car; he'll be here in a minute."

Taylor nodded silently. Trevor, watching her intently, realized that she'd somehow withdrawn into herself. And he wondered what it did to this sensitive, cheerful woman to look into the mind of a killer.

The rest of the family drifted in soon thereafter. They all seemed unusually subdued, and it took Trevor some moments to realize that they would remain near Taylor during whatever was to come, supporting her emotionally. And the silence of the normally talkative family disturbed him more than anything else.

Luke went to answer the summons of the doorbell, returning with a tall man in his mid-thirties who had graying black hair and intelligent brown eyes. As he was introduced to the detective, Trevor saw that his eyes were also very weary. Dave Miller sat down in a chair at right angles to Taylor and, though his lean face was unexpressive, he was clearly distressed.

"I'm sorry about this, Taylor. But we're at a standstill, nothing to go on, and if this creep follows the pattern he's established . . . random killings, nothing to tie the victims together, not a damn thing we can hold on to—"

"It's all right, Dave." She smiled at him, calm, quiet. "What've you got?"

From his pocket, the detective produced a plastic bag containing a black glove that bore ominous rusty stains on the fingers. He carefully rolled the top of the bag down so that it was possible to touch the material without touching the stains. "This didn't belong to the latest victim, but it was found near the body. If it's his—"

Taylor reached out to take the bag from him, her fingers closing over the exposed material. She fingered it for a moment in silence, then suddenly went deathly pale. The bagged glove dropped to the floor.

"Taylor?" Trevor wanted to reach out and hold her suddenly, but he feared to break her concentration or somehow further disturb her with unwanted interference.

She sent him a reassuring if strained smile and bent to pick up the glove again. "It belongs to the killer," she murmured almost inaudibly. Obviously unwilling to ask it of her, Dave nonetheless spoke gently. "Can you tell me where to look for him?"

A pulse was beating strongly in Taylor's neck, but her pale face was calm. She closed her eyes and sat for long minutes holding the glove. Then her eyes opened—feverishly bright eyes, Trevor noted in alarm—and she dropped the stained thing on the coffee table beside their unfinished chess game. Her hands rubbed against her jean-clad thighs in the unconscious gesture of wiping away dirt.

Huskily, she said, "There's an apartment building on the east side of town. An old one. The fire escape faces the street. And there's a windowbox with—with geraniums: second floor, corner apartment. I think he's in that apartment. I know he's in that building. It's somewhere near Maple Street."

The detective picked up the glove and returned it to his pocket, nodding. "I know the area. Taylor . . . thank you."

"Just get him, Dave." Her eyes were still feverishly bright. "Get him before he can do that again."

He rose to his feet. "I'll call and let you know."

Luke and Sara walked him to the front door, and Trevor only dimly realized that the others had also left the room; all his attention was focused on the white, stricken face and glittering eyes of the woman sitting stiffly, controlled, at his side.

"Taylor?"

She looked at him blindly, trapped somehow in a dark place of little creeping things and big stomping ones. "Why is it," she said in a reasonable, matter-of-fact tone, "that I can't cry when it matters? I wish it was the other way around. I wish I could cry when it mattered and not when it didn't."

Instinctively, Trevor reached out to enfold her in his arms, holding her rigid body in a comforting embrace. He said nothing, but only held her. A part of his mind noted that there was no "security blanket" this time, and that same distant piece of his intelligence realized that it was because she was rigidly locked inside herself. Not, he knew, because she didn't trust him with her vulnerability, but because, for her, there had never been an outlet for this kind of emotion.

"Why you?" he demanded, unconsciously fierce. "Why do you have to do this?"

In that same toneless, matter-of-fact voice, she said, "Because I'm the strongest. Stronger even than Mother or Daddy. It wouldn't be so bad if—if I could only *cry*."

The same dim part of his mind that saw so clearly and made him uncomfortable with what it saw spoke up now softly in his mind. And it sneered at him because he wouldn't recognize the fact that *he* could be her outlet for this painful, imprisoned emotion. With the best and most loving will in the world, her family couldn't help; she was a woman, and a woman would share the vulnerable part of herself only with the man she gave her heart to. *They* could see her pain but were helpless to ease it; *he* could see her pain—and refused to.

Holding her, feeling the stiffness of her body, Trevor fought a violent inner battle. The wall that stood between them was his, a conscious thing, and he knew now why he couldn't remove it.

She could read his mind.

So simple. He was an intelligent man; he knew why that very simple statement—fact—disturbed him so deeply. It was a human need to be seen, to be known, but it was equally important to be able, when necessary, to retreat into the privacy of one's own silent thoughts. And that primitive part of his mind shied violently from the knowledge that with Taylor there would be no solitude.

That was what belonging to Taylor really meant.

And guilt caught his arms to tighten around her as that dim sneering voice proclaimed that with him . . . she would be able to cry when it mattered. If the wall were down. If they loved.

He felt it, then, when that wall rose higher. And he felt something that might have been hope shrivel. Holding her motionless body tightly, he said, "You're tired. You should sleep." He was surprised at the even tone of his voice.

She pushed gently away from him, her face calm now, but the wonderfully honest eyes still curiously blind. "No. I'll have nightmares," she added simply. "I always do." She looked at their unfinished chess game, then smiled at him. "It's your move."

Truer than you know, he thought bleakly. Then, because he could do nothing else for her, he leaned forward to resume the game.

It was a couple of hours later when he rose to leave. Her eyes were no longer blind but calm and quiet. She said good night in something approaching her normal cheerful voice. But Trevor ached for her.

During the drive into the city to his apartment he fought inwardly, knowledge against desire, disquiet against the urge to at least *try*. If he could be sure that he was indeed the man for her—but he couldn't be sure. His emotions rioted until he didn't know what he felt.

He found a backpack just inside his front door and hoped his face was equal to Jason's perceptive eyes. His brother was lying on the couch, the room lit only by the glow of the television.

With an engaging grin, Jason said, "Your place is closer to the airport, and I have an early plane in the morning. D'you mind?"

"No, I don't mind. You've slept here before."

Abruptly, Jason sat up and turned on the lamp beside him, his green eyes fixed keenly on his brother's face. Oddly hesitant, he said, "I don't have to leave tomorrow, you know. I can stick around for a few days."

"Why should you do that?" Trevor asked, surprised.

"Just . . . in case you want to talk."

"I go back to work tomorrow, remember?" Trevor wondered

vaguely what his brother saw in his face to cause that younger face to go suddenly grim. "I'm fine."

"Are you?"

Pausing on his way toward the bathroom, Trevor looked levelly at Jason. "I'm fine. And you'll get on that plane if I have to put you on it myself. See you in the morning, Jase."

"Good night."

Trevor got ready for bed, sparing only a brief moment for a look in his dresser mirror. He didn't see anything in his own calm face, but it occurred to him as he slid between the sheets that he looked older than he'd thought.

In the morning, Jason said nothing more about deferring his vacation, but his eyes on Trevor were searching and troubled. Trevor noticed, but he said nothing. He put his brother safely on his plane and then went on to the law firm where he was a junior partner.

His work kept him busy, occupied. His attaché case loaded with briefs and notes, he worked long into the night at home. In the office he buried himself in legal tomes and made short, curt work of telephone calls. In court, one beaten prosecutor congratulated him on his coldly brilliant defense of his client, and another asked ruefully if he'd mind very much changing sides because the prosecutor's office could use some wins.

It wasn't until the end of the week that Trevor realized his secretary was creeping warily around him and speaking with unusual softness. Aware at last, he also saw that the entire staff was casting nervous looks his way.

He spent Friday afternoon with his hands folded atop his desk and his gaze focused on nothing. Thinking. For an even-tempered man to unsettle his entire office with his moodiness, his personal problems spilling over into his professional responsibilities, was unthinkable. But Trevor was not, as Jason had observed, a man who could long avoid facing up to problems.

D'you think you've forgotten her, fool? You know damned well you're being cowardly in not facing her. Cowardly in not telling her what's wrong. She got under your skin that first day, she and her ridiculous family. Got under your skin with those nakedly honest eyes. You don't want to hurt her. Even if you know you can't live with her. Because, for the two of you, it's going to take more than . . . love.

Trevor heard a ragged sigh escape into the silent room. He loved her. Another . . . simple . . . unquestionable . . . unbearable fact. He loved her, but he wasn't the man for her. The man for Taylor wouldn't feel this need to hide a part of himself from her.

The man for Taylor could laugh with her.

He wouldn't hide from her, Trevor silently answered to the silent voice in his mind.

He'd have to love that ridiculous family of hers.

Any man would love them.

She has honest eyes, the voice reminded stingingly.

Trevor sighed again. Honest eyes. An honest heart—and God only knew if she loved him; believing they'd marry "one day" was hardly a declaration of love. And if she did love him, what then?

He could hurt her so badly.

And hurt himself. He was already hurting, wasn't he? Wasn't that why he'd been biting the heads off his staff, why he'd been cold and decisive with everyone he'd spoken to? Why he'd brusquely shunned his brother's ready sympathy, turned a deaf ear to that willing one?

It occurred to him then that he, in his pain, had shut out everyone. Just as Taylor shut herself in with the pain her gift brought to her. Was that the real reason he'd ached for her pain? Because it reminded him of his own inability to share his pain with another?

The breakup with Kara—Jason had known, but they'd not discussed it then, and there had been no one else to talk to. Before that, the deaths of their parents in a plane crash, the tearing grief and shock. The struggle to raise a much-loved brother and take the place of two parents. The struggle of college and law school.

Except for the deaths of his parents, he regretted none of it. But it hadn't been easy.

Automatically, Trevor opened his attaché case and piled papers into it. Still thinking.

He was a lawyer, accustomed to looking for whatever would benefit his client. Bits and pieces, legal loopholes, careful maneuvering, an obscure precedent in a dusty book. Digging for the best out of a witness.

Now he was his own client. And dig though he had, he kept coming up against the wall in himself. He could willingly share a great deal with Taylor, but not the last dark corner of his mind. Not that place where old hurts were deeply buried alongside old fears and inevitable guilts. Not that place every sane mind needs apart from the rest where gremlins lurked in the dark.

He couldn't share that with her.

Trevor went home to a silent apartment. He took a shower, pulled on jeans and a light sweater. Twilight faded into night outside his windows, and he automatically turned on the lights. He turned on his stereo, putting in tapes he didn't listen to. When the doorbell rang, he went to answer it, still moving by rote. Until he opened the door.

"The mountain wouldn't come to Mohammed," she murmured.

She was leaning against the doorjamb gracefully, her slender figure set off by a clinging back dress; it boasted a deep V neck-line, a slit almost to her hip revealing one shapely leg, and had long, flowing sleeves. Her glorious hair was piled loosely atop her head. Diamond studs sparkled in her lobes, and a small diamond pendant lay alluringly in the valley between her breasts.

"I came to take you to dinner."

Before he could respond, she gestured slightly, and Trevor fell back in surprise as three white-jacketed waiters filed past him. Turning slightly, he watched as they set the table by the window with white cloth and candles, silverware, stemware—everything. They produced it all from the baskets they carried, finally un-packing several covered dishes and a bottle of chilled wine. Then, just as silently and efficiently, they filed back out of the apart-ment.

"Thanks, Eric," Taylor murmured.

The last waiter to leave sent her a quick smile and an "Any-time" in response, then they were gone.

Belatedly remembering his manners, Trevor stepped back and gestured for her to come in. As she moved past him, he caught the elusive scent of a truly devastating perfume. He shut the door and followed her into the living room, clearing his throat deter-minedly.

"Taylor, you—"

"French food," she interrupted blandly, turning to face him. "It fit my mood."

He stared at her. "Which is?"

She looked wounded. "Can't you tell?"

"Seductive?" he guessed.

"I'm glad you noticed."

Trevor cleared his throat a second time. It was impossible for him to be brusque with her, equally impossible to attempt a seri-ous conversation while she regarded him with that wickedly humorous look in her eyes. So he found himself falling back on the teasing, companionable mood he'd missed these last days.

"You could," he told her definitely, "seduce Mount Rushmore—all four of them—in that dress."

"What works on granite doesn't work on man?"

"This man is putty in your hands," he assured her in a rueful voice. "You came loaded for bear and found a puppy instead."

She giggled. "Then I won't have to strip down to the teddy to get your attention?" she added innocently.

To his throat-clearing, Trevor added swallowing. She'd caught him at a perfect time, while he was hovering between what he wanted and what he knew he couldn't have. He could have strangled her. Except that he wanted her in his arms worse than he'd ever wanted anything in his life.

"You ought to be spanked," he said finally.

She appeared interested. "I've never been spanked."

He caught her elbow firmly and steered her toward the table. "Let's eat."

Chapter Six

As Trevor politely pulled her chair out for her, he said, "Is this dinner part of your—uh—"

"Courtship?" She smiled up at him over one shoulder, vivid eyes gleaming with amusement. "Of course it is. Fine food, candlelight, the sexiest dress I could find in my closet." Her blue eyes became merrily critical as he moved toward his own chair. "You aren't dressed for the part, though—one disadvantage of surprises."

"My dinner jacket is at the cleaners," he apologized gravely.

"I'll forgive you."

"Thank you. What would you have done if I'd been . . . entertaining someone else?" he asked mildly, unfolding his napkin.

"You weren't." She watched him pouring the wine.

"But if I had been?"

"What do you think?"

He handed her a glass. "I think you would have innocently confided the date of our wedding to my guest."

Taylor lifted her glass in a little toast. "I probably would have. Or cried," she added reflectively.

"You're dangerous," he told her with some feeling.

She giggled. "Not really."

"Yes, you are. Any woman with a habit of innocently bringing home strange men is dangerous. Add to that a siren's eyes, a voice that could charm lions, a body that could move Mount Rushmore, a deadly ability to defend yourself, and—and—ESP. Dangerous."

Taylor lifted her fork and smiled very sweetly at him.

"And stop smiling at me!" he ordered, harassed. "I don't even know what I'm eating. What am I eating?"

"You know," she observed, ignoring his question, "for a man who claims to be fighting my—um—snare, you say the nicest things."

Trevor very pointedly ignored this, paying strict attention to his food. But finally his curiosity got the better of him. Half-glaring at her serene face across the table, he muttered, "D'you really have a teddy on under that dress?"

"Black lace," she confirmed gently. "And garters."

He blinked, forgetting to glare. "Garters? Do women still wear those things?"

"They do when they're out to seduce."

"Dammit, Taylor!"

"Just a friendly warning," she explained blandly.

Trevor drained his wineglass and filled it up again. Methodically.

She giggled again. "Well, I did—um—give notice of intent, Trevor. I warned you that I'd chase you."

"Wanton," he managed.

"Thank you," she replied cordially.

He fought manfully against his baser instincts. "Taylor, your father should have locked you in a tower when you were twelve."

"Like Rapunzel?"

"Yes. But your father should have kept your hair short."

"But my prince couldn't have reached me," she objected.

"My point exactly."

"You don't think I deserve a prince?"

"Let's say rather that it would take an extremely *unusual* prince to deserve you."

She thought about that. "I think I've been insulted."

"On the contrary."

Taylor smiled her sweet, mischievous smile and held out her empty glass to him. "Well, I think my prince is unusual enough to cope."

He hesitated before filling her glass. "First tell me how you hold your wine."

"By my thumbs," she confessed sunnily.

Trevor sighed and poured three fingers into the glass. "If I take you home drunk, your father'll kill me."

"I'm of age, darling," she reminded him.

The endearment caught him off guard, and when he met the blue eyes smiling at him across the table, he saw warmth behind the amusement. A steady, inviting, unsettling warmth. A very large part of him wanted nothing more than to cast aside the very real doubts he felt and allow instinct to take over. But he loved her too much to deliberately risk hurting her.

He broke free of her eyes, pushing his chair back and getting to his feet, glass in hand. He stepped down from the raised dining area into the living room and went over to the fireplace, a luxury feature few apartments in the building boasted. Setting the glass on the mantel, he reached for a box of matches. "Late in the year for a fire," he murmured. "But—"

"There's a chill in the air," she said softly.

Trevor made no response to that, bending to kindle the fire, but he was very much aware that she'd left the table. When he straightened from his task and turned, he saw that she had borrowed a couple of pillows from the couch and now sat on the thickly carpeted floor with her back to the love seat flanking the fireplace. One of the pillows was placed invitingly for him.

Retrieving his glass, he joined her with a reluctance born of the knowledge that his determination not to hurt her was no match for both his building desire—and her guileless "seduction." He found himself sitting beside her, one elbow resting on the love seat's cushion as he half turned toward her; her own position matched his, and she lifted her glass in a tiny salute, smiling, before sipping the ruby liquid.

"Taylor . . . we have to talk," he said, trying for firmness and hearing, without surprise, the rough unevenness of his voice.

"You want to talk about all your noble scruples," she murmured.

"Stop reading my mind!"

She looked surprised. "I didn't. I read your face."

Trevor got hold of himself. "Whatever. Look, we haven't known each other very long."

"No," she admitted, then spoiled the logic of this by adding simply, "but I feel as if I've known you forever."

He fought against being disarmed. "Still, the fact remains that we're virtual strangers."

"No," she objected, "we aren't strangers. And we have a great deal in common. We both like mysteries and baseball, old movies and animals, chess and jigsaw puzzles. We have the same tastes in music and politics. We both hate snails and peanut butter." She reflected for a moment, frowning. "The only things left to establish, I think, are if you mind taking out the garbage and if you sleep with the window open or closed."

Trevor now had a dual battle on his hands. He was fighting the baser instincts set alight by a combination of love, desire, and her intoxicating perfume, and he was fighting the laughter that her solemn, ridiculous conversation inevitably roused.

He cleared his throat. "Taylor—"

"Do you mind taking out the garbage?"

"No. Taylor—"

"Good. I hate it. Do you sleep with the window open or closed?"

"Which do you?"

"Open."

"I like it closed," he announced, perjuring his soul without hesitation.

"I'll adapt," she countered instantly.

Trevor choked. "Taylor, you—"

"Right or left side of the bed?" she asked briskly.

"I," he told her loftily, "sleep all over the bed."

"Well, I'm not very big. I imagine I could find a corner to curl up on."

"I hog the covers. You'd freeze."

"No. I'd just make sure the covers you were hogging contained me."

By now, Trevor's struggle was severe; he was holding on to control by force and fast-fading determination. "I snore!" he announced in a last-ditch effort to preserve them both from her recklessness.

Taylor patted his arm consolingly. "That's a shame. But I can put cotton in my ears, you know."

Trevor set his glass on the floor, buried his face in the love seat's cushion, and laughed until his stomach hurt. By the time he lifted his head, he felt inexplicably better, but the twinkle in the watching blue eyes sent his inner defenses jangling again.

"A *huge* tower!" he told her definitely. "And you should have been *beaten* every day and twice on Sunday!"

"I need a husband to curb my reckless ways," she told the ceiling soulfully.

"You need a cage!"

"I thought I needed a tower."

"That was before. *Now* you need a cage."

Abruptly, the laughter was gone, and she was gazing at him with huge, grave, honest eyes. "I need you," she whispered.

"Taylor . . ." he breathed, watching his hands reach for her, setting her glass aside, drawing her closer. "You don't know what you're doing."

She came into his arms with the naturalness of infinite trust, her own arms sliding around his neck. "But I do know what I'm doing," she told him throatily. "I know very well what I'm doing."

However much he mistrusted her certainty, however much his own doubts troubled him, Trevor could no more resist her than he could will himself to stop breathing. There was enough of his own determination left to hold desire rigidly in check, to make his kisses as gentle as they were hungry, but when her lips opened invitingly to his, control was shattered.

The insidious warmth crept over him, through him, and he felt a sense of well-being as strong as his desire. Her small hands threaded through his hair, and her slender body molded itself to his. Her mouth was wine-sweet to his exploring tongue, the golden flesh of her back satin beneath his hands as his fingers found the zipper of her dress and slid it down. The heady perfume she wore seemed to envelop them in a cloud and, joined with the kittenlike sounds she made, drove his desire higher in a spiraling, aching ascent.

She was in his bloodstream, a drug he desperately needed more of to satisfy a terrible craving. Never in his life had he felt such desire, such a simple, savage, boundless need. He wanted to lose himself in her, to become a part of her until there was only a sharing one and not a striving two.

Trevor was unaware of moving, yet realized on some observing level of his perceptions that they were lying together on the thick carpet. They were turned toward each other, so close he could feel her heart pounding in time with his, and he could feel her own need rising to meet his with a strength that denied her delicate body. Guided by instinct and hunger, his fingers blindly drew the dress off her shoulders and down her willing arms, the silky material gliding over her smooth flesh and the flimsy satin-and-lace confection she wore beneath it. Her hips lifted slightly to allow the dress its passage, and it slid down her legs to pool in glimmering folds until it was kicked away by careless feet.

He lifted his head at last, breathing roughly, unevenly, staring down at her slender form. The diamond glittered with her quick breaths; black satin and lace cupped her breasts lovingly and hugged her flat stomach and gently curved hips. The promised garters were frilly, silly things, stark black against her golden skin, and the sheer stockings they guarded turned flesh to silk. Her tiny feet were hosed only, the delicate sandals long since kicked away.

"God, you're so lovely," he said hoarsely, his gaze returning to her beautiful, fascinating face. The vivid eyes were dark with desire, fixed on his face. Her fingers lifted to trace his features gently, and an artless smile curved her lips.

"No one's ever looked at me like that before," she whispered wonderingly.

He kissed her fingers, smothered by his heart's thundering, aching all over with needing her. Tenderness warred with bemusement as he thought of her assured aplomb in "seducing" him; she could dress in sexy clothes and wear them as if seduction were an art she knew well, yet his own hungry yearning brought wonder to her eyes.

Unusual . . . God, yes, she was unusual!

"Sometimes I think you're twelve years old," he said huskily. "And other times . . . other times you seem older than you have any right to be."

Her arms encircled his neck, and her smile became a very feminine thing. "I'm old enough to know what I want," she murmured.

Vivid blue promises called him, snared him, and Trevor managed only a few words before banked, smoldering fire burst its bounds. "What you want—may not be good for you."

"I'll chance it," she whispered against his lips.

He was dimly aware of a niggling sense of unease, of doubt and uncertainty, but it all seemed far away and unimportant. Until he lifted his head again to see the trust shining in her eyes. Then the faraway stormed up and stared him down, his own conscience battering him.

Abruptly, feeling as if he left a part of himself in her arms, Trevor forced his aching body to obey him. He drew away from her, sat up. Back against the love seat, he stared into the fireplace blindly.

Taylor sat up slowly. She was gazing at him quietly. "Why?"

"Because you're so damned sure—" he burst out, halting when his voice broke raggedly.

Taylor nodded, as if to herself. "Because I'm so sure how it's going to end."

"And I'm not!" He gestured roughly. "Dammit, Taylor, d'you think I don't know you wouldn't make love with a man unless you were certain he'd be the father of your children one day? Of course I know it!"

"Of course," she agreed softly, eyes glowing.

"But *I'm* not sure that man is me," he said, gruff now. "And I won't—take a gift that might well belong to another man."

Taylor was smiling; in fact, she appeared on the verge of giggles. "You mean you won't play a Victorian rake to my Victorian heroine?" she asked unsteadily.

He stared at her for a moment, then choked on a laugh of his own. "God, did I sound that stuffy and noble?" he managed to ask.

She was too busy giggling to reply verbally, but she nodded enthusiastically, and Trevor joined her in laughter when he couldn't hold back any longer.

Taylor got her breath back first. "I'm so glad you found me crying in that park," she told him fervently.

He cleared his throat carefully of the final chuckle. "I haven't made up my mind whether I'm glad or not. But, stuffiness aside, you know what I meant."

"Yes." She smiled at him. "It's very gallant of you, Trevor, not to take advantage of me."

She's done it again, the little witch! Made me laugh when I ought to be feeling something else. God, she looks adorable in that teddy! Ruthlessly, he tore his mind away from how she looked. Or tried to. Whether she knew it or not, only her invariable habit of making him laugh saved her from ravishment. "Stop sounding so damned solemn—you'll set me off again!" he complained.

Plaintively, she went on, "After I *waited* for you all these years, *saved* myself for you, collected a *trousseau* in anticipation—"

"Did you?" he asked, intrigued. "Collect a trousseau?"

"I have my grandmother's handmade quilt and cast iron skillet," she said solemnly.

Trevor choked. "What—no wedding gown?"

"Mother's," she said serenely.

He carefully grasped sobriety and held on tight. "Enough of this. We have to be serious. This is a serious situation, Taylor."

"Agreed." She was frowning gravely at him now. "And I'm much appreciative of your understanding the seriousness of this situation."

He put his head in his hands.

"After all," she went on loftily, "we're adults. And this is the Age of Aquarius. Or maybe that was before. Anyway, we're certainly capable of resolving this very serious situation. We only have to be reasonable and logical about it." She blinked at him as he raised his head, adding severely, "Except that I don't want to be reasonable and logical. Let's be unreasonable and illogical. Let's make love."

Trevor pulled on a stern face. "You're a forward wench!"

"And you're a backward suitor!"

"Is that what I am?" he wondered, amazed.

"Yes!" She kept her mouth firm, but her eyes danced irrepressibly. "I went to a great deal of trouble to seduce you tonight, and you had to let your scruples rear their ugly heads. I'd planned on being a fallen woman by midnight!"

"You look like one now," he managed unsteadily. "Curled up like a cat on my carpet wearing nothing but that ridiculous bit of black lace. And garters. *Garters.* And not even the decency to ask for your dress!"

"Decency," she said austerely, "can go by the board. Besides, I asked Mother for advice, and *she* suggested the black lace and garters."

Trevor's mind boggled. "You asked your mother—"

"How to seduce you. Well, not that exactly, but what to wear. She said she caught Daddy with black lace and garters."

Searching in vain for words to express himself, Trevor finally uttered an elusive sound somewhere between a strangled laugh and a bear's growl.

"Something caught in your throat?" she inquired innocently, eyes limpid.

He picked up his discarded wineglass, drained it very scientifically, and, now better able to deal with madness, cleared his throat. "Do you mean to tell me that you told your mother you were going to seduce me?"

"I knew she'd be interested," she explained gravely.

"Oh," he responded carefully. "You knew she'd be interested."

"Certainly. And Daddy said—"

"Him, too," Trevor told the ceiling in a faint voice that suggested his cup was more than full.

Taylor ignored the interruption. "—that there was just something *about* black lace and garters. The male libido, I suppose."

"Do you?" He eyed her in utter fascination. "And that's all your loving parents had to say about the matter?"

"Well, when Mother suggested the teddy, Daddy said they were the very devil to get off—"

Trevor choked.

"—but Mother reminded him that Christmas presents wouldn't be half the fun to open if they weren't wrapped up in shiny paper. And after he thought about it, he agreed with her."

"I'll bet," Trevor said weakly.

"So then Mother gave me this necklace; she said it was meant to be a coming-of-age present, and tonight looked like as good a time as any. And Daddy told me to kick my shoes off at the proper moment, because they could get confoundedly in the way." Taylor looked thoughtful. "And since Mother started laughing when he said that, I imagine he spoke from experience, don't you?"

Trevor was laughing too hard to answer. He could picture that scene so vividly in his mind, seeing Sara's vague smile and Luke's absently paternal expression, both of them uttering their wonderfully unconventional, ridiculous, *absurd* advice in the most matter-of-fact way. In that moment, he would have traded his bank account for the privilege of having been present to see and hear them advise their firstborn in the art of seduction.

"And *now*," Taylor said sadly, "after they went to all that trouble, and I tried so hard to be sexy, *you* had to ruin everything with your silly scruples."

"Sorry!" he gasped.

"You should be! I've waited twenty-six years for you, buster—"

"Consoled by occasional strange foreign and domestic men," he pointed out meaningfully.

"That's beside the point. I was waiting for you to come along—and very patient I've been, too! There I was expecting a macho prince to come along and carry me off over his saddle, and instead I get Sir Walter Raleigh spreading his cloak over a puddle so I won't get my feet wet!"

Trevor went off again.

With no mercy, Taylor continued in the same fiercely put-upon voice. "I wanted more Don Juan—less Sir Galahad! I wanted the Black Knight instead of the White Knight! I wanted to be ravished totally—well, partially—against my will! I wanted a dash of James Bond and a pinch of Superman and a slice or two of the Lone Ranger—"

"A macho salad!" Trevor laughed even harder at the affronted expression she wore; it was belied by the wicked laughter in her eyes.

"And if we're going to talk about *decency*," she said roundly with only a faint quiver to betray her, "why don't we talk about a man who won't even let himself be decently seduced!"

"That's a contradiction in terms," he said a bit weakly.

"Not," she said, "in my dictionary, it isn't."

Trevor wiped his streaming eyes and tried to gather some vague sort of command over himself. He felt completely limp with laughter, utterly relaxed, and wholly incapable of logical thought.

"Feeling better?" she murmured suddenly.

Trevor stared at her. "You've been manipulating me, you little witch," he realized slowly.

"You were upset." Her lovely face was ingenuous. "And they do say laughter's the best medicine, after all."

He had a feeling his mouth was open and hastily closed it. He knew better than to doubt anything she'd said—particularly about her parents—but he realized his love had been playing him like a piano tuned expertly to her touch. "Three hundred years ago," he said ruefully, "you'd have been burned at the stake."

Her eyes gleamed at him. "Probably. But admit it—you do feel better."

Trevor sighed. "Yes, I feel better. I'm still not sure I'm the man for you, however."

"You laugh at my jokes," she pointed out. "And that's a more solid basis for marriage than most people ever find."

Just as she'd very nearly seduced him with black lace and garters, she now came close to performing the feat a second time. A part of him longed wistfully to share his life with a woman who could make him laugh—and feel better—in spite of himself. But there was still that part of him wary of being *too* well known.

She could read his mind.

Accordingly, he shied off again. "I'll grant that," he said carefully, "but I'm still not sure. And bear in mind, young lady, that I'll not be seduced against my will!"

"Funny, for a while there, I thought you were willing."

Trevor sent a mock glare toward her gently quizzical expression. "You know damn well I was, and stop baiting me!"

"Sorry," she murmured, still smiling.

"And now," he said sternly, "if you'll get de—uh—dressed, I'll take you home."

"I can't go home tonight," she objected.

He eyed her with foreboding. "Why not?"

"Because I'm supposed to be seducing you," she explained patiently. "If I come home before dawn, Mother and Daddy'll know I failed. Their very own daughter a failure as a temptress! Just imagine—they won't be able to hold their heads up again at their club!"

"Do they have a club?" he asked involuntarily.

"Of course they have a club, Trevor."

He got hold of himself again. "Well, no one else has to know, so they can hold their heads up."

"Trevor," she said in a very gentle, long-suffering voice, "you know my parents. D'you really believe no one else will know?"

He thought about it for a moment, then matched her tone of long-suffering. "I suppose they *would* consider it dinner-table conversation at that."

"Tennis-court conversation at the very least. And even if *they* can hold their heads up, *I'll* be utterly shamed! You wouldn't do that to me, would you?"

Trevor sighed, defeated. "If you'll promise me I won't face a shotgun wedding in the morning—"

"*Trevor!*"

"That," he said roundly, "is no promise!"

She giggled. "I promise. No shotgun wedding."

"I'm too limp to argue," he confessed wryly.

"Good. Listen, there's a dandy old movie on the late show tonight. D'you think—?"

"Why not?" He sighed again, then said in a stronger voice, "Now, since you're obviously too shameless to put your dress back on, I'm going to go find you a robe."

Taylor looked down at herself in some surprise. "I'd forgotten."

"I hadn't!" he said definitely, and he went in search of a robe with which to cover his love's distracting charms.

Chapter Seven

*I*t didn't take long to clear up the remains of Taylor's candle-light dinner. Items borrowed from her restaurant friend were washed and packed neatly back into their baskets so they could be returned the next day.

Then it was time for the late show.

A bowl of popcorn sat decorously between them on the couch. Taylor, who had categorically refused to don her dress on the grounds that what was comfortable for seduction was uncomfortable for television-viewing, was nearly swallowed whole by Trevor's blue velour robe. Legs crossed at the ankles and feet propped on his coffee table, she chatted amiably to him during commercials, clearly undisturbed by her failure to seduce him.

The violent emotions and laughter of the evening had taken their toll on Trevor. He divided his bemused attention between the TV screen and Taylor's profile, trying mentally to light a fire under those scruples of his so that he could insist on taking her home. But that fire would only sputter and die.

She'd forced his hand by coming to him, but he couldn't find it in himself to be sorry about that. Fighting his own desire to be with her had turned him into a restless, angry bear for five interminable days. He loved being with her. She turned his world upside down, but she made him laugh, and a dim part of him recognized that he hadn't laughed enough in his life.

No matter how determined he was to edge himself painlessly out of her life, he knew ruefully just how useless that determination was; if he'd had to fight only himself or only her he might have managed to walk away from her. He couldn't fight them both. And whenever he allowed himself to hope he might be able to live with her unusual gifts, a dark and primitive panic stirred in his mind.

It certainly occurred to him that he'd felt no discomfort in being with Taylor since that first day, but he couldn't deceive himself into believing the battle won. It might not have bothered him too much thus far, but there was a vast difference between a couple of weeks and thirty or forty years. And he knew himself too well not to be certain that he needed the privacy of his own mind.

Now, as they watched an old horror movie on television, he silently acknowledged the fact that he needed her, too. It was more than love, or at least more than he knew love to be. He was not fanciful, but he thought that the "more than love" he felt might well be an instinctive recognition of—a kindred spirit. More, perhaps. The other half of himself . . . perhaps.

Could he, with the best of intentions, with the best will in the world, walk away from that?

"You're getting upset again," she said softly.

"Stop reading my mind."

Her vivid, honest eyes gazed at him quizzically. "I don't have to read your mind; your face is grim."

"I'm a lousy companion, in fact," he said lightly.

"No. Just a troubled one. Are you . . . angry with me, Trevor?"

He blinked in surprise. "With you? No, of course not. Why should I be angry with you?"

Taylor's smile was a little crooked. "Well, I haven't exactly been conventional. In fact, as you said, I've been shameless. But have I been . . . wrong?"

"Wrong?" He bit back a sudden laugh. "Taylor, that's a hell of a question to ask me."

"Why?"

"Because I don't know right from wrong when I'm with you." Then he corrected himself wryly. "No, that isn't true. I know what's wrong, and it isn't you. It's me."

"Wrong for me, you mean?"

He nodded silently.

"But, why?" She half turned on the couch, folding her legs and resting an arm on the low back of the couch as she gazed seriously at him.

Her candid eyes drew the truth from him even though he was afraid it might well hurt her. "Because I'm—not comfortable with telepathy." He saw a tiny frown form in her eyes and tried to think of some way to make the truth less hurtful. "I've always believed there should be honesty in any relationship, but it's—unnerving to know I might as well speak every thought out loud. I catch myself putting up walls I shouldn't need, being guarded when I don't want to be. It isn't *you*, Taylor. It's me."

She reached for the remote control and turned the television off, then dropped it back on the coffee table and faced him again, and her expression was distressed. "Oh, Trevor, I'm sorry! I should have explained."

"Explained what?" He was gruff, feeling that he'd kicked something small and loving.

Taylor took a deep breath, clearly gathering her thoughts. "What being telepathic really means. I guess I didn't explain before now because it—it isn't *easy* to explain."

"You don't have to—"

"Yes." She gazed at him steadily. "I have to." A sudden and rueful twinkle lit her eyes. "You're perfectly entitled to sacrifice yourself on the altar of useless scruples, but I'll be damned if I'll let you sacrifice me!"

"What?" he managed, wondering when he'd lost the thread of the conversation.

"Well, maybe the choice of words was wrong, but you're putting up walls needlessly, Trevor. And if *that's* all that's standing between us, then I have to make you understand."

He nodded. "All right. But I don't see—"

"And neither do I," she interrupted firmly. "If you're afraid I'm constantly seeing into your mind, you're wrong. I've been telepathic all my life, and after twenty-six years I've learned to build walls—necessary walls—of my own. If I didn't, I'd go crazy."

"Because of the . . . mental chatter?" he asked.

"Yes. It'd be like standing in a huge room with people talking all around me; nothing would make sense, but it'd be *loud*. When I meet someone for the first time, a kind of door opens in my mind very briefly. Partly, I think, because telepathy is just another sense, and it's an old instinct to use all the senses in weighing up a stranger. But for me to deliberately open that door and look into someone's mind unnecessarily would be a horrible intrusion."

Trevor tried in vain to find the words to express the dark stirrings of panic he still felt. "But—you *can* read minds."

She seemed to realize what he meant. "Yes, but only the topmost level of consciousness. For instance, when we met, you were thinking of your brother, your job, and a restaurant you'd had dinner at the night before. Impressions from all of those were tangled in your thoughts; all I received was a *sense* of you made up of those impressions. No matter how hard I tried, I could never pull a complete thought out of your mind—just an impression of what you were thinking."

Taylor shook her head slightly. "If I'd worked all my life to sharpen that sense, maybe I could read coherent thoughts. But I can't. I can only see a tiny part of a very *surface* part of another mind. The majority of that mind is as hidden from me as it is from anyone with no ESP."

"You found that killer," he said, remembering the newspaper articles he'd read days before.

She paled slightly, her eyes going briefly dark. "The mind of a killer," she said in a low voice, "is very different from a normal mind. It . . . shouts. It isn't hard to focus on that kind of mind, but I still get only impressions."

Regretting his unthinking remark, Trevor attempted to draw her thoughts away from that dark mind she'd seen. "You always seem to know what I'm thinking," he said with forced lightness.

"Not what you're *thinking*," she corrected. "What you're *feeling*. I mean, I always know your—your mood. That isn't telepathy, Trevor. It's empathy."

More than a little startled, Trevor realized then that he was usually very aware of *her* moods. Empathy? Recognition of a kindred spirit? He put the thought aside and focused on one of the most insidious, pleasant, unnerving facets of her telepathy. "Whenever we touch," he said slowly, "I feel a strong sense of— of well-being. As if I were wrapped in a blanket."

"You, too?" Her honest eyes held a shy, delighted smile. "I thought it was just me."

"It has nothing to do with your telepathy?" he asked incredulously, all his doubts and preconceptions swaying on their foundations.

"I've never felt that before, so I don't think so." She leaned toward him anxiously. "Trevor, I haven't read your mind since that first day."

"You haven't?"

"No."

Impossible to doubt those naked eyes. He felt a heavy load lift from his shoulders. "Well, hell, why didn't you tell me?" he demanded wrathfully.

She laughed unsteadily. "How was I to know? Since I didn't read your mind, I just assumed you were bothered by my chasing you!"

Surprised yet again, Trevor said blankly, "I suppose I should have been, but, you know, that never bothered me at all."

"And you called *me* shameless! Being chased pandered to your ego, didn't it? Admit it!"

He grinned. "Well, I've never gotten flowers or candy before. It was a . . . novel experience."

Taylor lifted the bowl of popcorn between them, looking at him with a solemn expression and dancing eyes. "Do we really need this duenna anymore?"

He could hardly help but laugh. "No. *If* you've given up your intention of seducing me tonight. I still think we need a little time. Without walls between us now."

"If you insist. But I already know everything I need to know." She leaned over to place the bowl on the coffee table, then used the remote control to turn the television back on.

Trevor slipped an arm around her as she curled up at his side. "Oh, you do, do you?"

"Certainly. I know that you're a humorous, caring, sensitive man. I really don't need to know anything else."

"I thought you said I wasn't macho enough," he objected dryly.

"Only where your scruples and my virtue are concerned. Otherwise, you're perfect."

"I'll try to do better next time, ma'am," he murmured, humble.

Blue eyes glinted up at him before returning to the television screen. "I'll make certain of it," she said gently.

The late show turned out to be an all-night horror festival, and somewhere in the middle of it they both fell asleep. It was an easy thing to accomplish, since they'd stretched out during the second movie by mutual consent, both turned facing the set with Taylor's back to Trevor and his arms around her.

Trevor had never slept so well. He woke to bright sunlight streaming through the windows, hearing the murmur of an early news program on television and feeling the warmth of her in his arms.

It was, he decided, a very nice way to wake up.

"You *don't* snore," she murmured.

"That's odd. I thought I did."

"Liar."

"So I told one small white lie. *You* came here with the fixed intention of seducing me."

"I'm shameless, and you're a liar. Don't we make a perfect couple?"

"I plead the fifth amendment."

"Coward."

He laughed softly, tightening his arms around her. "I won't bother trying to defend myself on that one. Instead, why don't we have breakfast?"

"Does it occur to you that we spend a great deal of our time together either cooking or eating?"

"It crossed my mind. D'you suppose there's some Freudian meaning behind that?"

"Likely just hunger," she said practically. She sat up and swung her feet to the floor as he released her, looking down at him with a smile.

He gazed up at her for a moment, taking in the tousled chestnut hair and bright blue eyes. The robe's belt had worked loose during the night, the open lapels revealing black silk and lace; Trevor silently acquitted her of deliberate enticement, but he had to swallow hard before he could speak. "I might have known," he muttered in a long-suffering tone, "you'd look as beautiful in the morning as you do any other time."

Taylor leaned down and kissed him fleetingly, her hand lingering on his cheek. "Thank you, sir," she said gravely. "You look pretty good yourself—in spite of the stubble."

For the first time in his adult life, Trevor found a distinct pleasure in his fairly heavy morning beard; the tingling caress of her fingers was one for which he would have willingly let his razor grow rusty. "I have to shave," he said reluctantly.

"Only if you want to," she said. "I don't object to beards."

Dryly, he asked, "Is there anything you do object to?"

"Yes. Eggs in the morning." She stood up, absently drawing the robe's lapels together and tightening the belt. She stretched slightly, unconsciously luxuriating in the blissful morning action. "Do you like waffles?"

"Love 'em."

"Then if you have the fixings, that's what I'll make."

He got to his feet, stretching as unconsciously as she had. "I have the fixings, but you shouldn't have to cook; you're a guest."

"Forced on you against your will," she recalled soulfully. "Cooking will be my penance."

Trevor managed to swat her one on the fanny before she escaped, laughing, to the kitchen. He smiled after her for a moment, realized abruptly that he probably looked like a besotted teenager, then mentally decided not to give a damn. Feeling much more cheerful today than he had yesterday morning, he went off to shave.

He'd once heard a woman say that shaving to a man was like washing dishes to a woman—before electric dishwashers; it was an automatic, curiously soothing action, allowing the mind to range free. Trevor agreed that shaving tended to free the mind; he'd more than once worked out some tricky problem or legal question while gazing absently into a steamed mirror.

This morning, his mind focused inevitably on Taylor and their night together. The evening before was divided by his mind into four separate and distinct parts. Part one had been seduction, part two had been laughter, part three revelation, and part four an amazingly restful sleep. For the first two, he felt no surprise; seduction and laughter were quite definitely a part of their relationship. The fourth part amazed him only because he wasn't a gibbering idiot after holding her platonically in his arms all night.

Part three occupied his thoughts. Revelation. He never hesitated in accepting her assurances regarding the telepathy. She didn't read his mind, and that meant that there was no reason for the wall he'd built between them. However, he knew the wall still existed in a ghostly form, elusive and still vaguely troubling.

And he couldn't fully commit himself until he was certain that faint barrier posed no threat to them.

He pondered that wall as he shaved. It was formed of fear, he thought, a primitive and unreasoning fear of the unknown and the misunderstood. Applying logic in a determined attempt to breach that fear, he reminded himself that there was only a tiny part of his mind she could see into *anyway*. It helped, but the wall remained a nebulous threat.

Trevor thought he could deal with it eventually. Experience. A surer knowledge of Taylor gained through time. A gradual relaxing of the guards people inevitably raised against one another in the tentative beginnings of a relationship.

Wanting that relationship, he thought, would go a long way in helping. And he very badly wanted Taylor to become a permanent part of his life. She made him feel a better man than he knew himself to be, a fact he acknowledged with an inner rueful sigh. There were no rosy glasses blinding Taylor's honest eyes; she knew well that he was far from perfect. But she thought him perfect for her, and for that very unusual and fascinating woman to believe that of him was a compliment Trevor found both moving and bemusing.

Belonging to Taylor.

It meant laughing. And loving. It meant being known and understood, a fact that caused a faint uneasy quiver to disturb some deep part of him, but was, on some other level of himself, curiously pleasing.

But . . . could he ever know her that well? She was endlessly fascinating, his love, blessed with the gifts of humor and tolerance and honesty. Her unconventional upbringing had left her with few subtleties or feminine evasions at her command; she would never be blunt to the point of hurting another, but she'd always be honest, he knew.

Abruptly, superimposed over his own cloudy image in the mirror, he saw those honest eyes staring at him blindly.

"I wish it was the other way around. I wish I could cry when it mattered and not when it didn't."

A sensitive woman, her vulnerability for the most part hidden within her—like those unshed tears that mattered. A woman who was the calm, practical hub around which her ridiculous family turned, and yet who could herself become absurd at the drop of a hat. She was invariably cheerful, yet her psychic gift had shown her the darker side of humanity, had given her eyes to see into a madman's sick, murderous thoughts.

And not just one madman, Trevor realized painfully; she felt "a responsibility to do what I can to help." To help capture madmen, she'd willingly expose herself to those dark and twisted thoughts.

Automatically wiping way the steam obscuring the mirror, Trevor gazed into his own suddenly blind eyes.

She believed he was the man for her, and he realized then that he had never really considered their relationship from her point of view. "Sensitive," she'd called him. *Fool!* he called himself. He knew that he'd nearly had it once, nearly realized why she needed him—and it had thrown him into a blind panic.

She didn't need the dark gremlins hidden in his own mind; she only needed his willingness to share them.

That was all. All! If he could be willing to share his vulnerability, then she would share hers. It would not be an exchange of dark and guilty secrets, hurts, fears, but a simple knowing and understanding of them. Trust. Openness. And most of all . . . love.

Trevor had heard all the rhetoric. Times had changed. *People* had changed. Women could be strong and men sensitive. Women could be assertive and men understanding. Women could be forceful and men intuitive. But knowing it *could* be done was only half the problem solved.

Knowing that a man could cry made his unshed tears no easier than those a strong woman held at bay within her.

Taylor couldn't cry when it mattered, and neither could Trevor.

For her, he thought, the tears refused to come because her psychic abilities guarded her mind so carefully. For him, he knew, the tears a boy might have learned to shed had been deeply buried by a man's responsibilities. He'd been eighteen when their parents had been killed, his own shock and grief numbed by the necessity of raising his ten-year-old brother.

Jason had been able to cry, but Trevor, willingly accepting the role of parent, had buried his own tears, comforted Jason as best he could, and picked up the threads of their lives. And his brother would never know, although he might well guess, the sleepless nights and anxiety that had tormented Trevor. Their parents had left them far from penniless, but Trevor had struggled nonetheless in raising Jason and putting them both through school.

He regretted none of it, but he wished now that he'd allowed himself to share his brother's tears. For, having once accepted a stoic path, Trevor had found it impossible to retrace his steps. How could he be vulnerable when Jason had needed him to be strong?

How indeed.

But Jason had his own life now. And Trevor could see now how that first stoic step had molded his way of thinking. Even his choice of law as a career had reinforced the impassive surface of himself. How many times had he swayed a jury with emotional rhetoric while a part of him had watched analytically for the reaction he sought?

He'd learned to play with the emotions of others while keeping his own tightly bound in dark silence. Even his love for Jason had been an unspoken thing, proving itself in gruff gestures rather than words. Thankfully, Jason had seen through to the truth, Trevor thought.

And Taylor . . . Taylor. She called it empathy, this sensing of moods and understanding of them. She with the naked eyes holding the power to pull emotions from him and tease him into enjoying it. She had brought his emotions much closer to the surface—because *she* needed that as much as he did.

The other half of himself . . . the emotional, intuitive part of him buried for so long. They were, he realized with a sudden flash of insight, almost mirror images of each other—but reversed. His mind flew back to that first day. Taylor, on the surface a cheerful woman brought easily to laughter or tears, but underneath so very controlled because she'd been forced to build shields around her sensitive mind and heart. Trevor, outwardly controlled and stoic, calm and logical, but inwardly a caldron boiling with nearly fifteen years of suppressed love, laughter, and tears.

In a blink of time, Taylor had begun guilelessly to free those tightly bound emotions within him. And laughter, because it comes easiest, had fought its way free first. Love was struggling, but the chains binding it were snapping one by one. Tears would be the most difficult to free.

And Taylor, he realized slowly, had begun changing herself. There was now a curious blending of the very cheerful woman and the controlled one. Absurd as her humor sometimes was, there were deeper meanings to it now—such as when she had deliberately roused him to laughter to ease his troubled mind. And she had allowed him to glimpse the vulnerable part of her, to see her pain at a madman's thoughts, to see her diffidence at her own reckless "seduction" plans. The wonder at seeing herself reflected in a man's—his—passionate eyes.

Trevor grappled with the thoughts as he left the bathroom and headed for the kitchen. They could free each other, he realized dimly. Somehow, through an elusive but very real ... empathy ... they could free each other from cages only vaguely perceived.

He stopped in the doorway of the kitchen and watched her silently. She looked tiny and fragile in his robe, the sleeves turned back several times on her slender arms and the hem falling past her knees. Her hair was still gloriously tousled, the pins that had confined it last night now lost and unremembered. She was handling the waffle iron with the expert touch of a born cook and humming softly to herself.

He banked his thoughts carefully in his mind and stepped into the room. Whether those thoughts were right or wrong would only be proven, he knew, with time.

She looked over her shoulder at him, smiling. "I was afraid you'd cut your throat," she confided, neatly flipping the golden-brown waffles onto plates.

"Nope. Didn't even nick myself." It didn't surprise him to hear his own calm, bantering tone; with Taylor, falling into a companionable mood was rather like one foot automatically following the other.

They sat down at the breakfast table in the kitchen, and for a while conversation was limited to the mundane but necessary.

"Would you pass the butter, please?"

"Certainly. More coffee?"

"Thank you."

With the meal nearly finished, Trevor said, "Are you sure there'll be no shotgun wedding on the agenda?"

"I promised, didn't I?" she countered serenely.

He looked at her. "Under these circumstances with any other family, I'd be tempted to ask why not. With your family, I'm afraid to hear the answer."

Taylor's eyes were filled with mischief. "Well, I'm not saying that Daddy wouldn't rouse himself enough to defend his daughter's honor, you understand."

"Then why no shotgun wedding?" His gaze narrowed suspiciously. "If your father decks me the way he did the Frenchman—"

She laughed. "No, of course he won't. Trevor, you forget—my entire family's psychic. Daddy'll know the instant he sees me that my virtue is still very much intact."

Trevor blinked. Then, dryly, he said, "I *did* forget, dammit. You little witch. So they'll never be able to hold their heads up at the club, huh?"

After sipping her coffee, Taylor smiled seraphically. "I was worried about the *neighbors* seeing me."

"You were not. We agreed—I remember distinctly—that your parents couldn't resist telling everyone that you weren't, in spite of all efforts, a fallen woman. You were determined to spend the night here, weren't you? No, never mind answering that. It's obvious. Just tell me why." Trevor was looking forward to one of her ridiculous answers, and he wasn't disappointed.

"Well," she said seriously. "I was rather hoping to be ravished in the middle of the night. But you slept like the dead."

"Sorry," he managed faintly, fighting the desire to burst out laughing.

"You should be!" she scolded. "I even managed to get us both in a prone position on the couch—and you fell asleep. Asleep!" Frowning slightly, she asked quizzically, "Should I try a different perfume? Or maybe a lavender teddy instead of black?"

Trevor fought manfully. "Has it occurred to you that it wasn't a question of your—uh—seductiveness, but rather my willpower?"

"Was that it?" she asked, interested. "I didn't do anything wrong?"

"Nothing that I noticed," he said ruefully.

"We," she said firmly, "have to talk further about these noble scruples of yours."

"We've already talked about them. We're going to take the time to get to know each other—remember?"

"But I'm not getting any younger," she protested, aggrieved. "And I want babies!"

He eyed her, fascinated. "What'll you say next?"

"Whatever pops into my head." She grinned suddenly, the vivid blue eyes wickedly amused.

Trevor drew a deep breath and pushed his chair back. "I'm going to clean up in here, and you're going to get dressed—"

"You do want babies, don't you?" she interrupted briskly.

"A hint toward the stability of our future relationship," he advised in a careful tone. "Never—never—ask me loaded questions before nine A.M."

"All right," she said agreeably. "I'll ask again later."

"Much later."

"How much later?"

"Taylor, if you don't go and put your dress on right now—" He broke off and stared into the eyes watching him hopefully. "Witch!" he said feelingly. "Go get dressed!"

Laughing, she slipped from her chair and left the room.

Trevor found himself smiling like a smitten schoolboy again and shook his head at himself. A beautiful, seductive woman in his apartment wearing nothing but his robe and a black teddy, and he was ordering her to get dressed.

Ridiculous.

He was obviously losing his mind.

Jason would've split his sides laughing.

Chapter Eight

Trevor's willpower withstood the test of zipping Taylor's dress for her, but his finger-and-toehold at the edge of sobriety crumbled—as usual—the moment they entered her house.

With any other family, under the circumstances, Trevor would have accompanied her inside to explain her innocent all-night stay at his apartment; she was over twenty-one, but she lived at home and could have been expected, to some extent, to answer to her father.

However, this was the Shannon family. Trevor didn't go in with her to explain anything at all. He went because he wanted to be with her. And he went because he was curious to see the family's reaction.

Sara entered the hall from the den just as they came in the front door, and stood gazing at them with her vague gray eyes. Those seemingly hazy eyes took in Taylor's slightly rumpled appearance and blatantly innocent face, then shifted to Trevor's carefully grave face.

"Oh, dear," Sara said mildly but with distressed undertones. "Darling, you can't let it bother you. I'm sure you'll do better next time."

"I plan to, Mother," Taylor responded solemnly.

Trevor bit down hard on his inner cheek in an attempt to fight the laughter.

Sara peered at him, a little doubtful. "You mustn't think I'm being critical, Trevor," she said gently, "but I really think you shouldn't have disappointed the child. She was so looking forward to it."

He choked swallowing the laugh in his throat. He knew only too well that none of his rational arguments would have any effect on Sara, so he didn't attempt any. Holding his voice level with a tremendous effort, he said, "You are an unnatural mother, Sara."

"Am I?" She smiled at him. "I suppose so. But such fun for the children."

Luke wandered in just then, holding a distributor cap. He addressed his wife sternly. "What is this doing in the kitchen?"

"It fell out of the car," she told him.

"They don't just fall out," he objected.

"It did."

Her husband ran a hand through his blond hair, his abstracted expression holding the rueful acceptance of odd things occurring in his wife's orbit. "Well, I'll put it back later."

"The car runs without it," she observed.

He stared at her. "It isn't supposed to."

"It does."

Luke sighed. "It would for you. Not for anyone else. Hello," he added, apparently just noticing his daughter and Trevor. Before they could respond, his brilliant blue eyes became stern again. They focused on Taylor.

"Sorry, Daddy," she said meekly.

The frowning eyes lifted to Trevor, and he fought an instinctive urge to apologize as well. Instead, he met the gaze with all the severity he could muster in his own eyes.

Luke turned back to his wife. "We'll never be able to hold our heads up at the club," he said in a pained voice.

Trevor didn't dare meet Taylor's eyes.

"I know," Sara said seriously. "But I think it was more a matter of Trevor's willpower than Taylor's sex appeal."

Frowning at Trevor, Luke demanded, "Well?"

"Quite true," he answered faintly.

"Willpower," Luke told him in a ridiculously paternal voice, "is a very good thing—in its proper place. But you want to make sure you don't end up being stuffy."

Trevor nodded, not trusting his voice.

"Well, that's all right, then." Luke was cheerful again. "Can you drive a nail? I have to build a tree house for Dory."

"I can drive a nail."

"Then you can help me. Taylor, why don't we barbecue for lunch?"

"All right, Daddy." She sent Trevor a look brimful of laughter. "I'll go change and then see what we have to barbecue."

"Yes, do," he said absently, already taking Trevor's arm and leading him from the hall.

Trevor went.

The remainder of the morning and early afternoon flew by. Trevor managed not to bruise a thumb or nail his fingers to the tree while assisting Luke to build a tree house. They had barbecued chicken for lunch and a general family clean-up in the kitchen—which meant that it took twice as long to get everything put away neatly with the vaguely incapable "help" of certain members of the family.

Luke instigated a Frisbee game in the backyard and exhausted everyone but himself. They ended up sprawled in various positions beneath the trees, enjoying the shade and quiet as they watched the eldest Shannon industriously weeding a small flower bed in the shade.

Trevor shared the hammock with Taylor, drowsy and content. A part of him was a bit bemused, since she'd several times absently called him "darling." He looked around at the other peaceful members of the family—and one busy one—feeling very much a part of them. Dory was asleep with her head in Sara's lap, Jamie was stretched out nearby on her stomach with a book propped before her, and Jessie leaned against a tree with sheet music in her lap and her fingers playing an imaginary piano.

The blow, when it came, was as out of place in the peaceful scene as such blows always tended to be.

"Trevor."

He turned his head to respond to Luke's voice. Then slowly, he sat up in the hammock, feeling an inexplicable chill. He could feel Taylor's sudden tension as she, too, sat up, both of them staring at her father.

Luke was sitting back on his heels, garden tools overflowing the basket beside him. The tools and the flowers were forgotten. Luke was gazing at Trevor steadily, his brilliant eyes not the least abstracted and his handsome face unusually grim. His voice, when he spoke, held the same curiously chilling evenness that had caught their tense attention.

"Your brother's . . . hiking somewhere."

"In Wyoming."

Taylor softly asked the question Trevor couldn't ask. "What's wrong, Daddy?"

Her father continued to stare intently at Trevor—but through him somehow. As if he were seeing something else entirely. "Have you talked to him?" he asked slowly.

"Not since I put him on the plane Monday." Coldness was seeping all through Trevor, gripping his heart in sudden dread.

Very quietly, Luke said, "Maybe you'd better try getting in touch with him. There'll be a freak blizzard there tomorrow . . . and I think he's in trouble."

Trevor was hardly aware of slipping from the hammock and didn't realize until he was inside the house that he was tightly holding Taylor's hand. The warmth of her hand was the only warmth he felt; all else was coldness. He told himself fiercely that Jason was all right, that he was, even now, staying with his college friend in Casper as he'd planned to do the last few days of his vacation.

He told himself that, but the coldness held him.

It was difficult to think clearly, but Trevor forced himself to. He released Taylor's hand as they reached the telephone in the hall, silently grateful that she remained nearby. He met her anxious eyes, his own a little blind as he grappled mentally for the phone number only dimly remembered from other vacations. Desperation found the number, and steady fingers dialed. He kept his voice calm somehow when a worried voice answered far away.

"Hello?"

"Owen, this is Trevor. Is Jason—"

"Trevor! I've been trying to reach you since this morning."

"What's wrong?" Trevor asked steadily.

Owen sighed raggedly. "Jason was supposed to be back here in Casper yesterday morning. When he never showed, I got worried and called that lodge up in the mountains where he's staying. They sent out a search-and-rescue team, and they've alerted the Rangers. Trevor, there's snow on some of those high peaks, and a blizzard forecast for tomorrow. Jason must have gotten off the trails, or they would have found him by now. And with a storm coming—"

"I'll catch the first flight," Trevor said numbly.

"I'll meet you at the airport."

Trevor cradled the receiver slowly. He stared at Taylor, unable to force a single word past his blocked throat. But out of the fear gripping him rose a sudden terrible need to have her with him. He wasn't thinking of her psychic abilities, but only of her quiet strength. For the first time in his adult life, he needed a strength he couldn't find in himself.

Taylor stepped forward, her hand a comforting touch on his arm. "I may be able to help."

He nodded silently, then reached for the phone again as she hurried upstairs to pack. A toneless voice came from somewhere to book two seats on the next available flight to Casper, and he had to restrain driving impatience when he found that the flight left in two hours. By the time he hung up the phone, Taylor was back with a quilted jacket flung over one arm and a small bag in her other hand.

It was she who quickly and briefly explained the trip to her parents, both of whom were concerned and neither surprised. Luke said only, "He's alive, Trevor." It helped—but not much.

They were quiet on the drive to Trevor's apartment, where he hastily packed a few things. Quiet all the way to the airport and during the interminable wait for their flight.

Trevor paced while he could, then sat beside Taylor on the plane and railed silently at the time it was taking him to get to Jason. He hated the helplessness of not being able to do a damn thing to help his brother, gnawing anxiety tormenting him. And guilt.

Taylor's hand slipped into his as the plane finally took off, and when his fingers closed over hers fiercely, she spoke in a soft voice. "He'll be all right, Trevor."

He stared blindly down at their clasped hands. "I keep telling myself that," he said hoarsely. "I have to believe it. It's just been the two of us for so long. . . ."

"You raised him, didn't you?" Her voice was still soft, gentle. "Tell me about it."

He found himself talking, rapidly and disjointedly. Telling her things he'd not told a living soul until now. About Jason and about himself. About Little League games and parent-teacher meetings, broken arms and bloody noses. About the little anxieties of report cards and neat bedrooms, and the larger ones of late dates and accidents. About his own feelings of ineptitude in assuming the role of parent, his worry at the responsibility for another life. The sleepless nights and careful, anxious balancing of checkbooks.

He told her about teaching Jason to shave, to drive, to cook. About fishing trips and hiking trips and ball games. Sipping the coffee he couldn't remember ordering, he told her about raising a boy to be a man when he wasn't sure himself what it *meant* to be a man.

He told her briefly about a woman who hadn't been able to accept the presence of his brother in her life, and of Jason's only recently discovered feelings about that. He told her about the wrenching loneliness of Jason's college years and the final pang of seeing his brother a man grown and living apart from him.

And he told her of the guilt he felt now. Jason would have stayed in Chicago if he'd asked, not gone at all. . . .

"You couldn't have known."

"I put him on that plane!"

"You couldn't have known, darling."

"He knew I needed to talk—and wouldn't. He knew. He would have stayed if I'd asked. But I turned away from him. I couldn't talk to him. He saw me too clearly, and I couldn't bear that, so I put him on that plane."

"You needed to talk?"

Trevor nodded. He looked at her, forced a wry smile. "I was trying to come to terms with . . . how I felt about you."

Taylor didn't ask the question nine out of ten women would have asked. Not "How did you feel?" but a simple, "And you couldn't talk about that to him. I'm sure he understood, Trevor."

"But I've never been able to talk to him!" Trevor said savagely. "Not about anything that mattered. I've never told him I love him. I haven't even hugged him since he was a kid. God, I've made so many mistakes!"

"Jason's a fine man, isn't he?"

"Yes," Trevor said in a softer voice. "Yes, he is."

"Then your mistakes didn't hurt him. Trevor, you're human. You were a boy forced to be a man too soon, forced to shoulder his life as well as your own. But you did it. You raised your brother to be a fine man."

"I'm . . . proud of him," Trevor said, his voice almost inaudible. "And I've never told him that."

"You will."

"Unless it's . . . too late."

"It won't be."

He accepted that because he had to, needed to. And his own words set up an echo in his mind. *Too late . . . too late . . . too late. . . .* He looked at her, saw her clearly, and realized that it wasn't too late for one thing, at least. He heard his own voice emerge, queerly conversational but strained.

"I love you, you know."

Taylor smiled slowly, eyes glowing. "I'm glad. I love you, too," she said simply.

Trevor barely heard the pilot announcing their descent into

Casper; all his attention was focused on that beloved, fascinating face. "I couldn't tell you before. I was . . . afraid. I thought I needed time to . . . learn. Time to find out if I could give you what you needed."

"You have," she said, softly. "All I needed was your love, Trevor."

He realized then what he'd done. "All that about raising Jason," he said slowly. "I've never told anyone that before. I . . . needed to. But I never did. I was always afraid to . . . let it out."

"And now?"

With a sudden feeling of release, a feeling of burdens lifted, Trevor realized that the ghostly wall in his mind was gone. The fear and anxiety over Jason had driven him to talk, and he had instinctively reached out to the woman he loved. He looked at her wonderingly.

Taylor, gazing into that strong face that hid his vulnerability so well, felt the breath catch in her throat. He was looking at her, finally, as if he were finding what he wanted, needed, in her own face. As if, perhaps, he'd only just realized how much he needed. As if he were astonished and moved unbearably to see what he needed in her.

"And now I love you," he said huskily. "God, how I love you!" He leaned forward to kiss her tenderly. The vivid blue eyes gazing softly into his were brighter than ever, and he realized only then that she was crying silently.

"Taylor . . ."

She laughed shakily, one hand lifting to touch her wet cheeks. "I'm crying because it matters," she marveled. "Finally because it matters. Oh, Trevor, I love you so much!"

They had shoved the world aside for those few precious moments, but now it intruded again as the plane touched down and taxied toward its particular gate. But the warmth of their love

surrounded them both, cushioning against the chill of Jason's dis-
appearance. Wrapped in that love, they automatically gathered
their things and left the plane, Trevor's hand instantly catching
hers once the narrow aisle had been left behind them.

A blond young man waited restlessly for them just inside the
building, his lean face troubled and anxious. He greeted Trevor
with "No word yet," and responded politely to the introduction to
Taylor.

"I've chartered a helicopter to take us up to the lodge," he told
them as they worked their way through the crowd. "The search
teams are based there, coordinated by the Rangers."

It wasn't until they were in the noisy helicopter and lifting
high in the chill air above Casper that a sudden thought occurred
to Trevor. Using the headphones that made conversation possible,
he asked Owen, "Did Jason leave any of his clothes at the lodge?"

"I think so," Owen called back. "Why d'you ask?"

Trevor looked at his love, and she responded with a decided
nod. "The lady's psychic," he explained to Jason's friend. "Maybe
she can find a trail for us."

Owen turned in his seat to favor Taylor with a long, interested
look, then nodded. "I sure as hell hope so." He gestured worriedly
at the sun sinking rapidly in the west. "We'll have at best a couple of hours of daylight left. The teams can search at night, but it's
black as pitch up there. The Rangers'll probably want us to wait at
the lodge after dark."

"If we haven't found Jason by dark, they'll want in vain,"
Trevor said calmly. He looked down at Taylor again. "Can you
ride?" he asked quietly.

She nodded. "And I've ridden on mountain trails before."

He squeezed her hand. "I've been up here a couple of times
with Jason," he told both her and Owen. "I know the area almost
as well as he does."

Owen nodded, then hesitated before saying casually, "There's a doctor staying at the lodge."

Trevor only nodded in response, but his throat tightened. Almost instantly, he felt the warmth of the "security blanket" creeping over him. His own inner anguish had blocked that feeling until he had reached out to Taylor on the plane. Now he felt it wrapping him gently in strength and warmth, and he smiled down at Taylor, lifting her hand briefly to his lips.

"He'll be all right," she said firmly.

"Yes." He'd be all right. *He had to be all right.*

The helicopter touched down in a clearing near a rambling log building nestled in a high valley. A temperature quite a few degrees colder than they'd left in Casper greeted them as they climbed out of the machine and hurried toward the lodge together.

Inside, they found a comfortable "hunters' " lodge, the pine-paneled walls hung with hunting and fishing trophies, the people milling about in the large lobby-den mostly men. All were dressed for warmth and preparing lanterns and strong flashlights, and all wore grim faces.

A swift question from Trevor caused them to drop their bags by the casual desk and turn quickly toward a tall man, his heavy jacket nearly hiding the uniform beneath. Trevor introduced himself and his two companions, discovering that Owen knew the man in charge of the rescue teams.

The Ranger, whose name was Pat Carmichael, favored the two strangers with a fleeting but keen once-over from tired brown eyes. "There isn't much I can tell you." He was speaking directly to Trevor. "We know he headed north, and we've combed all the lower trails. It'll take time to cover the higher ground, and that's something we may be short of if the weather prediction's accurate—and I think it will be. I've lived in these mountains too long not to know a storm's coming. If snow catches the searchers up on the high trails . . ."

He didn't have to finish the statement; Trevor knew full well that the search would have to be called off in bad weather. "If we can borrow some gear and horses," he said evenly, "you'll have three more for the search."

"Those mountain trails are tricky—"

"We'll manage."

The tired brown eyes measured him thoughtfully, then glanced down at Taylor. "How about the lady? No offense, ma'am."

"None taken," she said promptly. "I can manage, too, Mr. Carmichael. In fact, I may be able to shorten the search. If Jason left some clothes here, that is."

"How's that, ma'am?" he asked mildly.

She met his inquiring eyes squarely. "I'm psychic," she said bluntly. "I may be able to point us in the right direction."

The Ranger seemed to weigh her small, determined self, then nodded slightly. "Never believed in that myself," he said, still mild. "But I've seen stranger things in these mountains. And I'd be a fool to turn down any help offered—if Mr. King here was to *let* me turn it down, which I doubt. You're welcome, ma'am."

Taylor nodded and turned to Trevor. "I'll get his room key and check on the clothes."

He watched her hurry away, the warmth of her presence still with him; he realized then that he'd never lose it as long as he had her. With the Ranger's earlier bleak words ringing in his mind, he badly needed that warmth.

"Think she can find him?" Carmichael asked quietly.

Trevor met the other man's intent gaze. "I think she can find him," he responded, just as quiet.

The Ranger nodded, accepting. "You'll all need heavier coats than those you have," he said. "Hats and gloves, too. This way."

Taylor came back downstairs just in time to shrug herself into the heavier coat Carmichael had found for her. It was a bit large but much warmer than her own quilted jacket. But she refused the proffered gloves. In her hand was a flannel shirt Trevor recognized as Jason's, and her eyes were more vivid than he'd ever seen them.

Carmichael protested her refusal of the gloves. "Ma'am, the temperature's dropping like a brick out there, your hands'll be frozen inside an hour!"

She shook her head firmly. "I have to be able to hold this—without gloves. I'll be fine."

Trevor took the gloves and silently put them in his pocket, as worried as the Ranger was about her hands but knowing better than to protest.

Sighing in defeat, Carmichael said only, "I suppose you know what you're doing, ma'am." He led the group outside, where a dozen horses waited, efficiently splitting the searchers into three groups and assigning the ground to be covered as well as a Ranger to each group. As Trevor had expected, Carmichael assigned himself to the three most concerned with Jason's well-being.

It would be a clear night boasting a full moon, a fact the Ranger wryly gave thanks for as he led the way from the lodge and up a gradually steepening trail. The horses were mountain-bred, carrying their riders easily and finding footholds where a goat would have balked.

The temperature dropped steadily.

Carmichael rode in the lead, with Taylor behind him. Then Trevor, with Owen bringing up the rear. It was still light enough to see without lanterns or flashlights, and they made good time for the first hour. Conversation was brief, dealing only with necessities. The Ranger kept in touch with the other search parties with a walkie-talkie, the negative reports drawing curt responses from him.

Taylor said almost nothing at all, but Trevor could glimpse from time to time her fingers moving over the shirt she held firmly. She rode easily, her slender body swaying to her horse's movements. She made no objection to the Ranger's choice of direction until they were slightly more than an hour from the lodge. Then, at a fork in the path they followed, she spoke up.

"Not that way."

Carmichael turned in the saddle as he halted his horse, looking at her searchingly through the gathering twilight. "That trail's no more than a rabbit lane, ma'am," he said, indicating the path he'd been on the point of ignoring. "It peters out after a hundred yards or so, and the rest is straight up. A man on foot—"

Fingering the shirt she held, Taylor pointed firmly with the hand grasping the reins. "That's the way he went."

"He wasn't wearing that shirt—" the Ranger objected, but was cut off fiercely.

"Not the shirt! *Him!* He went that way."

After a single glance at Trevor's face, Carmichael turned his horse toward the "rabbit lane." Clearly, though doubting the lady's judgment, he was unwilling to draw Trevor's defensive fire.

The trail narrowed as they moved along it, disappearing for good at the Ranger's estimate of a hundred yards. They had to pick their way cautiously, working around boulders and naked granite cliffs. The moon rose to provide some light, but flashlights were used more and more often to point ahead and search out obstacles. Taylor ordered a change in direction twice more, both times too definitely to invite argument.

And it was getting colder by the minute.

Three hours into the search, Taylor suddenly stopped her horse, her head moving in a horizon-sweeping gesture. "He's near," she said, the words misting in front of her face. "Close. Trevor—"

She didn't have to finish. *"Jason!"* he called out ringingly.

Echoes, then silence met their straining ears.

Taylor wasn't discouraged. She changed direction again, leading the way this time. After another hundred yards or so, she halted and glanced back at Trevor. Again, he shouted his brother's name.

Trevor strained to hear, all his concentration focused to catch the slightest sound. Was that—? Had he heard—?

She urged her horse forward, angling down a rocky slope with a sudden reckless haste.

"Be careful!" both Trevor and the Ranger shouted, urging their own horses to follow. They were only a few yards behind her when Taylor abruptly halted her horse and slid quickly from the saddle. And all three men reached her just as Taylor was lying flat on the crumbling edge of a ravine and peering down into the darkness.

"A flashlight!" she ordered breathlessly.

Carmichael halted Trevor as he started to cross the scant feet to the ravine's edge. "On your belly," he ordered tersely, handing the flashlight over. "And slowly; that edge could give way at any minute."

The edge . . .

Fear for her as well as Jason blocking his throat, Trevor lay flat and moved cautiously to her side. He flicked the flashlight on and pointed it over the edge, sweeping slowly along the bottom a good twenty feet below them. And the beam caught a red hunter's vest—necessary for a hiker wherever hunting was allowed—and eyes squinting out of a pale face. Taylor had been unerring; he was directly below them.

"Hey!" Jason called up to them in a faint voice.

Trevor had to swallow before he could respond. And relief made his response furious. "Jason, what the hell are you doing down there?"

"Mostly just lyin' here," Jason answered, rueful in spite of the exhausted voice. "Brother, you picked a dandy time to visit."

"Are you hurt?" Trevor called down, ignoring the humor although it made him feel better about Jason's condition.

"A few bruises and one slightly broken leg." Jason's voice faded toward the end of the sentence, then strengthened again. "I'm also a little cold and a lot thirsty—my canteen's empty, dammit."

"Hang on. I'll be down there in a minute," Trevor said, pulling Taylor with him as he eased back from the edge.

But in the end, it was Taylor who went down first.

While Carmichael summoned the other searchers and got the rope from his saddle, she was busy unfastening the backpack containing the first-aid kit from her own saddle.

"I'm a doctor's daughter, Trevor, and I've worked with him; I know as much as any paramedic. Besides, I'm the lightest, and we don't know how much that edge'll stand. Let me go down first."

Trevor argued, but the Ranger agreed with her once he heard her reasoning, and even Trevor was forced to give in when she briskly claimed experience in bellying down more than one mountainside at the end of a rope. So Taylor tucked two blankets and a thermos of hot coffee into her pack, and the men very cautiously lowered her over the edge.

She obviously knew what she was doing, making the descent quickly but safely.

A scant five minutes later, Trevor joined her in the narrow, rock-strewn bottom of the ravine, untying the rope and hurrying to kneel by his brother. He'd brought two battery-powered lanterns with him, and with both alight there was plenty of brightness.

Already Taylor had used her empty pack and Jason's shirt to pillow his head, and he was half propped up and sipping hot coffee gratefully, a blanket covering all but the leg she was carefully and gently examining.

"Brat!" Trevor said roughly, gripping his brother's shoulder.

Jason's face was pale with exhaustion, pain, and shock, but the gray eyes gleamed with indomitable spirit. "I know. And *such* a way to meet Taylor. Here I was out of chocolate bars and water, counting stars and hoping for rescue, and an angel lands beside me with blankets and coffee." Jason reached a shaky hand up to grasp his brother's. For the first time, his voice faltered. "I'm so glad you found me."

"Me, too," Trevor said huskily, feeling the warmth of tears on his cold cheeks. "You rotten kid, how're you going to dance at my wedding with a broken leg?"

"I'll dance if it kills me!"

Taylor looked up just then, her eyes traveling from one brother to the other. "No broken ribs," she told them cheerfully. "Just bruises and a broken leg. Jason, are you *sure* there was no blurred vision or dizziness after you fell?"

He nodded. "None. I landed on the damned leg and then rolled. So, no concussion?"

"I don't think so. And no compound fracture; it's a clean break. It needs to be set and splinted before you're moved." She looked at him seriously. "I've set bones before, but it's going to hurt like hell. I think we'd better wait for the doctor; he could give you something for pain. He was in one of the other search parties, wasn't he, Trevor?"

Trevor nodded. "And Carmichael's called him; he should be here in about an hour."

Jason laughed unsteadily. "I can wait. This is heaven after the last two days. Trust me to decide to go for a last hike the morning I'm supposed to leave, and then find myself rolling headlong into some godforsaken gully!"

Chapter Nine

The wait was slightly more than an hour. Warmed by the coffee and blankets, Jason was as comfortable as he could be. He insisted on hearing how they'd found him, and once he'd heard the whole story, he promised them both that he intended to shake Luke's hand. Then he pulled Taylor's head down and kissed her quite firmly, ignoring the stern rebuke from his brother.

"If you don't want her, I do," he said definitely.

Trevor gave him a mock frown. "I do want her." He looked at Taylor, adding silently, *God, do I want her!* And she smiled softly at him, clearly reading his thought without the need for telepathy.

Jason claimed their attention then by very seriously thanking Trevor for drilling the basics of hiking into him years before. "I left about dawn and was just planning a few hours up here. But you were always so rabid on the idea of being prepared that I automatically stuck a couple of sandwiches and a handful of chocolate bars into the backpack." He gestured to the somewhat frayed canvas pack lying nearby with a canteen. "And I made sure I had plenty of water. It didn't really start getting cold until a few hours ago; last night was pretty mild."

"So you've been just fine," Trevor said ironically.

His brother grinned. "Well, it could have been worse."

Trevor poured more coffee for him, then handed Taylor her gloves, feeling the increasing chill in the air. Jason was, as he'd said, in much better shape than he might have been. No apparent concussion or broken ribs, and he was dressed warmly enough— although if he'd had to spend *this* night with no added protection against the steadily dropping temperatures . . . What Trevor was most worried about now was getting his brother out of this ravine and down the mountain.

Against all predictions, it seemed that the storm was approaching more quickly than expected. The moon was gone, and they could hear the wind rising in the trees high above them. And after Trevor followed the path of a single large snowflake as it drifted idly into their lamplight, his eyes rose to meet Taylor's. Her face was calm, but he could read the worried frown in her steady gaze.

Just then, there was a shout from above, and they looked up, barely able to make out a bulky form being lowered over the ravine's edge.

"The doctor," Taylor said instantly.

And so it proved to be. Introducing himself cheerfully—"Just call me Doc and we'll get along fine"—he knelt beside Jason and began unpacking an emergency medical kit far more extensive than the average first-aid box. He was deft and gentle, examining Jason quickly and asking a few questions almost identical to those Taylor had asked. He concurred in her belief that there was no concussion and instantly requested her help when her background as a doctor's daughter was disclosed.

The shot he gave Jason might not have eliminated all pain, but it made the bone-setting at least bearable. The leg was splinted firmly as a collapsible basket stretcher was lowered to them, and Jason was carefully transferred, wrapped as warmly as possible, and strapped in.

After a shouted conference with the men at the lip of the ravine, a complicated arrangement of ropes was lowered to them. A sturdy tree branch hanging out over the gully bore the weight of Jason's stretcher, while allowing him to be lifted more or less vertically. Trevor went up with him on his own rope, one hand firmly holding the basket to keep it steady.

The Rangers and their rescue teams, experienced in a variety of mountain mishaps, effected this part of the rescue quickly and safely. With Jason and Trevor out of the ravine, ropes were lowered for Taylor and the doctor, and both were safely brought up.

As for the trip down the mountain, that would live long in Trevor's nightmares. The storm burst upon them when they'd gone only a few hundred yards, pelting them with a mixture of sleet and snow and freezing them with an icy wind. Half a dozen of the men had volunteered to help carry Jason, the rest sent back to the lodge with the horses. In spite of Trevor's anxious request for Taylor to leave with the mounted men, she remained with them for the most hazardous beginning of the descent, leading her horse ahead of the rest to find the easiest path.

But once the worst was behind and they were on the main trail back to the lodge, she mounted her horse and headed back after asking the doctor what exactly he wanted to have waiting for them at the lodge. Trevor kissed her briefly before helping her to mount, offering no protest at her decision to hurry ahead. He'd seen enough to know she was an expert horsewoman, and the thought that his love could become lost was one to be dismissed the instant it occurred.

Not his Taylor.

And she didn't, of course. As the warmth of the lodge finally closed around rescuers and rescued, it became obvious that Taylor had used her hour's lead to the fullest extent. Her help had been gratefully accepted by the lodgekeeper's wife in preparing hot coffee and soup, and Jason's room awaited him with a cheerful fire in the hearth and everything the doctor required by the bed. Jason was carried to his room and left with only her and the doctor in attendance, since there was no question of trying to transport the injured man any distance in the worsening storm.

The Rangers and their teams, most of whom had been searching without rest for more than twenty-four hours, paused only to gulp coffee and soup before heading for needed rest. They brushed off Trevor's heartfelt thanks as unnecessary, but all gripped his hand firmly before seeking their beds. Owen, too, was thanked for his help, and went off to get a room for himself and take a hot shower.

Outside the lodge, the storm howled viciously.

Trevor ignored the soup but drank hot coffee as he waited to hear the news of Jason. He was worried, concerned that his brother might need more care than the lodge could provide, but he'd formed a good opinion of the doctor. He spent the time of waiting in requesting the last available room for himself and Taylor, unable to suppress a rueful comparison of this night to last night. Their bags were carried up, and he found himself alone in the lobby-den.

The doctor came down just before midnight, snaring a cup of coffee before sinking down beside Trevor on one of the wide couches near the fireplace. "Constitution of an ox," he said briefly after a sip.

Trevor felt relief sweeping over him. "He'll be all right?"

"I doubt he'll even have a cold after spending a night up there. He was warm enough, and didn't have to go too long without food and water. I'd feel better if I could X-ray that leg, but it's a very clean break and he had the sense not to try to move it. He's sleeping now, and I expect him to sleep all night. I'll check on him during the night, but no one else needs to."

"Thank you—"

"I'll send you the bill." The doctor grinned at him, his weathered face cheerful. "For now, I've sent your lady off to have a hot shower, after which she's under orders to get something hot inside her. You do the same. This storm won't be letting up anytime soon, but your brother'll be fine up here until we can get him to Casper."

Trevor wasn't surprised when the older man brushed off a second attempt to thank him. Left alone again, he stared into the fire for a while, a little numb from the emotional battering of the day. Then he made a quiet request of the lodgekeeper's wife after apologizing for all the trouble. She responded by cheerfully disclaiming any trouble, complimenting him on "your lady," and assuring him she'd send a tray up to their room.

He stopped by Jason's room, going in to assure himself that his brother was indeed all right. Standing by the bed and gazing down at that sleeping face that was younger but very like his own, he remembered other night vigils, other injuries and childhood illnesses. Absently, he leaned over to tuck in a stray corner of the bright quilt, hearing his own husky voice in the peaceful quiet of the room.

"You've grown into a fine man, Jase. Maybe one day I'll be able to tell you how proud I am of you."

Green eyes opened to look up into his own, drowsy and warm with love. "You just did," Jason murmured. His hand fumbled to grip his brother's tightly. "But you've told me before . . . in different ways." The grip loosened as weariness and the painkillers pulled him back toward sleep, his last words almost inaudible. ". . . love you . . ."

Very gently, Trevor slid the hand back under the warmth of the covers. "I love you, too, Jase," he whispered. He straightened slowly, then turned away from the lamplit bed.

Taylor stood in the doorway watching silently, vivid eyes very bright and full. She was wearing a floor-length terry robe, having obviously just come from her shower. When he reached the door, she slid her arms around his waist in a fierce hug that he welcomed and returned, then spoke softly as they stepped out into the hall and pulled the door shut behind them.

"The doctor ordered hot showers; it's your turn."

He kept one arm around her as they moved down the hall. "And hot food; Mrs. Clay's sending up some of her—and your— soup."

She smiled up at him as they entered their room. It was a large and comfortable bed-sitting room with a huge four-poster bed, its covers drawn back welcomingly, near a curtained window, and a couch and small table set up to flank a fireplace a few feet from the door. The bathroom opened off one side, and the double closet off the other.

"If you feel like I did," she said, "you're probably cold to the bone. Go take your shower."

He did, standing under the hot water until his tingling skin protested. Then he dried off and pulled on his own terry robe. His fingers sufficed to comb his damp hair. When he stepped out into the room, he found Taylor sitting at the small table with a tray in front of her, sipping coffee as she stared into the flickering fire.

Trevor sat down across from her and firmly pushed a bowl of soup toward her. "Eat."

"I will if you will."

Smiling, he took the second bowl, and they both began eating. Nothing more was said until the soup was finished: then Trevor spoke first. "You must be exhausted."

"Oddly enough, no." Her smile was a little crooked. "How about you?"

"No. Just—relieved."

"I know. I'm so glad Jason'll be all right."

"We should call your parents," he said idly.

"I already did, while you were in the shower. Daddy knew Jason was all right, though."

Trevor chuckled softly. "I keep forgetting."

"Does it still bother you? My being psychic?"

Instantly, he rose from the table and went around to gently pull her to her feet, his arms closing round her. "We wouldn't have found Jason without you," he said soberly. "How could it bother me?"

"It did once," she reminded him, her voice diffident.

"Only because I didn't think I could share enough of myself with you. But now I want to share everything with you. I want you to share everything with me. I love you, Taylor. And I don't need any more time to be sure of that."

Her arms slipped up around his neck, and a smile slowly grew in her brilliant eyes. "If I were a scrupulous woman," she murmured, "I'd say something about catching you with your guard down. After a day like we've had, I've no right to take you at your word."

"But you aren't a scrupulous woman?"

"Not where you're concerned."

Trevor drew her even closer, feeling the warmth of her slender body against his. "Take me at my word, Taylor," he urged softly, huskily. "Today may have speeded things up, but I've known for a long time that we belonged together. I've realized that time isn't a commodity we can count on; I don't want to waste another moment of our time together."

She smiled, achingly sweet and inviting. "There's no candlelight," she whispered. "No French perfume. No black lace and garters. There's just a blizzard outside, and inside the scent of soap and the crackle of a fire."

He reached back to turn off the light switch, leaving the room lit only by that fire. "Much as I adore your parents, I think we can get along without their advice—tonight. We don't need seductive props, sweetheart." The endearment felt warm in his heart, right in his mouth.

He lifted her easily in his arms, carrying her slight weight across the room to the wide bed and then setting her gently back on her feet. His hands lifted to cradle her face, bending his head until the warm silk of her lips touched his. He felt her response growing, strengthening, even as his own desire, never absent, began to build achingly.

Like the first time he'd kissed her, Trevor felt himself opening to receive a warm, soul-deep radiance. It spread throughout his body, a bright and glowing fire, and this time he felt no panicked urge to draw away from that. Instead, he gloried in it, recognizing the truth of two minds and two spirits striving to become one.

He felt terry cloth beneath his fingers as he pushed the robe off her shoulders, then his own robe sliding to the floor. Lifting his head, he gazed down at the slender body painted by the firelight's golden touch, the breath catching in his throat, his heart pounding against his ribs. He lifted her again and lowered her to the bed, easing his own weight beside her.

"You're so beautiful," he whispered, only dimly hearing the ragged break in his own voice. "Taylor . . ."

The touch of her hands on his shoulders was silken fire, the murmur of his name in her throat a siren song of winging need. Blue eyes looked at him with trust and desire. If the wind howled outside the curtained window, it was a distant and unimportant thing, dimmed in the spiraling wildness of thudding hearts and uneven breaths. He was lost somewhere in a world containing only satin flesh beneath his hands and lips, and the fiery, radiant heat of desperate longing.

"Trevor . . ."

Lost, and he didn't care. Whispering he knew not what, except her name, always her name, he drew the soft curves and hollows of her body on his soul. His hands trembled with the strength of what he felt as they shaped and stroked, feeding his hunger. He was starving for her, the ache inside him growing until it was an unbearable hollowness.

His lips pressed hot, tender kisses over her face, her throat; endearments jerked from his own throat, from deep in his chest. The vibrant need for her breasts drew his mouth, intensified the hunger that couldn't be satisfied by mere touch or taste.

Trembling bodies moved restlessly, seeking satisfaction. Trevor could feel the feverish heat of her body beneath his hands and lips, even as his own body seemed to him an inferno. They were both burning out of control.

Brilliant blue eyes darkened with need gazed into his own, a soft plea reaching his ears. Desperate as his own need was, he moved sensitively, gentling her seeking body to accept him as a part of herself. And there was no awkwardness, only a smooth and tender joining, a possession that was hers and his and richly complete.

In the first instant's hesitation and savoring, in the momentary stillness, Trevor felt the soft, caressing touch of her mind as all senses opened to her. With quicksilver warmth and joy, her thoughts became his in a communication deeper than any he could have imagined. The stark aloneness of one mind became the unshadowed sharing of two, a breathless, joyous communion and recognition of spirit.

The fulfillment of mental bonding was a blinding glow, surrounding and feeding the physical passion, driving it higher and higher, driving them toward a consummation of the flesh. Need soared, their bodies matching in a yearning rhythm until they could go no higher, no further, until there was only a soul-jarring ecstasy and only each other to cling to. . . .

In the quiet of the room there was no sound but the soft crackle of the fire. Trevor held her close to his side, still dazed, stunned, still not quite certain he wouldn't wake in the morning alone both physically and mentally. But he could feel the softest touches in his mind, not an intrusion but simply an open door, an easy link with the mind of his love.

An open door.

Instinctively, tentatively, he sent a jumbled message through that door, a tangled, passionate declaration. And it was returned instantly to him in full, soft with love and an aching sweetness. He felt alight from within, warm as he'd never been before, and knew a sudden, heartfelt pity for the sense-blind majority of mankind.

To not know this—!

"I love you," he murmured, because there was still the inescapable human need to voice aloud what the heart knew so well.

She lifted her head to smile at him, the wonderful eyes brilliant. "I love you, darling. So very much."

He returned the smile as his hand lifted to stroke the vibrant silk of her hair. "You should have given me a good, swift kick days ago," he scolded gently. "God—I've been fighting *this*?"

Taylor rested her chin atop the hand lying on his chest, her own smile turning rueful. "I did try," she reminded him.

After a moment's thought, Trevor nodded slowly. "Yes. But I had to try as well, didn't I?"

"You had to meet me halfway. It was always your choice, darling. I knew we belonged together, and the emotional certainty was there by the end of that first day. But *you* had to be that certain."

"And on the plane," he realized aloud, "I . . . needed you."

"You were afraid for Jason," she said tenderly. "So afraid. You needed to share him—and you—with someone else. You had to talk about the two of you. You had to keep him alive in your mind, to fight the fear of losing him."

"And you?" He looked at her gravely. "You cried on the plane—because it mattered."

"You let me in," she said simply. "You trusted me with all the love and pain of your life. And you looked at me as if—as if everything you needed was me. With you beside me now, I think I'll always be able to cry when it matters."

He drew her head forward to kiss her gently. "This . . . mental link between us. Were you expecting that?"

She laughed. "Darling, in case you haven't realized it yet, you have powerful psychic abilities of your own!"

"I do?"

Taylor laughed again at his blankness. "You certainly do. I felt a touch of it in you that first day, but when you finally opened up . . . It's been locked inside you all these years, just waiting for an outlet. Haven't you felt moments of perception, flashes of intuitive certainty that you doubted at the time but that turned out to be accurate?"

Thinking about it clearly, Trevor realized that he had. Moments when he'd been certain how a jury would vote, moments when he had focused on some seemingly unimportant detail in a client's defense, only to find the entire case unlocked. "Good Lord," he said faintly. "Will I—will I be aware of it when it happens now?"

"Not at first," she said. "You'll automatically consider it just a part of your thought processes. I think you'll get stronger, though, now that you can let it out."

"I wonder if Jason—"

"Of course," she said casually, then giggled at his startled blink. "Trevor, because you had to be strong for Jason all those years, you gave him the chance to be vulnerable; there are no shields in his mind the way yours was shielded. And there's a bond between you that's more than blood. I think he reached out to you without even realizing what he was doing; otherwise, Daddy would never have picked up that he was in trouble. *You* were still guarding yourself, and I can never pick up a thought without physical touch of a person or object."

"I thought Luke was the precognitive one," was all Trevor could say.

"He is. But he's telepathic in a peculiar way. With all his children, and with Mother, it's an automatic, unthinking thing. With others, he's erratic. Jason reached out, and Daddy just happened to be the only one listening."

The central point of the conversation had Trevor a bit dazed. "So you're telling me that both myself and Jason are psychic?"

With a solemn face and dancing eyes, Taylor nodded. "You're the strongest, though. Jason could probably communicate pretty well with another psychic, one who knew how to reach. But you won't even need that, given time."

It was then that Trevor remembered two vaguely troubling encounters with her sisters, "Dory—and Jess. They both knew."

"Did they?" Taylor asked, interested.

He nodded slowly. "Dory asked me about my—my closed door." He looked at Taylor, unsurprised to see her comprehension.

"We use that so she'll understand better and learn to shield her own mind."

"I guessed that. But when she asked me about my own closed door, I just thought . . ."

"That since you weren't psychic, she'd confused no ability with the ability to *hide* ability?"

"Something like that. When I explained to her that I couldn't hear things the way she could, she . . . laughed. Then she smiled at me and said, 'You don't know.' I couldn't figure out what she meant. But now . . . she knew."

Taylor nodded. "Dory's going to be strong. And Jess?"

"When I denied being psychic, she didn't seem to believe me."

"Be sure to tell her she was right," Taylor advised calmly. "Jess has always felt a little left out—being less psychic, I mean."

"You knew that?"

"Of course. But it didn't do any good for any of us to reassure her. It was you encouraging her with the music that helped, darling."

Trevor shook his head a little helplessly. "I can't get over it. I'm psychic. I'm psychic?"

"You certainly are."

A little surprised at his bemused acceptance of this, Trevor suddenly found himself laughing.

"What's so funny?" she asked, smiling, knowing.

"Me," he said ruefully. "I was so worried about sharing my mind with you. But now, it's like—like I've been only half alive and never knew it."

"So was I," she confided quietly. "Building shields . . . locks yourself in as well as others out. There's a part of me no one's touched but you. Oh, Trevor, I never knew it could feel this way!"

"I'm very glad I found you crying in that park, love."

She snuggled closer contentedly, her head resting on his shoulder. Then, only a quick flash of mental laughter alerting him, her ridiculous sense of humor reared its head.

"It *would* have been nice if you'd chased me to Australia," she mourned.

"I wouldn't have done that in any case," he said stoutly.

"No?"

"No. I would never have let you start the trip."

A note of suspicion crept into her voice. "You wouldn't have?"

"Absolutely not."

"You'd have flung me over your saddle and galloped off with me?" Pleasure was growing in her voice.

"Something like that."

"You'd have put your foot down and *ordered* me not to go?"

"Closer."

"You'd have grabbed me and shaken me and *commanded* me not to go?" she asked delightedly.

Trevor bit back a laugh. "Definitely. I'd have stuck you in a castle, raised the drawbridge, and put alligators in the moat."

"Because—?"

"Because, you adorable little witch, I can't live without you."

Taylor sighed happily. "Prince Charming. At last."

He hugged her, then said suddenly, "I forgot."

"What did you forget?"

"To propose," he said wryly. "Of course, I realize that in the eyes of your family, the ceremony's only a formality."

"But a proposal's obligatory," she said in a firm tone.

"In that case, will you marry me, love?"

"I'll have to think about it."

"Witch."

She giggled. "This is so sudden! We haven't even known each other a *month*, for heaven's sake! I hardly know you, sir!"

Trevor made a rude noise.

She giggled again. "I couldn't resist."

"Neither can I. *Answer* me, for godsake! My heart and all my worldly possessions are at your feet! My castle beckons to you!"

"I never could resist castles."

"Is that a yes?"

"An unqualified yes, darling."

"I'm not Prince Charming, you know," he felt honor bound to point out.

"No, but you're *mine*," she responded serenely.

"And you're mine." There was a world of contentment in his voice.

"D'you think we should elope?" she asked, thoughtful.

"Are you thinking? I want a double-ring ceremony with all the flourishes, my love."

"Yes, but Trevor—my family."

"They can come," he conceded magnanimously.

"I'm serious! You *know* my family. It'll be the most absurd wedding in history."

"I know." He chuckled softly. "I wouldn't miss it for the world."

She laughed as well. "If you don't mind, I don't."

"Then all that remains is to set the date."

"June?"

"That's too far away," he protested.

"We're almost into May now, darling, and if you want a big wedding . . ."

He sighed. "June it is, then. Where would you like to go on our honeymoon?" He was vaguely aware that sleep was tugging at him, and her own voice held a touch of drowsiness when she answered.

"Anywhere, darling. As long as we're together."

"We will be, love. We will be."

Chapter Ten

Taylor pulled the young Siamese cat off the dining room table and put him firmly on the floor. "Pyewacket, you know better than that," she said absently. She barely heard the cat's disgusted "Hrrooo!" because she was busy deciding if she'd forgotten anything.

"Grandmother's china, best napkins, candles, wine . . ." She checked the wine in its terra-cotta cooler, then nodded, satisfied.

She went back into the kitchen, watching where she walked because Pye's favorite game was tripping his humans. The frustrated cat grumbled at her, but she gave him only a rueful smile. "You'd better hide when Trevor gets home," she advised. "You stole his best cuff link this morning, and he hasn't forgiven you for that." Pye's second-favorite game was stealing.

Taylor tasted from several bubbling dishes, added a few spices to one, then glanced at the clock on the wall. Good. She'd timed it perfectly. He'd be home any time now, and they had the whole weekend ahead. . . .

She reached for the phone as it shrilled a summons, amused even before she got the receiver to her ear. "Hello, Mother."

"Darling, does he know yet?"

"Honestly, there are no secrets in a family of psychics!" Taylor rolled her eyes heavenward ruefully. "I haven't told him yet, and I don't *think* he knows."

"Tonight?"

"That's what I've planned. How's Amanda, Mother?"

"Flourishing," Sara replied vaguely. "She kept us up last night, but your father's spoken to her. Dory says she's going to have green eyes. So nice and sweet. Different, too."

"Well, say hello to her for us."

"I will, darling. Oh, Taylor—"

"Yes, Mother?"

"Twins. Your father's sure."

"I was pretty sure myself," Taylor murmured.

"So nice. Lots of babies," Sara said. "Our love to Trevor, darling."

Taylor was giggling when she hung up the phone. She was still working as her father's receptionist but had gone to another doctor for her test; Luke didn't treat his own family except in emergencies. Still, there were no secrets in her family.

Leaning back against the counter, she thought back over the last months. Six months since the wedding, a week since her baby sister's birth. And only two weeks until Christmas. If Taylor hadn't been psychic, she would have considered it a good bet that her own babies would be born very near the first anniversary of her marriage; being psychic, she was positive. *On* the anniversary. June twentieth—a Friday.

Friday's child is loving and giving.

Perfect.

In fact, everything was perfect. She and Trevor had found this old house and restored it gradually during the past months, with help from Jason and from her father. She smiled suddenly, wondering if her husband had noticed his brother's fascinated interest in Jamie. Of course he'd noticed; Trevor missed very little these days.

Jamie was still a very young woman, but Jason had clearly made up his own mind. He'd wait for her, Taylor thought. Jamie kept her own counsel, but Taylor knew her sister. And wouldn't they make a wonderful couple—Jason so lively and Jamie so serene. Complicated explaining the situation to outsiders. Her husband's brother was also her sister's husband?

Oh, well.

She looked through the kitchen window at the snow blanketing their large yard and listened. Moments later, the back door swung open, admitting Trevor and a blast of arctic cold. He shut the door hastily.

"Why," he demanded wryly, "do we live in Chicago?"

"Because we both grew up here." Happily, Taylor went into his arms as soon as he shed his coat. She'd stopped wondering if each kiss would be as warmly dizzying as the last, content in the knowledge that it would.

How she loved this man!

The inner change in him had wrought an outward change as well. His gray eyes smiled now, gleaming with love and laughter. His lean, handsome face was relaxed and seemed years younger. He was quick to sense moods in those around him, quicker still to sensitively adapt himself to those moods.

Their love was large part of that, of course, but the jolting truth of time's fragility had also changed him. Trevor had learned in a single fear-filled day never to take time for granted.

Though all barriers had crashed into rubble that day, it hadn't been easy for Trevor. His growing closeness with Jason had been a tentative, sometimes awkward thing, but immensely rewarding. And just as difficult had been his complete acceptance of his own psychic abilities; that still startled him, and probably would, she thought, for a while yet.

His wife had no complaints at all. With her, Trevor had opened up instantly and completely. The door that had opened that blustery night in Wyoming had never closed, he as comfortable with it as she was. And the love and laughter they'd shared since that night only confirmed and enhanced what both felt.

He was looking down at her now in faint surprise after glancing through to the dining room. "Candles—wine." His arms tightened around her. "What's the occasion, love?"

"I could say it was my birthday," she teased.

"That's in April," he said firmly. "April first, as a matter of fact. Apt, I've always thought."

"You were disappointed to find that out," she reminded him, turning away to check her preparations for dinner. "You were hoping I'd been born on Halloween—to fit in beautifully with your witch theme!"

As if in conditioned response, Trevor bent to pick up the cat nattering at his feet. "Well, slightly disappointed," he said sheepishly, allowing Pyewacket to climb onto his shoulder. "And you didn't answer my question."

"Didn't I?"

"You grow more like Sara every day!" he said severely.

Taylor giggled. "Sorry." Not that he seemed to mind. "Actually, I just thought I'd try seducing you again."

"You did that last night."

"I did not. I distinctly remember you joining me in the shower. I didn't do a single thing to provoke seduction."

"If standing there with only a bar of soap in one hand and a washcloth in the other isn't provoking, I don't know what is!"

"*I* was minding my own business."

He matched her virtuous tone. "And *I* was merely betraying a perfectly normal husbandly concern. I thought you might have drowned."

She started laughing. "Oh, put the cat down and make yourself useful!"

"Yes, ma'am."

They never ran out of things to say to each other, so it wasn't until dinner had been finished and the kitchen cleaned that Taylor got around to her reason for the special meal.

The stereo was loaded with soft music, a fire kindled in the large old stone hearth in the den. Pyewacket had curled up in his basket near the fireplace, sleepy after his own dinner. And his two humans were sharing the large couch only a few feet away from him.

Trevor was sitting on the end of the couch, Taylor turned so that she half lay across his lap. One of his hands stroked her long hair, as he often did, and the other rested lightly but possessively on her hip.

Deciding that the time was right, she spoke casually into the peaceful silence. "Darling?"

The gray eyes smiled tenderly down at her. "Yes, love?"

"I asked you a question once. You said I should ask you later."

Trevor, not gifted with Jason's total recall, was puzzled. "I don't remember the question, but ask away."

She absently parted the top buttons of his shirt, her fingers seeking the crisp hair beneath. "I asked if you wanted babies," she murmured. Her attention fixed on his chest, she only lifted her eyes back to his when the silence had stretched.

An arrested expression held the slate-gray eyes, and his face was very still. "Taylor . . . ?" he breathed.

Her smile growing, Taylor nodded.

Trevor pulled her closer in a sudden fierce, gentle hug. "I do want babies," he said huskily. "Our babies." Then, whether through the ever-present contact they shared or through his own strengthening abilities, Trevor understood the rest. A slightly unsteady hand lifted her chin, and he gazed at her, bemused. "Twins?"

"I'm pretty sure." She laughed softly. "The doctor doesn't know that yet, but Mother called and said Daddy was certain."

He hugged her again, held her for a long time. "I love you, witch," he murmured. "So much."

"I love you too, darling."

"I'm so glad I found you crying in that park." He laughed suddenly. "You never have told me what you were crying about that day."

Taylor smiled, remembering. She didn't cry about unimportant things any longer. In fact, not counting the time she'd deliberately made herself cry to tease Trevor, that day in the park had seen her last unimportant tears.

Unimportant! Those tears had changed her life.

"I was crying because somebody had stepped on a rose."

Trevor shook his head, rueful, tender. "Somebody stepped on a rose, and I ended up married to a psychic—*and* finding myself psychic."

"Life's funny, isn't it?" she observed solemnly.

"Love"—he laughed on a sigh, his eyes full of silver warmth, the arms holding her gentle and strong beyond belief—"you've taught me the truth of that. Life is funny. And so much more now than I ever thought it could be."

Taylor lifted her face for his kiss, a part of her wishing she *had* been born on Halloween, just to make Trevor's life utterly perfect. But it was all right, really. She'd always be his witch. And an April witch had powers an October witch could never match.

Magic.

Eye of the
Beholder

To Leslie, my editor,
for her patience, understanding, and ability.
And for being my camera's lens
to focus what I see.

"That I should love a bright, particular star
And think to wed it."

—*William Shakespeare*
All's Well That Ends Well

Chapter One

"Marry me, angel, and I'll take you to faraway places!"

Tory stared blankly at the man standing on her front porch. He was leaning against the doorframe and staring off into the blue fall sky, showing her an admittedly handsome profile. He was roughly six feet tall, a copper-redhead with astonishingly bright green eyes, dressed in neat dark slacks, a cream-colored shirt open at the throat, and a gold sports jacket, and he looked to be in his mid-thirties.

And she'd never seen him before in her life.

It was just what she needed to cap off a truly distressing morning. With a detachment born of lack of sleep, she considered her appearance and decided that if the stranger would only look at her, he'd probably run screaming. She was wearing her old plaid bathrobe, which was badly tattered about the hem, ragged slippers, which made her feet look twice their actual size, and a towel wrapped turbanlike around her wet hair. And in her left hand, she clutched a percolator, cord trailing.

"I'd marry Attila the Hun if he'd only find my coffee," she told the stranger finally.

The man straightened in a hurry and stared down at her. "Who the hell are you?" he asked comically.

"Tory," she answered politely.

"Where's Angela?" he demanded.

"If you're referring to the lady who used to live here—and I gather you are—she doesn't anymore. Sorry to be the one to break it to you, but she's on her honeymoon. In Bermuda, I think."

"How could they get married without me?" he exclaimed, clearly aggrieved.

"It only takes two, you know. One to be the bride and one to be the groom."

"And one to be the best man," he added. "Dammit, why didn't they let me know?"

"I couldn't say."

He blinked, apparently seeing the percolator for the first time. "Coffee? Thanks, I'd love some."

Tory gave way automatically as he stepped into the house. She toyed mildly with the idea of calling the police, but the phone wasn't connected yet, and besides, the man seemed harmless. Sighing, she closed the door.

He was halfway to the kitchen by then, obviously familiar with the house. He made his way through the confusion of boxes and crates yet to be unpacked, still talking in that ridiculously aggrieved voice and apparently unconcerned that his listener was a total stranger.

"They could have reached me if they'd tried. I mean, I was only out in the desert; I wasn't on the moon. Was it my fault the sheikh decided he wanted another airplane and the ambassador was having kittens? Was it my fault everyone seemed to want to leave the Middle East on the same day and I had to bum a ride with an Air Force transport on a milk run? Was it my fault the last stop was D.C. and everybody wanted to leave *there* on the same day and I had to borrow Bobby's plane? Well? *Was* it my fault?"

Appealed to directly for the first time, Tory blinked and tried to absorb his confusing conversation. "Um . . . no. No, of course it wasn't your fault. Who could ever think it was your fault?" She gestured, only then realizing that she was still clutching the percolator.

"I can't make coffee without the pot. Here." He took the percolator and began filling it with water, adding darkly, "Phillip will blame me, if I know him."

"Phillip?" Tory made a determined effort to think. "Isn't that Angela's new husband?"

"And my brother." His hand dived into the nearest box and produced the coffee like a magician's rabbit. "Ah. Now you have to marry me; I've found your coffee."

"You weren't proposing to me," she reminded him, beginning to be amused by his leapfrog conversation.

"Well, I am now. Marry me?"

"No, thank you. I make it a habit never to marry men I don't know." Tory leaned against the counter and watched him spoon coffee into the pot with undiminished good humor. "Did you have a habit of proposing to your brother's fiancée, or was today a red-letter day?" she asked dryly.

"Oh, it was a habit. Started the day we met, actually. I told Angela that if Phillip hadn't caught her first, I'd propose. She told me not to let that stop me, so I proposed. She turned me down but said that it'd be good practice for me. So I kept proposing. I've come up with some pretty creative proposals," he finished in a self-congratulatory tone.

"I'm sure. Um . . . putting it as delicately as possible, didn't your brother object to all this proposing?"

"Of course not. Angela wouldn't leave him. He did say once that if I threw Angela across my saddle and galloped off into the night, he'd hunt me down like a mad dog. A gentleman's warning, you know."

"Uh-huh." Tory forced her mind into a higher gear; she was working toward full throttle but, at this rate, never hoped to get there. It did occur to her, however, that she was taking this uninvited guest with surprising calm. Probably lack of sleep. "If you're Phillip's brother," she said, "then your name is York."

"Devon York. And you're Tory—?"

"Michaels."

"So now we know who we are. What color is your hair?"

She was watching him unwrap coffee cups—and where on earth had he found them? His question sank in. "My hair?"

"All I can see is a purple towel," he explained apologetically.

"Purple?" Tory knew she sounded like an idiot, but she was trying to remember the events of an extremely confusing morning. She'd reached for the box of towels and grabbed the one on top—had it been purple?

"Black?" he guessed.

"What? Oh . . . yes, black." It set up a train of thought. "Your brother's dark," she said suddenly.

"Yes, he is. So's my sister. There was a redheaded Scotsman somewhere in the past, and occasionally he turns up and flaunts his genes. A throwback, I think they call it. I'm a throwback. Are your eyes gray or green?"

"Gray, usually," she answered in an absent tone, mentally conjuring an image of the tall, dark Phillip York and the merry, brunette Angela. They had certainly seemed devoted to each other, she remembered. Flaunts his jeans? No . . . surely he'd said *genes*. What on earth was wrong with her?

"How old are you?"

"Twenty-sev—" Abruptly, he had her full attention. "What's with the third degree?"

"Well, I'm drinking your coffee."

"Not yet, and so what?"

"I like to know a little about a woman when I drink her coffee and propose to her."

"Oh." For the life of her, Tory didn't know how to respond to that. She decided to let it pass.

He grinned suddenly, and the charm of that did something odd to her ability to breathe with normal ease. A little voice in her head announced mournfully that she really shouldn't have answered the doorbell.

"You're not with it this morning, are you?" he asked cheerfully.

Tory stared at him. The sense of ill-ease that had grown steadily all morning abruptly overwhelmed her, and she forgot that she was talking to a stranger. She began her little tale of woe slowly and steadily, but her voice increased its speed and lost some of its control by the end.

"I slept on a mattress on the floor last night, because when I got here—at midnight—I discovered that the movers hadn't put the bed up, and I didn't have a single tool to put it up myself. And my alarm clock, which was in the box right beside the mattress, went off at seven o'clock this morning. I fell off the mattress and nearly had a nervous breakdown, because the first night in a strange house is terrible, and then I tripped on the sheet getting up and fell into a box of books. By the time I turned off the damn clock, I wasn't about to go back to sleep, so I decided to take a shower. I didn't turn the water on until I got in; it was freezing, and I hate cold showers. When I got out, I couldn't find the towels for ten minutes, so I've probably caught pneumonia. And all my clothes were packed in sealed boxes except for this robe. My hair dryer short-circuited. The only slippers I could find were these—"

"Very fetching."

"—things. I nearly broke my neck on the stairs. I got lost trying to find the kitchen, and I was viciously attacked by the door to the basement. None of the light switches were where they were supposed to be, and it's *dark* at the crack of dawn. It took me twenty minutes to find the percolator, and I couldn't find my coffee!"

Her voice rose on the last word, the sound that of human tolerance pushed way past its limit. She took a deep breath, viewing his twitching lips and laughing eyes with real dislike. "No, I'm not with it this morning, Mr. York."

"Devon," he insisted politely.

She ignored that. "I'm so not with it that I let a stranger—obviously spending the odd day away from the asylum—come into my house, tell me strange tales about proposing to his almost-sister-in-law, arguing with sheikhs and ambassadors in deserts, bumming rides with transport planes, and borrowing other planes, and—and I let him make *coffee*!"

"I think you need a cup," he murmured, clearly trying not to laugh.

"There's no milk," she told him miserably, this last grievance threatening to overpower all the rest. "I hate black coffee."

"We'll work something out." He thrust a white handkerchief into her hand. "Take this."

Tory wiped her eyes and glared at him. "I don't cry," she announced coldly.

"Of course not."

"Don't patronize me, dammit!"

"I wasn't. Look, we can handle this one of two ways."

She wondered vaguely what they were supposed to be handling but felt too utterly limp to ask.

"Either you can borrow my shoulder, which I'm told is rather good at absorbing woes and cares of everyday life, or else you can sit down and put your feet up while I fix a much-needed breakfast for both of us."

"Can you cook?" Tory asked, feeling a faint flicker of interest.

"Certainly I can cook."

"Oh." She hiccuped and glared at him as though it were his fault. "Well, I don't want your shoulder," she announced defiantly.

"I'm crushed. Hold on a second." He disappeared in the general direction of the living room, appearing a moment later with a low-armed, high-backed chair that had been stuffed for comfort and covered in brushed velvet. He had one of her colorful throw pillows under an arm.

"You don't have very much furniture," he noted.

"I've never had a house before." She watched him position the chair in one corner of the large kitchen. "That doesn't belong in here."

"We'll put it back when we're finished. Now, have a seat."

Tory decided not to waste a glare. She sat down in the chair, tugging at the lapels of her robe as it suddenly occurred to her that only a frayed belt kept it in place and that she wore absolutely nothing underneath it.

Devon drew forward a sealed box marked BOOKS, placed the pillow on top of it, then wordlessly grasped her ankles and lifted them onto the pillow.

"I can do that," she muttered, alarmed at the breathless sound of her own voice.

"My pleasure," he said solemnly. Then he turned away and began searching through the various boxes piled in the room, finding what he needed seemingly by magic.

Tory wondered if she should protest his cheerful search through her belongings, but she couldn't bring herself to, somehow. It was quite a change for her to be taken care of like this, and she wasn't sure it was a good thing. Especially since she was aware that his offer of a shoulder to cry on had tempted her—very much.

And that was unnerving. Granted, she'd had a rough morning, and the preceding few weeks had been far from easy. But she was still annoyed by the weakness of tears. Because what she'd told Devon was true: She didn't cry. Not on the outside anyway. Not where everyone could see. And she was a very capable, reasonable, efficient woman. Everyone said so. Even though, she thought with mild irritation, "everyone" always qualified the statement by adding the rider, "for an artist, that is."

"Will this do in place of milk?"

She looked up hastily to see that he was holding several small packets of powdered creamer. She wondered, with a vague sense of annoyance, where he had gotten them and if he was the type of man who'd taken the Boy Scouts' motto of "Be prepared" for his own. Such efficiency was grating, particularly after her chaotic morning.

"I'll settle for it," she answered rather ungraciously.

"Great." He didn't, she noted, seem the slightest bit upset by her tone. He merely poured a cup of coffee, politely asked how she liked it, then handed her the cup.

"So you just arrived last night?" he questioned chattily.

"Mm." Tory was sipping the reviving coffee and watching him reposition boxes to clear space for cooking.

"From where?"

"Arizona," Tony replied, beginning to understand his verbal shorthand.

"Beautiful country out there," he offered.

"Yes."

"Why'd you leave? Or am I being nosy?"

Tory started to tell him that she'd left the West because she'd grown bored with deserts as subjects, but she answered his second question instead. "Of course you're being nosy; it seems to be a character flaw."

Devon accepted the observation philosophically. "Looks that way, doesn't it?" Before she could reply, he was going on cheerfully. "What d'you think of West Virginia?"

Reflecting silently that this man's bump of curiosity was a large one, Tory answered resignedly. "It's beautiful. I love mountains."

"So do I. Scrambled, fried, poached, or boiled?"

Tory blinked at the egg he was tossing lightly from hand to hand. "Um . . . scrambled, I guess."

"Good. No matter what I try, they always end up scrambled."

"Then why did you ask?"

"Good manners."

Sighing, Tory took another sip of coffee and forced her reluctant mind into the next highest gear. She crossed her ankles and watched him moving about the kitchen. Interest stirred to life inside her, and Tory told herself that it was entirely professional. Her instinctive eye for form, color, and movement was attracted by his unconscious grace and by the clean, masculine lines of his lean body.

Shunting the thoughts aside, Tory fiercely pulled her gaze away from him and stared down at her coffee. Uh-uh! Never again! Two years of painting deserts had done a lot to heal wounds, but she wasn't about to risk her hard-won peace by attempting another portrait—especially not a portrait of a man.

Rushing into speech to occupy her wayward mind, Tory said, "Let's have your vital statistics. Fair trade."

"Okay," he responded genially. "What d'you want to know?"

Tory lifted her cup in a whatever-you-like gesture.

Devon turned the bacon strips over and then began to break eggs into a mixing bowl. "Let's see, then . . . height, weight, serial number?"

"Cute," she murmured.

"In no mood for humor, I see."

"If you can ask that after hearing about my morning—"

"Sorry." He looked thoughtful for a moment and then, responding to her inquiring look, said gravely, "I'm trying to think of something really exciting to tell you so you'll say yes the next time I propose. Maybe if I likened myself to James Bond?"

"Not my type."

"Ummm, Horatio Hornblower?"

"I'd get seasick."

"The Scarlet Pimpernel?"

"Sorry."

"Heathcliff?"

"Too brooding."

"Don Quixote?"

Tory stared at him over the rim of her cup. "This is all very revealing, you know. Either you watch a lot of old movies or else you read a lot of books."

He grinned. "Both."

"Uh-huh. Look, why don't you just tell me who *you* are, and never mind the heroes of fiction."

"If you insist."

"I do."

"Remember that phrase; you'll have need of it later."

Tory blinked; it took her a moment to realize he was referring to something along the lines of "Do you take this man." She sighed. "Tell me about yourself before I start to think you're just an apparition in my nightmarish morning."

"Thanks a lot."

"You asked for it."

"I suppose. Okay, then. I'm thirty-two years old, single, reasonably well off. I can eat almost anything, never hog the blankets at night, and don't object to taking out the garbage. I can make beds, I never drop my socks on the floor, and I'm not addicted to televised sports. As you can see, I can cook, and I don't expect to be waited on. I'm also a dandy dishwasher. In fact"—he gave her a grin that was comical in its pleased surprise—"I'm perfect husband material."

Tory, elbow propped on the low arm of her chair and chin in hand, stared at him. Gravely, she asked, "Then why on earth are you still running around loose?"

"I don't know," he told her seriously. "I suppose because no woman has yet appreciated my sterling qualities."

"Those weren't quite the vital statistics I had in mind."

"Just thought I'd make my pitch, you know."

"It was wasted on me, I'm afraid."

"Determinedly single?" he queried with a lifted brow.

"Something like that."

"I'll have to see what I can do about that."

"Don't bother." Before he could respond, she asked casually, "What do you do for a living? You didn't say."

He looked wounded. "I have to leave something to the imagination. For the chase, you understand. Mystery."

Tory thought about that. "Who's chasing whom?" she asked politely.

"I'm chasing you," he told her cordially.

Chapter Two

Tory gazed at him, *thoughtful, considering. Any man, she decided finally,* who could say what he'd just said to a woman who looked as if she'd just been dragged by an ear through a hurricane was obviously a mental case. Accordingly, she humored him.

"I refuse to be chased on an empty stomach," she said mildly.

"Well, we'll fix that," he told her cheerfully, and he proceeded to finish preparing breakfast.

They ate the meal on a table made of boxes, since Tory had yet to acquire a kitchen table, and Devon York continued his questioning and more or less one-sided dialogue.

"Do you like animals?"

"Yes."

"Have any pets?"

"No."

"What's your sign?"

"You've got to be kidding."

"Well, these one-word answers of yours aren't very forthcoming, you know. What's your sign?"

"Taurus."

"No wonder you're answering in monosyllables."

"I beg your pardon?"

"Taureans are like that. Tranquil, serene. And fond of one-word answers." He studied her thoughtfully. "In fact, I'm surprised you cut loose a little while ago; your morning must have *really* been lousy."

"It was."

He grinned a little. "But you're back on balance now."

Tory pushed her empty plate away and leaned back, sipping her second cup of coffee and beginning to feel more human. "I'm getting there," she told him wryly. "And what's *your* sign?"

"Sagittarius," he replied cheerfully.

She filed the information away in her mind, although she didn't quite know why. "What are Sagittarians noted for?"

"Their charm." Devon got up and carried their plates to the sink.

Ruefully, she said, "You obviously don't believe in hiding your light under a bushel."

He was running water into the sink and efficiently dealing with the after-meal cleanup. " 'Course not. Faint heart never won fair lady . . . or something like that."

"Oh, are we back to that?"

"We never left it, fair lady."

Tory sighed. She watched him roll up the sleeves of his shirt—he'd tossed the jacket over a box some time before—and plunge his hands into the sudsy water. Idly, she wondered how she'd pose him, then hastily discarded the speculation. But her fingers were itching to pick up charcoal or pencil and begin a preliminary sketch. . . .

"You're staring at me," he noted, sending her a sideways glance.

"Just looking for the heart on your sleeve," she explained dryly.

He smiled modestly. "Love and a cough can't be hidden."

"You're a nut."

"I've been called worse."

"Doubtless by someone who knew you well."

"Ouch." He chuckled softly. "With one-word answers and one-liners, you're obviously tops."

"Practice," Tory heard herself say and, as if that wasn't enough, heard herself add, "with a man sharp enough to cut himself." She managed to end the admission on a note of absolute finality, irritated by her mind's refusal to let go of a painful memory.

She had looked away from Devon, and as she glanced back she encountered a suddenly keen, searching look from the vivid green eyes. The unexpectedness of it threw her for a moment, but then Tory hastily revised her impressions of Devon York. Obviously, she realized, here was yet a second man who was sharp enough to cut himself, and she felt wariness slipping into her mind.

Devon spoke quickly, the flash of shrewdness gone from his eyes as though it had never existed. In its place was the good humor of a moment before. "I sharpen my wits on dumb animals," he said solemnly. "That way I can convince myself I'm quicker than I really am."

The absurdity caught Tory before she could fully erect a wary mask, and she heard herself give a startled giggle.

He looked ridiculously gratified. Bowing from the waist with a certain style, he flourished a dishcloth and said sonorously, "Marry me, I beg of you," and added gravely, "I need that giggle; you're a terrific audience."

Tory stared at him for a moment, then looked to the ceiling for inspiration. "I don't know where we are, Toto," she murmured plaintively, "but it isn't Kansas."

"You didn't answer me," he reproved.

"Wanta bet?"

He looked hurt.

Tory relented and said mildly, "All right then. I'll marry you when it snows in Miami on the Fourth of July."

Devon leaned back against the counter and appeared thoughtful. "That's a very creative refusal," he said finally.

"I thought you'd appreciate it."

He rubbed the bridge of his nose reflectively. "I get the feeling," he said, "that this is going to turn into quite a contest."

Tory felt a sudden foreboding. What had she begun by allowing Devon York into her house? "Don't you have to get back to your desert?" she asked carefully.

He smiled. "No."

"Your job?"

"I'm flexible."

"You are *not*," she said strongly, "going to turn me into a vacation hobby! Audience or no audience!"

"I wouldn't think of it," he responded soulfully.

Tory stared at him suspiciously. "I don't believe you."

"O ye of little faith."

Curtly, she said, "I don't know you well enough to have faith— just well enough to be worried."

"Thanks a lot."

"Mr. York—"

"Please. I thought we'd at least gotten past that."

Tory looked at him, at the odd grin that did something to her breathing, and her unease grew even as she held firmly to a level voice. "Devon, then—"

"Thank you," he murmured.

She ignored the gentle irony. "You may have a flexible job, but I have quite a few things to do. I have to unpack and get the house in order, and then I have to go back to work."

"What d'you do?" he asked interestedly.

"I paint," she said after a moment, flatly.

He looked at her. "Really? What d'you paint?"

Tory was uncomfortably aware that there had been a second flash of shrewdness in his remarkable eyes. "Mostly landscapes and still lifes."

Devon snapped his fingers in sudden realization. "Most of those crates in there hold canvases, don't they?" he asked, nodding toward the den.

"Yes."

"You're prolific," he guessed.

Tory shrugged. "Active," she qualified.

He abandoned the subject abruptly. "Well, you'll need help unpacking," he said cheerfully.

"No—" Tory began hastily, only to be interrupted.

"I can set up your bed and help move furniture, and I'm first-rate at carrying boxes and hanging pictures. The yard needs some work, and there's that leaking pipe in the basement, too. Phillip has a house nearer town; I can use my key and borrow his lawn-mower and some tools—"

"Hold it!" Tory took a deep breath and fought down a sudden, inexplicable panic. She stared at this tall, maddeningly efficient stranger and wondered wildly if he'd decided to put down roots here. "Look, I appreciate the—the offer. Really. But I'm accustomed to taking care of myself. I *like* taking care of myself."

"That was before I came along," he said reasonably.

Tory struggled with herself. "I don't need your help," she said evenly.

He looked dismayed, and for the life of her, Tory didn't know if his expression was real or sham. "I wish you'd let me help," he said unhappily. "I'm at loose ends for a while, and with Phillip and Angela away I don't know a soul around here."

Tory felt herself weakening. She *knew* she was weakening yet couldn't seem to stop herself. It was that little grin of his, she decided irritably. It was a fallen-angel grin, a beguiling combination of charm, uncertainty, mischief, and defiance. *There's one born every minute!* she reminded herself ruefully, thinking that P. T. Barnum was a wise man.

"I can help?" Devon ventured hopefully, obviously taking note of the defeated gesture she'd made almost unconsciously.

She glared at him and muttered, "Why not."

"Terrific. Is it Victoria?"

"What?" she asked, completely at sea.

"Your name. Is it short for Victoria?"

"No."

"That's interesting."

Tory rubbed at a vague sort of ache between her eyes. "Look. Could you do me a favor?"

"Just ask."

"Leave."

Devon looked hurt.

Sighing, Tory said, "I can't deal with you this morning. Any other morning, I could probably make a stab at it. But not *this* morning."

He appeared to think it over, then demanded suspiciously, "Can I come back for lunch?"

Tory stared at him for a long moment. "If you bring it or cook it yourself," she said finally in a severely put-upon tone.

Devon lifted an eyebrow at her. "Thank you for that gracious invitation."

"You're welcome. Thank you for breakfast. Goodbye."

With undiminished cheerfulness, Devon rolled down his sleeves, donned his jacket, and left, begging her politely not to get up on his account.

Tory sat there for a long moment, a half-empty coffee cup in her hand. An absentminded swallow collided with giggles and caused a coughing fit, bringing relative sobriety. She rose to her feet and set the cup on the counter, thinking that she'd really better stop enjoying Devon York's company. It could get addictive. And since she'd twice seen evidence of an extremely sharp man beneath the genial facade, she thought that being addicted to Devon York's company could be a dangerous thing indeed.

When the doorbell rang at eleven that morning, Tory went to see if Devon had returned. No one else would visit her in this part of the country. But it wasn't Devon.

It was, instead, a delivery man bearing the most tremendous basket of long-stemmed red roses—bridal roses, she noted—that Tory had ever seen in her life. Bemused, she carried the huge basket into the living room and set it on a low table beside the French doors opening onto the patio. She made two discoveries then: one, that the flowers were scented silk; and, two, that there was a card.

The card was handwritten in a firm, curiously exact, block-printed style, undeniably masculine and shrieking of a logical, clear-thinking man of purpose. Tory had studied various theories regarding handwriting some years before out of curiosity and as a sort of offshoot of her artistic work. She had found the science fascinating and now automatically studied the handwriting before actually reading the words.

And she knew that if she had studied this handwriting knowing nothing about the man it represented, she would never have pictured Devon York as that man. This writing, she decided, be-

longed to a man who was sharply intelligent, extremely well ed-
ucated, concise, practical, and logical. Each stroke of pen revealed
self-confidence, assurance, pride bordering on arrogance, exacti-
tude, unerring logic, mathematical precision, and utter and complete self-control.

There was, in fact, little to remind her of the affable man who
had cheerfully cooked breakfast for her that morning. No creative
whimsy, no subtlety, no radical sense of humor—and *no* uncertainty.

Tory frowned and, almost as an afterthought, read the message. It was a quotation from Donne, and it represented a drastic
contrast between what was written—and *how* it was written:

> *Whoever loves, if he do not propose*
> *The right true end of love, he's one that goes*
> *To sea for nothing but to make him sick.*

Wandering over to her brick fireplace, Tory propped the card
up on the mantel and stared at it musingly. Then she looked beside the card at the mirror above the mantel, and at the reflection
there.

She saw a woman whose black hair fell in a long, loose page-
boy and gleamed with blue highlights, framing a face that was irritatingly heart-shaped and tanned a golden brown. Out of that
face shone eyes that were usually gray but sometimes green or
blue or violet or hazel, and that always looked too large for the
face they occupied. The nose was a snubbed affair, turning up at
the end and perfectly suited for the face even if its owner despised
it. High, flat cheekbones were a gift from a Romany ancestor, the
same one who had bequeathed her the raven hair and a tendency
toward introspection.

Tory knew, in fact, that she was almost a mirror replica of her paternal great-great-grandmother, who had been a Gypsy. An oil painting of her was still packed in its crate, waiting to be hung. Tory treasured the portrait because she had always felt such an affinity for the woman it represented.

Pushing Great-Great-Grandmother Magda from her mind, Tory continued her thoughtful scrutiny of herself. She was enough of an artist to know that her face was striking, enough of a woman to wish certain changes had been made.

Still, she thought with some satisfaction that Devon would be surprised when he saw her; the bedraggled, shell-shocked creature of this morning bore little resemblance to the woman now reflected in the mirror. Tory was not, she well knew, a woman who looked her best upon waking. The morning saw a bleary-eyed, pale face with no animation and no pretensions whatsoever to beauty. Only after coffee, a shower, and an interlude of walking about and waking up thoroughly did Tory feel human. And look it.

It was a highly vexing trait for one who had spent her life trying to disprove the popular theory that artists were vague, untidy creatures, irrational in mood and careless in habit. Tory prided herself on her logic and dedication to a profession she'd inherited a talent for, and on her rational approach to that profession.

Backing away from the hearth a few steps, she studied the rest of Tory Michaels as revealed by the tilted mirror. Too thin, she decided critically. Almost fragile, dammit. And the ribbed turtleneck sweater made of a soft, clinging gray wool only highlighted that unwelcome fragility.

Not surprising, all things considered, she thought. Working hard in desert heat and being one who never worried much about meals, she was bound to have lost a little weight. Still, she was hardly fragile, appearance notwithstanding. Tough. That was it.

She smoothed her palms down her jean-clad thighs and thought back to the childhood days when her father had called her a gazelle because of her long legs and habit of always rushing about. She'd never really grown into the legs, she thought a bit sadly. The early prediction of height had not materialized; she was only a little over five feet tall. And she never rushed these days; that meant wasted energy and was hardly efficient.

Tory sighed and stepped back to the hearth, returning to her study of Devon's card. It wasn't signed, but it was his, she knew. And she knew that the safest thing for her to do would be to lock all her doors and refuse to set eyes on the man again. Because if this card and her interpretation of it were to be trusted, he would have to be the most complex man she'd ever encountered.

She wasn't given to armchair analysis, but Tory trusted her impressions of people. Hers was a rational process of analysis, based on years of studying human beings and colored only slightly by what she studiously avoided terming "artistic intuition." And she had been wrong only once—when she'd allowed her emotions to influence her judgment.

Biting her lip, she turned away from the card and the puzzle-man it represented, returning to her unpacking. Clearing her mind, she carefully unwrapped a very old and delicate vase. It was, like Great-Great-Grandmother Magda's portrait, a part of her heritage. Tory sat cross-legged on the floor amid packing straw and wrapping paper, holding the vase and gazing down at it.

"Hello?"

Tory looked up swiftly, immediately recognizing the deep voice. "I thought you had good manners!" she accused.

"I rang the bell," Devon told her firmly. "You didn't hear it, I guess."

Getting up, she carried the vase over to the mantel and placed it carefully near one end. "I guess," she retorted, suspicion heavy in her voice as she turned around to face him. He was looking her up and down, and Tory was both pleased and irked by the surprise in his vivid green eyes.

"I knew there'd be an improvement," he said, "but I never expected an entirely new woman."

"Thank you!" she snapped before seeing the laugh in his eyes.

"You are a lovely woman, Tory Michaels," he said seriously, the laugh still present, but different.

"Um . . . thank you," she said again, uncertainly this time. Tory decided she really didn't want to consider how his expression had subtly changed; along that path lay the danger she sensed from this man. "I assume the flowers were from you," she said rather hastily. "They're beautiful. But why silk? That's an expensive gesture."

Devon had wandered over to the fireplace and was gazing at the vase she'd just placed there. "Ming," he noted almost absently.

"Why silk?" Tory repeated, disregarding his obvious knowledge of porcelain.

He looked down at her. "Because they last."

"Oh."

Devon gestured toward the card propped on the mantel. "What'd you think of that?"

"You mean your poetic turn of mind?"

"I mean my proposal," he corrected.

"You'd better get pills for seasickness."

He chuckled softly. "You think I'm going to sea for only that reason?"

"I think it'll be the only result of your trip."

"Well, I'm a good sailor. I'll take my chances."

Tory abruptly decided that their metaphorical little "trip" had gone on long enough. She turned and threaded her way among the boxes and crates, intent on completing the task at hand. "Are you sure you don't have to get back to your desert?" she asked over her shoulder.

"Positive. I can help you with this— Oh, wait a minute!"

With that disjointed utterance, he abruptly went out into the foyer, returning seconds later with a rather large box, brightly wrapped and tied with a big red bow, which he handed to Tory.

She felt the box shift in her hands and stared at the small holes—air holes, she realized warily—in the sides. "What's this?"

"A present. Open it."

Tory sat down on a large crate, the box resting carefully on her knees, and gazed up at him. "Will something jump out at me?"

"Probably."

"Devon—"

"Open it."

Cautiously, Tory slid the ribbons and bow off the box and even more cautiously lifted the lid. Then she began to laugh softly. "He's adorable!"

"He" was a red-yellow tabby kitten with huge brilliant green eyes and remarkably large pointed ears. Around his neck hung a somewhat bedraggled red bow, bearing obvious marks of curious little teeth. And he immediately left the box to cling to Tory's sweater and hide his face beneath her long hair. His purr was a startlingly bass rumble.

"Where'd you get him?" Tory asked, then added, "Him?"

"Him," Devon confirmed, grinning down at her. "And I got him from one of Phillip's neighbors. I've met her—Mrs. Jenkins— before; she breeds cats as a business. Anyway, she saw me loading tools and things and came over to ask if I knew anyone who might want a kitten. Of course, right away I thought of you—"

"Of course."

"—and I said sure. As soon as I saw this little fellow, I knew he was the one. And he was cheap." Devon started to laugh. "It seems that one of Mrs. Jenkins's prize-winning Abyssinians escaped the cattery and fell in with a ne'er-do-well tom whose only claim to royal blood was a possible smattering of Siamese. Mrs. Jenkins deduced that from the ensuing noise. Anyway, this little guy's the sole result of that memorable night. What'll you name him?"

"Oh, he'll name himself. Cats always do." Tory looked up at the man who was fast becoming less of a stranger. "Thank you, Devon."

Shrugging slightly, Devon said, "A house isn't a home until a cat's lived in it."

"Is that a proverb?"

"If it isn't, it should be." In the magical way that by now seemed customary, he produced a small carton of milk. "I've got some more stuff out in the truck—cat food, a litter box, and litter. I'll go get it."

Tory stood as he left the room, crossing to the window and pulling aside the drapes Angela had left, gazing out. "Truck?" she wondered aloud to her new houseguest. The answer was parked in her driveway, just behind her own gray Cougar; it was a four-wheel-drive pickup truck with a roll bar and a brilliantly swirling "sunset" paint job. A sense of familiarity crystallized as Tory realized it was Phillip York's truck.

She carried the kitten into the kitchen and poured some milk into a saucer, setting the kitten down to enjoy his first meal in his new home. Devon came in bearing cat food, which he placed on the counter, and a litter box and bag of litter.

"Where d'you want his box?"

Gesturing toward a small room off the kitchen, she said, "In the storage room, I guess."

Rapidly finishing off his milk, the kitten decided to explore and made a beeline for the living room and the fascinating clutter of boxes and packing materials expressly designed to provide hours of enjoyment for felines. Tory followed, fascinated by the kitten's fascination.

It occurred to her somewhat belatedly that although this second visit of Devon's had found her aware, alert, and awake, she had accepted his presence with the same curiously detached bemusement that had held her in its grip this morning.

It was an unnerving thought.

She discovered a new addition to the living room at that moment: a picnic basket. It was a large wicker affair, clearly designed to hold enough food for an army.

"Lunch," Devon explained, coming into the room and obviously following her gaze. "You told me to either bring it or cook it myself, remember?"

"So I did."

"Want to eat now or wait awhile?"

"Whenever you like."

"Now, then. I'm hungry."

Tory felt unnerved again, because she was becoming entirely too companionable with this man. "You're an insidious man!" she accused suddenly.

Devon, busily clearing a space in the middle of the living room floor, looked up at her with limpid eyes. "Which definition are you thinking of?" he asked, his voice soft. "Something spreading harm in a subtle manner? Or something beguiling and seductive?"

Tory couldn't think of a single damn thing to say in response to that. But she answered his question silently: *beguiling and seductive!*

"Well?"

She made a major production out of fishing the kitten from a crate filled with packing straw. "I should show him where his box is."

"You're stalling, Tory."

For some odd reason, it seemed as if she'd never heard her name spoken aloud before. She felt a mask beginning to grip her face. Guarded. Defensive. Wary.

"Actually," Devon said gravely, "I think *insidious* was the wrong word entirely. *Stubborn*, maybe. Or *helpful*. I like *helpful*. I like *being* helpful."

Tory didn't know whether to laugh or hit him with something. She sighed instead. "I'm going to show my new houseguest where his box is."

"You do that. I'll have this stuff ready when you get back."

She headed for the storage room. Several things occurred to her in the moments granted for reflection. She wasn't quite sure which man Devon York actually was: the genial, whimsical man . . . or the man who had looked up at her for a timeless moment with a shocking intensity in his vivid green eyes.

And she wasn't quite sure which she feared the most.

But what she was sure of was the fact that he meant to be a part of her life for at least a while. And, deny it though she would, she was tired of being alone.

Chapter Three

It was the genial, whimsical man who offered companionship during a curious little picnic in the middle of her living room floor; the brief flash of intensity in his green eyes might have been purely her imagination. Tory responded to him as calmly and as bemusedly as she had all morning, but a part of her perception was occupied in trying to probe beneath the facade he wore as easily as a second skin.

She knew that his straightforward good humor *was* a facade, or rather she sensed that it was. Although maybe his intensity was a natural part of him, a glimpse of brief, dazzling whiteness from one of a diamond's many facets. Whatever that hint of complexity was, it disturbed her—because it also intrigued her.

And she had no business being intrigued by Devon York. His very presence injected uncertainty into her life, stealing control from her and knocking her off the balance she'd achieved. He seemed to possess the uncanny ability to draw her emotions closer to the surface and away from her own guiding hand.

It bothered her. Badly.

"Earth to Tory?"

She blinked and hastily recalled her wandering attention. *Damn!* "Sorry," she murmured. "You were saying?"

"Asking, actually." His green eyes were unreadable for an instant before resuming their clear cheerfulness. "Are you a famous sort of artist?"

Tory almost laughed but managed not to. She was beginning to realize that Devon was, if nothing else, a peculiar kind of man; he could say or ask something in the most outrageous terms and yet sound perfectly grave. "No," she answered dryly, "I'm not a famous sort of artist. Art isn't the field to get into if one's after fame; Picassos aren't born every day."

"Ah." Momentarily distracted, Devon leaned sideways to fish the curious kitten out of the wicker hamper, where the remains of lunch reposed. He was spat at for his trouble, and placatingly gave the kitten a piece of drumstick to chew on.

Watching tiny feline teeth gnawing ferociously, Tory said, "Keep an eye on him so he doesn't get any bones; they could hurt him."

Devon nodded and stretched long legs out in front of him; they were both sitting on a gaily checkered tablecloth spread on the floor, backs against stout packing crates. He returned to the subject of art and fame. "I wondered. Your name's familiar, and for some reason I associate it with art."

"Jeremy Michaels."

Devon frowned only for a moment. "Now I've got it. And how could I forget! The experts have called him America's answer to Michelangelo; what he could express in sculpture has never been surpassed, before or since, by any other American artist—and by few in history. And he was also considered an expert in detecting forgeries in all forms of art; museums and collectors the world over trusted him to authenticate artworks." Devon looked at her steadily, questioningly. "And he was—?"

"My father." Tory smiled faintly. "So you see, I've been familiar with fame secondhand all my life. I don't care to experience it firsthand."

"*Because* your father was famous?"

"Maybe." She stared off into memory. "He told me once that fame was damnably easy to acquire—and damnably hard to control. But he did it." She smiled again. "Daddy's bathroom was completely mirrored. Not out of vanity, but out of humility. He said that after he'd stumble in there each morning and see the reflections of himself, unshaven, red-eyed, and wearing baggy pajamas, he never had to be reminded that he was . . . just a man."

Devon was watching her, not with the intensity she half dreaded, but with a curious *intentness*. "Did he expect you to follow in his footsteps and sculpt? Or did you feel that you had to paint to be different from him?"

"Neither." Tory was responding more to compelling green eyes than to his questions, and that bewildered her. "Daddy never pressured me. In fact, he gave me a lot of good reasons to avoid art altogether. I think he was pleased when I decided to paint, but I also think he would have been just as pleased if I'd chosen to paint houses instead of canvases. As long as I was happy with my decision, so was he."

"You're lucky."

Tory wondered if she'd imagined Devon's soft words, but she never had the chance to ask him. Briskly, he got to his feet and helped her to hers.

"Shall we unpack?" he asked politely.

Tory looked up into clear, unclouded green eyes and fought a sudden desire to hit him with the nearest handy object. Damn the man and his compelling, changeable, intriguing eyes! Like the smooth mirror surface of a lake they reflected calm and peace, then were abruptly disturbed by some pebble tossed in at random, causing ripples and changes . . . and puzzles.

Hastily, she pulled her hands from his. "Um . . . right."

If Devon hadn't realized early that morning that Tory Michaels was a complex woman, he very soon revised his initial impression of her. The first surprise had been the change in her physically: The survivor of the morning's war against wakefulness had become a beautiful woman whose entrancingly changeable eyes were vulnerable at first glance yet became guarded and controlled on closer inspection. There was a tense fragility about her that was reflected more in her stillness than in anything she said, and he had to fight, more than once, an instinct to take her in his arms and soothe the troubled, puzzled frown from her brow.

He was too wise a man to ask her point-blank what disturbed her; the very few probing questions he'd ventured had met with definite resistance. And so he bided his time, concentrating first on maneuvering his way into her life in the most unthreatening way he could think of, without bothering to question his own motives too closely. That she distrusted him he knew; her reasons seemed more the result of past experience than anything he'd done or said. He filed that realization away in his brain and went about the business of finding out what he could about her by observing her and what she surrounded herself with.

She was upstairs when he began to unpack some of the crates in the barren downstairs room she had chosen for a work area. The carpet had been torn up to reveal a dully polished hardwood floor, and the only saving grace of the room to Devon's way of thinking was the row of floor-to-ceiling windows with a northern exposure lining an entire wall. He knew enough about art to understand why she'd chosen the space, and although she hadn't requested his help in unpacking the crates holding canvases, curiosity drove him to it.

He hesitated only momentarily, hoping devoutly that she wasn't the type of artist who'd resent his handling her work, then began to pry open crates carefully.

He propped the unframed canvases against one wall as he unpacked them, halting only when the first half-dozen were done. Then he stepped back to really look at them. They were a series, he realized immediately, meant to be viewed in a group. All were desert scenes, with cacti as the focus of the work. At first glance they were simply beautifully painted representations of the stark loneliness and majesty of deserts, but then Devon looked again, more carefully, and he recognized the quality that set this work and Tory's talent apart from anything he'd ever seen.

As he studied intently, the first painting of a cactus became instead the primitive form of a weeping woman. Head bowed with crushing grief, shoulders slumped, she was as starkly beautiful as the desert surrounding her, and just as desolate.

Devon ached instantly for her.

The second painting of the series depicted a cactusman. Harsh, aloof, selfish, arrogant, there was cruelty and beauty in his face and pride in his stance. He seemed to gaze toward the horizon with the look of a conqueror, heavy-lidded eyes cold and calculating, and a clenched fist held delicate flowers crushed by unthinking, uncaring strength.

Devon hated him.

The third painting depicted two cacti rather than one; naturally they must have grown from a common root. Artistically, Tory had interpreted lovers being torn from one another's arms. The woman was half turned, falling away from the man, her face a rough, thorny portrait of bewildered, stunned despair. The man reached for her, but one hand was a fist and the other a claw, both punishing although they didn't touch the woman. And his face was, like the second painting, a portrait of cruel beauty.

Devon hated the man with a hatred that surprised him.

Refusing to look at the remaining three paintings in that moment, he strode to the wall of windows and stared out. Raking a hand through his hair, he was startled at the tremor in his fingers, bewildered to realize that the paintings of powerful, cruel emotions had moved him so deeply.

He remained at the windows for several minutes, then finally took a deep breath and turned to the fourth painting.

The woman again. No longer grieving, she stood in the bleak desert and stared into a fiery red sunset. Her shoulders were set squarely with determination, her head high. And her face—her beautiful, hurt face—was still and empty and set in ragged pride.

Devon swallowed hard and looked at the fifth painting. The man. But this man could only be pitied rather than hated. His beauty was a soulless thing, his pride and strength only crutches. His cruelty was unthinking but obvious. He gazed off at a distant mountain, seeing not the beauty but the obstacle, not the majesty but the inconvenience. He saw with his eyes but not his heart.

The sixth painting depicted two cacti standing some few feet apart. The lovers again. She stood with her back to him, her face oddly featureless this time; there was something unformed about her, a lack of personality. No, Devon realized suddenly, a lack of emotion. Her beautiful face revealed only indifference. The man stood watching her, his thorny face puzzled, his body stiff with anger and . . . fear? He seemed a man who had lost something he had never known enough to value and who was now confused by his sense of loss.

Devon knew instinctively that Tory's remarkable insight into these particular emotions came from experience. And the harrowing emotions she had captured in oil revealed a depth of feeling he hadn't expected to find in her. Under the heading of "artistic intuition," of course, artists were expected to feel things very deeply; Devon believed that Tory's paintings—these, at least—came straight from the heart. Her heart.

Talented though she quite obviously was, these six paintings represented a clear coming to terms with her own feelings; they cried out with the mute violence that Tory's own controlled stillness would reject.

He knew, with the certainty of perception and a sudden muted anger of his own, that these paintings had shed Tory's tears for her.

"I didn't ask you to open these crates."

Devon turned slowly to face Tory. He heard no anger in her voice, but instinct warned him that these next few moments would determine whether or not he had truly begun to carve a place for himself here. "No. D'you mind?"

She was standing just inside the doorway, leaning back against the jamb, and the wariness that disturbed him was present in her gray eyes. She glanced at the paintings. "Odd. You have them in the right order."

"D'you mind?" he repeated steadily.

"I suppose not."

He looked back at the paintings for a moment, then at her. "These are . . . extraordinary, Tory."

She inclined her head slightly, an abrupt gesture indicating thanks but also indicating a discomfort with the subject and perhaps even a trace of embarrassment for the naked emotions expressed in the paintings.

Devon probed cautiously, choosing to ignore—for the moment,

at least—her clear unwillingness to discuss the paintings. "They're incredible. I've never seen cacti used to represent people before."

"Anthropomorphism," she said flatly. "Attributing human characteristics to nonhuman things. But you know that."

Devon was almost certain she had brought up the concept to promote a very neat change of subject. But he refused to chase wild geese.

"You've captured such a wide range of emotion," he said, watching her face intently. "It's harrowing just to *look* at each painting."

"Wasted emotion," she said abruptly.

"No. Not wasted." He gestured slightly. "You've created a—a series representing growth. From despair to rebirth. It's a brilliant achievement, Tory."

"Thank you." She was still abrupt.

Devon saw that her wariness was increasing, her lovely face beginning to shut down into an impenetrable mask, and he instantly abandoned the subject in order to prevent that. "I'll leave the rest in here to you; I imagine you'll want the workroom to be arranged a certain way," he said cheerfully. "How about in the living room? The paintings in those crates?"

The brief, puzzled frown disturbed her face, then vanished. She pushed herself away from the jamb and started out to the foyer. "They're not my work; I want to hang them in the living room."

Devon followed. "Okay. I'll go get some tools from the truck. Back in a minute."

Tory heard the front door close behind him. She moved slowly into the living room, automatically fishing the kitten from the opened crate he seemed to be stuck in. She set him on the floor and absently scolded him for scattering packing straw everywhere, then knelt and continued with the unpacking that Devon's arrival, their lunch, and her trip upstairs to put away linens had interrupted.

Her hands performed the tasks without direction from her mind, because her mind was reliving what she had seen moments ago in the workroom. The humorous, affable Devon had not gazed at her paintings; he had looked at them, instead, with the intensity she had seen once before. And mixed with that had been the astute intelligence she mistrusted.

Sharp enough to cut himself. . . .

But he had thrown her off guard again, changing the subject instantly and distracting her attention. Damn the man. Tory gazed blindly down at a jade figurine for a long time, looking up only when she heard him returning.

"Got 'em," he told her easily, setting a toolbox down on the floor near the French doors. "I'll unpack the crates first; then you can tell me where you want everything."

"What d'you do for a living?" she demanded, ignoring his words.

Devon looked down at her with a raised brow. "What brought that on?" he asked.

"Answer the question," she requested, thinking of the shrewdness and sharp intelligence that were curiously at odds with his affability.

He stepped over to a crate, beginning to pry it open. "I'll let you guess," he told her maddeningly.

"Devon—"

"Hey!" He reached down suddenly to pluck the kitten from the left leg of his pants, where tiny claws were engaged in trying to climb. "Hang on to Dumbo here, will you? Try to convince him I'm not a tree."

Distracted once again, Tory accepted the kitten and held him in her lap. "Don't call him that," she said, pulling gently at the over-large ears of her new pet. "You'll hurt his feelings."

"He didn't do much for my leg," Devon pointed out politely.

"You can take care of yourself."

"So can he. Obviously."

Tory stared up into limpid green eyes for a moment, then announced firmly, "You changed the subject."

"Did I?" he wondered vaguely.

She sighed. "Look, if you don't want me to know what you do for a living, just *say* that, okay?"

"I don't want you to know what I do for a living."

"Why not?"

"Mystery."

"I think we've had this conversation before."

"It does sound familiar, doesn't it?"

Tory decided that two could play his game of innocent subject-changes. It wouldn't make her come out on top, since she *still* didn't know what he did for a living, but at least she stood a chance of keeping the dratted man as off balance as he kept her. "Whiskey," she said calmly.

"You feel the need for a drink?" Devon asked politely.

She held the kitten up to her neck, where he burrowed happily beneath her hair. "His name is Whiskey."

Irritatingly, Devon appeared as evenly balanced as always.

"S'fine by me. I won't ask how he happened to 'name himself' Whiskey, though."

Tory abandoned any further attempt to throw Devon off balance. There appeared to be a trick to the thing, requiring a mastery she didn't—yet—possess. "Careful with that," she directed as he began removing a large framed painting from the opened crate. "It's older than both of us." She set Whiskey to one side and shooed him gently away.

Holding the painting carefully, Devon stared at it for a long moment, then looked down at Tory. "She has to be an ancestor."

"Great-Great-Grandmother Magda."

He whistled softly. "You're the living spit of her."

"I know. And the odd thing is that nobody else in the family has ever looked even remotely like her. Daddy was a brown-eyed blond, and *his* father was a redhead."

"So you're a descendant through the male line?"

"Uh-huh. My great-great-grandfather—Magda's husband—was dark, too, but he was Irish-dark. Where Magda was born nobody knows; she was a Gypsy." Tory smiled suddenly. "And that ends the family history lesson for today."

Devon continued to study the painting. The resemblance, he thought, was truly remarkable. From the fine blue-black raven's-wing hair to the heart-shaped face and the eyes that seemed to subtly change color even as he stared, Tory was the living image of her great-great-grandmother. The painting had been done when Magda was roughly Tory's age, youth blending smoothly into womanhood. The clothing of an earlier era, curiously enough, enhanced the likeness. Magda's expression alone differed from Tory's. There was no wariness in the Gypsy's face, only the serenity of certain self-knowledge; there was no guarded firmness in her curved lips.

If Magda had ever been hurt by life, she had put it behind her and forgotten it.

Noticing his continued interest in the painting, Tory, puzzled, resumed the history lesson. "I never knew her; she died before I was born. Daddy said she was the stillest woman he'd ever known. Never nervous, never restless. And she adored her husband."

Devon took a deep breath and released it slowly. "You're lucky to have this. Not many of us can point to . . . tangible roots."

"Can you?" she asked, suddenly curious.

He shook his head slightly. "No. I never even knew my grandparents."

Tory, thinking of the rich lore handed down to her by generations, the stories and legends and personalities, felt sorry for Devon. What a lot he had missed out on!

"Where d'you want this hung?" he asked.

She pointed to the wall between two front windows. "There." She watched him carefully hang the painting, making sure its anchor to the wall was secure, and felt her interest in the man growing. This time she didn't try to deny that interest; she merely considered it.

Why did the man fascinate her? Because he was complex, a puzzle—she knew that. Because the affable and courteous gentleman he was on the surface masked, she knew, something else, something more intriguing. The urge to paint him had not diminished; she *did* ignore that. What disturbed her now was that her interest in him was the purely human and feminine attraction to the handsome and charming man standing just across the room.

Other than taking her hands briefly, he hadn't so much as touched her. And yet . . . Tory was almost painfully aware of his every move and gesture. She pondered that, trying to be analytical about it. Trying—and failing. She was too aware of the man to back off and view him objectively. She knew only that something about him, perhaps a hint of vulnerability she sensed more than saw, got to her.

And then, quite suddenly, Tory realized in disgust that she was being entirely too paranoid about Devon York. Whether or not she was attracted to him, Devon was simply a very nice, unusual man with time on his hands who'd decided to help out a lady in distress; after her description of her chaotic morning, he probably thought she needed a keeper. Perhaps he even felt— ridiculous, but possible—responsible for her just because she happened to have bought a house formerly owned by his new sister-in-law.

Whatever his reasoning, Devon obviously had nothing more on his mind than companionship and a means to wile away his— his what?—vacation? Anything else was just a product of her overactive imagination. Tory chided herself mentally and tried to relax. But that was difficult, because although Devon's attitude seemed perfectly straightforward, her own was becoming increasingly confused.

"Tory?"

"Hmm?" She blinked up at him. He had hung the portrait and now stood a couple of feet away, looking down at her. "Oh, sorry. You were saying?"

Devon looked hurt. "The least you can do is pay attention to my proposals!" he complained woefully.

She blinked again. "Sorry. I'm all ears."

In an aggrieved voice, he repeated his proposal. "I *said* that you really should marry me, because then I could share your ancestors. I mean, since I don't have any of my own."

"Of course you have ancestors," she said reasonably. "You wouldn't be here if you didn't. You just don't know who they were, that's all."

"Whatever. And you didn't respond to the proposal."

"Then I will. If you want ancestors, take up genealogy."

Devon shook his head. "You're cruel."

"I know. It's terrible, isn't it?"

He sighed heavily. "I'll say. Ah, well, what's next?"

Having finally decided to relax and enjoy Devon's relatively unthreatening company, Tory found the remainder of the day a lot of fun. They put the house in order in an astonishingly short time and without the exhaustion she would have suffered had she done the work alone. There was still a lot to be done, as Devon pointed out helpfully, but progress through each room was no longer impeded by crates and boxes.

Paintings and prints were ranged along the walls, propped up beneath the places where they'd later be hung; figurines, vases, and other ornaments were grouped together on tables and shelves, ready to be placed in as yet unacquired curio cabinets; Tory's sparse furniture was placed where she decided—for now, anyway—she wanted it.

Tory and Devon worked both together and separately during the day, more often than not, they busied themselves in different rooms. Devon had quickly discovered her rather extensive stereo system and had loaded the turntable with a stack of semiclassical albums. So music filled the house.

And laughter. Devon came in search of her at least once every hour, voicing a new and creative proposal and then retreating with a hangdog expression after hearing her polite rejection. He called out cheerful questions about her possessions from time to time, seemingly fascinated by the heirlooms being steadily unpacked. He found a stack of yellowed tarot cards and requested that she tell his fortune—being the great-great-granddaughter of a Gypsy, after all. Matching his solemnity, Tory promised to do so one day.

It was fairly late when they quit for the day and shared a hastily and jointly prepared supper of steak and salad. Conversation was cheerful, a bit weary, and very general—not a disturbing word or puzzling look exchanged between them. They shared the cleaning chores, still companionable.

And then Devon left with a promise to return in the morning and an easy good-bye.

Tory automatically made sure the house was locked up, double-checked to see that Whiskey had a bowl of kitten food in the kitchen in case hunger pangs attacked during the night, and then trailed up to her bedroom.

The bed was assembled, thanks to Devon, and neatly made, her clothing put away in drawers and closet. She took a hot shower, donned a filmy nylon gown, and went back into her bedroom to find that Whiskey had climbed onto the bed with what must have been a heroic effort and was waiting for her.

"If you get lost during the night and can't find your box," she told him sleepily as she drew back the covers, "don't wake me up."

Ignoring the order, the kitten squirmed beneath the covers and curled up at her side. His rumbling purr was muffled by blankets but still audible, and Tory giggled drowsily. She lay back on the pillows, then sat up again abruptly as she felt something hard beneath them. Cautiously sliding a hand underneath, she found a book.

It was a small, exquisitely bound volume of poetry. Love poetry.

Tory knew each and every book she owned, and she was positive this wasn't one of them. She opened it, puzzled, and discovered a bookmark placed precisely at the poem titled "How Do I Love Thee." The bookmark bore the glittering representation of a unicorn and the words "May all your dreams come true."

No matter how efficient or always-prepared Devon was, Tory was reasonably sure he wouldn't carry such a thing around in his pocket—which meant that he'd been a very busy man between his first and second trips to her house. She revisited one of her favorite poems and then read a few others, trying to convince herself that this was merely a continuation of Devon's exercises in creative proposing. Nothing more. Nothing more than that.

She almost convinced herself.

The next few days very nearly repeated the pattern of that first one. Devon always arrived reasonably late in the morning, giving Tory time to be up and awake, and he always brought food—prepared or ready to be—with him. He was preceded each morning by a delivery man bearing silk flowers of various types and arrangements, and nothing Tory could say in protest had any effect on the arrival of the gifts. And somehow, without her seeing him, Devon always managed to leave something beneath her pillow. A heart-shaped box of candy. A silk scarf. An I.D. bracelet with her name on one side and "My Bright Particular Star" on the other.

Tory had easily completed the quotation in her mind: "That I should love a bright, particular star and think to wed it." And she convinced herself yet again that he was still practicing his proposals. Just practicing.

Because Devon was rapidly becoming the best friend she'd had in years. He made her laugh. He kept her on her toes mentally, since she never knew when he'd suddenly turn shrewd eyes on her or when his deep voice would become suddenly intense. Those little "lapses" never lasted long, and they intrigued her because she had quickly realized that Devon was usually in complete control of himself.

But in spite of her uneasiness regarding those lapses, Tory thoroughly enjoyed his company. She was in no hurry to go back to work; he certainly seemed in no hurry. So they leisurely put her house in order and spent long hours talking about casual, unimportant things.

And if Tory realized, at some deep and vital level, that she was falling in love with him, she banished that half-formed realization from her heart and mind.

Because Devon never bestowed anything more than the most casual of touches, and it was quite obvious that he was merely a man with time on his hands. Nothing more.

And she banished any thoughts of love because, aside from his own obvious disinterest, she had no emotional energy to waste on a relationship; she needed all she had for her work. *That* emotional energy could be channeled into a useful outlet, and she knew all too well that any other outlet was a baited trap for the unwary.

Not for Tory Michaels.

She had gone through an emotional catharsis two years ago, and once was enough for her. The violence of her own feelings had shocked and frightened her, and she never wanted to experience another such loss of control. Ever.

Chapter Four

"*You promised to tell my fortune,*" he said firmly, handing her the yellowed tarot cards.

They were in her den, sitting on the comfortable couch before a newly built roaring fire. Whiskey was curled up on a pillow by the hearth, close enough to the fire to feel the heat but not close enough to burn his tail, and two half-empty wineglasses reposed on the coffee table. It was past nine o'clock at night, and thunder had been rumbling warningly for some time. Tory listened as the wind picked up outside, then looked at Devon. "You sure picked a good night for it."

"What we *really* need," he said in a theatrically throbbing voice, "is for the lights to go out."

At that exact moment, they did.

There was a deafening crash of thunder, and brilliant lightning lit their still faces. Then the wind howled eerily, and rain began to pelt the house as if in attack.

Mildly, Tory said, "Your timing is perfect."

"I'll be damned," he said blankly.

The firelight cast a flickering golden glow over the room, leaving corners in shadow, but even the darkest recesses were washed white when lightning bent its frowning glare on them.

"Sure you want me to read your fortune?" she asked wryly.

"I'm sure." Devon winced slightly as thunder crashed again, then looked at her. She was lovelier than ever in the fire's soft glow, and he found himself fighting urges even more powerful than those he'd fought for days. Resolutely, he kept his mind on the subject at hand. "But first, tell me if I should take this seriously or if it's just a parlor game. I mean, did you inherit more than black hair and strange Gypsy eyes from Magda?"

Tory turned the cards in her hands for a moment, staring down at them. The firelight had turned her eyes to silver and carved hollows beneath her cheekbones, lending her normally piquant face an air of mystery that was perfectly suited to the stormy night and his stormy emotions.

"I guess it depends on what you believe," she said finally, wondering if she should tell him that, Gypsy ancestor notwithstanding, she'd never tried to tell anyone's fortune before. Oh, she'd learned the most elementary rules for setting out the first several cards; Ouija boards and tarot cards had been something of a fad when she was a teenager. But aside from keeping a tarot deck, she'd never indulged in things mystical. She decided not to mention that little fact. Devon York wasn't the only one who could hanker for a bit of mystery, after all.

"What do *you* believe?" he asked softly.

She looked at him with limpid eyes and said in what she hoped was a mysterious voice, "I'm descended from a Gypsy, remember? I believe in a lot of things I can't see with my eyes or hold in my hands." She held out the cards to him, hoping her memory would serve her well. "Now, tap the deck and then cut it."

Wordlessly, he followed her directions.

Tory dealt the cards in a pattern on the coffee table, explaining what each card meant—of itself and in relation to those surrounding it—as she turned it faceup. It wasn't difficult to ad lib, since each card's illustration rather graphically reminded her of its most obvious meaning.

"Your past. Something divided. Strife. Opposition. Then— decision. Following a—new path. No, making a path of your own. Yourself still divided, still not whole. Your present. Suspension. A time of waiting. Still not whole. Your future, shown by three cards. The first, a storm, danger. The second, a journey. The third, the sun, coming gratification. An end of waiting. Wholeness."

When Tory turned up the next card, she fell silent, staring down at it. It figured, she thought wryly; she *would* have to turn up that particular card!

"Don't stop now," Devon murmured. He, too, was staring down at the card. He didn't know much about tarot cards, but he knew a representation of entwined lovers when he saw one.

Tory said nothing about that card, but she turned up the next one, flanking the card bearing the lovers. "This is your card," she said carefully. "It represents you." Then she turned up another card, placing it, also, next to the lovers. Hastily, she swept the cards up, saying a bit breathlessly, "And that's all."

But Devon had seen that last card; it bore the image of a dark-haired woman with mysterious eyes, and he didn't have to be a wizard or the descendant of a Gypsy to guess what it meant.

"So we're going to be lovers," he said calmly.

"You and a dark-haired woman, perhaps," she said instantly, shuffling the cards with restless, jerky movements. "Not me."

He reached out to cover her hands with one of his. "Shouldn't we be sure about that? Ready your fortune now."

Tory stared down at his hand for a long moment, then took a deep breath. "All right." She tried to tell herself the cards were virtually meaningless, superstition at best, but her inner arguments lacked conviction. She'd spent many a childhood hour watching her father sculpt and listening to his stories about the Gypsies—stories he had believed. And when one hears stories from a parent one adores, belief is automatic and enduring; part of her had always believed.

Forcing her fingers to be steady, she tapped the deck, cut it, and began to deal, speaking evenly.

"My past. Happiness. Then disillusionment. Solitude." She hesitated at the next card, then continued firmly, "Not whole. My present. Suspension. A—a time of waiting."

Dizzily, she wondered at the similarity of their fortunes. She knew it couldn't be wishful thinking on her part, since the cards could only be interpreted the way they fell. And her interpretation of them, she knew, was correct. She went on determinedly.

"My future. A storm. A journey. The sun, coming gratification. An end of waiting. Wholeness." She turned up the next card.

The lovers.

"The next card is me." She turned it up slowly, not surprised to see the dark-haired woman. She placed it beside the lovers, then turned up the next card and placed it on the other side of the lovers.

It was Devon's card.

"You see?" he murmured softly. "We are meant to be lovers."

Tory was determined to treat the matter lightly. "The odds against that must be astronomical," she said easily, sweeping the cards up. "I mean, two fortunes told, one right after the other, and both so similar. And the bits about storms. It's uncanny, isn't it?"

"Not if you believe in fate and Gypsy fortune-telling."

She slid the cards back into their box and placed it on the coffee table. "We live in the twentieth century, Devon," she said a bit more breathlessly than she'd intended. "Fortune-telling belongs in carnival sideshows. You don't really believe—"

"Don't I?"

Quite suddenly, she found herself hauled against the solid wall of his chest, and through the thin material of his shirt she could feel an erratic pounding that must have been his heart. Her fingers moved instinctively, probing the muscled firmness covering that heart. And then she realized what she was doing. "Devon—"

"I believe," he murmured huskily, his lips feathering lightly along her jawline, "in fortune-telling, my little tzigane, my little *zingara*. I believe. Especially when it only confirms what I've felt myself since the morning I saw a plaid robe and a purple towel and strange Gypsy eyes."

"You—you never showed it," she managed weakly, aware that her head was tilting back to allow him more room to explore and unable to do a damn thing about her body's reaction. "Deceiver . . . you're an unscrupulous, conniving, deceitful—"

"Hungry man," he finished with a low laugh. "Hungry for a *zingara*'s touch."

"What . . . does that mean? *Zingara*?" She was stingingly aware of his lips moving toward the corner of her own like a whisper of promise. And she knew she should be thinking very seriously about what was happening, but somehow that seemed impossible. Later. She'd think about it later. *When it's too late to think!* her mind sneered—but she didn't listen.

"It's Italian for Gypsy," Devon murmured, his lips hovering just above hers. He guided her gently back until she was lying on the couch with him stretched out close beside her, their bodies pressed together. "I've never kissed a *zingara*," he breathed.

Tory stared, wide-eyed, even after his lips touched hers. His face was so fascinating, half in shadow and half glowing golden from the firelight. . . . And then her eyes drifted closed as a warmth having nothing to do with the fire began spreading through her.

He was gentle, almost hesitant, as if he felt that to move too quickly would be to frighten her. His lips moved tentatively over hers, probing, shaping, listening with other senses. His tongue traced the sensitive inner surface of her lips in a searching little caress that brought the blood pounding to her head.

Resistance had never been on Tory's mind, and although the sneering little voice within her idly condemned her for it, she could hardly help but respond. This fascinating, changeable man had somehow turned the tables on her yet again, knocking her off balance with his sudden desire. Her fingers slid up his chest, curling to dig into his shoulders as emptiness yawned abruptly inside of her.

Her mouth bloomed beneath his, warming, becoming hungry. The woodsy scent of his cologne filled her senses, transporting her in time and place to enchanted forests where elves laughed and Gypsies danced. The warmth of those pagan campfires ran hotly through her veins, igniting feelings she'd not known existed within her. And she knew now why Magda smiled with such serene mystery in the portrait, knew now what the Gypsy woman had also known.

She had never felt this way before.

Not even with . . .

Tory gasped as his lips left hers to burn a trail down the V neckline of her sweater, striving desperately to push the half-formed realization out of her mind. Nonsense. She barely knew this man.

But his lips were a brand against her flesh, a brand of possession, and she could feel the tremor in his body answer her own. Thunder rumbled outside as his fingers slid beneath the sweater to touch the soft, quivering skin of her stomach, and his hand was a live wire to shock and ignite.

Too fast, it was happening too fast, and somehow they had to slow down. . . .

"*Zingara* . . ."

The distraction came rather suddenly and from an unexpected source, and Tory felt an overwhelming urge to giggle. "Um . . . Devon?"

"Hmm?"

"Why are you wearing an earring?"

His head lifted abruptly, the hand beneath her sweater transferring its attention to his ear, where her fingers still toyed gently.

"Ah, hell," he muttered, clearly torn between disgust and chagrin. "I forgot all about that!"

It wasn't much as earrings went—just a golden loop so fine as to be virtually invisible. Tory hadn't even noticed it until her searching fingers had encountered it. "I *have* to know why you're wearing an earring," she said solemnly.

Devon sighed, then smiled ruefully down at her. "Not because I wanted to, believe me. I was . . . uh . . . made a sort of honorary member of a tribe, and the earring is the . . . badge of membership. It would have been an insult to refuse, and afterward I just forgot the damn thing."

"Tribe?" She stared up at him, bemused. "Of Indians?"

"You could say that. Strictly speaking. It was in South America a few months back."

After a moment, and very calmly, Tory said, "If you don't tell me right now—this very minute—what you do for a living, I shall quite probably kill you."

"It's very dull," he evaded.

"Devon."

"*Very* dull. No mystery."

"Devon!"

"Hell. I'm an archaeologist."

Tory gazed up at his face, seeing there an odd sort of defensiveness, and she added another piece to the puzzle this man was. After a moment, she said dryly, "I'd hardly call deserts, sheikhs, ambassadors, and honorary memberships in native tribes *dull*."

He looked at her, one green eye brilliant in the firelight and the other in shadow, and the tension she had seen in his face seemed to drain away. "You wouldn't?" He hesitated, then added doggedly, "It usually is, you know. Dull. Hours of repetitive work, usually with little gain. Living in tents. Wearing a ton of dust or sand in your clothes. Eating out of cans because God only knows what's in the local community stewpot."

"Studying the past," she said softly. "Piecing together a culture dead for centuries. Touching a life that was. Dull? Oh, no, Devon—not dull."

She touched the tiny golden earring that so nearly matched his golden flesh, and her vivid imagination conjured an image of another pagan campfire, this one surrounded by faces solemn with ceremony. She smiled suddenly. "Did it hurt?"

His fingers moved to lightly fondle one of her own pierced lobes. "You tell me," he said wryly.

"It did!" She laughed.

"Damned right!" Then he sobered, gazing down at her with a curious wonder in his face. "Why didn't I meet you ten years ago?" he mused softly.

"What was her name?" Tory asked quietly.

He was obviously startled. "Her?"

"The woman who convinced you your work was dull."

"Oh. Her. Lisa." He touched her face gently, "And you're a very perceptive lady, *zingara*."

"I just hope she—didn't hurt you too much," Tory said a bit uncertainly, wondering at her own words.

"I survived."

Before Tory could question him, Devon had turned the tables on her yet again. "And what about you, *zingara*? What was *his* name?"

"Who?"

"The cactus-man. The man with the beautiful, cruel face who hurt you."

Laughing a little shakily, she said, "We seem to be a perceptive pair tonight."

"Tory . . ."

She took a deep breath, keeping her arms around his neck because there was an odd security in that and because the pagan fires that had warmed her blood still flickered beneath his verbal probing. "His name was Jordan. And he hurt me only because I was too blind to see him for what he really was."

"And do you still hurt because of him?" Devon asked quietly.

Tory hesitated, then answered honestly. "No. But he left me . . . wary."

"Wary enough to fight the cards' prediction?" He watched her face intently, looking for a return of the mask. But it didn't return. Instead, she looked up at him with a new vulnerability in her Gypsy eyes, and he felt his heart lurch inside him.

"I don't know, Devon."

And she didn't know. Not that. All she knew was that she would be taking a huge gamble if she let Devon into her mind and heart. Because once that happened, she'd never be rid of him. Unlike Jordan, Devon would become a part of her, and she knew it.

She'd carry him with her all the days of her life. Already he was under her skin. . . .

"Then we'll take our time, *zingara*." He kissed her very gently with no demand, his fingers smoothing the fine black hair away from her face. "We'll take all the time you need."

Tory stared up at him, feeling the pagan pounding in her veins, and marveled at his patience. Or perhaps he just didn't feel the same desire that she did? " 'You're a better man than I am, Gunga Din,' " she said tremulously.

Devon looked at her, his green eyes probing with the shrewdness that no longer surprised her. Then, softly, he said, "There's another quotation from Kipling. 'Through the Jungle very softly flits a shadow and a sigh—He is Fear, O Little Hunter, he is Fear!' I've seen that shadow on your face, *zingara*. I don't like it there. I don't want it there. So I'll wait. Even if I have to lash myself to a mast in the meantime."

Just as softly, her eyes gazing into the jewel-green brilliance of his, she said, "Ulysses had himself lashed to a mast so he could hear the siren song but not go overboard to his death."

Devon nodded. "Don't you know?" he murmured. "You're a living siren song, little *zingara*. But it isn't death I fear; it's seeing you turn away from me. So. I wait."

Tory was bewildered by his quiet intensity, by the stark truth in his eyes. It was almost as if— But no. He hadn't mentioned love. Only desire. Her body curved into his as he stretched out fully beside her; they both faced the fire in the hearth, and she could feel his heart beating strongly against her back, feel his breath stirring her hair, feel his powerful arms wrapped around her. But she could no longer look into his face, and for that she was grateful.

She listened to the inner voice now, listened to the warnings her mind had been screaming, heard but ignored, for some time now.

Devon York was a dangerous man.

An insidiously dangerous man.

And she was a fool.

What did he want of her? Obviously he wanted to know her in a way only one other man had known her. He wanted her, and he was prepared to wait for what he wanted. Why? Because she didn't think his profession dull and boring? Ridiculous. That was ridiculous. Because the cards foretold that they would be lovers? Even more ridiculous. Devon was certainly a rational man, an intellectual man; he wouldn't put faith in such nonsense as tarot cards. Even if they *were* read by the descendant of a Gypsy.

Tory stared fixedly at the fire's golden flame until everything but that became hazy and unreal.

He wanted her.

He would wait.

He loves me . . .

He loves me not . . .

The flames wavered before her eyes, filling her vision and her mind. It didn't matter, really. Not really. Because, of course, she didn't love him. She wouldn't let herself love him. He was a complex, deceptively unthreatening man who bore scars. The distaste and probable ridicule of the woman who had thought his profession dull had left scars. How deep those scars went, she had no idea. But they existed. Chinks in his armor.

He was a strong man, was Devon York. Intelligent, witty, honest, determined, perhaps even ruthless in his own deceptively quiet way. And that strength attracted her, intrigued her. But it was his vulnerability, the chinks in his armor that she feared. Strength could be met with strength, but vulnerability . . . vulnerability could not be defended against. It was the most devastating weapon of all, the one that would defeat her in the end if anything did.

Not, of course, that she loved him.

That was absurd.

Remember the saying, her sneering inner voice warned: *Fool me once, shame on you. Fool me twice, shame on me.*

Was she going to allow herself to make another emotional judgment that would devastate her? Would she let her hard-won rationality be overborne by the fleeting pleasures of reckless love?

No, Tory Michaels didn't intend to be fooled twice. And God knew that Jordan had come into her life just as unthreateningly as Devon. With his charming smiles and his witty remarks, he had effortlessly captured her interest and her love. And when that love withered and died a painful death in the face of stark truth and understanding, it was Jordan who emerged unscathed. Not she.

Blinking, Tory brought the fire back into focus. Well, she decided firmly, this time she would emerge unscathed. Except that there wouldn't be anything to emerge *from*, because . . . No. No, there *would* be something to emerge from; she was already involved with Devon.

All right! she thought fiercely. All *right*, then! She couldn't deceive herself into believing she wasn't attracted to the man; why not name that attraction *desire* and be done with it?

But it would be all right. Just a brief interlude before Devon returned to his deserts and ruins and she to her art. Just a brief interlude, and God knew she was entitled, wasn't she? She should take him at face value, accept the warmth and companionship and desire he offered, and remain heart-whole when it was over.

And she could do that.

If she didn't fall in love with him.

Tory felt his heart beating against her, felt the even rise and fall of his chest that meant he was probably asleep, and she wondered again at his control. Devon York seemed a man superbly equipped to walk confidently through life, scars notwithstanding. A man in complete control of himself and his life. A man almost perpetually on balance.

She listened to the thunder rumbling outside, to the rain and wind and to her misgivings and fears. She looked down at the arms holding her securely, aware that the pagan fire within her, though banked by rational thoughts, still smoldered.

And when sleep claimed her sometime later, it brought no counsel.

Always reluctant to face a new day, Tory fought waking as long as possible. When she did finally manage to unglue her eyelids, she noticed several things. The first was that Whiskey had apparently decided sometime during the night to bed down on her chest, since he was curled up mere inches from her chin, sound asleep. The second that she was on the couch, lying mostly on her back. The third was that it was a sunny, stormless morning.

The fourth was that Devon still lay beside her; he was poised on an elbow and was smiling down at her with what she irritably felt to be an ungodly amount of morning cheer.

"Good morning," he murmured.

"Hello," she responded blearily.

"It's a beautiful day," he offered.

"Interested in a rebuttal to that?"

Devon laughed.

Tory winced; it just wasn't decent, she thought, to be so bright-eyed so early in the day. "Is today really *necessary*?" she wondered plaintively. "Couldn't we skip it and go straight to tomorrow?"

"That's not the way it works," he explained solemnly.

"It's the way it should work. In fact, today should always be outlawed in favor of tomorrow."

"You sound like a poster I saw once."

"Oh?"

"Uh-huh. It ran something like: 'I'd like the day better if it began later.' "

"I'll drink to that."

"The sun isn't over the yardarm yet."

"It must be over the yardarm *somewhere*."

"This is true."

Quite abruptly, Tory remembered the night before, and it must have shown on her face or in her eyes because Devon immediately leaned down and kissed her gently, the scrape of his morning beard an oddly sensuous little caress.

"Don't panic on me now," he murmured.

"I never panic," she managed staunchly.

"I know." He was smiling. "You never panic and you never cry. You're a tough lady, aren't you, *zingara*?"

"Very tough." Tory didn't know whom she was trying to convince: Devon or herself.

"Then tell me, tough lady, what're you afraid of?"

Tory stared up at him, aware that she was in no shape to answer that very pointed question in anything but a very revealing manner. But he was looking down at her gravely now, and she suddenly decided that it might, perhaps, be best to lay her cards on the table for him to see.

"You," she said starkly.

A frown drew his brows together. "Why?"

She searched through the list of reasons, condensing all of them, finally, under one neat heading. "Because I don't understand you."

"Is that so important?" he asked with a quizzical half-smile. "I don't completely understand you either, *zingara*. But we have time."

"Do we?"

"Sure."

Tory remembered her advice to herself of the night before and decided somewhat grimly to follow it. She'd take him at face value and accept what he offered. And if a part of her was still intent on understanding him, then so be it. She wanted to understand her friend.

Before he became her lover.

Chapter Five

Tory stood in the kitchen, drinking coffee and staring down at Whiskey as he hungrily lapped his breakfast. Devon had solemnly asked to borrow her razor and then gone upstairs to shave, while she had contented herself with brushing her hair and starting the coffee.

She was, of course, only just beginning to wake up now. And when he came into the kitchen a few minutes later, she instantly said, "Never, *never* ask serious questions before I've had my coffee. It's unfair and ungentlemanly."

"Want another shot at the question?" he asked politely.

Tory sighed. "No. Just don't do that to me again."

"My word of honor. Now, how about breakfast?"

"How about it?"

He chuckled softly, gazing at her with bright eyes. "It's up to me, huh?"

"You *know* I hate cooking," she said patiently, "at the best of times. And breakfast is hardly the best of times. Don't expect the impossible, pal."

Devon sighed in manful long-suffering. "I guess I'd better get to work, then."

"You do that."

Laughing, Devon opened the refrigerator and began removing items for breakfast. "By the way, since you're obviously waking up now—"

"I'm working on it."

"—I just thought I'd offer to marry you. I mean, since I compromised you by spending the night here and everything."

Tory fiercely steadied her heart by reminding herself that Devon was simply still "practicing" his proposals. "In another life," she said calmly.

Breaking eggs into a bowl, Devon laughed again. "It's a good thing I don't have ego problems," he said philosophically.

She poured another cup of coffee for herself, then one for him, adding dryly, "Besides, I could never marry anyone who's so damned cheerful in the morning. It's indecent."

"If I learned to sleep late, would you marry me?" he asked anxiously.

Tory fell back on a proverb: "You can't teach an old dog new tricks."

"I'm not an old dog!"

"The point stands."

Devon caught her hand after she set his coffee on the counter, drawing her close to his side and bending his head to kiss her with deliberate thoroughness. "I'd be happy to learn from you," he murmured.

"Um . . . the bacon's burning," she said, wondering with a definitely put-upon feeling how her arms had worked themselves up around his neck.

His smile glinted at her before one hand slid down to pat her briefly on the fanny. "All right, *zingara*, have it your own way."

As soon as he released her, Tory retreated to the counter across the room, picking up her coffee cup and frowning at him. "Ungentlemanly!" she accused a bit breathlessly.

Devon was unrepentant. "All's fair, tough lady. All's fair."

If Tory had vaguely supposed that there would be little change in Devon's behavior after his briefly unleashed passion of the night before, she very quickly discovered just how wrong supposition could be.

For one thing, the intensity she had seen only occasionally until now became an ever-present thing in his green eyes; he looked at her more often, and the warmth of that intensity was unsettling. And for another thing, his touch-me-not attitude of the first days vanished as if it had been a figment of her imagination; he couldn't seem to stop touching her, however casual that touch might be.

He kept her unsettled that day. He made her laugh, often in spite of herself. He treated her as if she were a cherished treasure one moment and a sparring partner the next. He was alternately a pal and a lover, joking one moment and kissing her until she was dizzy the next.

And Tory found herself swept along helplessly in his confusing wake.

"You're being ungentlemanly again!" she accused after one rather potent attack on her equilibrium.

Devon managed to look both wounded and triumphant at the same time. "I never claimed to be a gentleman."

"And I never claimed to be an idiot! Devon—"

"D'you realize your eyes sparkle when you're annoyed with me?"

"I'll bet they *threw* you out of that desert!"

"Sticks and stones."

She narrowed her eyes at him. "Careful. The life you save may well be your own."

"Marry me and I'll take you away from all this."

"Are you kidding? With you around, there's no place to go but crazy!"

"Now you've cut me to the quick."

"I don't think you *have* a quick. Except—Devon!"

"What?"

"Quick hands! For heaven's sake . . ."

"Kiss me, Kate."

"I'm not Kate, and you're not taming a shrew, dammit."

"I'm beginning to think that I am. . . ."

Tory enjoyed the good-natured fencing, the innuendos; she wasn't about to deny, even to herself, that she enjoyed his kisses and his touch. But she was still puzzled and a bit unsettled by at least one facet of his personality: his control. It was always there, always present beneath the banter and the intensity. She didn't know why it bothered her so much, except perhaps because she felt he was holding back something of himself.

And that brought echoes of her relationship with Jordan and the qualities in him she'd not seen until it was too late. She knew it was hardly fair of her to expect Devon to bare his soul while she kept her own tightly wrapped and hidden, but her instincts for self-preservation urged that very one-sided arrangement over fairness.

So she held on to her willpower, resisting both him and herself, playing with fire but never coming close enough to be burned. And that night, as in the nights that followed, a part of her wished Devon would lose his control—not only because she distrusted it but also because his loss of control might well free her from the decision he awaited so patiently.

A decision she was still unwilling to make.

But she came to realize, reluctantly, that he had meant what he said about waiting. And that his control, like a solid protective wall with spikes on top, was going to withstand the test of time.

After four days, she came very close to breaking.

He was kissing her good night at her door, as he had every night, and Tory wasn't looking forward to sleeping in her lonely bed. "Why don't you throw me over your saddle and gallop off into the night?" she demanded plaintively.

His hands linked together loosely at the small of her back, Devon smiled down at her. "Why don't you throw yourself over my saddle, and we'll gallop off into the night," he suggested softly.

Tory glared at him. "Whatever happened to the hunter's instincts?" she muttered irritably. "Yours ought to be quivering by now."

"They are," he confirmed affably. "But I'm the hunter who waits, remember?"

"Why?"

"Why do I wait?" Devon laughed softly and branded a last hard, possessive kiss on her lips. "You'll have to make like Kipling's mongoose, *zingara*: Go and find out. 'Night." And then he was gone.

Tory fought a childish impulse to kick the door. Sighing, she wandered into the living room, picking Whiskey from where he lay in her favorite chair and sitting down with him in her lap. She watched her hands shake for a few wry moments, then stared up at Magda's portrait.

The Gypsy woman, smiling with her serene, mysteriously knowing gaze, stared back.

"I'm acting like a child, Magda," Tory murmured. "I *know* I'm acting like a child. I'm an adult, for godsake. An observant, analytical artist. So why do I feel threatened every time he reminds me it's my decision? Why do I want *him* to be responsible for whatever happens between us?"

Magda continued to smile serenely.

Tory went on trying to sort out her own thoughts and motivations.

"Am I afraid of making the choice because of what happened with Jordan? Do I want someone else to blame this time if it all goes wrong? Or . . . do I somehow trust Devon more than I trust myself? He has ancient eyes, Magda, ancient knowing eyes, as the Gypsy men must have had. I think he sees me in a way no one else ever has. And when I look at him, I see . . ."

What did she see? A strong man. A vulnerable man. A laughing man. An intense man. Sensitivity. A subtle ruthlessness. Tenderness. Passion. A man who walked like a cat or a king. A master gamesman who knew when to hold his cards close to his chest. A man who stole her breath and left her dizzy. A man who continued to send flowers each day so that now her new house was bright and cheerful with their silky color and permanence.

Sighing, Tory pushed the reflections from her mind. She felt restless; she knew she'd be unable to sleep. After a moment, she rose and carried Whiskey in search of something to occupy her mind, returning to her chair with a thick volume of poetry. Then she determinedly bent her mind to memorizing certain pertinent verses—just in case Devon continued to practice his proposals.

And when she finally did wander up the stairs to her bed and to sleep, she dreamed of a mysterious Gypsy man with copper hair and ancient green eyes who threw her over his saddle with a lustful laugh and carried her off into the night . . .

"Stop *sending me flowers!*"

"Is that any way to say good morning?" Devon asked, wounded.

Tory stepped back to let him in the front door, gesturing wordlessly toward the living room. She found words, though, very aggrieved ones, and they followed him from the foyer. "Look. I appreciate the thought. I really do. However, not only is it costing you a fortune, not only have I become a joke to the delivery man, and not *only* have you sent the florist into creative fits by demanding a different bouquet every morning—but *I'm running out of room!*"

Devon didn't respond to her tirade until he got a good look at the latest floral offering, and then he burst out laughing.

It sat on the floor with a fascinated Whiskey staring at it, and it looked like nothing so much as a floral tribute a winning thoroughbred could expect. The red roses were shaped into a perfect horseshoe.

"Did I win the Kentucky Derby or what?" Tory wanted to know, staring at the offering.

Devon was still laughing. "Sorry. I knew the florist looked a bit ruffled when I told him I wanted something different, but I never thought his creative powers would be so limited."

"You can hardly blame the man; have you *counted* the arrangements you've had sent? Devon, please. Please stop sending the flowers."

"If you insist," he said woefully.

"I do." And when he instantly opened his mouth to speak, she neatly spiked his guns. "And, yes, I'll remember that phrase—*if* I ever have need of it."

"You will," he said, undaunted.

Wistfully, she said, "Once, just once, I'd love to see you knocked off balance. I'd love to see you lose control."

"Be careful what you wish for." Devon's eyes went over her quite deliberately from her raven hair to her loafer-clad feet, taking in her snug jeans and gray cowl-neck sweater along the way. "You may get it."

Tory felt flushed and uncertain, and for one tremulous moment she very nearly caved in. Then the moment passed. Reluctantly, and leaving behind it tendrils of restless desire, but it passed. She reached desperately for normality and found it with a sudden responsibility.

"Oh, Phillip called. He tried his house first, but you must have already been on your way here. The number's by the phone; he said he needed to talk to you right away." She looked wryly at Devon. "He also said you'd called him shortly after meeting me and told him you needed his house for a while. He was very amused."

Devon didn't have the grace to look guilty, just cheerful. "Sure. I told him I'd met a knockout lady and planned to stick around."

"Uh-huh."

"Did Phillip say what he needed to talk to me about?" Devon was already reaching for the phone.

"Just something about a favor." Politely, Tory started to leave the room.

"Stay, please." He was dialing but spared a moment to raise an eyebrow at her. "I like looking at you."

Tory plucked Whiskey out of their favorite chair and sat down with him in her lap, sending Devon a halfhearted glare. Then she listened while he spoke to his brother.

"Phil? Yeah, I just got here. Of course not—although why you'd be calling your brother on your honeymoon—What? Well, no, I haven't even listened to the radio lately. Oh, that's funny. All

right, get serious. Yeah. I see. Of course I will. Look, it's no problem; I still have Bobby's plane. I forgot you didn't know; it's a
Lear, so there's no problem with the distance. Yeah. Hang on a
minute, Phil."

The rather abstracted gaze Devon had fixed on Tory sharpened.
"Honey, d'you have an atlas?"

"Sure." Tory went immediately to get it, bringing back a ruler
as well, since she'd guessed what he needed. Her foresight won a
quick smile and a kiss on her hand from him, and she retreated to
her chair in some confusion, unsure whether it was the smile, the
kiss, or his absent endearment that had shaken her.

Devon made some quick calculations with the map and ruler,
then continued his conversation with his brother. "It's no problem, Phil. A bit over a thousand miles from Huntington to
Bermuda, then about the same to Miami. Sure. I'll clear it with
Bobby. Well, I don't know about that; I'll certainly try. Right. I'll
call before I take off and give you an ETA."

He hung up and immediately placed a second call, still gazing
at Tory. But his gaze was now more thoughtful than abstracted.

"Bobby? Listen, friend, when d'you need your plane back? I
got distracted, and answer the question. That soon?" He did a few
more calculations on the notepad by the phone, frowning slightly.
"What? No, no problem, it's just that I need to make a quick trip.
Bermuda, then Miami and back. Phil needs to get to Miami, and
there's some kind of snafu down there; he can't even charter a
plane. Yeah. I think I can make it. Right. Hey—I owe you one.
Okay, so I owe you a few! Bye."

Tory couldn't stand it anymore. "Who is Bobby?" she asked
curiously.

"Hmmm?" Devon's eyes laughed suddenly. "Well, he's a dis-
placed Englishman whose family happened to make a fortune
mining diamonds in South Africa."

After a moment of recalling certain newspaper and magazine articles, Tory voiced a small question. "Lord Robert? The playboy?"

Devon chuckled softly. "That's him."

Tory shook her head bemusedly, but Devon's next brisk question quickly recalled her attention.

"How would you like to take a little trip?"

She blinked. "A *little* trip?"

Devon was smiling, but his eyes were very intent. "Well, maybe not so little. I'm really being selfish in asking you, because it probably won't be a fun trip. We'll be in Bermuda and Miami just long enough to top off the tanks with fuel; I'll be fighting the clock all the way, since Bobby needs his plane soon. Phil and Angela will be aboard only to Miami; he has some business to take care of, and she's staying down there with him for the next couple of weeks."

Tory wondered briefly at Phillip's need to get to Miami so quickly and at Devon's willingness to instantly fly to his rescue; they were obviously very close, but since she hardly knew what drove either man, it was useless to speculate.

In any case, a more immediate problem loomed.

"Devon, what about—"

"We can drop Whiskey off at Mrs. Jenkins's until we get back, although it won't really be long. We should make it back by late tonight, if you think you can cope with the tiring trip."

"It's not that. I just—"

"Please, *zingara?*"

There was a curious effect when Devon said *please*, Tory discovered somewhat grimly. His tone never altered, but the one simple word spoken by him caused her to instantly abandon her judgment, all objections, and her common sense. It did not bode well for her peace of mind.

"Devon, I—"

"Please?"

"Oh, hell."

Less than two hours later, Tory found herself buckled securely into the co-pilot's seat of a gleaming Lear jet, consciously willing herself to relax after the takeoff; it was the only part of flying she hated.

"That wasn't so bad, was it?" Devon asked cheerfully.

"Keep your eyes on the road," she directed instantly.

He laughed but complied; he was rather occupied in any case by the demands of getting them to cruising altitude and on the correct heading. Tory watched him intently, gaining confidence from the ease with which he handled the duties of pilot. He was obviously expert and experienced at it, and she felt the last remaining bit of tension drain away.

The sound of the engines disturbed them very little in the cockpit, and once the jet had leveled off, she ventured a hesitant question. "What does your brother do for a living? I only met him briefly and haven't thought to ask since then."

Devon relaxed in his own seat, his eyes checking over dials and gauges with the automatic attention of someone who knew exactly what he was doing. "Phil's a corporate attorney. He played professional football for a few years after college—quarterback—then retired at a ridiculously young age to go to law school. The owner of his team tried every inducement you could name to get him to stay on, but Phil wasn't having any. He wanted to be a lawyer. Now he's one of the top corporate attorneys on the East Coast."

"And the trip to Miami?" she asked, still hesitant.

"Business. One of his clients has recently acquired some kind of company down there, and they're having legal problems. Phil has to straighten the situation out as soon as possible."

"I see." Tory glanced out to find only a thick blanket of cotton-candy clouds beneath them, then looked back at Devon. "He's older than you, isn't he?"

"Four years. Our sister—Jenny—is squarely in the middle. She's married and lives in Seattle."

"Are you an uncle?"

"Uh-huh. Niece and nephew."

Studying him silently, Tory wondered if this was quite the time to ask something she was reasonably sure would shake him off his balance. Being an artist, she was always interested in people. She had contained her curiosity about Devon's family until now; having sensed a faint reserve in him regarding one member of his family at least, she hadn't wanted to pry. But now her curiosity ate at her, because she very badly needed to understand the man Devon's life had shaped him into.

She took a deep breath. "Your parents?"

He answered casually. "My mother died when I was very young. My father's retired and lives in San Diego."

"And he . . . didn't want you to become an archaeologist." It wasn't a question. When Devon's head turned sharply, his surprise was evident.

After a silent moment, he turned his eyes back to the "road." He seemed about to speak, then finally cleared his throat and said huskily, "A *very* perceptive lady."

Tory waited silently; he would talk about it or he wouldn't.

Devon stirred restlessly and made a few minor adjustments to the aircraft. When he began speaking, his voice was neither affable nor intense, but simply quiet. "My father is . . . a very strong-willed man. He wanted certain things for his family—and from his family. He respects physical ability, a strong sense of competition . . . and winners. He always wanted to be an athlete himself; an injury sidelined him during his first year of college. The ambition never really died; years later, he just transferred it to his children.

"When Phil came along, he was the perfect son from our father's point of view. Athletic, competitive, and incredibly *good* at anything he turned his hand to. He enjoyed sports, but he wasn't driven the way our father was. In fact, I think he played pro football more to satisfy Dad than himself." Devon fell silent.

"And when you came along?" Tory questioned softly.

Automatically checking his instruments again, he continued wryly. "When I came along, I proved to be a major disappointment. Even when I was small, I was always more interested in looking at rocks than throwing them. Sports bored me. I didn't believe it was necessary to compete against anyone but myself. Dad . . . pushed."

His voice warming suddenly, Devon went on. "If it hadn't been for Phil, I don't think I'd have been able to stick it out as long as I did. He was a buffer between Dad and me. He defended my right to choose my own way and drew Dad's fire away from me time after time. And whenever Dad pointed to Phil's trophies and asked why I couldn't duplicate his achievements, Phil always stepped in to remind him that they were just symbols of fleeting moments, quickly forgotten, and that my scientific work would be remembered long after those trophies grew tarnished and dull.

"And I think Phil's decision to retire from pro football and pursue his own ambitions as an attorney helped me to go my own way."

Tory understood much better, now, why Devon had been so completely willing to fly to his brother's rescue. He was the kind of man who'd feel a debt after a childhood of Phillip's support and understanding. It was, she thought, a measure of his own strength and generosity of spirit that he had never hated the older brother who had clearly been the favorite son. Devon felt, instead, beholden to his brother for his support, and quite obviously loved Phillip very much.

She swallowed the aching lump in her throat, unwilling to question its existence. "What about your sister?" she managed.

Devon grinned just a little. "She very quietly and calmly decided to go her own way—and she did. No fuss, no bother. Jenny was a strong girl; she put herself through college. Phil and I helped when we could—and so did Dad, once he realized she knew what she was doing—but she did most of it on her own. She's a teacher now. History."

"Do you . . . see your father?"

"Oh, sure." His voice was ruefully affectionate. "We buried the hatchet years ago. He's still not terribly interested in my work, but I think he respects me for what I've achieved. We see each other several times a year, whenever the family gets together or when I get the chance to visit."

Tory stared at the clean lines of Devon's profile, thinking of her own father, the man she'd adored and respected intensely, and the lump rose again in her throat. Even though Devon and his father resolved their differences, she knew it couldn't have been easy for Devon. Without consciously willing the action, she reached out to touch his arm. "I'm sorry, Devon."

He looked at her, and it was as if a fleeting touch of gratitude had passed from him to her. Then he was smiling. "The past is past."

Soberly, Tory said, "No. It's like our shadows—always chasing after us."

"I suppose." He was smiling, green eyes glowing warmly. "But I'm glad you decided to . . . stand in my shadow for a while. I'm glad you came along with me, *zingara*."

A course change demanded his attention, and Tory clasped her hands together in her lap and gazed blindly out at the cotton clouds.

Vulnerability. Chinks in the armor.

The father who had scorned his goals in life, who had belittled his chosen profession. A woman who had thought that same profession dull.

Tory thought of the complex man beside her who had bared at least a part of his soul to her, and she ached. Had it been the father, she wondered, who had unintentionally sparked such vast control in the son? A control necessary in deflecting scorn and ridicule? A control that rarely showed the intensity of a determined man hovering just beneath it?

She thought of the sensitivity of poetry and flowers and a kitten, of the humor that sharpened her wits and brought laughter bubbling to her throat. She thought of ancient green eyes and patient waiting.

And she thought that Devon had been right to warn her against wishing for something. She had gotten her wish: She had seen him off balance, seen the shadow of his past chasing after him. The chinks in his armor. More than that, though, she had seen him with different eyes, new eyes. Not the woman's eyes or the artist's, but a curious blend of both; for a fleeting moment, she had seen Devon as clearly as she ever would unless she painted him.

Unless she loved him.

Chapter Six

They were on the ground in Bermuda for just slightly more than an hour; it took only that long to top off the fuel in the Lear's tanks and to get Phillip and Angela York safely aboard. Devon insisted that Tory stretch her legs while he went after his brother and sister-in-law, reminding her that they still had quite a trip in front of them.

She had brought her passport just in case, but no one asked to see it; she merely strolled around on the tarmac and watched the refueling procedures. Once back on board and after being reintroduced to Phillip and Angela, Tory was both amused and unsettled to realize that both had eyed her rather thoughtfully.

Amusement won out when Phillip, obviously lying through his teeth, announced that he and his wife were bored with each other's company; Angela immediately asked if she could ride up front with Devon, leaving Tory in the luxurious cabin with Phillip.

Tory waited until they were in the air and leveled off before loosening her seat belt and turning to him with a gentle smile, fully aware that the affection Devon felt for his brother was returned; Phillip quite clearly wanted to find out what kind of woman his brother was involved with. "You want to pump me now or wait awhile?" she asked dryly.

Phillip looked sheepish. "Is my curiosity that obvious?"

"Uh-huh." She smiled. "But nice, too. You really take care of your brother, don't you?"

"We take care of each other," he said firmly.

She studied him for a moment in silence. The similarity between them was unmistakable: They were much of a height; each had green eyes beneath batwing brows; each displayed a stubborn jaw and a determined chin. Phillip was dark, though, and his green eyes were more of an emerald color. And if he lacked that lurking, compelling intensity of his brother, he made up for it with sheer good-humored charm.

"I guess you got into the habit," she said finally, "with your father the way he was."

Phillip's eyes sharpened. "Devon told you about that?"

"Yes."

Whistling softly, he said, "That's a first."

Tory felt a bit uncomfortable beneath his scrutiny and tried to pass it off lightly. "That sounds like I'm the latest in a long line of ladies."

"No. Oh, no. That's never been Devon's way. He makes friends hand over fist, but his work generally manages to keep him occupied. And then there was—" He broke off abruptly.

"Lisa," Tory said quietly.

"That, too," Phillip murmured, obviously referring to the fact that Devon had told her of Lisa. "Yes. She—she wasn't good for him. He realized that pretty quickly; my brother's no idiot. But it hurt. It left him wary. And I know he's damned tired of defending his way of life to those he cares about." He sighed. "Lisa thought his work was dull; she made no secret of that. And she was jealous of his complete dedication and of the time his work took him away from her. She was hardly the type to pack up a sleeping bag and go with him to some dig in the back of beyond!

"Other than that, as far as I know, their relationship was fine. Devon's work was the stumbling block." Phillip shrugged resignedly. "With Dad . . . well, things were harder because both Devon and Dad knew Devon was a born athlete."

Tory listened intently, realizing she would gain a slightly different perspective from Phillip. Devon had not spoken of himself as a "born athlete."

Phillip went on musingly, "He could handle any sport, but his heart wasn't in it. He never needed to be the fastest in track or the most valuable player in football or baseball. To Devon, sports were for exercise and fun—and Dad took the fun away. He even gave up karate—he studied it more for the discipline, I think—after earning a black belt, because Dad started pushing him to compete."

"Didn't your father realize how brilliant Devon is?" Tory asked incredulously, unable to comprehend how anyone, particularly a parent, could ignore the vivid intelligence in those green eyes.

"That didn't matter," Phillip said simply. "Dad respects aggression and competitiveness over everything else."

Tory stirred restlessly. She didn't want to hear this; it made her ache inside. Ache for Devon. Childhood pains hurt the worst and the longest, and she ached now for a little boy who'd been unable to satisfy his father. And she didn't want to think about what her feeling that pain meant.

"But they get along now?"

"Oh, sure," Phillip said, sounding uncannily like his brother

"We're all adults now. In fact, the family ended up being pretty close, considering the distance between our respective homes."

She stared out the window.

"Tory?"

"Yes?" She looked at him, waiting.

He smiled a little crookedly, but his eyes were grave. "I know it sounds both impertinent and corny, but—"

"What are my intentions toward your brother?"

"Something like that."

Tory spoke slowly, searching for words. "Phillip, I—I don't want to hurt Devon. I certainly don't want him to defend his profession to me; I think it's fascinating work. Beyond that . . . I just don't know. You see, I'm wary, too."

Phillip didn't seem surprised. "I thought so. It's in your eyes."

She decided rather hastily that it was past time to lighten the conversation. "I don't think I like that," she commented with a frown.

He was nothing if not quick; he followed her lead instantly. "Wear dark glasses," he suggested gravely.

"I have a feeling that wouldn't be at all effective against the Yorks," Tory said definitely.

Phillip laughed and, as easily as that, they began talking about casual, unthreatening topics.

A few minutes later, Phillip went forward and traded places with his wife, who came back to sit with Tory.

Angela was a lovely brunette with sparkling brown eyes and a cheerful, irrepressible personality. Like Tory, she was a small woman, unlike Tory, she moved and spoke quickly. Collapsing into the seat beside Tory's with a long-suffering sigh, she said, "We should be in Miami before long—if Phil doesn't get us killed, that is."

Startled, Tory said, "He's flying the plane? Is he licensed?"

"Nope. He doesn't know the first thing about flying," Angela said cheerfully. "Devon's giving him instructions now. Let's hope they both pay attention to what they're doing."

Tory realized something abruptly. "Aren't we flying the edge of the Bermuda Triangle?"

The two women stared at each other for a moment.

Angela giggled a bit nervously. "I *hope*," she said, "they're paying attention to what they're doing! And did you really have to say that just now?"

"Sorry. It popped into my head."

Angela looked at her with bright eyes. "Well, I'm sure neither of *them* believe in a Devil's Triangle. The question is, do either of *us* believe in it?"

"No," Tory said firmly after a moment's thought. "We don't believe in it, either."

"Oh, good. Then I can relax." Angela smiled at her. "So tell me. Have you thrown a rope around Devon yet?"

Prepared for the question or something similar, Tory remained unshaken. "Hardly."

"Has he thrown one around you?"

"No," Tory answered with more certainty than she felt.

"Uh-huh."

"Stop smiling at me, dammit."

"It's just that you sound so awfully sure. And so awfully familiar," Angela said apologetically.

"Familiar?"

"Mmm. Just the way I did—a few months ago."

"These York men," Tory muttered. "They were born to cause trouble."

"Isn't that the truth! And the worst of it is that they'd be hurt and horrified if we told them just how much trouble they cause."

Tory rested an elbow on the armrest, propping her chin in her hand and staring broodingly out the window. "At least with macho we knew where we stood," she said cryptically.

Angela giggled. "Right. Squarely behind the eight ball!"

Sending her new friend an amused look, Tory said, "Okay, okay—three cheers for women's lib. It freed us. It freed them. We can be tough; they can be sensitive. Which leaves us with a nice round of confusion for all."

"And no game plan."

"Exactly. It took men and women two million years to establish clearly defined roles, and a single generation to wipe them out. Not, mind you, that I totally agree with those ancient roles, but—Look. Our grandmothers knew exactly what to expect from life; they might not have liked it, but they knew what roles were supposed to be theirs. Look at us. We're a generation on a guilt trip. We feel guilty if we have a career, guilty if we *don't* have a career, guilty if we have kids and can't live up to the Supermom image. Guilty if we *don't* have kids.

"We've been brainwashed by media hype and politics, and now we're torn between what we *think* we're supposed to be and what we feel we *want* to be. Our grandmothers looked for security in their men, but we're supposed to be secure in ourselves."

Tory blinked suddenly. "Hell. It must be jet lag coming on. Am I making sense?"

"No," Angela said politely. "But you rather neatly changed the subject. Or did you?"

Tory sighed. She looked at the other woman for a moment, sensing sympathy and an open hand of friendship, and she wasn't really surprised to hear her abstract confusion pouring out in specific detail.

"Maybe I didn't change the subject. It's not easy being a woman, is it? There are no rules anymore. I don't feel that I . . .

fit in anywhere. I don't want to be the prototypical clinging vine, stuffed with emotion and basing all decisions on the way I feel. But I also don't want to be so—liberated—that I begin to believe I don't need anyone at all."

She smiled a little wryly. "I don't want to care for him, Angela, I really don't. I don't want to be vulnerable again. It isn't that I don't trust Devon; sometimes I think I trust him more than I trust myself. But I know that if I—if I let myself care for him, and it goes wrong somehow, I don't think I could stand it. I've gotten used to being alone. And I know that if I let him into my life, if I let myself care for him, nothing will ever be the same . . . and I'll have to learn to be alone all over again."

"Are you so sure you'd be alone?" Angela asked softly.

Tory gazed broodingly out the window. "Physically . . . maybe not. Maybe he'd stay, or want us to be together. But *emotionally* . . . I'd be alone. I don't know how to extend myself to him that way, and I'm afraid to try. Afraid he won't be there, or that he won't be what I think he is."

"The risk goes with the territory."

"Yes." Tory took a deep breath. "But I'm not sure I want to take that risk." She shook her head suddenly and sent a wry smile to her new friend. "It's amazing, isn't it? I mean the convolutions we put our emotions through. Or is it just me?"

"Oh, no." Angela laughed ruefully. "D'you know, when I finally caved in and told Phil I loved him, I was absolutely furious? I was crying and swearing—in fact, I all but hit the man! He didn't know whether to hold me or run wildly in the opposite direction."

"He obviously made the right choice."

"Well, I think so—although I wasn't too sure that night!" Angela sobered abruptly. "You know, Tory, it's all very well to talk about choices and whether or not we want to care for someone, but in the end we don't seem to have a lot of control in the matter. And then, there's Devon; it's a risk for him, too. What if he decides to take the risk and *you're* not there?"

At that moment, Phillip came into the cabin, sparing Tory the necessity of answering Angela's question. And she was glad, because she had no answer to give.

Phillip smiled cheerfully at Tory. "Devon wants you up front— for luck, he says."

Tory rose to her feet, grateful when Angela asked the question uppermost in her mind.

"What's wrong?" the other woman demanded instantly.

"Just a little rough weather coming up," Phillip answered easily.

The two women looked at each other, and Angela said mournfully, "The Devil's Triangle."

"Superstition," her husband told her firmly.

Angela frowned at him. "I hope somebody doesn't find that written down years hence in a book of famous last words."

Tory went hastily toward the cockpit, leaving the couple to argue the point. She strapped herself into the copilot's seat, sending Devon an anxious look. "Should I have updated my will before we left?" she asked with forced lightness.

He smiled reassuringly. "We'll be fine. It looks worse than it'll feel to us, believe me."

For the first time, Tory glanced forward, and she bit back a gasp at what she saw. In the distance, far too close for comfort, reared an enormous thunderhead. The sun was completely hidden behind it, and lightning was flashing within it. It looked about as unfriendly as any type of weather possibly could.

Tory hesitantly voiced her worst fear. "That isn't a hurricane, I hope?"

"No, just a low-pressure area. Hell of it is, we can't get above it, and it's just too big to go around. Ergo, we fly through it."

"Great."

Devon smiled again. "Don't worry. I've been through worse."

"Yeah? When?" Tory was trying to keep her mind off the fast approaching storm.

"Last year," he replied instantly. "And in this jet, too. Bobby'd flown down to Central America, where I was working on a dig. When he decided to leave, he discovered that his pilot had come down with Montezuma's Revenge—or the Aztec Two-Step, if you prefer." Devon grinned at her. "Anyway, he asked me if I'd fly him home. It was fine with me, especially since a virtual monsoon was soaking the ruins."

"What happened?" Tory asked, wincing slightly as they began to enter the storm and rain lashed the jet viciously. "Or would you prefer to keep your mind on flying?" she added hastily.

"No problem," he said, laughing as he intercepted a doubtful glance from her. "Really. We're perfectly safe." He made a minor adjustment to their course, then said, "What happened? Well, about halfway over the Gulf, we had the misfortune to encounter last year's worst hurricane. If we'd thought to check the weather before taking off, we would have gone around the thing, but no one down there in the boonies offered to warn us. Anyway, we made it."

Tory was silent for a moment, nearly hypnotized by the eerie sight of lightning arcing in the surrounding clouds. The clouds themselves formed an almost smothering image of a dirty gray blanket wrapped around the jet, lanced with electricity and driving rain.

She fought to keep her voice level. "Bobby's interested in archaeology?"

"His hobby. He funds expeditions a couple of times a year."

"I meant to ask before"—Tory turned her head to look at him—"why Bobby's so generous with his plane."

"We're friends," Devon said.

Tory's gaze sharpened as she heard the touch of evasiveness in his voice, and she very nearly forgot the storm. "That's isn't the whole reason, though, is it?" she guessed.

After a sidelong glance at her, Devon appeared to become fascinated by the instrument panel.

"Devon?"

He shifted his weight in obvious discomfort and muttered, "You wouldn't believe me."

"Try me," she suggested, becoming more and more intrigued.

Sighing, he said, "Well, Bobby seems to think he owes me."

"Why?"

In the tone of one pushed inescapably into a corner, Devon said, "Because of a curse."

Tory blinked. "A curse?" She thought for a moment. "You mean, like the curse of King Tut's tomb?"

"Sort of. Aztec, though, not Egyptian."

Silently absorbing his very embarrassed tone, she swallowed a giggle. "I see."

"It's more of a joke than anything else," Devon said with rather heavy emphasis. "We don't actually *believe* in the curse, of course."

"Of course."

"Just a dumb joke."

"Uh-huh. Did you, uh, actually save him from this curse, or was it something more . . . nebulous?"

Devon sighed. "What I actually *did* was to keep him from being brained by a falling idol. Bobby decided I'd saved him from a curse. It's been a sort of running joke for years."

The jet shuddered just then, buffeted by strong winds as they entered the most violent part of the storm, and they dropped the subject of curses. It was almost as dark as night now, lightning flashing and thunder crashing even above the sound of the jet's engines.

While Devon was somewhat occupied with handling the craft, Tory suddenly remembered what the cards had predicted. "A storm," she murmured, more to herself than to him. "Danger."

Devon glanced over at her and, proving that he'd seen that little fortune-telling episode as something more than the joke she'd meant it to be, said, "Apparently you're more intuitive than you know."

Tory stirred uneasily. "Coincidence."

"Was it?" Devon studied her profile for a moment, then began speaking very deliberately. "I never thought much about intuition. I never thought it was something I'd ever feel myself; I suppose because I'm a scientist. But since I met you, I've been aware of . . . insights that have surprised me. Some of it, I suppose, can be explained rationally. Your paintings, for instance. What I saw in them could have been, perhaps, seen by anyone because of your sheer talent.

"But there've been other things, all of them connected to you. For instance, I've finally figured out why you're wary, Tory."

Tory knew what was expected of her, but she had to swallow before she could force the words out. "Oh? And why's that?"

"You don't trust your emotions. You don't trust your emotional *judgments*."

Highly conscious of the storm raging all around them, Tory wondered if the tension she felt could be attributed solely to the weather. "Emotion just clouds a—a situation."

Devon was silent for a moment; then he spoke softly. "Emotion is necessary, Tory. Without it, logic would be cold and rationality would be lifeless. D'you know the concept of yin and yang?"

She nodded. "Yes. It's symbolized by a circle with a curved line through it: One side is the passive, feminine; the other, the active, masculine."

"And it means," Devon said firmly, "that neither side is whole without the other. You should think about that, Tory. We were never meant to be either one or the other exclusively. I never realized I was intuitive until I met you. Perhaps you should begin to understand that you'll be . . . incomplete without your emotional, intuitive qualities."

Tory remained silent, but she was thinking about what he said. The storm raged on outside the plane, eerily beautiful and deadly, while her own personal storm raged within.

She was still thinking when they touched down in Miami, far beyond the storm.

Tory and Devon had dinner with the other couple—a rather hasty dinner since they were on a tight schedule—and then left the lights of the city behind as the Lear lifted up into the night.

Although she had thoroughly enjoyed the meal and the convivial conversation, Tory had been forced to make a determined effort not to lapse into long silences. She knew that the hours spent in the jet had something to do with it, but she also realized that her restlessness and abstraction couldn't entirely be blamed on anything other than herself.

Magda's gift of introspection made it impossible for Tory to postpone her ruthless self-analysis; she was by nature one who would always question her own thoughts and emotions. But doing so this time brought her no closer to an answer.

Could she trust her emotional judgments? Was Devon right in believing that emotion and intuition were necessary? She had long believed that her work was based on some kind of science—on technique and logic—but had her own intuition played a larger part than she'd been willing to admit?

Could the answer really be that simple? Hadn't her image of

Jordan been based on emotional judgment? And hadn't it taken the "science" of her art to prove the fallacy of that image? Or had she drawn on a deeper intuition that was, in fact, the basis of her art?

She stared out into darkness, aware that the man at her side sent her searching glances from time to time, aware of the faint light in the cockpit and the odd intimacy of being along with him in darkness and so high above the earth. She sat perfectly still, remaining utterly silent as the truth rose up within her, drawn by his perception or unleashed by her own, too powerful to deny or ignore.

It was already too late. Too late for choices, for denials, for analysis. Too late for making a decision—any decision at all.

She was in love with Devon York.

"Tired?"

His voice came to her gently across the narrow space between them, and Tory turned her head to look at him. She felt, oddly, as if she were looking at him for the first time. Her voice, when it finally emerged, sounded normal to her. "A little."

"We'll be home soon," he said, still gentle.

Home.

Tory took a deep breath, attempting to disperse the fog that seemed to grip her mind so totally. It didn't do much good, she decided, but at least she was able to keep her voice level and calm. "Yes. I suppose it'd be better to wait until tomorrow to pick up Whiskey. I mean, since it'll be fairly late when we get back to the house."

"We'll get him tomorrow." Devon shot her another glance, wondering again what had happened to upset her. Although her voice and face both reflected calm, the fingers twisting together in her lap betrayed a restlessness he'd never seen in her before. And something in her eyes as she'd looked at him just then bothered him. *She looks so lost. . . .*

He wanted to take her in his arms and comfort her, and he didn't stop to question why. She intrigued him, this tough lady with the strange Gypsy eyes and the wary soul. Her piquant face drew his eyes like a lodestone, and her very presence commanded his instant and total awareness.

Devon had never thought of himself as a patient man, and he saw no great virtue in the fact that he had not pressured her into a relationship she was clearly hesitant to begin. He was sure only that he wanted her to be as certain about her feelings as he was about his. And the desire he felt for her was a living thing inside him.

He looked at her again, feeling his body quicken in response, and then ruthlessly turned his attention to the craft he piloted. Time. They had time. And he meant to convince Tory Michaels that he belonged in her life—no matter how long that took.

Tory didn't think much during the remainder of the trip. She was in a kind of limbo and didn't try to disturb that. A sort of peace had come over her when she realized that she loved Devon, and she was content, for now, with that peace. In admitting the possibility of necessary emotion, she had given a name to her feelings.

They dropped the Lear at the airport in Huntington in the hands of the pilot Bobby had sent from D.C. to fetch it, then drove Phillip's truck up the winding mountain road to her house.

The silence between them had lasted too long to be comfortable; she knew Devon was puzzled by it, but she could find no words to explain to him. She could only invite him in for a drink and then stand in silence before the cold hearth in the living room as she sipped hers. And she was vaguely surprised to realize that he was restless and uneasy, pacing the room as if searching for something he couldn't find.

"I enjoyed the trip," she said finally.

"Good. I'm glad you went with me."

Silence again.

"Is something wrong?" he asked suddenly.

Tory glanced up to find him standing before her; then she looked back into her brandy. Inwardly acknowledging what she felt was one thing; she had no intention of voicing her feelings aloud. Not now. Not yet. "There's nothing wrong," she murmured.

"No?" He looked at her steadily, then deliberately eased off. "That's good. Listen, *zingara*, you're really going to have to marry me. Otherwise, my brother'll think you're toying with my affections."

She smiled just a little but still didn't look at him. "Remember Byron: 'When a man marries, dies, or turns Hindu, his best friends hear no more of him.' You wouldn't want that to happen."

"Byron was talking through his hat," Devon told her definitely. "The man was cynical and chronically bitter. And you evaded my proposal again."

Tory strove desperately for lightness and normality. "Well, I just don't know. You'd have to have several necessary qualities before I'd even *consider* marrying you."

"For instance?"

"Can you get a taxi in the rain?"

"Of course. Although it's not a very useful talent around here."

"Hmm. D'you like the window open or closed at night?"

"I'm flexible."

"I don't suppose you do windows?"

"In the spring and fall," he said instantly.

Tory tried to think of something else, something trivial and playful. But she couldn't. She was too stingingly aware of his lean body so close to her own, too aware of that damped-down pagan fire smoldering within her. And too aware of the fact that, teasing notwithstanding, his proposal-practicing now made her heart ache.

Words just wouldn't come.

When the deafening silence between them had stretched into minutes, Devon hesitated, then softly recited a verse from Lewis Carroll:

> " 'The time has come,' the Walrus said,
>   'To talk of many things:
>   'Of shoes—and ships—and sealing wax—
>   'Of cabbages—and kings—
>   'And why the sea is boiling hot—
>   'And whether pigs have wings.' "

Tory knew what he was saying. And she had come to know this man well enough to be sure he would not give up until he discovered why they had been saying meaningless things.

"Cards on the table," he said quietly. "What's wrong, *zingara*?"

Chapter Seven

She reached up to set her glass on the mantel, then looked a him finally, finding words that were inadequate but all she had. "I promised myself—after Jordan—that I wouldn't get involved again. The price is too high. It seemed to me that turning two people into . . . emotional punching bags for each other was just insanity."

"It doesn't have to be that way," Devon objected firmly.

"No?" Tory smiled a little wryly, aware that the long day and the rawness of her emotions had left her vulnerable. "Maybe not But the risk . . . I need my emotional energy, Devon. Contrary to popular opinion, suffering doesn't make an artist great; an unhappy artist is no more productive than an unhappy individual in any line of work. And I have to paint. D'you understand that? I *have* to."

Devon nodded slowly. "I understand that. And I understand that you've been hurt, and that you're wary." His face was very

still, the vivid green eyes direct and honest. "But, Tory, I don't believe I'd be bad for you. God knows I can't be very objective about
that, but I honestly believe you need me as much as I need you.
And I can't walk away from that. Give me a chance, *zingara*. Give
us a chance."

"And I thought that's what I'd been doing," she managed unsteadily.

"And?" he questioned quietly, setting his glass on the mantel.

Tory swallowed hard, then said starkly, "I hate it when you
leave me, and I hate myself for feeling that way. Dammit, I'm getting involved again, and I don't want to!"

"Shh." He reached out abruptly, pulling her into his arms and
holding her tightly. "You're tired—"

"I'm tired of being alone," she said huskily, her arms slipping
around his waist of their own volition. "I'd gotten used to it, and
then you came along, and now I can't stand it anymore."

"Tory . . ."

"Stay with me," she whispered almost inaudibly.

Devon went still for a moment, then drew away just far
enough to turn her face up and gaze into gray eyes gone a smoky
violet. "If only I could be sure you know what you're doing," he
breathed.

"Don't you understand?" She conjured a small, crooked smile
from somewhere. "That's the problem: I know exactly what I'm
doing."

He stared at her for a moment, then said fiercely, "I won't hurt
you!"

"Then don't leave me."

"Tory . . ."

His hesitation, oddly enough, sealed her own decision; his control sent hers winging into oblivion. The only thing she was sure
of was that she wanted this night with him. She wanted all the

nights she could hold in her mind and in her heart. And if some tomorrow demanded a price of her, she would pay it—tomorrow. Tory threw her love and her fate into the laps of the gods. She turned her face, touching her lips to his wrist and feeling the tiny pulse there beating wildly. "Please stay."

Devon's breath caught harshly in his throat, and his green eyes blazed with a savagery that showed only there. Hands still framing her face, he bent his head slowly until his lips gently teased hers apart. His breath becoming hers, he whispered, "I need you . . . God, how I need you . . . if you're sure, Tory . . ."

Her arms moved to encircle his neck, her fingers toying briefly with his golden earring. "I'm sure," she murmured, molding her body to his and feeling her senses beginning to whirl.

His mouth slanted across hers, driving, possessive, as if he would take everything she had to give and still need more. It became almost a battle as they fenced with living blades, an explosion of desire more powerful than either of them had expected.

Tory clung to him as he swept her up into his arms, her fingers locked in his hair. She knew he was carrying her up the stairs to her bedroom, and she felt oddly cherished being held in his arms as easily as if she were a child. But the feelings inside her were hardly those of a child.

Devon set her gently on her feet beside her wide bed, bending to fling back the covers and turn on the lamp on the nightstand. A soft golden light spilled over the bed and over them, leaving the room's corners shadowed and isolating them in intimacy. He lifted his hands again, holding her face as his lips rained warm kisses over her closed eyes, her cheeks, her brow. Tory's fingers pushed the jacket from his shoulders and, as he shrugged it to the floor, searched out the buttons of his shirt.

It had become impossible to breathe, yet Tory scarcely even noticed. Her sweater was tossed aside; she couldn't remember if he had removed it or if she had. His shirt fell to the floor as she stepped out of her shoes and kicked them aside. Clothing lay where it fell, neither of them caring.

Hands spanning her narrow waist, Devon drew her forward slowly, his lips feathering lightly down her throat and past her collarbone, tracing the lacy border of her bra to the shadowed valley between her breasts. What little breath Tory could command caught in her throat, her body shivering beneath his touch. She felt her jeans sliding over her hips, and then he was lifting her easily and placing her on the bed.

Reluctant to lose his touch for even a moment, Tory forced her arms to release him, lying back on the pillows and watching him with passion-drugged eyes as he flung aside the remainder of his clothing. He symbolized the pagan fire in her blood, the hard planes and angles of his lean, powerful body riveting in the lamplight. He was as handsome as a blooded stallion and twice as dangerous, and she wondered dizzily why on earth she had waited so long for this night.

He came down on the bed beside her, accepting the silent invitation of her open arms with a low, husky groan. Shaking hands smoothed away her delicate underthings and then stroked fire into her awakened flesh as his vivid green eyes raked her body hungrily.

"Oh, God, you're beautiful," he said raggedly, his hot breath drawing a throbbing need from some core within her even before his lips touched her.

Tory bit her lip on a gasp, her hands gripping his shoulders fiercely. Ripples of fire scalded her body, burning her nerve endings raw as his avid mouth surrounded the pointed need of her breast. Her heart thudded beneath his caress, expanded, pounded in her ears. She held on to him, almost afraid because he seemed the only reality in a world teetering on the brink of madness.

She could never afterward pinpoint exactly when the devil was born inside her, but somehow it sprang into life. A feminine devil, a fire-devil, it took hold of her mind with a relentless grip and released a molten passion as old as the cave. And it freed her in some mysterious way, loosening the restraints of hesitation, doubt, and shyness. She became something she had never been before, something primitive, and the craving in her body and mind drove her recklessly.

And Devon's control couldn't stand against the onslaught.

Her hands and lips explored his body feverishly, learning him in a way she'd never known a man before. She went a little crazy, submerging herself in this new discovery, this enchantment of the senses. Her caresses drew hoarse groans from his throat and shudders from his body, his whispered encouragements growing strained and finally frantic. And still she teased and incited.

The bulk of physical power lay easily with Devon, but it was her fire-devil that finally snapped his control and drove him over the edge.

The storm erupted with all the force of nature's fury, pulling them into a crucible's white blaze. They moved with the grace of dancers and the lethal power of jungle predators, loving and warring with an intensity only a breath away from madness.

And then there was only that, only madness, and only each other to cling to. They cried out with one voice in torment, in delight as the crucible finally released them . . . tested in the fire and not found wanting.

Exhausted, drained of everything save incredulity, they lay entwined on the lamplit bed. As if a massive earthquake had shaken them, aftershocks continued to send tremors through their bodies. Devon had drawn the covers up over them, and he held Tory close to his side as if in fear of losing her somehow, almost compulsively stroking her hair and the arm that lay across his chest.

"My God," he murmured at last.

Tory rubbed her cheek against his shoulder, still stunned and wide awake. She didn't know what had happened between them, but she had never felt so close to another human being in her life.

"You are . . . something else, *zingara*."

"You're not so bad yourself," she said huskily, reaching for airiness because she couldn't handle anything else in that moment.

Devon followed her lead instantly. "I hope you'll respect me in the morning," he said, anxious.

She giggled. "I always knew you were easy."

"I guess that's why you threw yourself at me."

"Obviously."

"You were carrying coals to Newcastle, you know."

"You're amorous by habit, huh?"

"By nature, actually. Just call me Lothario."

"Hmm. What does that make me?"

"That's a loaded question."

"Funny."

"Well. You're my conquest."

"Oh? You should never confuse women with trophies."

"Was I doing that?"

"Definitely."

"Sorry. Then you can be my consort."

"Only if you're a prince or a king."

"Am I not?"

"No. You're my shining knight."

"Right. Your shining knight on a donkey."

"Whatever works."

He hugged her suddenly. "And you're my angel. Even if you *don't* have a halo."

"Halo?" She reached toward her head and felt around. "Damn—it's gone. Did you steal my halo?"

"Well, I needed a souvenir."

"Give it back."

"No way. It's hard enough to cope with a 'bright, particular star' without worrying about hanging onto a halo-bearing angel."

Tory giggled suddenly. "Uncle! The honors go to you. I think faster vertically and clothed."

"You're no slouch horizontally and unclothed, let me tell you."

"Devon!"

"Thinking. I meant thinking."

"Uh-huh."

"Really. Of course, you're also exceptionally good—"

"I'll take it as read," she interrupted firmly.

He chuckled. "Ambiguous phrases."

"The whole conversation's lousy with them."

"Then how about an explicit statement?"

"What?" she asked guardedly.

"It's raining."

Tory started laughing.

"Got you, didn't I?" Devon was clearly satisfied.

"I should learn not to try to guess what you're thinking," she responded, resigned.

"Guess what I'm thinking now."

She gasped and murmured rather uncertainly, "You—um— aren't you tired?"

"Not that tired," he said huskily, smoothly shifting position until he was propped up on an elbow beside her. His hand continued to move seductively over golden flesh, and his lips began to probe her jawline. "How about you?"

Tory didn't bother to answer. Not with words.

Quite some time later, Devon reached out a long arm to turn off the lamp. "*Exceptionally* good," he noted in a drained, sleepy voice.

Tory smiled drowsily, lying securely close to his side, the steady sound of his heart beating beneath her ear lulling her to sleep.

Tory knew she was awake, but, like every morning, she resisted opening her eyes until the last possible moment. Only the rather abrupt awareness that Devon was awake finally prompted her to stir; he was stroking her hair very lightly and, if her hazy memories of the night were correct, she realized neither of them had budged an inch in sleep.

She moved very slightly and felt the instant response of his arm tightening around her. "You're a snuggler, aren't you?" Her voice, heavy with sleep and amusement, was muffled against the tanned flesh of his throat.

"I'm a what?"

"A snuggler. Someone who snuggles. In bed. I've never slept with a snuggler before."

"Good." He tilted her chin up, kissing her softly. "Good morning."

Tory gazed into impossibly green eyes, thinking vaguely that it must have been weariness that had caused her to act the way she had last night. God, had that really been she? That wanton woman? She felt heat suffuse her throat and steal up her face.

Devon chuckled softly. "Don't look so horrified, *zingara;* you'll hurt my feelings if you wake up every morning wearing that ex-pression!"

"It's not that," she denied almost inaudibly. "It's just that I—that I've never—"

"You've never—?" he prompted softly.

"Felt that way before."

"Neither have I."

She looked at him a little shyly. "No?"

"No." He traced the curve of her lips with a gentle finger. "To-gether we make magic, tough lady."

Tory laughed shakily. "The cards were right."

Devon's fallen-angel smile lit his eyes. "I hate to say I told you so, but—"

"But you can't resist!"

"It's a quirk in my character," he explained apologetically.

"You seem to have a lot of those."

"I beg your pardon."

"You do. Insatiable curiosity, the patience of Job, a nutty sense of humor, and the control of a saint."

"Those don't sound like quirks."

"They are. They don't—they don't mesh." She was only half teasing, her mind still puzzled by the complex, conflicting quali-ties of this man.

"Look who's talking."

"I don't conflict," she stated in surprise.

He started laughing, a soft, rueful sound. "Oh no? Sweetheart, as far as I'm concerned, you're the most fascinating mystery since Stonehenge."

"I am?" Her voice was blank.

"Definitely. And it just might be worth the rest of my life to eventually figure you out."

A part of Tory wanted to ask him to explain that remark, but a

larger part just wasn't ready for even an elusive verbal commitment. Besides, Devon seemed to be having no problems with energy this morning, and somehow or another, she forgot to ask
him anything at all. . . .

They shared a shower when they found the strength for it, then
went downstairs, where Devon once again demonstrated his ability to prepare breakfast and keep her giggling at the same time.
And Tory found, somewhat to her surprise, that mornings were
really enjoyable with the right company.

Nobly insisting on doing her share by cleaning up, Tory restored the kitchen to order while Devon went to pick up Whiskey
from Mrs. Jenkins. She finished some time before he returned,
and, feeling the long overdue itch in her mind and fingers, fetched
her sketchpad from the workroom.

It was a warm and sunny day, a sample of Indian summer, and
fresh air beckoned. She threw open the French doors and stepped
out onto the patio, looking at the view of rolling mountains and val-
leys that had originally sold her on this house. Making use of one of
the redwood lounge chairs Angela had left with the house, Tory sat
down and propped the sketchpad on her upraised knees. She stuck
one charcoal pencil into the accustomed spot above her right ear and
used a second pencil to begin shaping a mountain on paper.

She stopped, the sketch incomplete, only moments later. Something nagged at her, tickled like a feather in her mind. She stared
at the paper mountain, battling silently, then gave in with a quick
sigh.

Only the first step, she assured herself resolutely. There was no
danger in that, no danger in committing to paper the qualities she
saw in him. The first step never revealed much, after all, just surface appearance and perhaps a trick of expression.

The first step . . . .

Turning the heavy paper, she abandoned the mountain, and smoky lines and curves began to appear on the clean page. Slowly at first, jerky with reluctance, her movements gradually smoothed and quickened. She sketched entirely from her mind's eye, staring fixedly at the emerging portrait.

The man had broad shoulders, his head well and proudly set on a strong neck. His thick hair was a little windblown, his head tilted ever so slightly to one side. A faint smile curved his rather hard mouth, revealing humor but something else as well, something elusive.

Tory closed her mind to all things elusive and went on sketching.

High, well-formed cheekbones. The nose just a bit crooked, the jaw stubborn. Flying brows. Eyes . . . eyes that were strikingly, vividly *alive* in the lean face, and very direct.

She stared down at the likeness of Devon for a long moment, then slowly closed the pad. Hugging it to her breast, she gazed out over the mountains, unseeing. "There's beautiful scenery," she murmured to herself, not even seeing it. "And all the heirlooms for still lifes. There's Whiskey. I don't *need* to paint you, Devon. I'll just . . . I'll just enjoy you for as long as you stay with me. If you leave—*when* you leave, I'll paint you. It won't matter if it hurts then."

And it just might be worth the rest of my life to eventually figure you out.

"Ambiguous," she muttered as the memory of his words rose to her mind. "He could have meant anything."

The sound of the truck pulling up near the house yanked her from thought, and she immediately rose and went inside, closing the French doors behind her. She slid the sketchpad and pencils into the drawer of the corner table, turning away just as Devon entered the room.

"Your cat," he announced dryly, "very nearly caused a major pileup a little while ago. He *would* try to climb onto my shoulder while I was driving." He handed her the maligned feline, adding firmly, "We'll get him a carrier."

"Don't *you* like to see where you're going?" Tory defended, scratching behind Whiskey's outsize ears in welcome before setting him on the floor and watching him scamper off toward the kitchen.

"I," Devon responded unanswerably, "am not a cat."

Tory started to tell him that he walked like one, but she bit back the words. She reminded herself fiercely to keep things easy, but before she could follow through he had reached out abruptly and hugged her. Hard.

Returning the hug with interest, she smiled up at him. "What was that for?"

He shook his head slightly, as though puzzled by his own action, and said a bit gruffly, "You look so lost in the morning."

"It's afternoon," she pointed out lightly.

"Yes, but you're still wearing your lost look."

"I have this system for facing the day," she explained solemnly.

"Which is?"

"I delay it as long as possible. Then I stagger around doing my impersonation of a zombie for a while. Then I drown myself in coffee. Somewhere in all that, the day becomes reality for me."

He lifted a quizzical brow. "I don't recall you staggering this morning."

"That's because I was leaning on you."

"And after I left, you backslid?"

"Exactly."

"You need a keeper."

"Not at all." Tory slipped out of his arms and went to sit on the couch. "What I really need are some answers."

"To which questions?" he asked politely, joining her on the couch

Intending both to satisfy her curiosity and to keep things light she said, "Well, I've been wondering. I know what an archaeologist *does*, but what I don't know is how you make a living at it D'you teach? D'you have a grant or work for a museum?"

"All of the above. I'm a consultant for a museum in D.C. at the moment. And I'll begin teaching again this winter at a nearby university."

"Nearby in D.C.?"

"Nope. Nearby here."

She tried not to think of Devon being so near if their relationship didn't last. "So no more desert?"

"Not for a while. I usually spend a few months a year at a dig. He was smiling at her, adding innocently, "Lots of interesting subjects for an artist at a dig."

"I'm sure."

"Really. Just think of it. Beautiful sunsets. The wind whining through the ruins of an ancient civilization. Pieces of the past."

"Right," she said noncommittally. "But I still have questions So tell me about your work."

Apparently realizing that she was honestly interested, he did He told her about past digs, enlivening the details of methodical work with descriptions of people he'd met and fascinating places he'd seen. He talked seriously about some lasting impressions he'd gotten, such as of the Sahara: "A beautiful, haunting, dying land." And cheerfully about other impressions: "You should ride a camel; it's an experience not to be missed. I've never felt more insignificant in my life than when one of the creatures stared at me. Talk about daunting!"

He told her about sandstorms and flash floods, boiling days and freezing nights. About the patient sifting of dirt and the labor of digging down through layers of time.

Tory was fascinated, keeping him talking by asking questions and listening intently. They gravitated to the kitchen later to prepare a late lunch, the conversation branching off along various similar paths. Tory had seen many of the world's major cities, having studied art in Paris and traveled with her father, and she now contributed her own observations and impressions.

They were more relaxed with each other than they had ever been, and when the conversation—and everything else—abruptly changed, it caught Tory completely unaware. She had her back to Devon and was tossing the salad while he was across the room turning steaks beneath the broiler.

"Marry me," he said suddenly.

Tory was already turning toward him, one of the quotations she'd memorized on the tip of her tongue, when the hoarseness of his voice struck her. She looked at him, her smile fading, seeing an odd, solemn alarm on his face, and feeling her heart lurch.

"You're serious," she whispered.

He nodded jerkily. "I'm serious. Odd, when I finally proposed for real, I could only think of the words. All that practicing shot to hell."

Chapter Eight

Tory was neither *controlled enough nor insensitive enough to re-*spond lightly, especially when she could see how shaken he was by his own words. And she couldn't sort out her own tangled emotions enough to make sense of them. But one thing was clear. She had to make him understand the fear she barely understood herself.

"I want to show you something," she said finally.

Devon looked at her for a long moment, apparently realizing that she was not changing the subject, then nodded. "All right."

She turned off the oven, then led the way to her workroom. Devon had not been in the room since that first day; Tory had un-packed the remainder of her finished canvases and arranged her equipment and supplies herself. She said nothing when they en-tered the room, but merely pointed to one corner, where the sun-light slanting through the uncurtained windows shone brightly on canvases leaning against the walls.

Devon hesitated only briefly before approaching the paintings. "Is this my answer?" he asked quietly, gazing at her.

"In a way." She took a deep breath. "I can't think about marriage, Devon. Not now."

"Marriage? Or marrying me?"

"Both."

He leaned a shoulder against the wall, sliding his hands into the pockets of his slacks and continuing to stare at her. He ignored the paintings. "What about last night?" he asked tersely.

Tory knew he was disturbed and confused; she wanted to run to him, cling to him, tell him she loved him. She wanted to respond to the vulnerability she saw so clearly in his remarkable eyes.

But that final blowup with Jordan haunted her. Her bewilderment and despair, his vicious lashing-out because of her belated honesty. The pain of losing a love that had never really been hers.

Devon wasn't Jordan; he could never, she was sure, lash out at anyone in viciousness or cruelty. But still Tory resisted the commitment of three small words and an open heart. She had a choice to make first, a choice between two potential heartaches: Paint Devon now and discover if what she felt for him was real, or allow her love for him to become even more deeply embedded in her heart before being forced to paint him.

Either way, she risked the agony of losing a love that was already far more important to her than Jordan's had ever been.

"You know what last night meant to me," she said finally.

"I thought I did. It looks like I was wrong."

Tory almost reached out to him then, responding instantly to the thinly veiled pain in his voice. But her fingers twined together in front of her, and her feet remained rooted to the floor. "No. No, you weren't wrong," she said unsteadily.

"Then why won't you marry me?" he asked, adding fiercely, "I said I'd never hurt you, Tory, and I meant it."

"I know. I know that. Please, Devon, can't we just let things go on the way they are?"

"Why?" he asked flatly.

"Because I need . . . time."

"I thought we'd gotten past that."

She had no answer, or at least no answer she thought he'd understand. And she tried desperately to lighten the moment. "Just my luck to find the only man around who *wants* strings."

He didn't smile. "And rings, and promises. I was never looking for an affair, Tory."

"You weren't looking for marriage, either."

"Not consciously when I knocked on your door that first morning. Maybe not even when I was—practicing proposals. But I think that in essence I was. I think I've always wanted to marry you."

She fell back on the practical, the sensible. "You don't know me."

"I'm *learning* you, Tory; I'll know you if you'll only give me the chance."

"You see? We need time."

He stared at her for a long moment, and then his face tightened almost imperceptibly. "Well, let that be a lesson to me," he said evenly. "I guess that, like the boy who cried wolf, I proposed one time too many."

Tory took a jerky step toward him and stopped. "Devon, you're a part of my life." She tried to keep her voice steady and knew that she failed. "I'd—miss you terribly if you left me. But right now I don't know what I'm feeling, and I can't seem to think very clearly. All I know is that I can't . . . make another mistake. The last one cost me too much. I have to be *sure*. Can you understand that?"

Abruptly, Devon's stiff pose relaxed, and he came swiftly across

o draw her into his arms. He was no longer the taut stranger who
ad very nearly frightened her. "I'm sorry, sweetheart," he
>reathed huskily. "I'm sorry. I was rushing you—and after I
>romised not to. Don't cry, *zingara*—I can take anything but
hat."

To her vague surprise, Tory realized that she *was* crying. She
lipped her arms around his waist and held on tightly, burying
ier face in the smooth fabric covering his shoulder. "Tough ladies
lon't cry," she said with watery humor, her voice a little muffled.

"That's what I thought," he chided gently. "It looks like neither
>ne of us is batting a thousand today."

"It's just training camp," she explained, finally lifting her head
o smile uncertainly up at him. "We'll do better during the season."

"I hope so," he said wryly, reaching for a handkerchief to dry
ier cheeks. "We could hardly do worse."

"Oh, I don't know," she murmured, memories of the night be-
ore rising in her mind. "We've gotten some things right."

Devon's eyes darkened, his thoughts apparently running on
he same track as hers. "We certainly have," he said, kissing her
vith a sudden fierce passion.

Tory lost her breath somewhere during the interlude and
lidn't really care. She threaded her fingers among the copper
strands of his hair, her mouth blooming beneath his, only dimly
iware that her fire-devil was etching yet another brand of possession.

"You and your ancient eyes," she managed after regaining her
>reath.

"My what?" he asked, smiling quizzically, his green eyes still
lark and compelling.

"Ancient eyes. Gypsy eyes."

"You're the one with the strange Gypsy eyes, *zingara*," he
murmured.

Tory, her fingers idly toying with the almost invisible earring, smiled suddenly. "No, you're the Gypsy. Ancient eyes and a golden earring and the charm of Lucifer himself."

Her mention of the earring brought a sheepish expression to his lean face. "Hell, I forgot the thing again. Would you mind taking it out for me?"

"Yes, I would mind. I like it."

"Tory—"

"Besides"—Tory choked back a giggle as her exploring fingers discovered something else—"you don't seem to have a choice at the moment. I don't have anything small enough to cut it."

"What?"

"Well, didn't you notice anything about it when they put it in?"

"All I noticed," he said definitely, "was that it hurt. Why d'you need something small enough to cut it?"

"Because it's a sealed loop, Devon. And part of that pain you remember may have occurred when they used heat to solder it."

"Dammit!"

"Maybe you'd better forget it again," she suggested.

He sighed. "I suppose I could find a discreet jeweler?"

"Good luck."

"Ah, hell."

"And, you know, even if a jeweler cuts it, the edges are going to be ragged; it'll probably hurt to take it out."

"You cheer me up any more," he said, deadpan, "and I'm not going to be able to stand it."

"Sorry."

"I am not," he muttered, "going to be very popular in certain places wearing an earring."

"You'll be *very* popular in other places, though."

He stared at her.

"Native tribes and such," she clarified innocently.

"Uh-huh."

"And if you're invited to any masquerade parties, you have at least two choices of costume now: Gypsy or pirate."

"Tory . . ." he began dangerously.

"I'm only trying to help."

"Stop trying to help. Please."

"Well, I think it's cute."

Devon winced. "Why don't you just shoot me and put me out of my misery?" he suggested mournfully.

She hugged him. "I have so much fun when I'm with you."

"Good." He grinned. "I'm glad I'm useful for something."

"Fishing?" she asked.

"I'm not too proud. And just as soon as I find the right bait, I'll catch you, tough lady."

"Coming from a liberated man, that sounds suspiciously like treason," she observed thoughtfully.

"Am I liberated?"

"Certainly. Men can be sensitive, and women can be tough. And one day it'll work out nicely."

"But not now?"

"Things are a little confused. You may have noticed."

"I thought it was just me."

She giggled at his wistful tone. "Hardly. We're all confused."

"Oh. Well, my planning to 'catch' you may sound like treason, but it doesn't stop the plan. I'm going to make myself indispensable to you, *zingara*. One way or another."

"You don't have far to go," she said honestly, and then abruptly remembered something. "You called me something else once," she said slowly. "Not *zingara*, but something else."

Devon nodded immediately. "Tzigane. It means Gypsy. In French it's *gitane*."

"D'you speak Italian and French?"

"Nope."

Tory smiled just a little. "Odd that you know those words, then."

He was smiling, too. "Not odd at all. Fate always intended me to fall for a Gypsy."

"Seriously. How do you happen to know so many words for Gypsy?"

His smile fading to something elusive, he murmured, "You'll think it's weird."

"So what else is new?"

"Funny."

"Okay, okay. Just tell me."

"I don't remember."

"What?"

"I don't remember how or why I know the words. I just know."

"That's weird."

"Uh-huh."

Tory stared at him. "I mean, really weird. Like the cards that night." She frowned. "I sense your fine hand in this somehow."

"I could hardly have stacked the deck when you were fortune-telling," he observed reasonably. "You handled the cards."

Tory conceded the point reluctantly. "True. But those words—"

"I swear, solemnly swear, on my *honor* that I can't remember when or how or why I learned the words."

"Devon, this is definitely weird."

"Fate."

She stared at him, suspicious but shaken nonetheless.

"Didn't you want me to look at those paintings?" he asked idly.

Tory nodded slowly.

"Shall I?"

"Please." She watched him begin examining the paintings, and then, frowning, she left the room. Returning moments later, she announced calmly, "They're real. The words. I looked them up. French and Italian, and they both mean Gypsy. Are you *sure* you didn't look them up after we met?"

"I'm sure," he answered absently, obviously intent on studying the paintings.

Tory shook her head bemusedly and leaned against a table holding jars of brushes and tubes of paint, watching him. The sunlight caught him in a golden halo, the earring he wore reflecting a brilliant pinpoint of light from time to time, throwing a sudden shower of sparks as he moved suddenly. It suited him, she thought. Then she frowned as she stopped to turn her mind over, vaguely noticing something underneath it.

Her father's deep voice swam up through memory, cheerfully reciting something he'd heard at Magda's knee, something the Gypsies believed in above all else and never questioned.

"If your true love wears a golden earring, then he belongs to you."

She bit her lip and stared at Devon, realizing that it was too late, that it had always been too late to spare herself potential pain. He belonged with her. He belonged to her—even as she belonged to him. Emotional judgment or not, the feeling was too powerful to ignore.

In novels, Tory knew, the "point of no return" was often discussed at great length and suitably shadowed with pretty words. It was important in that a corner had been reached by the characters who traveled a suddenly one-way corridor. No going back. "Unto the breach, dear friends . . ."

And in a love story, the heroine would be wide-eyed, possibly tearful, and suddenly consumed by the realization that she was fathoms deep in love and couldn't swim, poor dear. She would gaze at the hero with hungry eyes and promptly sink all her scruples, abandon all her principles, and dissolve willingly into the raptures of love.

It didn't happen like that with Tory.

She watched as he repeated the gesture that had inexplicably stopped her heart, a ridiculously common gesture seen anywhere. Long brown fingers raked through copper hair. Restlessly, abstractedly, creating attractive disorder out of attractive order. He was a big man, loose-limbed, powerful but slim. His copper hair shone like a beacon. His face was strong and somewhat arrogant, with a nose that had been broken at least once and possibly more than once. His jaw bordered on the stubborn; his mouth was hard and yet possessed sensuality and humor and an elusive something else within its slight curve; russet bat-wing brows provided a strangely touching symmetry for his rough face.

Detached, somehow distant from herself, Tory studied him. As if, she thought vaguely, that other artist, the one who had made him, had decided to carefully contrast the finished and the incomplete. The hard face, with its crooked nose and stubborn jaw, was not yet finished. It would acquire lines of time and character, grow leaner with passing years. But his brows, she somehow knew, had been perfect from birth.

And Tory knew, in that moment, what was happening to her, and she acknowledged it completely and finally. She was perfectly still and utterly silent, listening for the sounds of scruples sinking and principles abandoned, waiting for the rapture that didn't show itself with a hint or a whisper.

Was it like that, then? she wondered. She was still herself, with scruples and principles intact, but raw and oddly untried.

You know how to swim, she reminded herself firmly. You've been in over your head before, and you survived. You made it to the shore and, dammit, you pulled yourself out!

Tory looked down at her hands as if she'd never seen them before, spreading the long fingers, studying a smudge of charcoal marring one knuckle. And wondered, defeated, when she would paint—try to paint him.

She looked back at him. He was studying the paintings, paintings of people rather than places or things. Precious few of them. They were mostly of women and children, with a smattering of men she'd asked to pose for her because of their interesting faces. Old men. Two of her character studies were missing, although, of course, Devon had no way of knowing that. The painting of her father, done entirely from memory, was on loan at the moment to a gallery in New York where his very first showing had been held.

The portrait of Jordan was still crated and stood in a corner, untouched.

Devon turned from the last painting, one of an old man with the dignity of years and cares on his face, and gazed at her, his eyes bright. "D'you accept commissions?"

She nodded.

"Would you accept one from me?"

She looked at him and said very softly, "I won't paint you." And her voice had the sound of a whisper that wanted to be a scream, a shriek of protest against what had to be.

"Am I unpaintable?" he asked with comical seriousness.

Tory didn't laugh. She half turned away from him. "You're . . . eminently paintable," she said, realizing in her distant observation of herself that her voice had gone somewhere else.

Devon crossed the room to her, and as she looked unwilling up at him, she saw again that he was a perceptive man—or that she looked like hell.

"Something's hurt you," he said abruptly, the perfect bat-wing brows drawing together and his big body tensing as if preparing to do battle.

Tory did laugh then, a soft, almost soundless laugh that would do, she thought as a substitute for tears. "I won't paint you," she repeated, gazing up at the finished brows and the unfinished face and the eyes that were worried for her.

He frowned harder. Large hands rose to rest on her shoulders. "What is it?" he asked in a new voice. "What's wrong?"

She lowered her gaze to the third button of his shirt, studying with the fixed stare of memorizing. Russet hair, because the first two buttons were unfastened. Tanned flesh beneath. Hard muscle beneath that. A heart beating somewhere beneath that, beating with strength and force and certainty. "I . . . need to be alone, Devon," she said, and his name echoed in her ears and her mind.

He was silent for a moment; then his hands tightened gently. "I can't leave you," he said. "Not when you're like this. Not when I don't understand what's happened."

He won't even let me drown decently.

"I need to be alone," she repeated steadily.

"Look at me," he commanded, oddly rough.

"I need to be alone." She felt like a character from a grade-B movie.

"Tory."

Her scruples and principles were still flying proudly, she thought, but her willpower was nil. She looked up at him.

His breath caught suddenly. "What is it?" he pleaded softly. "Tell me what's wrong!"

"You wouldn't understand," she told him sadly.

"Try me."

Fumbling mentally for words she didn't have, Tory unwillingly released a part of herself and wanted to cry out when she felt it emerge. Too soon. God, too soon. She hadn't meant to tell him this, but he was entitled to know. He had to know. Hadn't that been why she'd brought him in her to show him the paintings?

"I painted a man once," she heard that bruised part of herself reveal in a gritty voice.

Devon was very still. "So that's it. That's why you wanted me to see the paintings," he murmured, adding quietly, "Tell me about it."

"I painted him because I loved him," she said in the strange voice that was rusty with disuse. "And I *couldn't* paint him . . . because I loved him. Because I loved him, I saw him with a lover's eyes. And because I painted him, I saw him with an artist's eyes. He was suddenly . . . two men. I tried to paint what I felt, but I suddenly felt differently about him." She shook her head, trying to untangle the threads of hard-won knowledge.

Devon spoke slowly. "You loved him . . . *until* you painted him. Is that what you mean?"

Tory almost laughed in wry appreciation. How neatly he had condensed months of pain! But she didn't laugh; she nodded. "I should have known better," she mused tiredly. "I made up my mind long ago to paint honestly, and that's something I never compromise on. When I painted him, the . . . illusion of lover was gone."

Slowly, because he seemed to want—need—to understand, she tried to explain. "For most people, seeing others is like looking 'through a glass, darkly.' The glass is murky, unless and until enough knowledge is gained to see clearly."

"What you're saying," he said thoughtfully, "is that we see a distorted image of those we look at. We can't see them clearly until we know them well enough to see what's there."

She nodded. "Yes. But an artist—a good one—can somehow bypass that stage of learning. It's as if an inner eye opens out of the intense need to *see*. With each stage of the portrait, each brush stroke, the image becomes clearer. Until, finally, there's no illusion."

Very gently, Devon said, "Has it occurred to you that if there'd been no illusion, your honesty wouldn't have changed anything? That if there'd been no illusion, the lover and the artist would have seen the same man?"

"Yes," she said remotely. "It occurred to me. *After* I realized that I'd allowed an emotional judgment to cloud what I saw."

"Tory—"

"I let my feelings control me, Devon. I relied on them. I believed in them. And I was wrong—*wrong* to do that. It took the truth of the painting to show me just how much I'd let my feelings influence me."

Devon took a deep breath. "And what," he said neutrally, "does all this have to do with your painting me?"

For a moment, a split second, Tory felt cornered, trapped like a terrified wild thing. Then the moment passed. Her eyes held his steadily, and she could feel the vulnerability that he had to be seeing in her. "You know damned well what is has to do with you," she whispered nakedly.

"Tory . . ." His voice was unsteady.

She stepped back abruptly, unwilling to let him say or do anything irrevocable until he understood. Wrapping her voice in tight bindings of control, she said, "If I paint you, everything could change. And the thing is, I may have to paint you. I want you to understand that."

In a voice every bit as controlled as hers, he said, "I want *you* to understand something, Tory. I only know how to be one man: myself. There's no illusion."

Tory finally allowed her fear to see the light of day and reason. "But what if I've built an illusion myself? the way I did before . . ."

"You're stronger now," he said.

Stingingly aware that neither of them had yet said words of love to each other, she realized then that they wouldn't. Not then. Not yet. And she found herself wondering with an unfamiliar tenderness about this man who could accept the unspoken with no demands.

"I hope so," was all she said.

Very softly, Devon said, "Why don't you show me the last painting."

She looked at him for a moment, then sighed in resignation. "Why not. At least you'll see how brutally honest I am. It's over there." She nodded toward the corner and Jordan's painting.

Devon went to the crate, using the tools still in the room to pry it open. But before he slid the painting out, he looked at Tory with an odd hesitation. "Most women," he said slowly, "would have destroyed it."

"Not if they were artists. And not if it represented their best work," she said steadily. "That's the irony of it, really. It's the best thing I've ever done."

After a moment, Devon nodded, accepting that. He slid the painting from its crate and propped it against the wall on a low shelf, then stepped back to examine it.

Wholly a character study, there was nothing to detract attention from the man himself; the background was shadowy, obviously a room but undefined and lacking personality. But the man . . .

He was raven-haired and blue-eyed, tanned and fit. And he was a beautiful man. His features were classically perfect, his smile charming. But a closer inspection revealed the flaws that Tory's brush had captured so unerringly. Vanity was stamped in the set of his head, selfishness and cruelty in the curve of his lips. The blue eyes were empty, surface only with no beauty beneath the sheen. Arrogance bordering on insolence curved his lifted brow.

Quietly, Tory said, "I haven't touched it since we split up. It's an honest painting, Devon. With the best will in the world, I couldn't make him as beautiful as I thought he was."

Devon turned to look at her, his eyes oddly bright. "I don't sup-pose he's anywhere around here?"

"No. He said he was going to Texas; I don't know where in Texas. Why?"

Taking a deep breath, Devon said flatly, "Because if I'm going to feel threatened by something, I'd rather I could punch it out."

Tory laughed in spite of herself, then sobered. "You shouldn't feel threatened by him, Devon. When I think of him at all, I think of him as a mistake. Nothing else."

"He hurt you."

"I hurt myself. I was in love with the idea of being in love, and I saw a man who didn't exist. It's over, Devon. I promise you that."

"Then paint me," he said softly.

She stared at him.

"I'm not afraid of what you'll see, Tory."

"*I'm* afraid," she said starkly.

"We both know you'll have to paint me sooner or later. You'll never be sure. *I'll* never be sure. We can't have that uncertainty standing between us."

"Not yet," she whispered pleadingly. "I can't paint you now."

Devon came to stand before her, framing her face in warm hands. "Why not now?" he asked gently.

Tory's heart caught in her throat, and she swallowed painfully. She closed her eyes for a moment, words welling up from depths she'd never expected to reach, all the denials and confusion of this day and all the other days melting away.

"Because I love you," she said raggedly. "I love you, and I'm afraid of losing that. I'm afraid of losing you."

Chapter Nine

evon pulled her instantly into his arms, holding her tightly. "I thought I'd never get you to say it," he breathed.

"I haven't heard *you* saying anything," she objected, feeling tearful again and wondering with some distant, laughing part of her mind if the dratted man had turned her into a watering pot.

"Sheer terror," he admitted on a shaky laugh. He drew back just far enough to look down at her. "Of course I love you, *zingara*— why else d'you think the proposal was for real?"

Accepting his handkerchief, Tory dried her eyes and said reasonably, "How should I know? You could've just wanted a place to rest your weary head."

"I have an apartment in D.C. and half-interest in a large farm in Virginia," he said calmly. "I'm also gifted with a father, a brother, a sister, and a lot of friends. It's not a place I want, sweetheart; it's you."

She looked up at him a little uncertainly, but every doubt dissolved when Devon abruptly and with deeply satisfying enthusiasm demonstrated just how badly he wanted her. Emerging from the embrace with the dizzying sensation of having narrowly escaped drowning, Tory wondered what on earth she'd been worried about. And then she remembered.

"Devon . . . about my painting you . . ."

"We'll take things one step at a time," he said immediately. "I'm a patient man; I can wait." He grinned at her. "And in the meantime, I'll just have to think up a proposal you won't be able to refuse."

"You did all right the last time," she murmured. "In fact, you did better than all right. You did perfect."

Devon hugged her. "I'm going to remind you that you said that," he said. "Later."

The steaks had dried up in the oven, of course, and the salad had wilted; they started the meal again from scratch. And they had fun. Whiskey was underfoot and in the way, stubbornly maintaining in the face of all disagreement that Devon's leg was a tree to be climbed. He also seemed fascinated by the oven and had to be restrained time and again from roasting himself in his curiosity.

As for his two human companions, they had faced the problem standing between them, and if not solved, it was at least understood and clearly seen by both. They might have been lovers for years in their familiarity, and brand-new lovers in their fascination with each other.

So much had happened since they had boarded a jet for Bermuda and flown together in storm and darkness; they had finally reached an interlude of merely enjoying each other in every sense of the word. Love and laughter filled the house and brightened worsening fall weather.

"I *should make you rake leaves*," she told him sternly one day.

"I think the leaves add a nice touch; we should leave them be."

"You don't care one way or the other—you just don't want to rake them!"

"That's slander."

"Is it?"

"Yes. You're calling me lazy."

"I have endless admiration for your energy, believe me."

"I seem to recall your saying something similar this morning," he murmured.

"Uh-huh. Before *and* after you served me breakfast in bed."

Laughing, he said, "I had to wake you up somehow. You know, I really think I should invest in a set of jumper cables to get you started in the mornings."

"You're doing just fine with your native inventiveness," she said dryly.

"You approve of that, huh?"

"Well, so far, it's been . . . interesting. To say the least."

"Is that what you were this morning? Interested? I was under the distinct impression I'd tangled with a wildcat."

"Turn a woman into a feline, you should expect to get scratched."

Devon choked on a laugh. "Sweetheart, I'm corrupting you! You keep saying things that seem to shock the hell out of you."

"My God," she said faintly, "you *are* corrupting me. If this goes on much longer, I won't be able to trust myself in public!"

"Not to worry; we'll build ourselves a new world and not shock anybody."

"That does not help. I'm being advised by a man wearing an earring."

Devon advanced purposefully. "That remark, my darling love, was unfair and unworthy of you. And I shall take great pleasure in punishing you suitably for it. I'll cage my wildcat yet!"

"Don't count on it!"

"Just let me find the thumbscrews."

"Devon!"

"No? Then I'll rely on my native inventiveness."

"Devon!"

Tory *was slowly gaining insight into Devon's apparent contradic*tions of character, and that delighted her not only because she wanted to understand the man she loved, but also because she was gaining those insights as a woman rather than as an artist. It was not the resolute, absolute stripping away of layers that her logical artistic eye would have done, but rather a gentle and gradual perception woven out of conversation and observation.

His patience, she realized, was the result of both a child's stoicism under the strain of a stern father, and a man's dedication to a painstaking and demanding profession. The subtle ruthlessness was also, oddly enough, a result of those same traits; Devon had learned the hard way to fight for what he wanted—although his fight would never be a cruel one.

The humor and intensity that seemed to conflict were actually, she came to understand, perfectly in step with the man Devon was. He was a man who felt things deeply, but his very control usually hid those feelings. The intensity escaped occasionally through his remarkable eyes. But his humor was the outlet he most often employed, and that was understandable, since laughter had always been a substitute for strong emotions.

Tory understood that when she remembered, all at once, the morning they had met. Devon's amusing conversation had neatly drawn her attention away from what had been his very real disappointment in missing his brother's wedding. And she recalled other occasionas when both she and Devon had reached hastily, as with one mind, for humor because there was too much feeling to be entirely comfortable.

It made her ashamed, that realization, because she had been too self-absorbed to understand that Devon's laughter, like her own, had channeled powerful emotions into a niche more easily approached.

It made her ashamed, and it caused her to reach out emotionally with an openness she had never known in herself. She was vulnerable, but so was he; she knew she could hurt him just as he could hurt her.

And so she encouraged the lightness and humor, seeing it now for what it really was. And if their mood or conversation drifted into a more serious vein, she encouraged that as well, realizing that they had, each for different—and similar—reasons, locked far too much of themselves inside.

She had done so because her painting had demanded an inner focus, a concentration every bit as exclusive as Devon's control. He had done so because as a child he'd been denied a father's support and understanding, and as a man he, too, had developed a concentration and single-mindedness for his work.

They were both unpracticed in reaching out emotionally—but they were getting better, she thought. And they were enjoying the time spent in learning.

I think you've gained about ten pounds," Devon said judiciously.

"Surely you jest."

He laughed. "Don't look so horrified, love. You need to gain another ten pounds or so as far as I'm concerned."

"I think I'll skip lunch."

"You will not."

"Look, fella, you should know I don't like being ordered around."

"I'll make a note of it."

"Why do I get the feeling I'm being ignored?"

"If you were being ignored, love, you wouldn't have gained ten pounds. It wasn't *your* cooking that did it."

"So I never learned to cook. I had more important things to concentrate on."

"There's nothing more vitally important than starving to death."

"Very funny. I cooked last night."

"Is *that* what that was?"

"You're treading a very thin line, you know."

"And you're perfect, even if you can't cook."

"Guile will get you nowhere."

"What about charm?"

"Sorry."

"A pitiful stare?"

"Nope."

"If I apologize?"

"You're getting warm."

"If I abase myself?"

"On target."

"You're a tough lady."

"Devon? Why did you lift me up? And where are we going?"

"We're going to negotiate, my love."

"I'll never relent. *Never*."

*   *   *

But, of course, she did.

Tory had fallen in love totally against her will, fighting and denying every step of the way. She had recognized her own feelings only gradually, and the fear of being hurt again had delayed the realization even more. But she knew how she felt now, and because she'd gotten to know Devon, she trusted those feelings as being real.

It had surprised her to discover that what she had felt for Jordan had been, as she'd told Devon, only a love of being in love. Inevitably comparing this time with Devon to the early days with Jordan, she saw finally, ruefully, that there *was* no comparison.

There had been silences between her and Jordan, long silences during which neither had found anything to say. He had laughed at her rather than with her, puzzled more often than not by the quick, dry humor she'd inherited from her father; his own wit had been sardonic and sharp—sharp enough to cut himself—but it was instinctively sly rather than thoughtful. With the conversational ball in his court, Jordan had all too often missed the shot. He had found nothing endearing in her reluctance to face the morning, expressing only impatience and irritation. There had been no understanding of her need to paint, but only a surface, selfish pride in the fact that she was "artistic."

His job in the glittering world of advertising had involved gimmicky slogans and glamorous parties where he'd used his charm to best effect. He had "worked" the room with her on his arm, always managing to mention her father's famous name and to heavily imply ties between himself and the art world.

God, what a fool she had been! In love with a beautiful face and a charming smile, hypnotized like some idiot adolescent with a hopeless crush!

But Devon . . .

There were few silences between them, and those were companionable and comfortable. He laughed with her constantly, responding with an instant understanding to her words and her mood. And Devon *never* missed a conversational ball. He teased her about her morning doldrums, her inability to cook more than the least complicated of dishes, and her occasional moodiness; and somehow, he always sparked her own sense of humor and made her feel good about herself.

He delighted in her unintended off-color remarks, clearly taking an enormous satisfaction in the freedom she felt to say what she liked to him—even if she was still vaguely horrified by her own unguarded tongue. He couldn't be in the same room without being near her, or near without touching her. And he held her in the night as though afraid of losing her.

Tory had very quickly discovered, partly through the continued existence of her fire-devil, that the only time Devon could hide no part of himself from her, the only time he truly lost control, was when they made love.

She was slower in realizing that she, too, bared her soul in his arms.

It was more than passion, more than desire. They would cling together, their murmured voices barely human, sharing the harrowing intimacy of gazing into each other's souls. No walls, no barriers, no shells to hide away in.

And with every night of sharing, the words became easier.

"Devon?"

"Hmm?"

"I love you."

"I'm glad, sweetheart. I love you, too."

"You were right, you know. We make magic."

"Mmm. Want to cast a few spells?"

"You're incorrigible."

"Insatiable."

"That, too."

"But you love me."

"But I love you. I can't think why."

"No?"

"No. Yes. Ancient eyes."

"Well—"

"And an earring."

"Tory."

"Sue me. I think it's cute."

"And will you explain to our children why their father wears an earring?"

"Of course."

"How?"

"I'll tell them that he's actually the reincarnation of a Scottish Gypsy—"

"And howls when the moon is full?"

"I'll tell them that when they're older."

"God help me."

"And then I'll tell them that their father seduced me with ancient eyes and blandishments. And an earring. That he flew me in a Lear jet along the edge of the Bermuda Triangle. That he cooked breakfast for me when he barely knew my name. That he conjured up a storm and made the lights go out just so I'd tell his fortune."

"I'll never live any of it down."

"Trust me; they'll love the story."

"They'll love their mother. They'll lock their father up."

"Only when the moon is full, darling."

Devon was very still for a moment, then tightened his arms around her as they lay in the lamplit bedroom. "D'you know that's the first time you've called me that?" he mused huskily.

"I like the sound of it," she whispered.

"So do I." He hesitated, then said slowly, "I know we haven't really talked about it, and I know we're taking one step at a time, but, Tory . . . d'you want kids?"

"I . . . yes. Yes, I do. I always regretted not having brothers and sisters."

He hugged her. "I want kids, too. Although I don't know what kind of father I'd make."

"I know," she said whimsically. "You'd be the kind of father who'd always cope with crises in just the right way. You'd mend a broken doll or a toy airplane, bandage a skinned knee, build a tree house. You'd tell stories at bedtime and answer questions patiently and help with science projects. You'd dry tears and comfort broken hearts . . . and always be there when they needed you."

Devon turned her face up and kissed her tenderly. "Thank you," he whispered.

She smiled at him. "Don't thank me. That's just the kind of man you are, darling." And she knew then, beyond doubt, that Devon was indeed just that kind of man.

There were two people inside her—the woman and the artist—and the eyes of one didn't usually see things with the eyes of the other. But Tory realized in that moment that love, real love, had given her an insight equal to, if not surpassing, what she now recognized as her artistic intuition.

She suddenly had no doubts, no doubts at all, that if she were to paint Devon tonight or ten years from tonight, the result would be the same. It would be the portrait of a complex man with red hair and green Gypsy eyes. A man whose humor belied his intensity and whose control could be knocked into splinters by the love of a fire-devil.

A portrait of the man she loved.

"I always loved you," he said suddenly, hoarsely.

Tory looked at him questioningly, wondering at the intense certainty in his deep voice.

Devon stroked her cheek with fingers that weren't quite steady. "That first morning, when I looked at you, I knew I had to stay here. I didn't stop to ask myself why. You looked up at me with eyes that changed color and were wary, and I had to stay. There was something . . . fragile about you, something bruised and vulnerable. I wanted to hold you. All the time, I wanted to hold you.

"I had to be part of your life from the very first day. You . . . intrigued me. Your Gypsy eyes were gray and so solemn, but they turned blue when you laughed, and when I held you in my arms they were purple and mysterious . . . they way they are now."

Tory listened, still and silent and moved almost unbearably by the longing in his voice.

"I hurt when I saw those first paintings. They were so lonely, so bleak and beautiful. I looked at them, and I knew then how badly you'd been hurt. I wanted to find the man who'd torn those paintings out of you, and I wanted to break him apart with my bare hands." He drew a deep, shaken breath. "I'd never felt that strongly before."

"Devon . . ."

"And then the night you told our fortunes, the night you slept in my arms, I knew something was happening to me. You made me laugh even when I wanted you so badly that I ached with it. You smiled at me, and my heart"—he laughed suddenly, ruefully—"my heart went belly-up like a beached whale!"

In spite of herself, Tory giggled unsteadily.

He traced the curve of her lips with a tender finger. "That smile. You have Magda's smile, did you know that? Gentle, mysterious . . . as if you know something the rest of the world hasn't quite caught on to."

He smiled himself, the elusive quality Tory had so often seen and had never been able to put a name to lurking just beneath the surface. "And something you never quite caught on to yourself—

mornings. Gray eyes solemn and puzzled, you wander around like a lost waif from another world. Every morning I want to—to give you something to hang on to, because I can't help being afraid you'll slip away from me.

"God, Tory, I'm so afraid of losing you," he said, suddenly ragged. "I wake up in the night because I'm afraid you've gone. I've spent my life looking for you, and now that I've found you . . ."

The sound of his voice was the raw sound of a saw biting into wood, and Tory couldn't bear it any longer. She rose up on an elbow until she was half lying across his chest, raining warm kisses on his face. "I love you," she said fiercely. "I love you with everything inside me!"

Devon swallowed hard, his arms holding her tightly. Teeth gritted to keep back the fear lodged in his throat, he said very steadily, "I can't lose you, *zingara*. Tell me I won't lose you."

"You won't lose me," she said unwaveringly.

Green eyes more brilliant than any emerald gazed up at her. "You haven't painted me," he reminded, control torn by jagged hope.

"I don't have to," she whispered.

"Tory, love, I want you to be sure. It'd kill me if it all fell apart one day—"

Her fingers touched his lips, cutting off the painful words. "Darling, I've loved only one other man in my life: my father. I didn't have to paint him to see what was there. I don't have to paint you."

Devon waited, still, holding his breath as her sensitive fingers traced each feature as though she were blind and saw only through touch.

"I see what's there," she said huskily. "What will always be there. I see strength, humor, understanding. I see a man who makes me laugh, and cry, and sometimes hurt inside . . . because I

ove him so much. I see a man who brought me flowers, poetry,
nd a kitten. A man who looks at my paintings and sees what they
ost me. A man who holds me when I feel lost.

"I see ancient eyes, Gypsy eyes, and they're branded in my
oul." She kissed him softly but fiercely. "Devon I see *you*. I see
he man I love, and nothing will ever change that!"

Devon groaned deep in his throat, holding her as if he'd never
t her go. "I love you," he breathed.

"Enough to marry me?" she asked shakily.

"I thought you'd never ask." He kissed her, desire laced with
everence, and Tory lost herself in the wonder of his touch.

W*hy don't we stay awake and watch the sun come up,"* he
murmured a long time later.

Tory's chuckle was muffled against his neck. "Suits me. As long
s I don't have to *wake* up and watch it."

"Well, I'm all for skipping tomorrow, if you like. We'll just go
n with tonight."

"That doesn't make sense," she observed thoughtfully.

"Sure it does. Think about it."

She did. "It doesn't make sense."

"So what d'you expect in the middle of the night?"

"Rationality."

"You can forget that. I'm barely sane, let alone rational."

"Why're you barely sane?"

"Love does that to me."

" 'Lord, what fools these mortals be'?"

"Something like that."

"You can still back out of the wedding, you know."

"No way. In fact, love, I'm perfectly willing to wake up a
reacher right now."

"We have to have blood tests and wait three days."

"I'll borrow Bobby's Lear again and fly us to Nevada."

"The anxious bridegroom."

"You betcha. I'm afraid you'll change your mind."

"Like you said, darling—no way."

"Caught at last, eh?"

"In spades. I'm a disgrace to women's lib."

"Does that bother you?" he asked politely.

"Not really. As long as they don't brand a scarlet letter on my blouse."

"Which letter?"

"*W*—you know, for wife."

"I wouldn't let them do that."

"My hero."

He was silent for a moment. "Tory?"

"Hmm?"

"Will you go with me on a dig next summer?"

"I'd love to, darling."

"It'll probably bore you to death," he warned carefully. "And the living conditions won't be a bed of roses."

"Well, you never promised me a rose—"

"Don't say it!"

She giggled. "Sorry, darling."

"You should be."

"My middle-of-the-night humor. Not top form, I'm afraid."

"I'll make allowances."

"That's big of you."

"I know."

She punched him weakly in the ribs. "You're a terrible man and I don't know why I love you so much."

"Fate was smiling on me."

"You think so?"

"Definitely."

"Good. Fate was smiling on me, too."

"Then we agree. Fate was smiling on both of us. We, of course, had nothing to do with it."

"Nonsense. We helped. A little." She giggled as he swatted her lightly on the fanny. "All right, more than a little."

"A lot," he said firmly. "I'm not about to let fate take all the bows."

"Whatever you say, darling."

"I say it looks like the sun's coming up."

"It is, isn't it?"

"Mmm. I'll give it another hour or so before I call Bobby."

"Devon . . ."

"You'll be my wife before nightfall, wench."

"Darling, we have to sleep—"

"We'll sleep while the jet's being flown to Huntington."

"You're awfully sure he's going to lend it to you."

"My love, when Bobby hears why I need the jet, he'll not only fly to Huntington himself but will probably destroy airline schedules by pulling rank to get Phil and Angela on the next flight to Nevada."

"Good Lord," she said faintly, rising on an elbow to stare down at him.

Devon was smiling. "Are you game?"

Slowly, Tory matched his smile. "Vegas?"

"Vegas."

"Can we stop off at a casino on our way from the chapel?"

"You think we'll be lucky?"

"Darling, how could we miss? We're on a roll."

Chapter Ten

Devon set the cases down on the floor in the foyer, huffing mockingly as he looked over his shoulder at his wife. "What've you got in these things, *zingara*—rocks?"

"Yours may have rocks in them, since you packed them. Mine contain only clothes and a few pounds of sand." Tory shut the front door with her foot, setting down her case of supplies and equipment and carefully propping a canvas—hidden by draped cloth—against the wall.

"What *is* that?" Devon wanted to know, asking the same question for the tenth time at least.

And for the tenth time, Tory was evasive. "Oh, just something I filled time with while you were at the site."

Since she had shown him her various sketches of the dig, the workmen, and the surrounding scenery each day, Devon was more than a little interested in finding out which subject she had committed to oil. But he had hardly wasted the months of their marriage in remaining in any way ignorant about his wife, so he bided his time. She would show him the painting when she was ready to and not before.

"All right," he said cheerfully. "I'll wait. And, for the record, I didn't bring rocks home in my cases. We dropped those off at the museum, remember?"

She came to slide her arms around his waist, smiling up at him. "I remember. You *would* insist on introducing me to the curator and then boring him silly with an account of your wife's artistic brilliance."

"Sue me. I'm proud of you."

"I never would have guessed."

Before he could respond, a feline howl shattered the peace and rudely attracted their attention. And before they could move, Whiskey had launched himself from the newel post at the bottom of the stairs and landed neatly on Devon's shoulder.

He winced. "I think he missed us."

Laughing, Tory reached up to remove the cat. "Remind me to thank Angela and Phil for keeping him for us—and for bringing him back up here."

"I'll also remind you to trim his claws," Devon said ruefully, massaging his shoulder.

Over Whiskey's loud purring, Tory said serenely, "His enthusiasm's part of his charm, darling." She stood on tiptoe to kiss his chin. "Like yours."

Smiling, Devon watched as she headed for the kitchen to check on food and water for their pet. He bent to pick up the cases, nobly resisting an impulse to peek beneath the cloth hiding the mysterious painting before taking their bags upstairs.

By the time he came back down, Tory had thrown open the French doors to let the warm air in and reveal the late-summer scenery, and she was on the phone talking to Angela.

Allowing the side of the conversation he could hear to wash over him, Devon just stood and gazed at his wife. Like the artifacts he had devoted most of his life to, Tory's secrets had required long study and delicate handling to understand. And he had found her as fascinating as anything representing a culture long past.

Her tense fragility was gone now, replaced by serenity. Her Gypsy eyes were still changeable, mysterious, but no longer wary. And though she would never be a morning person, the months of their marriage had given her a sense of security that was reflected most strongly in the fact that her "lost" look was now a brief, fleeting thing.

He had seen her happy, passionate, angry, loving, puzzled, amused. He had seen her after a fall into a muddy river and after a horrendous trip by camel in desert heat. She had knelt beside him under the burning sun to stare in fascination at pottery shards, and stood laughing in a pouring rain that very nearly washed them away. He had seen her cope resolutely with insects and reptiles, easily with scientists and workmen, and cheerfully with students, half of whom had developed fierce crushes on her.

And he had watched as she sat on uncomfortable walls in ruins and on the shifting sands of dunes, her sketchpad on her knees and charcoal pencils in her teeth, behind her ear, and in her fingers as she worked furiously to catch some trick of expression or a workman's face or the last rays of a setting sun.

She slept on airplanes, on trains, or in cars, but never while traveling over water. She spoke flawless French and had a knack for picking up dialects. She loved horror novels and was perfectly capable of scaring herself half to death while reading one, yet she never hesitated to get up and go looking if she heard a strange noise at night.

He could clearly remember being shaken on finding her gone

one night, only to discover her outside feeding a stray dog that had wandered into their camp.

She would, he had rapidly found out, make a pet of any creature that looked at her with sad eyes—and never mind that it could be dangerous. They had spent two weeks on the Serengeti Plain in Africa visiting a friend of his, and Tory and a *lion* had conceived an immediate fascination for each other. A wild lion. A big wild lion.

It was enough to give a husband nightmares.

And when Tory had requested at least a fleeting trip into the Sahara—"since we're in the neighborhood"—she had somehow managed to win the affection of the most obnoxious camel it had ever been Devon's misfortune to encounter; the creature despised him and followed Tory around like a puppy.

She had gotten a dandy sketch out of one incident during which that evil animal—she'd named him Spot—had cornered him in a tent. The sketch showed the creature's hindquarters protruding from the opening while Devon escaped through a nonexistent rear flap. And the sketch was captioned, in Tory's fine script: My Hero.

Some hero, he thought with amused disgust.

Unless she meant the camel. . . .

Devon looked at her now as, entirely unconscious of his scrutiny, she laughed at something Angela had said, and he could still hardly believe she was his wife.

His Tory, his *zingara*.

Devon looked toward the wall opposite Magda's portrait, where Tory's painting of her father now hung. He studied the man whose blond hair was only lightly sprinkled with silver and whose brown eyes reflected the serene self-knowledge of his great-grandmother and his daughter, the man who had mirrored his bathroom because he never wanted to forget that he was, after all, only a man. And Devon sent a mental salute winging off to that man, for himself and for the daughter he had raised with such grace.

"Why're you staring at Daddy?"

Devon looked back at his wife, his Tory, finding that she had ended her conversation with Angela and now watched him quizzically. He smiled at her. "Just thanking him for the marvelous daughter he and your mother produced."

Tory sank down on one end of the couch. "You're in one of your moods," she observed wisely.

"I don't have moods," he protested firmly, going around to sit down beside her.

"Oh, yes, you do! Like when you're staring at one of your relics. You know, long ago and far away."

"That isn't a mood; it's utter and complete fascination."

"If you say so."

"I do."

"I still think it's a mood, though."

"Stubborn. I have a stubborn wife."

"The pot's calling the kettle black. Besides, you're supposed to overlook my little faults."

"Oh?"

"Of course. I overlook yours, after all, and what's fair is fair."

"Zingara?"

"Yes, darling?"

"You're playing with fire here, you know that, don't you?"

"Are you going to turn me over your knee?" she asked, interested.

"Don't tempt me."

"I wouldn't dare." She smiled at him sunnily. "You could always send me to bed without supper."

"So you'd break your neck on the stairs sneaking down to

rummage in the refrigerator during the night? And, speaking of which, shouldn't we make a trip to the store to stock the thing? I distinctly remember cleaning it out before we left."

"No problem. Angela stocked it for us this morning."

"I have a noble sister-in-law."

"I think so, too."

"How's she doing?"

"Mother and baby are doing great. A couple of months to go, and you'll have another niece or nephew." Tory laughed. "Angela's a bit impatient; she says she feels like a blimp."

"I can imagine," Devon said thoughtfully.

"I doubt it."

With a saintly air, he said, "Look, *I* didn't decide that women should have the babies."

"No, but I'll bet you think it's a dandy arrangement."

He considered for a moment. "Anatomically speaking, yes."

Tory giggled.

"I'm serious!" he scolded.

"I'm sure." Tory swallowed another giggle, then leaned over to trace a seductive finger down his cheek. "Darling . . ."

He looked at her warily. "Uh-huh?"

"You're not *too* tired, are you?"

Devon fought to hide a smile. "It all depends on what you're after."

"Well, we have all the makings for spaghetti, and since yours is so much better than mine . . ."

"You can't," he said, deadpan, "make spaghetti. Edible, that is."

"Exactly," she said instantly. "So maybe you could?"

"Maybe." He reached to lift her easily into his lap. "And just what'll you do for me in return?"

Tory linked her fingers together behind his neck. "Anything," she said enticingly.

"How about the Dance of the Seven Veils?"

"I don't think I know that one."

"Improvise," he suggested gently.

She considered for a moment, then nodded decisively. "You got it."

"And I'm looking forward to it."

Laughing, Tory kissed him lightly and said, "Hold up your end of the deal first, pal. And while you're getting started in the kitchen, I'll go upstairs and see how much dust I can sift from our clothes."

Devon rose with her still in his arms, then set her gently on her feet. "You do that." He watched her disappear up the stairs, then headed into the kitchen to deal with spaghetti and a curious feline.

Less than ten minutes later, Tory erupted into the room with a delighted smile on her face. "How did you slip it into the case without my seeing?" she demanded without preamble. "*I* packed for us. And how did you keep me from seeing it when we went through customs?"

"The same way you kept me from seeing that painting." Devon laid aside the knife he'd been using to chop ingredients for the sauce and grinned at her. "I had a private word with the official."

Tory wrapped her arms around his waist, squeezing the comical-looking stuffed camel between them in her enthusiasm. "I love him, darling. Thank you." She giggled suddenly. "I'm surprised you found a spotted one!"

"It wasn't easy, believe me," he said dryly, returning the embrace—and then some.

Her wonderful eyes glowed up at him with purple mystery. "I love you," she said softly, intensely. "And I'd love you even if you *didn't* give me presents."

"You mean I could have saved myself a few bucks?" he exclaimed in mock horror.

"Oh—fix your spaghetti!"

"Your spaghetti," he reminded her politely. "And that's what I
was doing until a crazy lady burst into the room waving a camel
at me."

Laughing, Tory blew him a kiss and returned to her unpacking.

Hours later, coming into their bedroom after his shower, Devon was
riveted by the sight of his wife waiting patiently for him. There
was nothing unusual in that, of course, except that she seemed to
be in an unusually fey and sultry mood.

She lay back against banked pillows, the covers neatly folded
down to reveal cream silk sheets he'd never seen before—and
didn't really pay much attention to now. Because Tory was wearing one of his recent "presents," and she did things for that black
silk and lace teddy that should have been, and probably were,
against the law. It contrasted starkly with her smooth golden
flesh and molded her slender body with a lovingly seductive
hand.

Devon let out a long, low wolf whistle.

"Thank you," she said, solemn.

He cleared his throat and asked huskily, "Should I ask questions, or just accept a gift from the gods?"

"What you should really do," she murmured, "is deal with the
champagne. I'm not very good with corks."

He noticed only then the bottle of champagne leaning in a silver ice bucket on the nightstand and the two goblets beside it.
Slowly crossing the room, he sat on the edge of the bed and
reached for the bottle, never taking his eyes off his wife. "The
spaghetti was hardly worth this, love."

Tory smiled. "This is . . . in the nature of a celebration. It's been
almost a year since that fateful morning you knocked on my door.

And since we'll be in D.C. on the actual date, I thought we cou celebrate a little early."

She reached for the goblets as the cork popped explosivel holding them while Devon poured the sparkling liquid. He r placed the bottle in its bucket, accepted a glass from her, and the lifted it in a salute.

"To you, *zingara*. To us."

The glasses clinked softly, and purple eyes melted into gree ones as the wine was sipped. Tory obeyed the gently guiding hai at the nape of her neck, leaning forward slowly until she cou feel as well as hear his whisper.

"I love you so much. . . ."

His lips moved on hers tenderly, growing fierce with desire a most instantly. Her free hand slipped down over his chest, his lea stomach, finally touching the towel knotted at his hip, and she r luctantly forced her mind back to the surprise she had planned carefully for tonight.

When his kisses trailed down her throat, she managed to s huskily, "I have a present for you."

"You certainly do," he breathed.

Tory set her glass on the nightstand, threading her finge through his hair and gently forcing him to look at her. "I have present for you," she repeated firmly.

Devon sighed, his green eyes still dark and passionate. "I better be good, wench," he growled.

"I'll, uh, let you be the judge of that."

He set his own glass on the nightstand, wondering at the dif dence in her face. She touched his cheek briefly before noddi toward a point over his shoulder.

"It's there."

Devon turned slowly, looking toward the corner. He had r ticed nothing particular there when he'd come into the room; l entire attention had been fixed on her. But now he saw. The soft glow of a lamp on a small table lit her gift where it hung on the wall, and Devon wasn't even aware that he'd risen from the bed until he found himself standing before the painting she had so carefully guarded from his curiosity.

In the background was the stark beauty of ruins shadowed by an afternoon sun, their ancient tumbled walls mute testimony to old knowledge. In the foreground, the focus of the work, stood a man, his eyes narrowed against the red sun, his collar open to the faint breeze. He held a clay figurine in his hands, its surface cracked by time. But his attention was focused somewhere else, at what a viewer could only imagine.

Fascination was written on the man's face, intensity in his vivid green eyes. His strong mouth was curved with humor, sensuality, and an odd bemusement. There was an honest grace in his stance and knowledge in the strong hands holding the figurine.

And Tory's brush revealed other traits as well. Determination. Patience. Sensitivity. There was an elusive vulnerability in the lean face, and the intensity of his green eyes held a deep and abiding love.

"I remember that day," Devon said in a voice that seemed to come from deep inside of him. "I looked up, and you were standing there watching me."

"Yes." Tory waited, almost holding her breath.

Devon came slowly back to the bed, sinking down beside her. "Is that what you saw when you looked at me?" he asked thickly. "That—that—"

"That beautiful man," she whispered. "Holding time in his hands and gazing at me with so much love in his eyes. That's what I saw. It's what I always see. It's why I had to paint you."

Devon reached to take her hands, holding them in his own unsteady ones as he bent his head over them. Pressing soft kisses into her palms, he whispered, "Thank you, love. It's a priceless gift."

"I only painted what's there, Devon. Don't thank me for that."

He smiled at her, green eyes bright and full. "Then I'll thank you for a doubly rare and precious gift, love. I'll thank you for giving me the opportunity to see myself as you see me. And I'll thank you for loving what you see."

"Devon . . ."

"My beautiful love . . ."